DEADLY PURSUIT

Books by Irene Hannon

DEADLY PURSUIT

A NOVEL

IRENE HANNON

FIC
HANNON
2011

Revell

a division of Baker Publishing Group
Grand Rapids, Michigan

© 2011 by Irene Hannon

Published by Revell
a division of Baker Publishing Group
P.O. Box 6287, Grand Rapids, MI 49516-6287
www.revellbooks.com

Printed in the United States of America

Library of Congress Cataloging-in-Publication Data
Hannon, Irene.
    Deadly pursuit : a novel / Irene Hannon.
       p.   cm. — (Guardians of justice ; #2)
    ISBN 978-0-8007-3457-2 (pbk.)
    1. Stalkers—Fiction. 2. Social workers—Fiction. 3. Law enforcement—
Fiction. I. Title.
PS3558.A4793D43 2011
813'.54—dc22   2011017328

11   12   13   14   15   16   17   7   6   5   4   3   2   1

To my husband, Tom—
who proves to me every day that a man
doesn't have to jump into raging rivers to be a hero.

1

Heavy breathing.

That was all she could hear.

No voice.

No background noise.

Just a palpable presence on the other end of the line.

Again.

Despite the warmth of the early May breeze wafting through her kitchen window, an icy shiver snaked down Alison Taylor's spine.

She glanced at the number displayed on caller ID. Compared it to the one thumbtacked to the small corkboard beside her phone. The one she'd jotted down after the second call.

It didn't match. But it looked vaguely familiar.

She grabbed a pen and wrote down the new number.

"Who is this?" She tried to sound poised. Unruffled. In control. But the tremor in her words betrayed her.

A sudden click as the line went dead was the only response.

I do not need this!

As she slammed the portable phone back into its holder, a startled yelp at her feet summed up Bert's reaction to her frustrated—and futile—gesture.

Bending down to pick up the fourteen-pound mutt she'd rescued from the animal shelter last summer, she winced as a twinge of pain radiated down her leg. Lately she'd begun to forget about the steel rod inside. And that was a positive sign. It meant her recovery was progressing. But moments like this reminded her it wasn't yet complete.

And maybe never would be.

As Bert wriggled and stretched his neck to lick her face, his unrestrained affection helped chase away her sudden dejection—and uncoil the knot of tension in the pit of her stomach.

"Missed me while I was at work, did you, big guy? How does a walk sound on this beautiful St. Louis afternoon?"

The word *walk* set off another round of ecstatic slurping.

Chuckling, she set him on the floor again, moving more carefully this time. "Okay, okay, I get the message. Let me grab your leash and we'll—"

The phone rang again, cutting her off midsentence.

Her heart stuttered, then tripped into double time as she edged toward the counter to check caller ID. She should have done that before answering the last call too. But Bert's enthusiastic welcome-home greeting had distracted her.

One glance at the display, however, set her mind at ease. Her two brothers had a tendency to be annoyingly overprotective, but she could handle them better than she was handling the anonymous calls. Especially Cole.

Bert nudged her leg when she picked up the phone, and she gave him a pat. "In a minute, big guy. Be patient." As if. A rueful grin tugged at her mouth. Bert had many virtues, but patience wasn't one of them.

"Hi, Cole." She grabbed the leash draped over a coat hook by the back door. "What's up?"

"Not much. Just checking in. How's my favorite sister?"

"I'd take that as a compliment, except I'm your only sister."

"Are you evading my question?" Concern sharpened his tone.

She let out an exasperated sigh. "No. I was making a joke. The accident was a year ago, Cole. I'm fine, as I keep telling you and Jake. Although I have to say, our big brother hovers less since he and Liz got engaged three weeks ago. Maybe I need to find you a good woman too."

"Very funny."

"I'm serious. You're thirty-five. You ought to have a wife and family by now."

"You're thirty-four, as of a couple of weeks ago."

She clicked the leash on Bert's collar, fighting back a wave of melancholy. If all had gone as she'd expected, she might have been married by now—as they both knew. Instead, her dreams of a husband and family had been shattered that fateful night a year ago.

"Alison . . . I'm sorry." Contrition and self-reproach etched Cole's words. "Sometimes I speak before I think."

"No kidding." She took a deep breath and lightened her tone. "However, my experience with David is ancient history. Besides, I have Bert now. Not a bad trade-off, if you ask me."

Hearing his name, the dog gave her a hopeful look and began vigorously wagging his stubby tail, his whole body quivering in anticipation.

"Who wants to go for a walk, by the way." Alison leaned down to pat him again, favoring her bad leg. "So if there's no specific reason for your call other than to harass your little sister . . ." She let the words trail off, preparing to hang up.

"Actually, I do have another reason."

At the trace of nervousness in his voice, Alison's antenna went up. Her brothers rarely displayed even a hint of uneasiness. As a deputy U.S. marshal, Jake was a take-charge kind of guy—on and off the job. Cole wasn't far behind. She'd been the victim of his brother-to-sister interrogations on numerous occasions, and she pitied the suspects who faced his official, on-the-job grilling. Police detectives didn't come any sharper—or more relentless—than Cole Taylor.

When the silence lengthened, she prompted him. "You mentioned another reason?"

"Right. Here's the thing. Remember me telling you at your birthday brunch that we were getting a new detective?"

"Yes."

"Well, he started this week. Nice guy. My age. A former

Navy SEAL. He's spent the past four years with the NYPD—two on the SWAT team, two as a detective. His name's Mitch Morgan."

Silence fell again, and Alison frowned. Bert was tugging on the leg of her slacks now, his initial excitement over the prospect of a walk giving way to the necessity of a walk.

"Look, Cole, spit it out. Bert's sending me an urgent message here."

"Could you let him out in the backyard?"

"Is this going to take that long?"

"It might."

Huffing out a breath, Alison unclipped the leash and reached for the doorknob. "Fine. But I have one disappointed dog here. He was all geared up for a walk." Bert shot out the instant she opened the door and took off at a gallop for the nearest tree.

"Okay." She swiveled back to the kitchen. "You have my full attention. Continue."

"First, promise you won't say no right away."

Uh-oh.

Alison knew where this was headed, and she had no intention of going down that road again. "You're not trying to fix me up with this guy, are you?"

"Not for a lifetime. Just an evening."

"Yeah? Are you willing to take a lie detector test on that?"

"Hear me out, okay? Can you do that much at least?"

Picking up on his frustration, she bit back the retort that sprang to her lips. Cole's efforts to shore up her social life might be annoying, but they were well-intentioned.

"Sure. I can do that. As long as you know that when I decide to date again, the man will be of *my* choosing. Not one of the guys you and Jake have been trying to set me up with for the past six months."

"They were nice guys."

"I can handle my own love life."

"This isn't about your love life. It's about helping a guy out for one night."

10

Drat. People in need were her Achilles' heel—and both her brothers knew that. Positioning this as a favor to someone else was an excellent strategy.

Score one for Cole.

"Okay." She might as well give up the fight. "What's the deal?"

"He needs a date for his cousin's wedding reception on Saturday night."

"You don't need a date for a family event."

"You do if you're a very eligible male and you don't want every married female relative shoving single women at you."

Good point.

Her resolve wavered.

"Will he expect me to dance?"

"I can tell him you don't dance if you want me to, but I bet you could. I hardly notice the limp anymore. Come on, Alison. Help the guy out. He's only been back in town two weeks, and he's spent most of his free time doing some long-overdue repairs on his dad's house. And here's the other thing—his father will be riding with you to and from the reception. So it's not a real date. But having you there will keep predators away from Mitch."

"Maybe he wouldn't mind a few predators."

"Yes, he would. He told me almost the same thing you did. That when he's ready to jump into the St. Louis social scene, he'll choose his own dates. That's why he's not looking forward to having single women steered his way by well-meaning relatives at the reception. So what do you say? Can I tell him you're willing to step in for the night and be a defensive shield?"

Defensive shield?

Not the most flattering role she'd ever played.

On the other hand, she had no plans for Saturday night. Why pass up a free meal, the chance to do a good deed, and an opportunity to dress up? Especially in such a safe setting. A guy couldn't get too amorous with his father in tow, even if he was so inclined. And this one didn't sound like he was, anyway.

"Okay. If he wants a date for the evening, I'll go."

"Great. I'll check with him tomorrow and let you know what he says. You won't regret this."

"I hope not, brother dear. Because if I do, your name is mud."

Why did I let Cole talk me into this?

As he sat in his car outside Alison Taylor's small suburban bungalow, Mitch ran his finger around the collar of his dress shirt and wished he could ditch the tie. Or better yet, ditch this whole evening.

If he had it to do over, he'd never have gotten into that conversation with Cole on Tuesday. The one about meddling female relatives who can't stand to see a guy stay single. And he sure wouldn't have agreed to take his new colleague's sister to this shindig when Cole had brought it up again on Wednesday, even though his colleague had picked up the tab for their burgers after work. He'd rather fend off a dozen women on the make than try to entertain one who was still too distraught to reenter the social scene a year after breaking up with her boyfriend. She was going to be a barrel of laughs.

But once Cole had mentioned an accident his sister had been in and said it would lift her spirits to get out, he'd been a goner.

His colleague's largesse—plus the soft heart beneath his own tough-guy veneer—had done him in.

Resigned to a boring evening, he slid out of the car and considered the suit coat hanging on the hook above the door in the backseat. Should he bother putting it on?

Nah. It wasn't like he was trying to impress a real date.

As he strolled up the concrete walk and climbed the steps to the porch, a muted, high-pitched yapping heralded his arrival. Some froufrou dog, no doubt. He'd lay odds the pooch was a nipper too.

Bracing himself, he pressed the doorbell.

Thirty seconds later, at the sound of a latch being pulled back, he pasted on a smile and gritted his teeth.

Look at it this way, Morgan. In three hours, max, it will be over. You can find an excuse to . . .

The door opened, and Mitch's mouth almost dropped open. Wow.

The wallet-sized family shot Cole had shown him, taken at his mother's birthday party last fall, hadn't come close to doing justice to Alison Taylor's classic oval face or her model-like cheekbones. To eyes as blue as a summer sky. To lips that were full and soft—and slightly parted, as if she, too, was surprised.

Her smile wavered, then steadied as she held out her hand. "Mitch, I presume."

He reached out and enfolded her slender fingers in his. At some peripheral level, he realized she was about five inches shorter than his six-foot height. But he was more intrigued by the way the late-afternoon sun was gilding the highlights in her shiny, dark blonde hair. Worn parted in the middle and tucked behind her ears, it fell just shy of her shoulders before turning under to frame her perfect face.

Double wow.

Alison Taylor was drop-dead gorgeous.

Clearing his throat, he restrained the urge to loosen his tie. Too bad he hadn't donned his jacket after all. "Guilty."

A tug on the cuff of his slacks caught his attention. Welcoming the excuse to regroup, he looked down.

"Bert!" Alison scolded the golden fluff ball at his feet, bending to scoop him into her arms. "Sorry about that." The skirt of her black cocktail dress was made of some kind of floaty fabric that billowed around her as she dropped down, emphasizing a waist that was impossibly small.

It took him a second to find his voice. "No problem."

She wobbled as she started to rise, and he reached out to steady her. "Careful."

"Thanks."

Once upright, she cuddled the dog close, a slight flush suffusing her cheeks. "I meant to put him in his cage before you got here. Come in and make yourself comfortable." She stepped back and gestured to the living room. "This will just take a minute. Will your dad be okay in the car?"

"My dad?" He tried to shift gears, but Alison's blue eyes got in the way.

"Yes. Cole said he'd be joining us tonight."

"Oh. Right. That was the original plan. But his sister and her husband are in town for the wedding, so he decided to ride with them."

Her eyes narrowed. "When did the plans change?"

"Thursday afternoon. My dad called me at work."

"Did Cole know that?"

"I think I mentioned it to him yesterday. Why?"

"It's not important."

Pressing her lips together, she turned on her heel and headed toward the kitchen.

But as Mitch took a seat on one of the side chairs in her living room, he sensed Cole's lapse was, indeed, important.

And he had a feeling it didn't bode well for his colleague.

You are dead meat, dear brother.

Alison latched the spacious cage in the basement, unmoved for once by Bert's pleading whine to be released.

Cole had known as of yesterday that the man's father wouldn't be part of the date, and he hadn't bothered to give her an update.

He was going to pay for this. Big-time.

Resting one hand on the cage for leverage, she straightened up. He was going to pay for something else too.

He'd failed to disclose that the bureau's newest detective was hot.

Very hot.

Okay, so maybe a guy wouldn't think in those terms. But all

he'd offered when she'd asked him on Thursday what Mitch looked like was that the man had brown hair and was tall. Pretty sketchy for a guy who dealt with detailed descriptions every day on the job.

He could have told her about Mitch's velvet brown eyes. Or his broad shoulders. Or his firm chin with the tiny Cary Grant cleft. Not to mention his potent presence, which radiated strength and integrity and leashed power.

No way did she believe Cole's reticence was an oversight.

On the other hand, why should she care, when the handsome man waiting upstairs was hers for the evening? She slipped her fingers into the cage and gave Bert's ear a distracted scratch. This could turn out to be a lot more interesting than she'd expected. Not that she'd ever tell Cole about her change of heart. Overprotective brothers might be bad.

But I-told-you-so-ing brothers were worse.

Seated at a small table tucked into one corner of the noisy VFW hall, where a rowdy duck dance was in progress, Mitch took a sip of soda. It was the first time he and Alison had been left alone. His relatives had all paraded by to say hello—and from their interested looks, it was clear they assumed he was on a real date rather than a mission of mercy.

Truth be told, he was beginning to wish it was a real date.

If it was, though, he wouldn't have brought Alison here. He'd have taken her to some classy place for a sit-down dinner instead of the roast-beef-and-mostaccioli buffet that was the standard fare at weddings in his family. A quiet place where they could have had a real conversation instead of trying to shout over a DJ who seemed to have only one volume setting on his equipment: deafening.

Not that Alison appeared to mind the down-home festivities or the noise. She'd chatted with everyone who'd stopped by, the epitome of graciousness. She'd impressed his father, who'd given him an approving wink when she wasn't looking.

And if her tapping foot was any indication, she was enjoying the silliness on the dance floor.

But he didn't want their evening to end with a duck dance.

Taking a final swing of soda, he leaned toward her. "You ready to head out?"

She looked at him in surprise. And unless he was way off base, there was a touch of regret in her eyes.

That was encouraging.

"Whenever you'd like to leave is fine, but we've only been here an hour and a half. Will your family be disappointed if you don't stay longer?"

"I've talked to everyone I need to, and trust me. In this crowd, my absence won't even be missed. Give me a minute to say good night to my dad and wish the bride and groom well, okay?"

"Sure."

He said his good-byes as quickly as he could, and as he wove back to their table she gathered up her purse and shawl and stood.

Taking her arm, he led the way out of the noisy, crowded hall. Just as they reached the deserted foyer, the duck dance ended and the DJ switched to the Nat King Cole/Natalie Cole rendition of "Unforgettable."

His step faltered.

"Did you forget something?"

At Alison's question, Mitch looked down at her. If she wasn't Cole's sister, if he hadn't been railroaded into this date, he wouldn't be hesitating over his next move. But he usually avoided being anything more than friendly to setup dates—and sisters of colleagues.

He'd already decided to break that rule when he'd opted for an early departure, though, and he wasn't going to rethink his decision.

"No. But it just occurred to me that I never invited you to dance."

A flicker of . . . distress? . . . darkened her irises to cobalt for a fleeting instant. "I don't dance much anymore. Cole was

16

supposed to mention that." Her eyes did that squinty thing again. Like she wasn't happy with her brother.

He ignored the reference to his fellow detective. It was always safer to stay out of family battles.

"Because of the car accident?"

Her grip on her small clutch purse tightened, wrinkling the black fabric. "Cole told you about that?"

"No details, if that's what you mean."

She hesitated for a moment before responding. "The accident did a number on my leg. It's not a hundred percent yet."

He'd wondered why she'd had trouble rising earlier in the evening when she'd dropped down to pick up her dog. Now he understood.

"Your walking doesn't seem to be impaired, and a foxtrot doesn't require much more than that."

She stared at him. "You know how to foxtrot?"

"My mom insisted. She said knowing how to dance would impress girls." He grinned. "Are you impressed?"

"Very."

He held out his hand. "Why don't we give it a try?"

Catching her lower lip between her teeth, she considered him. "I haven't danced in quite a while."

He gave her his most persuasive smile. "This isn't *Dancing with the Stars*, Alison. There aren't any judges watching us. Besides, I'm rusty too. My last couple of jobs haven't offered me much opportunity to enjoy the finer things in life."

The smile worked. She set her purse and shawl on a nearby folding chair, then stepped into his arms.

And into his heart.

At least that's what it felt like.

Jolted, Mitch did his best to focus on shuffling his feet to the beat of the music. But it was hard to concentrate with Alison's soft curves nestled against him. With her faint floral scent filling his nostrils. With her silky hair soft against his jaw and her breath a warm whisper against his throat.

"You don't seem the least rusty to me."

17

Her slightly unsteady comment refocused his attention.

"And your accident didn't impair your dancing ability." He eased her closer. She didn't protest.

After that, there didn't seem to be any need for words. They just moved in perfect unison to the music, as if they'd danced together many times before. As if they belonged together.

It was like no dance Mitch had ever experienced.

And he didn't want it to end.

Eventually, though, the song would wind down. But perhaps the evening didn't have to.

"I noticed they were setting out the wedding cake as I was saying good-bye to the bride and groom." He kept the comment casual as he dipped his head to bring his lips closer to her ear—and her silky hair. "I can grab a piece for you if you like, but I know a better place for dessert, if you're game."

He detected a very faint hesitation in her step, as if she'd been taken off guard by his impromptu invitation.

"Can I tell you something?" With her cheek resting against his jacket, her uncertain question came out muffled.

"Sure."

"I didn't want to come tonight."

A smile tugged at his lips. "Can I tell you something back? I didn't either."

"Cole told me you wanted a date to deflect advances from interested females. That I'd be a defensive shield."

That was news to him. It seemed his new colleague had played on both their sympathies.

"And he told me your social life's been lacking since you broke up with the guy you were dating."

She stiffened in his arms but kept moving to the music. "Did he tell you why we broke up?"

"No."

She relaxed a little. "I plan to have a long talk with my interfering brother."

The song came to an end, and Mitch slowed his steps, then reluctantly released her from his arms. The bright overhead lights in the foyer didn't provide one shred of romantic ambiance, but as he stared down into Alison's eyes, he could have sworn he heard a violin somewhere. How nuts was that?

"I wouldn't be too hasty." His comment came out husky, and he cleared his throat. "This evening might turn out okay after all. Even if we were both manipulated into it."

"I'm not certain that's a good thing." She wrinkled her nose. "Watching Cole gloat won't be pretty."

He plucked her filmy lace shawl off the chair, chuckling as he draped it over her shoulders. "We don't have to give him a lot of details." After retrieving her purse, he took her arm and guided her toward the exit.

"Trust me, I don't plan to."

"So can I interest you in a detour for some dessert?" He pushed the door open, and they strolled toward his car. "I haven't been to Ted Drewes in years, and I won't feel like I'm really home until I have a strawberry concrete."

At the mention of the landmark South Side frozen custard stand, she gave him a suspicious look. "Did Cole tell you I like Ted Drewes?"

"No. This was my own idea. So you're a Ted Drewes fan?"

Her features relaxed. "Isn't everyone? Okay. I'm sold."

Once he settled her in his car, Mitch slipped his jacket off his shoulders, grinning as he circled around to the driver's side.

Now this was what he called a date.

A real one.

And if all went well, perhaps it would be the first of many.

2

Alison scooped the last bite of custard out of her cardboard cup, closed her eyes, and licked the plastic spoon as she leaned against the side of Mitch's midnight blue Accord. "Perfect!"

"I couldn't agree more."

Detecting a smile in his voice, she looked over at him. He was leaning against the car too, his long legs crossed at the ankles . . . and his gaze was fixed on her.

Under his blatant—and appreciative—perusal, heat rose on her cheeks. "Are you flirting with me, Mitch Morgan?"

"Guilty as charged. And not the least repentant." His smile broadened to a grin.

"We hardly know each other."

"There's a way to fix that."

She tapped the spoon against her empty cup and watched a stretch limo pull up in front of the simple custard stand. Streetlights had turned the ten o'clock darkness into daylight, but the crowds milling about paid scant attention to the wedding party emerging from behind the tinted privacy windows. It wasn't an unusual occurrence.

But being here with a handsome man—who made no secret of his interest—was out of the ordinary. Ted Drewes had been too plebian for David, and he'd never been in any hurry to advance their relationship.

Mitch, on the other hand, struck her as a man who went

after what he wanted with single-minded determination—and didn't waste any time doing it.

That sent a little thrill zipping through her. But it also scared her.

She turned back to him, deciding to repay honesty with honesty. "I'm not a fast mover, Mitch."

"I can be patient. If it's worth my while." He held her gaze, his own never wavering.

She blinked. "You don't mince words, do you?"

"Your old boyfriend did?"

"Let's just say he was a bit more . . . discreet . . . in his intentions."

"His mistake. What does he do for a living?"

"He's an attorney. For the Legal Aid Society."

"That figures. It's hard to get a straightforward or decisive opinion from a lawyer. Let me pitch that for you." He tugged her cup from her fingers and set off across the parking lot.

Watching the fabric of his dress shirt grow taut across his broad shoulders as he tossed the empty containers into the trash bin, Alison felt a faint flutter of excitement in the pit of her stomach. She hadn't experienced anything like this since the early days of David's courtship. Even then, there had never been such tangible chemistry.

But chemistry could be dangerous. Especially with a man who might view relationships in a far more casual light than she did. So she didn't intend to get carried away. Better safe than sorry, as the old adage cautioned. She needed to take things slow and easy.

As he rejoined her, he touched his tie. "Do you mind if I loosen this? The transition to jacket and tie has been tough. I peel off the formal attire as soon as I get home from the station and avoid it entirely on weekends."

Alison firmly banished that image from her mind. "No problem."

He tugged on the knot of silk at his throat and let out a relieved breath. "Better." Leaning back beside her against the car, he shoved his hands in his pockets and shot her a rakish grin, producing a dimple in his cheek that matched the one in his chin. "So tell me about Alison."

She lifted her shoulders. "There's not much to tell. I grew up here. Got a degree in social work at one of the local universities. Landed a job in the Department of Social Services Children's Division, where I've been for the past twelve years. Compared to my brothers, I lead a quiet, boring life."

"Doing important work. Hard work. The unsung hero kind of stuff." He studied her in silence for a few beats. "You must see some bad situations in your job."

When was the last time a man had looked at her with such absolute focus, as if she was the most important thing in the world?

She couldn't remember.

But she liked it. A lot.

Slow and easy, Alison. Remember?

Right.

She eased slightly away. "No worse than what you've seen, I'm sure."

"Watching adults inflict damage on each other isn't fun, but seeing innocent children get hurt . . . that's a whole different ball game. How do you deal with it?"

He'd homed right in on the most troubling part of her job. The part that sometimes gave her nightmares.

"Not always very well. There are nights I lay awake worrying about children who've crossed my path. Wondering how they're being treated. If they'll end up on the streets." She frowned and tucked her hair behind her ear. "I love children, and seeing them in bad situations tears me up. They're so vulnerable, so easily victimized. Someone needs to see that justice is served on their behalf. To protect them. The job seemed like a good fit."

"Is it?"

"Yes. Most days."

"Cole tells me your oldest brother is a U.S. marshal. Interesting that all of you went into justice-related fields."

She smiled. "My dad can take the credit for that. He was a beat cop who did his very best every day to protect the innocent and defend justice. The world lost a good man when he died too young five years ago." Her voice hoarsened, and she swallowed. "I think all of his children inherited the justice gene."

"Not a bad legacy to pass on." Mitch folded his arms across his chest. "And what do you do at the end of the day to unwind?"

"Cook. Knit. Garden. I used to love to swim too, but that's still a little tough. I'm easing back into it, though. And since last summer, Bert has kept me occupied—and entertained."

His brow rippled for an instant—then smoothed out. "Oh yeah. Your dog. I'm sure he's a fine companion. But dogs do have their limitations."

She ignored his implication and turned the tables. "Now that you know my life story, tell me about Mitch Morgan. You grew up in St. Louis, right?"

"Yep. In a small house not too far from here. As a matter of fact, I'm living there now while I look for an apartment."

"What brought you back?"

"My dad. He had to have bypass surgery recently, which was a very tangible reminder that he's getting older—and that times change. I wasn't around much during the last years of my mom's life. I regret that now. So I wanted to be here more for him."

"You must have been a close family."

"We were. We used to call ourselves the Three Musketeers. I arrived long after my parents had given up hope of ever having a family, and I suspect that contributed to the closeness. We weren't wealthy in a material sense, but I had a very rich childhood."

A man who loved his parents. Who had his priorities and values straight.

Nice.

"How did your dad feel about you coming back?"

He gave her a crooked grin. "Happy on one hand. Guilt

ridden on the other. He thinks he's taking me away from my glamorous life." The grin faded. "Actually, he did me a favor. The so-called glamour was waning."

"Cole said you were a SEAL."

"For eight years."

"That's impressive."

He shrugged. "I liked to swim. I liked excitement. I wanted to serve my country. Being a SEAL seemed like the best way to accomplish all of that."

"Was it?"

"Yeah."

"So why did you leave?"

"My enlistment was up. And I'd seen enough action."

"So you took a quiet job with the NYPD SWAT team."

He quirked an eyebrow. "Cole must have been a font of information."

"Maybe he hoped your intriguing background would entice me to go out with you."

"It must have worked."

"Nope." The wedding party passed by, close enough for her to hear one of the groomsmen tease the newlyweds about getting started on the large family they wanted. A wave of melancholy washed over her, and she tuned out the conversation. "You know what clinched the deal? When he said you needed my help to dodge matchmaking attempts at the wedding."

"Ah. You have a soft heart."

"I thought we were talking about you?"

"I'm changing the subject."

"I noticed. Very smooth, sailor."

One side of his mouth hitched into a half smile. "I like a woman who can hold her own in a verbal sparring match."

Her neck grew warm. "My brothers don't."

"That's not what I hear."

"Yeah?" She shot him a skeptical look.

"Yeah. Cole sang your praises the night he used the sympathy card to convince me to take you to the wedding."

"You must have a soft heart too."

"Let's keep that our secret, okay?" He pushed off from the car, pressing the heel of his hand against the edge of the roof as he angled toward her. "And as far as sympathy goes, just for the record, that guy you were dating needs it more than you do. He lost out big-time when he let you get away."

His comment filled her heart with warmth, chasing away her momentary melancholy. *Slow and easy, Alison.*

She summoned up a pert smile. "Cole should have warned me about your silver tongue. You have some great lines."

"I happen to mean that one." All levity vanished from his face. "Why did you two break up, anyway? If you don't mind me asking."

For some reason, she didn't. "He couldn't handle the long-term consequences of my accident. I had some . . . permanent damage."

Twin furrows appeared on Mitch's brow. She knew he was debating whether to ask the obvious follow-up question—and saved him the trouble by answering it.

"I had serious internal injuries." She dropped her voice and tugged her shawl tighter. "David wanted children, and I'll never be able to have them."

The noise continued around them in the parking lot, but all at once it receded into the background. As if a clear curtain had dropped, insulating them from the world around them.

"He left you because of that?"

The chill in Mitch's eyes—and his grim tone—took her off guard. "Having a family was important to him."

"Hasn't he ever heard of adoption?"

"That wasn't for him."

He didn't respond. With words, anyway. Instead, he twined his lean, strong fingers with hers. "His loss."

Her throat tightened. "Thank you. And for the record, I'm over him, despite what Cole might think. I have been for several months."

"Good. That leaves room for someone else to step in."

He hadn't said "me." But the implication was clear.

He squeezed her hand, and when he relinquished it, she missed his touch at once.

"Are you ready to call it a night? I promised to take my dad to church in the morning, and he likes the early service."

"Yes." She moved aside as he opened the door, then slipped into the car. All the while trying to analyze what had just happened. She'd never shared so much personal information with anyone on such short acquaintance. Nor felt such a strong attraction.

This was crazy.

Things were happening way too fast.

And now she had a dilemma on her hands. What should she do if he tried to kiss her good night?

If that issue was bothering Mitch, he gave no sign of it as he drove her home. His hand was steady on the wheel, his posture relaxed, his banter laid-back.

She, on the other hand, was a mass of nerves. By the time they pulled up in front of her house, she couldn't even remember what they'd talked about during the drive.

After braking to a stop, he switched off the ignition. "Sit tight. I'll get your door."

He slid out of the driver's seat, and a few seconds later her door was pulled open. Once she was on her feet, he took her arm and guided her up the concrete path toward her porch.

Still waging an internal debate about how to handle their parting, she took no notice of her surroundings as she groped in her purse for her keys—until Mitch spoke.

"Looks like you have another admirer."

She paused at the bottom of the three steps. What appeared to be a bouquet wrapped in green floral tissue lay in front of her door, illuminated by the light from the decorative lanterns on each side.

Stymied, she gaped at it. "Who on earth would be sending me flowers?"

"I think you've been holding out on me."

At his teasing comment, she ascended the steps. "Trust me . . . I haven't."

Mitch followed, bending down to retrieve the bouquet before she could reach for it. As he lifted it, the tissue gapped open to reveal the flowers inside. All of them wilted. The roses and carnations and daisies were not only well past their prime, their heads were drooping into the brown-edged filler fern.

Alison had never seen a sorrier bouquet.

"How strange." She pulled her shawl closer around her. "This wasn't here when we left, and it's not warm enough yet to kill flowers that fast. They must have been delivered looking like that."

When her comment produced no response, she looked up. Twin creases had appeared on Mitch's brow.

"Let's go in for a minute, okay?" He nodded toward the door.

So much for her quandary about how to handle a romantic overture. Based on his grim expression, the last thing on his mind was a good-night kiss.

In silence, she fitted the key in the lock.

He followed her across the threshold to the tune of loud beeps, shut the door behind them, and stuck close as she hurried to the back door to turn off the security system she'd activated before they left. An excited, muffled bark from the basement broke the stillness after the alarm went silent.

"I need to let Bert go outside for a few minutes."

"I'll go down and get him." He set the bouquet on the kitchen table and started for the basement door.

Her first inclination was to say she'd handle it. But in light of the unsettling vibes she was picking up from both Mitch and the creepy bouquet, she curbed that auto response. A solo trip to the basement wasn't all that appealing tonight.

Sixty seconds later, a happy yip from Bert and a rattle from the cage preceded the sound of mad scrambling on the steps. A heartbeat later, Bert scooted past her legs and careened through the kitchen. Mitch rejoined her at a more sedate pace, flashing a quick grin.

"There's no energy shortage in this house."

An answering smile tugged at her lips as she crossed to the back door and flipped the locks. No sooner had she cracked the door than Bert zipped past, disappearing into the shadows at the edge of her patio, past the range of her security lighting.

"He'll scratch on the door when he's ready to come back in."

Mitch gave a brief nod, then gestured to the bouquet. "Mind if I see whether there's a card?"

"Help yourself."

He crossed to the café table in the small bay window and tore off the taped-together tissue. The cloying scent of decaying vegetation wafted toward her, and she took a step back.

Exposed to the light, the bouquet looked even more pathetic. As Mitch shifted it around, three withered petals from a lily, their color fading into transparency, drifted to the floor.

"No card." Mitch straightened. "Any idea who might have sent them?"

She started to shake her head. Stopped. Frowned.

"You know . . . I have gotten three weird phone calls in the past couple of weeks. Maybe there's a connection."

"Define weird." He pinned her with an intent look.

"All I hear is heavy breathing, then the person hangs up."

"And you have no idea who might be behind those either?"

"No."

"Have you told Cole?"

She grasped the back of a chair and lifted her chin. "No. I figured it was just a teenage prank, or someone who gets their kicks trying to scare people. If I tell Cole or Jake about it, they'll turn it into a major case squad issue, insist on sleeping here at night, and escort me to and from work. They've always been overprotective, but since the accident last year they've been treating me like a fragile butterfly. I love them for caring, but I've had enough hovering to last a lifetime." She waved a hand at the bouquet. "This kind of stuff isn't dangerous. Just annoying."

"Harassment is against the law. We could trace the calls."

"There's no need to do that. I have the numbers from the last two calls, thanks to caller ID."

She crossed the kitchen and removed the small piece of paper from the corkboard by her phone. "I didn't write down the number from the first call, but I have a feeling it came from the second number. It looked familiar when it flashed on caller ID." She walked back and handed it to him.

After a quick glance, he flashed her a smile. "You've noted dates and times. Excellent."

"My brothers trained me well."

"It's odd that your caller isn't using call blocking." He studied the numbers.

"I thought so too. I guess he's using public phones."

"Probably. But he's still taking a chance. These calls place him in a certain spot at a certain time. There might be witnesses who could identify him."

"He doesn't seem to be worried about that."

"The question is, why not?"

"I haven't a clue." She considered the flowers. "You know, it's possible those are unrelated to the phone calls."

"Possible, but not probable. The timing's too close to be coincidental." He fisted his hands on his hips. "And I don't like the fact that this person has physically shown up at your house."

She didn't either, though she wasn't about to admit that. She had state-of-the-art locks, well-placed exterior lighting, and an excellent security system. Cole had taken care of those defensive measures before she'd moved in two years ago. She also had Bert. Her best alarm system. Safety had never been a concern.

Until now.

Not that she planned to admit that either.

"I'm sure it's just some prank, Mitch. I'm not worried."

His gaze dropped to her white-knuckled grip on the back of the kitchen chair beside her. She loosened it at once—but it was too late.

"Okay, maybe I'm a little worried. But I don't want to over-react. There might never be another incident."

"That's true. In the meantime, though, why don't I check out these numbers? That might be all it takes to solve the mystery."

She bit her lower lip and shot him a warning look. "I don't want Cole in on this."

"I'm okay with that. As long as it's not an official investigation." He withdrew a business card from his pocket. "Once we have the phone locations, we may be able to get a squad car there fast enough to spot the caller if you hear from him again. At the very least, the officer could ask around, see if there are any witnesses." He held out the card. "Will you promise to call me immediately if he bothers you again? Day or night?"

As she took the card, their fingers brushed. The brief touch of warmth from his helped chase the chill from hers.

"I hate to bother you with this."

"It's no bother. Promise you'll call either me or Cole."

"I'd rather call you."

"I'd prefer that too." He smiled.

A jolt of electricity zipped between them, and Alison was grateful when a scratch on the door signaled Bert's return—and diffused the charged atmosphere.

By the time she let him in, reset the locks, and turned back to Mitch, he'd picked up the flowers. "Why don't I get rid of these?"

"No argument from me. There's a trash can in my garage. Through there." She indicated the door that led from the kitchen into the attached single-car structure.

He rejoined her moments later, brushing off his hands. Rather than stop in the kitchen, he continued toward the front door. "I should be going."

She followed. "I had a nice evening."

He paused at the threshold to smile at her. "I did too. In fact, I'm hoping it's not a onetime event. Are you by any chance free for dinner next Friday night? I can promise you a better dining experience than roast beef and mostaccioli."

He was asking her out on a real date.

This night was turning out far better than she'd expected. Despite the flowers.

"I'd like that. Very much."

His smile heated up a few degrees, and the room suddenly grew too warm. She let the shawl slip from her shoulders but resisted the urge to fan her face.

"I'll be in touch to arrange the details. In the meantime, be careful."

"You sound like Cole."

"I'm not sure I want to be compared to one of your brothers."

She grinned. "Trust me. I don't think of you as a brother."

He volleyed with a chuckle—and a look that was most unbrotherly. "That's nice to hear." He winked and opened the door. "Good night."

"Good night."

She set the lock, then peeked through the peephole, watching as he walked through the shadows with a spare, easy grace that had no doubt served him well as a SEAL. Wondering how many hearts he'd broken. A man like that didn't make it to his thirties without leaving more than a few in his wake.

And she didn't intend hers to be one of them.

Been there, done that.

But she wasn't averse to moving forward either. Slow and easy, of course. After all, he was a handsome, charming, intriguing man. And they'd clicked tonight—in spite of Cole, not because of him. Even though her brother would take the credit if things worked out.

"But his gloating would be a small price to pay, don't you think, Bert?" She scooped her furry companion into her arms and walked down the hall to her bedroom.

In reply, Bert snuggled close and made a contented sound deep in his throat.

She could only agree.

3

At the sudden ring of her phone at noon on Sunday, Alison jerked toward it, sending an arc of water from the pitcher in her hands spewing across the floor.

Delighted with the dandy new game, Bert leapt in the air and skidded through the elongated puddle, careening into her legs with an enthusiastic yip.

Muttering under her breath, Alison grabbed the counter to steady herself as the phone continued to ring.

"Cool it, Bert. This isn't a game."

He cocked his head, spared her a quick, "Oh yeah?" look, and continued to cavort in the water.

Huffing out a sigh, Alison set the pitcher down and checked caller ID. Although that sequence of digits had never before appeared on her readout, she knew who was on the other end. She'd memorized Mitch's cell number after he'd left last night.

Her heart did a little flutter as she wiped her palms on her jeans, picked up the phone, and said hello.

"Alison, it's Mitch. Everything quiet over there?"

"Yes." She climbed onto a stool next to the counter as Bert made a flying leap into the puddle and skidded across the floor, delivering another series of excited barks. "Relatively speaking, anyway."

"Your pooch sounds wound up."

"Yeah. I spilled some water as the phone rang and he dived right in."

A deep-throated chuckle came over the line. "Do you need to corral him?"

She regarded the frolicking dog. "I'll let him have a couple more minutes of fun."

"Speaking of fun . . . I enjoyed last night."

Turning her back on the havoc in her kitchen, she gave Mitch her full attention. "I did too."

"And I'm looking forward to Friday. Shall I pick you up around seven?"

"Perfect. What's the attire?"

"I plan to wear a jacket."

"What? No tie?" A smile teased her lips.

"I will if you prefer."

"I'm flattered you'd make such a sacrifice in my honor. But I'll let you off the hook this time."

"You have my undying gratitude."

"Wow . . . you're awfully easy to please."

"Hold that thought." He let her mull that over for a few seconds. When he spoke again his tone was more serious. "I also called to let you know I had our Communications Bureau research the numbers you gave me. As you suspected, they're public phones. I did a drive-by this morning. One's outside a quick shop in South County. The other's at a gas station about a quarter mile from your house."

Some of her lighthearted mood evaporated. "What does that tell us?"

"For one thing, we should be able to get a squad car to either location pretty quickly if he calls again. Both of those areas are well patrolled. Keep my number handy, okay?"

"I will." No need to tell him she had it memorized. "So what's on your agenda for the rest of the day?" Bert dived into the water again, and she grabbed him by the collar as he slid by, giving him a stern look. Fun time was over. "Be a good boy, okay?"

"Sure. But you'll have to define good."

At Mitch's teasing comeback, warmth crept up her cheeks. "I was talking to Bert."

"Oh. Too bad." He gave an exaggerated sigh. "To answer your question, I'll be painting. The porch on my dad's house is long overdue. There's a lot of other stuff that's been neglected too. He always used to stay on top of maintenance, but it's gotten away from him since his bypass. He tries to keep up—in fact, he does too much—but his energy level isn't what it was."

"Will that improve?"

"Yes. If he takes care of himself. But he's not doing the best job of that. The first thing I did when I got home was stock the kitchen with healthy food. All he had was canned soup and frozen dinners and artery-clogging junk."

"Sounds like your work is cut out for you."

"True. But on a brighter note, I have Friday to look forward to. Although it seems a long way off. Any chance I might be able to talk you into a Ted Drewes run some night this week?"

Bert growled low in his throat and shook his head, dislodging her grip on his collar. He bounded away to play in the water again.

"Rats." She shot the pup a dismayed look.

"Not the most enthusiastic response I've ever had to an invitation." Mitch's amused voice came over the line.

"Sorry. Bert escaped." She surveyed the tile floor in disgust. "While you're painting, I'll be mopping. And yes to Ted Drewes."

"Great. I'll call you soon. Give Bert a pat for me."

She eyed the pooch, who seemed to sense that playtime was about over. He'd retreated to the corner of the kitchen and was watching her warily.

"Bert is in big trouble."

He chuckled. "Don't be too hard on him. He's a cute little guy."

"Good looks don't excuse bad behavior."

"I'll remember that." She could hear the grin in his voice. "Talk to you soon."

As the line went dead, she found herself smiling. Bert gave a tentative wag of his tail and tipped his head, his expression hopeful. She slid off the stool, gingerly crossed the wet floor, and scooped him up. One look into his happy brown eyes and she was a goner. Which was bad. If she didn't start exerting some discipline soon, he'd be hopeless. Maybe it was time to think about an obedience class.

But she'd worry about that tomorrow. Because at the moment, her thoughts were on another pair of brown eyes.

And a trip to Ted Drewes with the man who owned them.

"Are you gonna eat that last toasted ravioli?" Cole directed the question to Jake, who sat across from him at the table in the cozy restaurant.

"You can have it. Unless Liz wants it." Jake turned to his fiancée.

"Are you kidding? I don't think I'm going to eat for three days. Good thing we only come to The Hill for Italian food every other Sunday or the seams on my clothes would be straining."

"As if you have to worry." Alison grinned at her soon-to-be sister-in-law. With her svelte figure and long blonde hair, she definitely did not fit the stereotype of a federal judge.

"You should talk." Cole popped the entire ravioli into his mouth. "You could stand to put some more meat on your bones." The words came out garbled as he chewed.

"Talking with your mouth full is bad manners. And I've gained back most of the weight I lost after the accident."

"Yeah?" Cole ignored the reprimand and gave her a skeptical glance.

"Yeah. And if I keep going to Ted Drewes, I'll put on the rest in no time."

The instant she uttered the words, she knew she'd made a tactical error.

"You've been going to Ted Drewes without inviting us?" Jake gave her a wounded look.

35

"Just once."

"When?"

"Recently. Liz, did you ever lock in a florist for the wedding?"

"Whoa. Not so fast." Cole leaned forward. "Who'd you go with?"

"You have marinara sauce on your chin." Alison flicked a finger in Cole's direction, then refocused on Liz—hoping her brother would take the hint and drop the subject. "So, did you—"

"Wait." Cole wiped off the sauce with a napkin, dashing her hopes. "Why aren't you answering my question?"

"What is this, the third degree?" Liz cast a sympathetic look toward Alison. "You're off duty, Cole."

"I'm curious myself." Jake took a sip of his iced tea, his dark eyes watching her over the rim.

She felt like the proverbial bug under a microscope.

"And you're off duty too, Jake." Liz elbowed him gently in the ribs. "Alison has a right to a private life."

"That reminds me—how was the date?" The question from Cole, delivered with a smirk, drew everyone's attention.

"What date?" Jake redirected his attention to Cole.

"I set her up with our new detective last night."

Jake's eyes narrowed. "What do you know about this guy?"

"He's a former Navy SEAL. Came to us from the NYPD."

"A lot of those guys are hard partiers."

"Mitch is okay. He has his head on straight."

"Yeah?"

"Yeah." Cole glared at his older brother. "You think I'd send Alison on a date with someone I didn't trust?"

Alison reached for her purse in disgust. "I'm out of here."

"Wait." Jake's hand shot out, keeping her in place. "Was this guy a gentleman?"

Pulling free of Jake's grasp, she glared at her brothers. "Yes. And for the record"—she sent a deliberate glance toward Cole—"it wasn't a date. I was doing a favor for a new guy in town who needed a companion for a family wedding reception. As for Ted Drewes, we stopped there on the way home. End of story."

Sort of.

"What did you mean when you said if you *keep* going to Ted Drewes?" Cole squinted at her. "It sounded like another trip is in the offing."

"Gracious." Liz looked at the two brothers, then at Alison. "You weren't kidding when you told me how overbearing they could be."

"Overbearing?" Jake frowned at his intended.

"Yes. Overbearing. Both of you." Liz aimed that comment at Cole. "Alison is a big girl. She can take care of her own social life. If I was on the bench, I'd rule both of you out of order."

Alison grinned. "You are so welcome in this family, Liz!"

"Thank you." She grinned, settled back in her chair, and tucked her arm in Jake's. "Now, let's talk about the flowers."

As the women debated the pros and cons of stock versus delphinium and roses versus orchids, the two men's eyes began to glaze over.

Changing the subject had been an excellent strategy.

But even though the topic of her love life had been set aside for the evening, Alison knew it would come up again.

Because she knew her brothers.

In this case, however, their concerns were misplaced. While their acquaintance was brief, Alison sensed Mitch was a man of honor and integrity. A man who could be trusted to protect secrets—and lives. A man who knew how to deal with the hard stuff in life without losing his soft heart.

A man who might be destined to play an important role in her future.

And that was one insight she had no intention of sharing with her brothers.

"Sorry, Bert. But Ted Drewes calls." She secured the clasp on Bert's cage in the basement and tuned out his pleading whine. Since Mitch had called last night to set up this outing, it had dominated her thoughts. She'd zoned out for most of the Wednesday morning staff meeting today, and this afternoon she'd driven right by the turn she'd made countless times on home visits to one of the families in her caseload.

On the plus side, however, neither Cole nor Jake had bugged her about Mitch since Sunday night.

The muffled ring of her phone wafted down the basement steps, and she ascended as quickly as she could, wondering if Mitch had been delayed. She grabbed the handset just before the answering machine kicked in.

"Hello?"

The only response was heavy breathing.

Her heart began to hammer, and Alison groped on the counter for her cell phone, tapping in Mitch's number with an unsteady finger.

As soon as he answered, she depressed the mute button on her home phone. "Mitch, it's Alison. My mystery caller is on the other line."

"Which number is he calling from?" His question came out in a clipped, no-nonsense voice she'd never heard before.

She recited it.

"That's the South County location. I'll get a squad car over there. Talk to him. Try to keep him on the line. I'm five minutes from your house." The line went dead.

Alison lifted her finger off the mute button. She could still hear breathing.

"Look, can you tell me why you're doing this?" She tried for a conversational tone, searching for some way to prolong the contact. "Is there something you want? Do we know each other?" She paused. The heavy breathing continued. "Listen, I got your flowers. They weren't in great shape. If they were fresh when you picked them up, you ought to tell the florist and get your money back. It wasn't hot enough to make them wilt that much in such a . . ."

A hum on the line told her he'd hung up.

Caught off guard by a sudden unsteadiness in her legs, Alison resettled the phone in its cradle and eased onto a stool by the counter.

All the while praying the patrol officer would arrive in time to find her caller and put an end to these distressing disruptions in her life.

As Mitch strode up the path to Alison's house, the front door opened.

She'd been watching for him.

He closed the distance between them and slipped inside, shutting the door behind him as he gave her a quick scan. "Are you okay?"

"Of course." She tried for a smile, but the tremble in her lips refuted her words. As did the quiver in her hand when she tucked her hair behind her ear.

The latest call had rattled her. Badly.

"Dispatch sent two cars that were in the vicinity. I haven't heard anything back yet. How long did you keep the guy on the line?"

"A little longer than usual. But I doubt it was long enough."

"It's possible he . . ." His phone began to vibrate and he pulled it out of its holder. "Morgan."

He listened as dispatch gave him the bad news. "Okay. Thanks."

"He was gone, right?" Alison crossed her arms over her chest.

"Yeah." He slid the phone back onto his belt. "But they're going to ask around and see if anyone noticed who used the phone. Unfortunately, it's in the parking lot, and areas of transient traffic often aren't very productive. The guy's luck will run out one of these times, though."

"Unless he gets tired of his game and quits first."

"That could happen too." He smiled, determined to ease the tension in her features. "Ready for Ted Drewes?"

"Sure." Her answering smile seemed strained. "Let me grab my purse and set the alarm."

He waited while she retreated to the kitchen, and thirty seconds later he heard her punching her code into the keypad. A loud series of steady beeps echoed through the house as she rejoined him.

After opening the door, he waited while she exited, noting that her fingers were still unsteady as she fitted her key in the lock.

She'd warned him on their first date that she wasn't a fast mover, and he respected that. Yet he couldn't resist the impulse to take her hand as they walked toward his car. It was a gesture of comfort more than attraction, and he hoped she'd see it as such. To be safe, however, he reinforced his motivation with words.

"You know, most prank calls aren't dangerous." Her fingers were icy, and he rubbed his thumb over the back of her hand.

"I know." She didn't pull away. Good. "But they're unnerving."

"No argument there. With your excellent home security, though, you don't have to worry about being safe here. And I'm only a phone call away."

She aimed a rueful look in his direction as he leaned down to open the car door. "You got a whole lot more than you bargained for when you agreed to take me to that wedding, didn't you?"

He straightened up, giving her delicate sandals, her slim Capri slacks with the flirty little notch on the bottom of each leg, and the soft knit top that emphasized her trim figure an appreciative, unhurried perusal. His gaze lingered on her full lips and sky-blue eyes.

"Yeah, I did."

A soft blush rose on her cheeks. "Are you flirting again?"

"What do you think?" He grinned at her and leaned closer.

"I think you're moving too fast for me."

"Well, we can't have that." He eased back and gestured to the car. "No more flirting. Tonight, anyway."

For the next two hours, as he drove into the city, ate his

frozen custard standing in the parking lot with the hordes of other St. Louisans who'd made the same pilgrimage, then drove her home, he did his best to keep that promise. But it wasn't easy. Especially when he walked her to the door at the end of the evening and the urge to kiss her good night undermined his resolve.

As if reading his thoughts, she shot him an uncertain look. "Do you want to come in?"

"Do you want me to?"

"Yes—but I'm not sure that's wise."

He propped a shoulder against the siding beside the door and studied her. "Because you don't trust me?"

"No. Because I don't trust myself."

He gave her a slow smile. "Are you flirting with me, Alison Taylor?"

"No." Her expression remained serious. "I'm being honest. There's a lot of chemistry going on here."

"You think?" He lifted his hand and brushed a few stray strands of hair off her face.

She sucked in a breath. Swallowed. "Yeah. But I got hurt badly with someone I thought I knew very well. Someone I'd dated for over a year and was considering marrying. That experience left me very cautious—and less confident about my instincts."

"You know what? My instincts have rarely let me down. And they tell me you have great instincts." Slowly . . . reluctantly . . . he withdrew his hand. "However, I do understand where you're coming from. I'm not the most patient man, but as I said the night we met, I'm willing to wait for something worth waiting for." He gestured to the door. "Go on in. I'll stay here while you turn off the alarm."

A loud beeping greeted them as she opened the door, and he waited on the threshold until it ceased. Moments later, she rejoined him.

"I'll take a quick walk around the outside of the house before I leave."

She frowned. "Do you think that's necessary?"

"Can't hurt. Are we still on for Friday at seven?"

The parallel grooves on her brow eased. "Unless you want to back out."

"No way." He reached up and touched her cheek. "Good night."

"Thank you for another nice evening—and for understanding."

"Hey . . . if empathy earns me brownie points, I'll work even harder on it." He flashed her a grin. "See you soon."

Lifting a hand in farewell, he did a quick circuit of the house. The gate to the fenced yard was latched, and there was no evidence of uninvited visitors. All appeared to be quiet.

Yet he was as unnerved by the calls as Alison, despite his truthful reassurance that such pranks weren't usually dangerous. Because most pranksters didn't leave flowers—wilted or otherwise.

There was more to this incident than someone just wanting a few sick laughs at Alison's expense. He knew that intuitively. And as he'd told Alison, he trusted his instincts.

Meaning this game wasn't over yet.

4

Not again!

Alison jerked to a stop as she approached her front door on Thursday night. Another bouquet wrapped in floral paper rested against it.

Despite the humid evening warmth, a chill rippled through her.

Bert, clearly confused about why they'd paused this close to the door after completing their ritual bedtime walk, gave an impatient tug on his leash.

"Hang on a sec, Bert."

He tilted his head and aimed a quizzical look her direction. As if to ask what was wrong.

And from his perspective, nothing was, she realized. If any shady character was lurking about, her little guy would have alerted her. He always barked at strangers. So whoever had left this latest present hadn't hung around.

Nevertheless, she approached the porch and ascended the steps slowly. Although she kept a firm grip on Bert's leash, she let him get close enough to the tissue-wrapped sheaf to give it a thorough sniff. After a few pokes with his nose, however, his interest shifted to a moth bobbing around his ears.

As Bert pranced around in pursuit of the fluttering insect, Alison edged toward the door. Toeing the package aside, she fitted her key in the lock, removed Bert's leash, and let him scamper inside while she bent to pick up the flowers.

The last bouquet had been heavy. This one was light.

Too light.

Keeping it at arm's length, she crossed to the porch swing and set it on the slatted seat. As an owl screeched in the wooded common ground behind her house and the light from the lanterns on either side of the door cast ghostly shadows, she was transported back to her childhood. To the days when she'd been afraid that monsters lurked in the gloomy fringes of light.

Except she wasn't a kid anymore. And she would not allow herself to be spooked by a few weird phone calls and some wilted flowers. She wouldn't give her stalker that satisfaction.

Mustering her courage, she leaned over the bouquet, grabbed a corner of the paper, tore it open—and stopped breathing.

As she stared at the contents, two things immediately became clear.

Her stalker had succeeded in spooking her after all.

And she needed to call Mitch.

Now.

Twenty minutes later, as Mitch strode up the walk toward Alison's front door, it opened to silhouette her slender, jeans-clad form.

Bypassing her latest gift, which still rested on the porch swing, he moved toward her. "Everything quiet since we talked?"

Bert let out a yip at her feet, and she bent to pick him up, cuddling him close to her chest. "Except for this little guy, who decided to play tug-of-war with me when I dropped a dish towel. He wasn't happy about losing, and he was very vocal about it."

One corner of Mitch's mouth quirked up, and he leaned closer to give Bert a quick pat. "Why don't you go back inside and shut the door? I'll join you in a minute." He gestured to the lanterns. "With the lights on out here, this porch is like a stage."

Casting a nervous look into the darkness beyond the circle of light, she nodded and slipped back inside.

Once the door closed, Mitch approached the swing and surveyed the two items left by her stalker, framed by the torn tissue. They were exactly as she'd described them.

A sheaf of dead, brittle roses, spray painted black, adorned with a lopped-off ribbon containing the X-ed out word *Beloved*—meaning they'd been salvaged from a funeral home dumpster . . . or from the top of a fresh grave.

And a bingo card, one number marked off with a skull-and-crossbones stamp.

A muscle clenched in his jaw. There were two possible motivations for a gift like this.

A very sick sense of humor.

Or a vendetta.

The first one made him mad.

The second one scared him.

Poking through the flowers, Mitch saw nothing to indicate who had sent them. The bingo card yielded no clues either. It was standard issue, the kind used at bingo nights all over the city. But it was new—suggesting someone had bought a pack for this express purpose.

There was a slim chance they could ID the culprit from fingerprints, if the guy hadn't worn gloves while handling it. But considering the evidence backlog at the county lab, the odds of getting a gift from a prankster processed were nil.

He heard the door open behind him, and Alison poked her head out. "Find anything helpful?"

"No." He crossed the porch and entered the house, closing the door behind him. "But I'm going to knock on a few doors where the lights are on and see if any of your neighbors happened to see someone suspicious on your property. You found these about half an hour ago. How long were you gone on your walk?"

"Less than twenty minutes."

He checked his watch. "So they were left sometime between nine and nine thirty. While I take a stroll, you might want to think about letting Cole in on this. And before you say no"—he held up his hand when her lips flattened into a mutinous line—"hear me out. Your 'admirer' is persistent, and this latest gift has an overtly threatening tone. Cole's been around a lot longer than I have and knows most of the beat officers. A request from him to beef up patrols on your street will carry a lot more weight than one coming from me. And having a cop car cruise by here more frequently isn't a bad idea."

A flicker of annoyance sparked in her eyes, telling him she still wasn't crazy about getting her brother involved. But she was also smart, and he hoped common sense would override her initial emotional reaction.

The sudden, resigned slump of her shoulders told him it had.

"Okay. I'll tell Cole. This weekend. The three of us are driving up to Chicago on Saturday morning for a Mother's Day celebration. We'll have plenty of time to talk about it in the car."

He thought about pressing her. He'd prefer to have a patrol car drive by a few times tonight, since she lived near the end of a quiet, dead-end street. But he let it go. She did have excellent security, and while the frequency of contact seemed to be accelerating, the likelihood her stalker would be back tonight was small.

"That should work. I'll take my walk now and stop back in before I leave."

She shoved her hands into her pockets. "I'm sorry to ruin your evening. I should have waited until tomorrow."

"You didn't ruin my evening." At her skeptical expression, he summoned up his most convincing smile. "You know what I was doing when you called? Cleaning the grout in my dad's bathroom. Trust me—I was thrilled to have an excuse to put that job on hold."

The hint of a smile teased her lips. "If you're trying to make me feel better, it's working."

"Good." He grasped the knob. "Lock up. I'll be back in a few minutes."

Once he heard the dead bolt click into place, he set off for the house next to Alison's, where a light was burning in the living room and he could see the flicker of a TV screen. He didn't have much hope anyone had seen anything, but it was worth asking. He didn't like the direction the stalker's messages were taking, and he'd rather head this thing off than let it escalate to a more serious—and dangerous—situation.

As it very well could.

Fifteen minutes later, when a knock sounded at Alison's door, Bert barked and raced toward it.

As she followed her canine friend, she didn't hold out a lot of hope that Mitch had learned anything useful. Except for one young couple at the entrance to the street, her neighbors were all older couples or widows. The small two- and three-bedroom bungalows tended to draw empty nesters. Like the Harrisons on her right, who always had the TV going at full blast; they never heard any neighborhood noise. Or Marjorie Evans, the widow on her left, who was hard of hearing and spent most of her time in the back room, listening to classical music and making quilts that she sold at a consignment shop. Or the O'Learys across the street, who were on their annual trip to Ireland.

One peek at his face through the peephole confirmed her assumption.

She swung the door open. "No luck, right?"

"No. The only house nearby with lights on was next door, and neither the man nor his wife heard or saw a thing. I can have a patrol officer swing by tomorrow and ask a few more questions at the other houses."

"I doubt that will produce any leads. Almost all my neighbors are older. They tend to close their shades as soon as it gets dark and go to bed early."

"It can't hurt to ask around, though."

They were still standing in the hall, and Alison gestured toward the living room. "Can I offer you a drink before you leave? I put some coffee on. I also have diet soda."

"I don't want to keep you up on a work night."

In light of her latest "gift," sleep was the last thing on her mind. She intended to defer retiring until she was a lot more tired, and she wouldn't mind Mitch's company in the interim. But it was a work night for him too. And he had other responsibilities.

Curbing her selfish impulse, she pasted on a smile. "Well, I appreciate you coming by."

He studied her for a moment with that discerning gaze of his. "I think I will have some coffee."

She let her fake smile flatten. "You don't have to stay to keep me company."

"It's either you or back to the grout." He grinned.

"Wow." Her lips twitched for real this time. "You sure know how to sweet-talk a girl."

Grinning, he followed her into the kitchen, Bert on his heels. He claimed a chair at the café table in the window and leaned down to scratch the pup under the chin.

She poured him some coffee, then withdrew a soda from the fridge. As she joined him at the table, she cast a glance at her pooch. Eyes closed, he was blissfully soaking up Mitch's attention. If he was a cat, he'd be purring in contentment.

"I think you've made a new friend."

"He's a cute little guy."

"Who's spoiled rotten, I'm afraid." She flipped the tab on her soda, releasing a whoosh of carbonation.

"How long have you had him?"

"I rescued him from the pound last summer."

"After your accident?"

"Yes." She took a long swallow of her soda and cast an affectionate look at the pup who'd won her heart with his unconditional love and distracted her with his antics through long, pain-filled days. "I needed a pick-me-up, and Bert fit the bill. He's seen me through some rough times."

"How rough?"

At Mitch's quiet question, she transferred her attention to him. He was focused on her just as intensely as he'd been that first night at Ted Drewes. As if every word she said mattered to him. It was the kind of look that could turn a girl's head. Make her care too much, too fast. Unless she was very careful. *Slow and easy, Alison.*

"I was hurt very badly." She rose before he could ask the obvious follow-up question. She needed to buy herself a few moments to think about how much she wanted to share. To figure out how much she *could* share without putting her heart at risk. "Will you excuse me for a minute? I threw some laundry in the dryer downstairs while you were making your circuit of the neighborhood and I need to get a few blouses out. Ironing is not on my top ten list of favorite activities."

"No problem." He took a sip from his mug, watching her over the rim.

And as she escaped to the basement, she had the disconcerting feeling he knew exactly why she'd needed to put some distance between them.

As Mitch waited for Alison to return, he took another sip of coffee, then grimaced and pushed it aside. He liked a strong brew, but this would dissolve wallpaper paste.

Bert nudged his leg, and he bent down to scratch his ear again. Entertaining as the pup was, though, he was far more interested in the dog's owner.

He couldn't remember the last time a woman had intrigued him this much. Maybe never. His job had always come first, and dating had served only one purpose—a chance to unwind and a brief respite from the pressures of his job. Nothing serious, no strings attached. That's how he'd liked it.

Until now.

Frowning, he tapped his finger against the table, producing a hollow thump. Odd. With Alison, his job came second—unless it related to keeping her safe—and strings didn't sound so bad. His instincts also told him that with her, serious wasn't an outcome to be avoided but cultivated.

That was a little scary.

Based on the way she'd hightailed it out of the room, she seemed to agree. Except he got the distinct feeling she found the notion even scarier than he did.

The sound of footsteps on the basement stairs alerted him to her return, and he shifted toward the door. With only seconds to develop a game plan, he decided to go for the direct approach.

"So what did you decide?"

She shot him a startled look as she shut the door. "What do you mean?"

"About whether or not you're going to share the details of your accident."

Expression wary, she crossed the room and retook her seat. "How do you do that?"

"What?"

"Look into my brain and see what I'm thinking."

He grinned. "Would you believe me if I said it was part of SEAL training?"

"No."

"In that case, I guess I'll have to be honest." He linked his fingers on the table and leaned closer. "The reason I know what you're thinking is because we're soul mates."

Her eyes widened briefly, then narrowed. As if she was uncertain about his sincerity.

"I'm dead serious, Alison."

Once more, her eyes widened. "You did it again."

He lifted his hands, palms up, and settled back in his chair. "I rest my case."

"Then how come I don't always know what *you're* thinking?"

"Because I've had a lot more practice guarding my thoughts. Thanks, in this case, to my SEAL training."

She toyed with her soda can, her expression speculative. "Okay. I'll admit I was debating that question."

"What did you decide?"

"You don't know?" She rested her elbow on the table, propped her chin in her hand, and shot him a teasing smile.

He grinned. "Cute." Settling his own elbows on the table, he steepled his fingers and grew more serious. "My instincts tell me you're going to tell me the story. That you trust me. And you *can* trust me. I promise you that."

Several beats of silence passed while she mulled over his comment. Finally, after taking a drink of soda, she set the can to the side and snapped her fingers at Bert. He bounded over, jumped into her lap, and wiggled into a comfortable position, resting his chin on her thigh. As if he'd been through this drill many times.

"Okay. I'll give you the basics. A year ago I was broadsided at an intersection by a drunk driver. My left leg was broken in two places, and I have a metal rod as a souvenir. I was on crutches for quite a while. My pelvis was fractured too, and I had blunt trauma injuries to my abdomen. Bad enough to require a hysterectomy. I was in physical therapy for months, and I still do strengthening exercises for my leg every day." She stroked Bert as she spoke, seeming to take as much comfort from the rhythmic gesture as her pup did. "On the plus side, other than never being able to have children and being a little underweight, I've made a great recovery. Now you know the whole story."

Not quite.

While she'd given him a lot of detail on her physical injuries, which had been far more severe than he'd thought, she'd also left much unspoken. What of the emotional toll the accident had wrought? The man she'd been in love with had walked away in the midst of her ordeal, and her ability to have children had been stolen from her. For a woman who'd chosen a career in child protection because she loved kids, the latter trauma alone would have been devastating.

Yet she'd picked herself up and carried on. Without a trace of self-pity, as far as he could tell. It took strength and grit and determination to move past an experience like that, and she'd exhibited all three in spades.

His first inclination was to pull her into his arms, tell her how special she was. But the potent chemistry between them already had her spooked. An impulsive action like that could send her running. And he couldn't take that risk. So he confined his response to words.

"You've had a tough time. I admire you for coping as well as you have."

She lifted one shoulder, dismissing his praise. "A lot of people have far worse problems. I know that firsthand, from going to rehab. Seeing the struggles other people had just to stand up, let alone walk, gave me a lot of perspective. As did prayer."

"Gaining perspective from rehab I can understand. Less so from prayer."

Her hand stilled on Bert's back and she frowned. "That surprises me. Didn't you say you take your dad to church?"

Uh-oh.

From her demeanor and the tone of her question, he could only conclude that Alison's faith was very important to her. Unfortunately, his relationship with God was lukewarm, at best. Had been for years. If he told her that, though, he suspected he could be shooting himself in the foot. Yet he couldn't lie.

"I do, but I don't stay for the service." He spoke slowly, choosing his words with care. "I haven't seen a lot of evidence that God takes much interest in our world. Or listens to prayers."

"You mean because he doesn't stop devastating hurricanes or effect miraculous cures? That kind of thing?"

She'd pretty much nailed it, though putting into words his reason for turning away from the faith of his youth sounded too simplistic. He shifted in his chair. How had they gotten into this, anyway? Religion and faith weren't topics he was comfortable discussing. But since he'd pushed her to talk about her accident, he supposed he owed her an answer.

"I've never thought about it in quite those terms, but yeah, I guess that sums it up. I've seen some bad stuff in my life. Stuff God could have prevented if he'd wanted to. Including your accident. Why would a caring, compassionate deity rob you of the ability to have children, when you obviously love them so much?"

A flash of pain rippled across her face, and he clenched his teeth. *Way to go, Morgan.* "Forget I asked that, okay?"

"No." She looked down at Bert and resumed her rhythmic stroking. "It's a fair question. There is injustice in the world. God doesn't will it, but he does permit it. And that injustice does make a lot of people turn away from him." She lifted her chin, her expression earnest. "But I believe he can bring good out of every instance of suffering and evil, if we let him. If we just put our trust in him, listen with an open and humble heart, and get out of his way, good can come from bad."

He tried to hide his skepticism. "Those words sound nice, but what positive outcome was there from your accident?"

A gentle smile tugged at her lips, and her gaze locked with his. "I met you."

Jolted, he stared at her.

"If I hadn't had the accident, I might be married by now. To the wrong man. Even if I wasn't, Cole wouldn't have gone out of his way to set me up with you. He's only started taking an active role in my social life since David and I split. So our paths might never have crossed. That would have been a shame, don't you think?"

He found his voice at last. "Yeah."

"I can also answer your question from the perspective of distance." She dislodged Bert from her lap, much to the pup's annoyance. Leaning forward, she clasped her hands on the table. "A year ago, I thought my world was ending. I couldn't see God's plan for me. As I've learned, it often takes time for a clear purpose to emerge. To see how one thing leads to another."

Okay, she had a point. His father's situation supported her theory too. When Mitch had gotten the call about the emergency bypass surgery, he'd seen nothing positive in the news. Sitting by his dad's bedside, watching the once-strong man he'd always looked up to struggle with simple tasks, helping him through the first couple of weeks, had been one of the most difficult things he'd ever done. Yet it had forced him to reevaluate his lifestyle. Had reminded him of the importance of relationships—and the danger of taking them for granted. And it had brought him home. Where he'd met Alison.

It seemed many events—good and bad—had worked to bring them together. And perhaps God's hand had been in it.

"That's food for thought, anyway." He took a sip of his coffee.

Her features tightened in frustration, as if she knew she hadn't convinced him. "I don't want to oversimplify things. There are many times when God's purpose and plan aren't clear. I may never know why some bad things happen, but I trust God does. That allows me to accept the bad as well as the good, even when I don't understand it."

Mitch knew all about trust. It was the bedrock of a SEAL operation. He'd put his life into the hands of his teammates on multiple occasions without a single qualm. But they deserved it. They'd proven their loyalty and dependability. The concept of trusting in some distant deity was a different matter altogether.

"Trust is hard for you, isn't it?" Alison's quiet words were more comment than question.

"Not with people who've earned it."

"God did. On Calvary."

He had no comeback for that.

Instead of pressing her advantage, Alison gave him a Mona Lisa smile that told him he wasn't the only one with mind-reading skills. But much to his relief, she offered him an out. "I think I'll be able to sleep now. Thanks for hanging around."

"I have a feeling I should be thanking *you*. And I'm sure God is grateful too." He flashed her a quick grin and stood. "Do you have a large plastic garbage bag? I want to save that bouquet."

She wrinkled her nose, but rose and pulled one out of a drawer. "What's the point? We trashed the last one."

"That one didn't feel as ominous—and it didn't have a bingo card with it." He took the bag. "Do you have a spot in your garage where we could store this?"

"Yes. There's a shelving unit on the far wall that's half empty."

"Clear evidence you haven't been here long." He tried to tease away the renewed tension that had crept back into her features. "You should see the shelving in my dad's garage. Not to mention the basement. There's forty years of stuff crammed into every available nook and cranny."

She gave him a rueful smile. "We had the same situation when my mom sold her house and moved to Chicago to live with her sister. Jake was out of town, so Cole and I tackled the job of going through everything while Mom supervised. I vowed never to accumulate that much stuff."

"Junk is insidious. I'll have to check back in forty years and see how you fared. Unless I happen to still be around."

"I think that might be a possibility."

Surprised at her candor, he raised an eyebrow. "For someone who claims to be a slow mover, that's a very interesting remark."

A soft blush suffused her cheeks and she bent down to give Bert a pat, hiding her face from his view. "You're right. Ignore it."

"No way. I'll take whatever encouragement I can get. I'll be back in a minute."

After exiting through the front door, he did a quick scan of the neighborhood. Not much was visible beyond the pool of light cast by the lanterns. And there was very little chance Alison's stalker had hung around. But if he had, Mitch wanted him to see she had the company of an able-bodied man on a regular basis. That might do more to discourage him than anything else.

Unless it was someone with a bizarre fixation, who wanted Alison for himself.

That scenario could be dangerous. Very dangerous.

But he wasn't going to go there. Yet.

After easing his hand under the brittle bouquet, he lifted it and slid the dead, black roses into the plastic bag. Once he'd deposited it on an empty shelf in her garage, he returned to the kitchen and nodded toward the front of the house. "Show me out?"

"Of course."

Reaching for her hand, he twined their fingers together in a gesture that had nothing to do with comfort. If she was already thinking about them as a couple forty years out, he figured he could risk this step.

She didn't pull away, and when they stopped by the door he turned to her. "A word of advice. Put the nighttime walks with Bert on hold until we get this thing sorted out. And call me if anything seems suspicious to you or you get another message of any kind from your stalker."

"Stalker." Her brow wrinkled. "I hadn't thought of him in those terms."

"He's kept this up long enough to qualify for that term. We're not dealing with a couple of teenage kids getting their kicks after some clandestine beer drinking party."

"I guess not."

He touched her cheek. "Be careful, okay?"

"Okay."

"I'll see you tomorrow at seven." Without waiting for a reply, he leaned down and brushed his lips across the satiny skin of her forehead.

Battling the impulse to dip his head lower and claim her lips, he started to pull back. But much to his surprise, she tightened her clasp on his hand, stood on tiptoe, and touched her lips to his.

Before he could recover enough to turn it into a real kiss, however, she took a step back.

"I'm still a slow mover." Her words came out breathless. "But I have to admit you're playing havoc with my resolve."

"Should I apologize?" He shoved his hands into his pockets to keep them out of trouble.

"I'm not sure." She took another step back and wiped her palms on the denim fabric of her jeans. When Bert trotted over, she picked him up and cuddled him in front of her. Almost like a shield.

"I don't think I will." He grinned at her and opened the door. "Lock up. And be ready for a night on the town tomorrow."

He pulled the door shut behind him, and once he heard her slide the lock and twist the dead bolt, he headed down the walk toward his car.

Wishing he didn't have to leave.

Counting the hours until tomorrow night.

And hoping the beefed-up patrols would be in place before Alison's stalker paid another visit.

5

"So how come you're not out with that pretty little gal you took to Kevin's wedding? That would be a far better use of your Saturday night than cleaning grout in your father's bathroom."

Wedged into a corner of the porcelain tub in the master bath, Mitch twisted toward the doorway. Walter Morgan had always been a strong, sturdy man who thrived on physical activity, and his job in the construction industry had kept him in shape his entire life. Even after he'd retired fifteen years ago, he'd maintained his trim physique. So his new, fragile gauntness—a souvenir of his recent surgery—sent a jolt of worry through Mitch every time he looked at him.

"I thought you were watching a movie."

"I was. But I've seen it before, and I'm tired of sitting around." Walt stuck his hands in the pockets of too-baggy slacks that were held up with a belt buckled in the last notch. "I think I'll trim the bushes out front before the light fades."

"That's on my to-do list for tomorrow, Pop. I'll get to it."

"I know you will. And I appreciate all you're doing. But I didn't have a heart attack, and I'm not an invalid. The doctor said it was okay for me to be more active now."

Mitch didn't miss the subtle, stubborn tilt in his father's chin. Nor the flinty determination that sparked to life in his eyes.

He bought himself a moment by wiping his hands on a rag.

58

With every day that passed, his dad had been getting more restless. More adamant about tackling chores. That was a positive thing—to a point. It meant his energy was returning and he was feeling better. Trouble was, Mitch thought he was pushing too hard. He'd tried every argument he could think of to convince his father to take things slower, but to no avail.

Like last Tuesday. He'd come home from work to find his dad patching drywall in a room slated for painting. On Wednesday, when he'd stopped in at the house unexpectedly at lunchtime, he'd discovered his father in the backyard, digging in the as-yet-unplanted vegetable garden. They'd come close to arguing that day.

"Why don't you fix us some dinner instead, Pop? You could steam some of the broccoli I bought yesterday and fire up the grill for the chicken breasts." So far, his father had demonstrated negligible interest in cooking. Mitch was hoping that before he moved out, he'd break his father of the habit of relying on high-fat, artery-clogging prepared meals.

"Why don't you do that while I take over your job?" Walt countered.

"What? You don't trust me?" Mitch tried to tease him into compliance. "I learned from the best carpenter and construction guy in the business."

It didn't work. His father's eyes narrowed, the way they used to when Mitch was a kid and Walt wasn't happy with some shenanigan he'd pulled.

"You know, sitting around feeling useless is as bad for a man's heart as too much cholesterol. Or working too hard. The ticker's fine, Mitch. You've talked to the doctor. I'm recovering from surgery, not a heart attack."

"I know." He'd had several long conversations with the doctor throughout the ordeal. "I just don't want you to wear yourself out. Or put too much strain on your heart while your body's trying to regain its strength."

"I appreciate that. But you're turning into a mother hen." He propped a shoulder against the door frame and shoved his hands in his pockets. "I've been on this earth for seventy-five years, son. The good Lord will take me when he's ready. Not a day before, not a day after. So there's no sense worrying about something you can't control. Let's just trust his timing on this, okay?"

Trust.

The same word Alison had used on Thursday night in reference to the Almighty.

He'd been thinking about it ever since. And about the sustaining strength—and peace—her faith gave her. He was beginning to sense that somehow he'd missed the boat on the whole faith thing. Pop's quiet expression of faith only reinforced that growing conviction.

"Mitch?"

At his father's prompt, he summoned up a grin. "Sorry. My mind wandered for a minute. I just don't want you to rush your departure, okay?"

"I'm not in a big hurry to leave, myself. Especially now that you're back. I have to admit, it's been a little lonely around here since your mom went to her reward. It sure is nice to have two of the Musketeers together again." He blinked and cleared his throat. "You never did answer my question about that little gal, Alison."

He should have known his father wouldn't let that subject drop.

With an indifferent shrug, he turned back to the grout. "She went to Chicago with her brothers to visit her mom for Mother's Day."

"Ah." He gave an approving nod. "She sounds like a loving daughter. And loving daughters make excellent wives."

Mitch shot an exasperated look over his shoulder. "I just met her."

"Doesn't take long to know if it's a fit. After one date with your mom, I knew she was the one for me."

This was not a conversation Mitch wanted to have. Time to change the subject. Again. "What service are you going to tomorrow?"

"Nine. Unless you'd rather sleep later. You put in some long hours on that case last night."

That was true. The homicide investigation that had pulled him back on duty and nixed his date with Alison had kept him on the move until almost noon today. But he'd catch up on sleep tonight.

He shook his head. Cleaning grout and going to bed early on Saturday night. His SEAL buddies would never believe it.

"The early service is fine." He refocused on the tile. "I might even go with you."

That bombshell was met with silence.

He risked a peek out of the corner of his eye. His father was staring at him.

Walt pursed his lips and cocked his head. "Why the change of heart? You've said no every time I've asked you to go with me since you've been back."

"I drive you there anyway." Mitch lifted one shoulder and tried to downplay his visit. "I decided I might as well hang around instead of making two trips."

"Hmm." Another moment of silence. "This wouldn't have anything to do with that pretty lady, would it?"

Walt Morgan might not yet be at full physical strength, but there wasn't a thing sluggish about his mental processes.

"She did get me thinking about it."

A soft chuckle sounded behind him. Mitch ignored it. But as his father turned to exit, he heard his comment loud and clear.

"All I can say is, there's a lot of potential when a woman can get a man who's avoided the Lord for years to go to church."

Mitch wished he could think of a zinger to toss back, but nothing came to mind. For one simple reason.

His father was right.

The whole weekend had been a bust.

As they crossed the Mississippi River from Illinois into Missouri and passed the Gateway Arch, Alison checked on

Bert, who was sleeping in his travel cage on the backseat beside her. At least one occupant of the car had had a relaxing trip. Huffing out a sigh, she ticked off all the things that had gone wrong.

First, Mitch had had to cancel their date Friday night when a homicide had required his attention an hour before he was supposed to meet her. Cole had been involved in that case too. Several county detectives had spent Friday night and Saturday morning tracking down suspects and potential witnesses.

Second, because of that, the three of them had ended up leaving for Chicago much later than they'd planned. Jake had done the bulk of the driving while Cole slept—and snored—in a corner of the backseat.

Third, an hour after they'd arrived at the two-bedroom condo their mother shared with her sister, she'd declared she was tired and gone to bed. That had surprised all of them, since Eleanor Taylor had always been the life of the party. But when she called their hotel the next morning and told them she'd spent the night throwing up, it made sense. Aunt Catherine, they learned, had been ill for a couple of days on the cruise the two of them had just taken. She'd obviously passed the bug to her sister.

So they'd gone to church with their aunt, taken her out to brunch, visited a bit with their mother—from a distance, at her insistence—and left after she'd fallen asleep twice during the conversation. They'd promised to return in June for a belated Mother's Day celebration.

In between all that, Alison had found herself dodging questions from her brothers about her relationship with Mitch.

Definitely not the most relaxing weekend she'd ever spent.

Nor was it going to get better. She'd promised Mitch she'd tell her brothers about the stalker while they were gone, and at the rate Cole was driving, he'd be pulling into her driveway in less than fifteen minutes.

Now was the time.

Taking a deep breath, she tried for a casual tone. "By the way, I meant to tell you guys about something that's been going on for the past couple of weeks."

Cole shot her a hopeful look in the rearview mirror. "Does this have anything to do with Mitch?"

He would home in on that. "Not directly."

"I tried asking him a few discreet questions about the two of you while we were working the homicide into the wee hours of Saturday morning, but he sidestepped every one."

She knew all about Cole's version of discreet, and she cringed. "Maybe because it's none of your business?"

"I'm your brother. That makes it my business."

"What's going on that you want to tell us about, Twig?" Jake twisted in his seat and grinned at her.

"When are you going to stop using that adolescent nickname?" She gave him an annoyed look.

"Never. It's cute. Besides, it fits as well now as it did when you were a gangly twelve-year-old."

She narrowed her eyes. "Don't start with the weight thing again."

"Did I mention weight?" He feigned a picture-of-innocence look. "So what's up?"

Her pulse took a leap and she moistened her lips, praying they wouldn't make a big deal out of this. "Nothing important. But I figured you guys, being law enforcement types and all, would be interested. Believe it or not, I've gotten a few of those heavy-breathing kind of calls lately. Some people have no life, that's all I can say."

Her brothers exchanged a look. One she knew far too well. She braced herself as Jake shifted into U.S. marshal mode. "When did this start?"

"A couple of weeks ago."

"How many calls have you gotten?"

"Four."

"We can trace them, Alison. Why didn't you tell us sooner?"

"I thought he'd get tired of the game and stop calling. Besides, there's no need to trace them. The numbers showed up on caller ID."

"Numbers? As in plural?" Cole caught her eye in the rearview mirror.

"Yeah. Two."

"Give them to us. We'll check them out."

This was where it was going to get tricky. She clasped her hands in her lap.

"No need. They're both public phones. One at a quick shop parking lot in South County, the other at a gas station about a quarter mile from my house."

Jake frowned at her. "How do you know that?"

"Mitch looked into it for me."

Her reply was met with five seconds of dead silence.

"You told Mitch and not us?" This from Cole. In an ominous voice that made it clear he was not happy about being left out of this loop.

And he was going to be less happy after he heard the rest.

"Yeah. He happened to be there when the first bouquet came."

Her brothers exchanged another one of those looks. In some silent communication she wasn't privy to, Cole handed the interrogation over to Jake. Which was fine with her. Jake wasn't as prone to fly off the handle as his younger brother.

"Okay, Alison." He turned toward her again, his voice calm, his eyes probing. "Instead of feeding us this scenario in bits and pieces, why don't you just give us the whole story?"

So she did, finishing by answering the questions she knew would come next. "And before you ask, I have no idea who might be behind the calls or the flowers. Nor does there seem to be a pattern to any of this."

Cole flipped on his turn signal and moved into the exit lane of the highway. Her exit. In five minutes she'd be home. She'd timed this well.

"The thing is, Mitch thought it might make sense to ask the patrol officers to drive by my house more frequently until this guy gets tired of his game. Since you know them all, Cole, he said you might be able to pull a few favors and get a little more coverage. Not that I think it's necessary, but I told him I'd ask you about it."

"You know, this is really interesting." Cole made a left turn. "When Jake and I try to watch out for you, you get all huffy and independent. Then this new guy shows up, and you fall right in line with his suggestions. I wonder why."

She ignored the comment.

"Alison?" Cole prompted.

"What?"

"You didn't answer my question."

"I didn't hear one."

He shot her an annoyed glance in the rearview mirror.

She ignored that too. Bert began to stir, and she poked her fingers through the cage to stroke behind his ears. "We're almost home, boy."

"Where's the latest bouquet, Alison?" Jake spoke up.

"In my garage."

"Is the bingo card with it?"

"Yes."

"I want to take a look at it."

"Mitch already did that. There's nothing that identifies the sender."

"I still want to take a look."

"So do I," Cole chimed in.

"Fine. Look all you want."

The conversation petered out as Cole pulled into her driveway. Once he set the brake, she pushed open her door and circled the car to retrieve Bert. By the time she got there, Jake had already jockeyed the cage through the door.

When she reached for it, he angled away from her.

"I've got it, Alison."

The firm set of his jaw told her arguing would be useless.

Retreating to the trunk, she arrived to find Cole pulling out her overnight case. He blocked her approach with a broad shoulder, swung the case out, and started for her front door.

She planted her hands on her hips. "You know, this is exactly why I don't tell you guys anything," she called after them. "You go into this superprotective mode that drives me nuts."

"The appropriate response is 'thank you.'" Cole threw the retort over his shoulder.

Frustrated, Alison glared at their backs. She did appreciate their help, but why did they have to go overboard? When would they realize she was strong and independent and perfectly capable of handling her life on her own?

Never.

She sighed at the depressing reality. The truth was, they were always going to think of her as their kid sister. Throw in their law enforcement backgrounds, and she was doomed.

One of these days, she was going to have to make her peace with that.

But today wasn't that day.

They were waiting for her at the door when she joined them. After fitting her key in the lock, she pushed through and headed for the beeping alarm. They followed, and as she deactivated it, Jake opened Bert's cage.

"You want this in your bedroom?" Cole hefted the suitcase.

"Yes."

"Basement?" Jake lifted the cage.

"Yes." They started to turn away. "And thank you." She owed them that, but she had to dig deep for the words.

Cole shot her a grin over his shoulder.

"You're welcome, Twig." Jake winked at her.

Ignoring the wink, she opened the back door and let Bert out. Once her brothers reappeared, she led them into the garage and gestured to the bagged bouquet on the shelf.

"Have at it."

She watched from a few feet away as they examined the dead flowers. From her vantage point, she had only a side view of their faces, but *grim* was the best word she could think of to describe their expressions. And they got grimmer after they extracted the bingo card and exchanged another look.

Finally, Jake gestured to the bouquet and addressed Cole. "You done?"

"Yeah."

"Okay. Let's go inside."

He slid the bouquet into the bag, added the bingo card, and settled the bundle back on the shelf.

Alison led the way in, swiveling around to face them in the center of the kitchen, hands clasped in front of her. "So what do you think?"

"I don't like the fact this guy's been on your property." Twin creases appeared on Cole's brow.

"I don't like the dead funeral flowers. Or the bingo card." Jake propped a hip against her counter and shoved his hands into the pockets of his jeans. "Or the implied threat."

"That's what Mitch said."

"I'll get the patrols beefed up within the hour." A scratching noise sounded on the back door, and Cole opened it to admit Bert, who bounded past his legs. "You still taking your evening walks with Bert?"

"Mitch suggested I put those on hold for a while."

"I agree." Jake directed his next question to Cole. "You okay with the security at the house?"

"Yeah. I checked the place out before she moved in and added some enhancements." He took a step toward her. "I'm going to ask the patrol officers to go by the quick shop and the gas station more often too. Next time this guy calls, I'm hoping one of them will be close by and we'll get him. Call me—or Mitch—the instant you know the guy's on the line. Okay?"

"Okay. Trust me, I want him caught as much as you do. And one other thing." She included Jake in her next comment. "I don't want Mom told about this. There's no point worrying her. Promise you won't say anything."

"I've been through this drill before." Cole's lips settled into a flat line. "And I didn't like it then."

"From someone on the receiving end of your good intentions, I second that." Jake folded his arms across his chest.

"You know why I made Cole and Mom promise not to tell you about my accident, Jake. You were in Iraq. On a Special Operations Group assignment. People were shooting at you every day. My problems could have distracted you. If you'd gotten hurt—or killed—I would have had to deal with guilt for the rest of my life, wondering if that's why a bullet got you. Besides, there was nothing you could have done to help me."

"I could have offered moral support."

"I had Cole and Mom for that. And I have you and Cole this time. So promise you won't tell Mom."

Her two brothers did another one of those silent communication things. At last, Jake nodded. "All right. We'll do this your way. But if she ever finds out about this, we'll be toast."

"There's no reason she ever will. I have a feeling the problem will be cleared up within the week."

"I hope you're right." Cole started toward the door, stifling a yawn. "Let's go, Jake. I still need to catch up on the sleep I lost Friday night."

"Okay. I promised to stop by and see Liz, anyway."

Alison followed them to the door, where Jake gave her a hearty bear hug. "I'll call you tomorrow."

"Me too." Cole leaned over and kissed her cheek as Jake exited. "So what are your plans for the rest of the evening, what little is left of it?"

"I have a case file I need to review for a custody hearing tomorrow."

He made a face. "Sounds like fun."

"It's better than spending the wee hours of a Saturday morning dealing with a dead body."

"Different strokes . . ." He shrugged, then wiggled his eyebrows. "Maybe you'll hear from Mitch. Ted Drewes would be a lot more exciting than a case file."

She pushed him out the door. "Good night, Cole."

The sound of his laughter carried through the heavy wooden door as she closed it.

Bert claimed her attention with a yip, and she bent down

to pick him up. "I have impossible brothers, you know that, my friend? Even if they mean well."

He snuggled close, and she stroked his fur as she wandered toward the kitchen in search of caffeine. A cup of tea would help her stay alert as she prepped for the hearing.

But Cole was right. A trip to Ted Drewes with Mitch would be a whole lot more fun.

6

It wasn't fair.

Fuming, Alison stomped down the corridor at the Family Court building, forcing herself to take a few deep, calming breaths. She'd done her best to present the situation at the Callahan home accurately, then given a strong recommendation that the interests of the children would be best served by allowing them to remain with their mother. But the judge hadn't been convinced, thanks in part to the vindictive but convincing testimony of Stan Orton, the superintendent of Ellen Callahan's apartment building. A man, according to Ellen, who hadn't been happy when she'd rejected his overtures.

Unfortunately, a broken glass pipette had been found outside her back door, which hadn't helped—despite the negative results of Ellen's drug test and her insistence that she knew nothing about the drug paraphernalia.

Judge Strathman had zero tolerance for anything that connected kids and drugs. Even if the connection was tenuous, at best.

And the fact was, the children had been alone when the police officer responded to the hotline call. Abandoned by the neighbor who'd promised to watch them for her, Ellen had said. A neighbor who had since gone missing.

Now the two siblings—ages two and four—would remain

in foster care, separated from the mother they loved, pending further investigation.

It stunk.

Days like this made her wonder if she'd picked the wrong profession.

A buzzing vibration next to her rib cage alerted her to an incoming call, and she dug into her shoulder purse with one hand, juggling her case file with the other.

Her fingers closed over her cell phone, and she pulled it out, pressing the talk button. As she greeted the caller, she cast a look back at the courtroom, her focus still on the hearing.

"Alison? Mitch. Am I catching you at a bad time?"

Turning away from the courtroom, she spotted an empty plastic chair in the corridor ahead and aimed for it. "I've had better days. I just got out of a hearing that didn't go the way I hoped it would."

"I'm sorry to hear that."

"Unfortunately, the children are the ones who'll suffer. But I'm not giving up." She sank onto the chair, balancing her case file on her lap.

"That doesn't surprise me."

His words warmed her, lifting her spirits. "How'd you get my cell number, anyway?"

"Cole. He gave it to me after he finished reading me the riot act for not telling him about the stalker."

She huffed out a breath. "Sorry about that."

"Trust me, I can handle him. I've been dressed down by navy officers who make Cole look like a rank amateur."

A smile tugged at her lips. "You should tell him that."

"I did."

Laughter bubbled up inside her. "I wish I could have seen his face."

"He got a little red."

"I'll bet."

"But he ended up grinning about it. Now we're best buddies. It's a guy thing."

"Must be." Sometimes Alison wondered if she'd ever figure out men.

"I know this won't make up for our missed dinner on Friday, but if you have a few minutes, we could grab a quick lunch."

"Where are you?"

"Walking toward the Family Court building as we speak. Cole and I were in Clayton because of the homicide investigation, and before he took off he mentioned you were here too."

Securing her purse on her shoulder, Alison stood. "Sold. I'll meet you at the front door in five minutes."

As she ended the call and dropped her phone back in her purse, she caught sight of Ellen Callahan walking the other direction down the hall. Alone. Shoulders drooping.

Her smile faded.

Separating the woman from her children had been wrong, and she intended to do everything she could to bring about a reunion sooner rather than later.

As the distraught mother disappeared around the corner, Alison walked toward the elevator, recalling a similar case four years ago. At twenty-one, Nicole Larson had been younger than Ellen. She'd had only one child, a three-year-old son named Kyle, when Alison met her. Yet she, too, had been doing her very best to provide for him. Then she'd fallen for the wrong guy. Trusted him to love Kyle as she did. And she'd paid the price with the loss of her son for more than a year.

The door opened and Alison edged into the crowded elevator, her mind still on Nicole and Kyle. In general, she tried not to get personally involved with her clients, knowing that could lead to emotional bankruptcy.

But that case had been different. From the day she'd found Kyle scavenging for food in a discarded McDonald's bag in the stairwell of an apartment she was visiting as part of a home study for a different client, she'd felt a special responsibility for him. Especially when she'd asked where he lived and he'd pointed out a doorway down the hall, where a man who had all the signs of a meth addict was conducting a suspicious transaction with Kyle's long-haired male caregiver.

Rather than take Kyle back, she'd kept him close and watched through a window at the end of the hall as the guy left, jotting down his license number. Then she'd called the police. Eventually the long-haired guy had come looking for Kyle, but the boy had clung to her and she'd stood her ground against the irate man until the police arrived.

Half an hour later, Kyle's caregiver had been in custody, his customer had been arrested, and Kyle had become a ward of the foster care system.

But Nicole had been so determined to straighten out her life that Alison had found herself going above and beyond to support the young mother. It had been well worth the extra effort, though. Nicole had completed her GED and now had a receptionist job with a decent salary. She lived in an apartment she didn't have to share with rats. And based on her annual photo Christmas card, Kyle was flourishing. Last year, the picture had shown him, gap-toothed and smiling, on a camping trip with his mom to Quivre River State Park.

Alison was confident that given the chance, Ellen Callahan would do as well for her children. And in the days to come, she intended to put in as many hours as it took to make that happen.

"Sorry, Alison."

"No problem."

Yes, it was a problem. Frustrated, Mitch pulled out his phone for the fourth time during their impromptu lunch at the outdoor café. So much for the few quiet moments he'd hoped to share with her. Of the thirty minutes they'd been together, he'd spent more than fifteen on the phone. And there wasn't a thing he could do about it. The homicide case was getting hotter. As he jotted down the names of two more persons of interest while his sergeant dictated them, he knew the lunch was a bust.

After tucking the phone back into its holder, he adjusted the knot on his tie and gave Alison an apologetic look as he signaled for the waiter.

"I need to go."

She dabbed at her mouth with her napkin and responded with a rueful smile. "I know. I've been around law enforcement types long enough to recognize the signs. It was a noble thought, though."

As the waiter approached, Mitch pulled out his credit card and handed it to the man. "One of these days we're going to have that nice, uninterrupted meal I promised you."

"And in the meantime, there's always Ted Drewes."

He grinned. "You're a good sport, Alison Taylor."

She bent to retrieve her case file. "I understand about duty calling. I have some more work to do this afternoon on my case too. I'm not going to rest until I get this resolved."

After listening to her impassioned narrative about what had happened at the Family Court hearing this morning, he didn't doubt that.

"It sounds like you have a challenge on your hands, given the superintendent's claim that he witnessed neglect. Plus the evidence of drugs."

Her lips settled into a resolute line. "I do. But she's clean, and I believe her claim that she had no idea her new neighbor was into drugs. I saw no evidence of mistreatment, and the four-year-old didn't tell me anything that would suggest she was an inattentive mother. Just the opposite." Distress tightened her features. "The look on her face when she got the news that her children were being placed in foster care tore my heart out. I can't believe that guy would be vindictive enough to rip a family apart."

The waiter returned with the credit card slip, and Mitch scrawled his signature. "Spite and bitterness are powerful motivators."

"I know. But even after a lifetime of exposure to the justice field, man's inhumanity to man never fails to appall me."

"That's because you're a nice person, with integrity and compassion and a strong sense of right and wrong. Don't ever change." He covered her fingers with his, giving himself a few seconds to enjoy the clear, vivid blue of her irises and the elegant sweep of her cheekbones.

She flicked a glance at their hands, and a faint flush crept over her cheeks. "You're very good for my ego."

"Maybe you'll keep me around for a while, then." He grinned at her, but he was more than half serious.

"I think that's a strong possibility. After all, you indulge my love of Ted Drewes."

"And I promise another trip very soon." He rose, and she followed suit. "Maybe even tonight. To make up for the rushed lunch."

As he followed her from the restaurant, his phone once more began to vibrate. Pulling it out again, he grabbed her hand. She turned, her expression quizzical, and he gave her fingers a quick squeeze. "Another call. Where are you parked?"

She gestured to the right.

"I'm the other way. I'll say good-bye here."

"Okay. Good luck with the case."

She tugged her hand free, lifted it in farewell, and set off down the street.

The sidewalks were crowded with the noontime lunch rush, but he kept her in sight as long as he could, his mind only half on the call. She looked very professional in her pinstripe suit. But he liked how the businesslike severity was softened by a discreet slit in the slim skirt and a touch of lace on the camisole in the V of the tailored jacket.

A slow smile lifted his lips as she stepped off the sidewalk and hurried across the street, the slit revealing an enticing length of leg with each stride. And as he eased sideways to gain a better line of sight, he was glad Cole wasn't privy to the thought that had just flashed through his mind.

Because if he had been, Mitch knew he'd be dead meat.

75

The phone was ringing when Alison arrived home late that evening. She'd spent the afternoon checking to make sure Ellen Callahan's children were adjusting to their foster homes, trying to track down the neighbor who Ellen claimed had been babysitting, and talking to the reference her client had provided—Ellen's boss. All of this while trying to juggle several other crises, complete two scheduled home visits, and catch up on paperwork. The only thing she wanted to do now was kick off her shoes, put on some soft jazz, and take a long, hot bath.

Exhaustion had even stolen a bit of the luster from the notion of an excursion to Ted Drewes with Mitch.

Dumping her briefcase on the kitchen table, she hurried toward the phone. But as she started to reach for it, the number on caller ID registered.

She froze.

Her stalker was back.

As she picked up the landline, she fumbled through her purse for her cell phone.

"Hello?" She punched in Mitch's number as she spoke.

Heavy breathing.

"Look, I know you're there. Why won't you talk to me?"

Mitch answered on the other phone.

Depressing the mute button on the portable, she spoke softly into her cell. "The stalker's on my home phone. Calling from the South County number."

"We'll get a car there right away. Keep him on the line as long as you can."

Mitch broke the connection.

Cell phone still in hand, she moved back to the counter, picked up the remote, and pressed it to her ear.

He was still there.

"You know, this game is starting to get old. If you don't quit calling, I'll have to change my number. And you can stop with the presents too." She tried to think of something that might keep him on the line, but the only idea that came to mind turned her stomach. If this guy was some pervert, though, it might intrigue him enough to prolong the call. She tightened her grip on the phone. "Well, if you're not going to talk, I think I'll take a shower." She walked down the hall as she spoke and entered the bathroom. "Want to listen?"

The breathing continued.

Reaching into the tub, she twisted the faucet. "And now I'm going to put the phone on speaker and set it down on the vanity. Have fun."

She tapped the speaker button, laid the phone down, leaned close, and listened.

He was still there. She could hear his labored breathing even over the shower spray.

Maybe her ploy had worked. Maybe he'd still be there when . . .

The line clicked and went dead.

Slowly, Alison shut off the water and straightened up. He'd stayed on longer than in any previous call.

But had it been long enough?

As Mitch pulled into the parking lot of the convenience store, a quick look in the rearview mirror showed Cole hot on his trail. He'd phoned Alison's brother as soon as he'd called dispatch.

Three patrol cars were in the lot, and a small crowd had gathered on the sidelines. The officers were clustered around a figure near one of the cars, but Mitch couldn't see the guy.

Nevertheless, it looked as if they had their man.

Finally.

After braking to a stop, he slid from his car as Cole angled in sharply beside him. The other detective was out of the door almost before his unmarked Impala jerked to a stop.

"This looks promising." Mitch set off for the small group.

"Yeah." Cole fell into step beside him.

One of the patrol officers saw them coming. With a word to the other two, he broke out of the huddle and met them halfway.

"We have a little problem."

Mitch frowned. "He's not our guy?"

"No. He's our guy. No question about it. He was halfway across the lot when we arrived, but a couple of witnesses said they saw him on the phone at the time in question."

"Then what's the problem?" Cole gave him an impatient look.

Suddenly one of the other two officers moved to the side, giving the detectives a clear view of the perpetrator.

Mitch exchanged a glance with Cole. And read his own thoughts in the man's surprised expression.

This wasn't at all what they'd expected.

Pacing the kitchen, expecting a call any minute that would tell her the outcome of the race to catch her stalker, Alison nevertheless jumped when her phone rang.

As she lunged for it, Bert nipped at the hem of the jeans she'd put on while she waited. Apparently he thought the sudden move was a new game.

"Not now, Bert." She shook her leg to discourage him as she checked caller ID.

It was Mitch.

She didn't bother with preliminaries. "Did you get him?"

"Yeah."

Her immediate rush of relief was tempered by an odd nuance in his tone. "What aren't you telling me?"

"Let's just say we're surprised. Do you know a guy in his midtwenties named Erik Campbell?"

She searched her mental rolodex and came up blank. "The name doesn't ring any bells."

"He has Down syndrome."

An ID badge containing a first name clicked into focus. Along with a face.

"Does he work as a bagger at the Schnucks grocery store near my house?"

"We haven't determined that yet. All we've been able to figure out is that he lives in a group home not far from here. We have a call in to the house manager. She should be arriving any minute. He's too upset to talk to us."

Alison slid onto a stool at the counter and combed her fingers through her hair. "This doesn't make sense. I've known Erik since I moved here and started going to that store. He's a very nice guy—always pleasant and polite. And there's this sweet innocence about him . . . I can't believe he'd do anything malicious."

"Those dead roses and bingo card weren't warm and fuzzy."

"I know. It's a huge disconnect." She bit her lip and tapped her finger on the counter. "Something's not right here."

"There are witnesses who saw him making the call, Alison. By the way, an officer will be arriving at your house shortly to pick up the roses."

"Okay." She played with the cross that hung on a gold chain around her neck. "Look . . . do you want me to join you? He might talk to me. We always chat when I'm at the store."

"I'll hold that offer in reserve for now. Let's see what we can find out first. You'll also need to think about whether you want to press charges."

The notion turned her stomach. "That will depend on what you learn, I guess. But I can't imagine taking that step. There has to be an explanation for this." The doorbell rang and she slid off the stool. "I think the officer is here."

"Okay. I'll be back in touch with more information soon."

While the uniformed officer waited in the tiny entry area, Alison retrieved the bag from the garage. Once she handed it over and locked the door behind him, she wandered back to the kitchen. Bert danced around her ankles, trying to entice her to play.

"Later, Bert." She bent down and gave him a conciliatory scratch behind the ear.

She didn't know Erik Campbell all that well. Their contact was limited to the few words they exchanged if he happened to be working during one of her visits. On her last few visits, though, he'd stopped bagging an order halfway through at an adjacent checkout line to come over and take care of hers.

How—or why—that translated to silent phone calls and weird bouquets was beyond her. But she hoped Mitch would get to the bottom of it.

Because despite the witnesses to tonight's phone call, something didn't ring true.

"Erik's still very upset, Detective Morgan. I don't know how much you'll be able to get from him until he calms down."

Mitch didn't need Dorothy Walker, the group home manager, to tell him that. At her suggestion, he and Cole had reconvened with her and Erik in the living room of the home a few blocks from the quick shop. The other five residents had been diverted to the TV room to watch a movie, but the switch to familiar surroundings hadn't lessened Erik's agitation. He was huddled in a corner of the couch on the far side of the room, keeping tabs on their discussion.

"We can wait a little longer to talk to him, Ms. Walker, but we do have to get some answers. There are witnesses to tonight's phone call. And the other phone used to make the harassing calls is at a gas station across the street from the Schnucks where Erik works."

Dorothy shook her head, her expression troubled. "This is so unlike him. He's such a gentle spirit. A few weeks ago he found a baby bird that had fallen out of its nest and he took meticulous care of it. He's always the first to offer assistance when any of the residents needs help too. I wish I had his patience." She sighed. "This doesn't make sense."

"What can you tell us about his background?" Cole joined the conversation.

"Erik's twenty-five and a model resident. He's never given

us one bit of trouble. Until his mother died of cancer nine months ago, he lived at home with her. Prior to her death, she made these living arrangements for him. He's on the higher-functioning end of the Down syndrome scale."

"How long has he worked at Schnucks?" Cole asked.

"Six years. We're talking with the store now about transferring him to a location closer to the home. That way he can take the bus to work. But we wanted to give him a chance to adjust to the loss of his mother and his new living environment before further disrupting his world. For now, we drive him to and from work."

"Any problems on the job?"

"None. The store loves him because he's so friendly and always tries hard to please. Too hard, in fact. When someone is unhappy with him, he gets very upset and tends to withdraw—as you can see. However, under normal circumstances, he communicates very well." She checked on Erik again. "I'm certain there's an explanation for his actions."

The doorbell rang, and Cole turned toward it. "That's probably the officer with the flowers. I'll get them."

"Keep them in the foyer for now, okay?" Mitch instructed.

As Cole exited, Mitch sized up Erik again. "Ms. Walker, I had a cousin with Down syndrome. In a lot of ways, Erik sounds like Justin. I think I may be able to get some answers without upsetting him further."

"As long as I can join you, I'm fine with that. I want him to feel he has a friend nearby."

"That's not a problem."

She led him over to the couch. Erik shrank deeper into the corner as they approached. Mitch chose a chair at a nonthreatening distance, while Dorothy sat beside Erik.

"Erik, this man would like to talk to you for a minute, okay? He's a detective. I'll be right here the whole time. He thinks you can help him by answering a few questions. And I know you like to help people."

She conceded the floor to Mitch, and he leaned forward with

a smile. "Hi, Erik. I'm Mitch Morgan, and like Ms. Walker said, I'm a detective. I'm sorry the policemen scared you at the quick shop. They didn't mean to do that. But someone has been calling Alison Taylor on the phone from there, and she asked us to find out who it was. She says you bag her groceries sometimes at Schnucks. Do you know who I'm talking about?"

Erik looked over at Dorothy, and she gave him an encouraging nod.

"Alison is nice." His words came out shaky and laced with fear.

"Yes, she is." Mitch waited, giving Erik a chance to offer more.

"Some people . . . never talk to me. Some people act like I'm . . . not even there. But she always talks to me. She even told me her name."

That sounded like Alison.

"I called her a few minutes ago. She said she didn't believe you would do anything to scare her."

"I didn't mean to." Erik leaned forward, his features twisted with distress. "I just wanted to talk to her. I looked her name up in the phone book, but I couldn't . . . get the words out. My mouth got . . . all tangled up."

"What did you want to say to her, Erik?" They already had an admission of guilt. Now he needed to find out the motive. But Mitch was inclined to agree with Alison. There'd been no malicious intent in the young man's actions.

"I just wanted to tell her I liked her, and to say thank you for always being nice to me."

"Is that why you left the flowers too?"

His head bobbled up and down. "Yes. Susie at the store was going to throw them out. But I thought they were . . . still pretty. She said I could have them, and she let me wrap them up in that fancy green paper." His tone shifted from enthusiastic to crestfallen. "But Alison . . . didn't like them. She said they were . . . all wilted. That made me feel real bad."

"Is that why you sent the black roses?"

His face went blank. "Huh?"

Mitch was used to reading criminal types, many of whom were experts at faking—and hiding—emotion. Erik wasn't in that league. And his confusion appeared to be genuine.

Glancing toward the door, where Cole was watching the scene from a distance, he motioned him in. "Bring the roses."

Alison's brother retreated to the hall, reappearing moments later with the bouquet. After handing it to Mitch, he backed off a few feet.

Pulling away the green paper, Mitch set the bingo card on top of the stems and held the bouquet out for Erik to examine.

The young man took one look and recoiled. "Those are dead. And ugly."

"Yes, they are."

"And that card is . . . scary."

"Did you send these to Alison, Erik?" Mitch kept his tone conversational.

"No! That might scare her!"

His aghast expression, and the sincerity in his eyes, convinced Mitch that Erik was telling the truth.

Leading him to a conclusion Cole clearly shared, based on the furrows denting the other man's brow.

Two different people had targeted Alison for attention.

Erik's innocent contact had been well-intentioned, if unsettling.

But the dead, black roses and ominous bingo card weren't innocent. Nor well-intentioned.

A flicker of fear flamed to life in the pit of his stomach.

"Is Alison mad at me?"

At Erik's distressed question, Mitch redirected his attention to the young man sitting across from him. Handing the bouquet back to Cole, he tried for a reassuring tone. "No, Erik. She's not mad."

"Are you sure?"

He thought about Alison's offer to come over, and the concern that had softened her words. There was no chance she'd press charges after hearing the details about her secret admirer's actions. "Yes, I'm sure. But from now on, just talk to her at the store, okay? That way she won't be scared."

"Okay."

Mitch rose. After assuring Erik she'd be right back, Dorothy followed him to the foyer.

"I'm sorry about this, gentlemen." She pitched her voice low. "I'll have a discussion with Erik tonight about appropriate ways to express affection. He's been quite bereft since his mother's death, and I can see how he'd latch on to friendly overtures—and misinterpret them. Please let me know if there are any further calls."

"We will. Thanks for your cooperation." Mitch turned to Cole. "Ready?"

"Yes."

They didn't speak again until they were in Cole's car, retracing their route to the quick shop so Mitch could retrieve his own vehicle.

"I'm more worried now than I was before."

At Cole's terse comment, Mitch looked over. The man had a white-knuckled grip on the steering wheel, and the set of his jaw was grim. If Alison thought her brothers had hovered before, she was about to find out what real hovering was.

And her brothers weren't the only ones who were going to be sticking close.

"Yeah. This puts a whole different spin on the situation."

"We need to talk to Alison. Probe harder. She must have ticked somebody off, despite her claims to the contrary."

"Why don't you let me see what I can find out?"

Cole shot him a narrow-eyed look. "Why you?"

"It might help preserve family harmony. I've gotten the impression she thinks you and Jake are a tad overprotective." It was a logical suggestion, if not entirely altruistic.

His colleague considered the offer, then let out a disgruntled sigh. "Okay. You have a point. But I want to know what she says. Tonight."

"You got it."

Cole pulled up beside Mitch's car. "I'm going to make another call to patrol. I want more drive-bys."

"Good idea." Mitch opened the door. "I'll talk to you later."

Once behind the wheel of his own car, Mitch checked on Cole across the parking lot. The other man was already on the phone. Beefing up patrols.

The sooner the better.

Because even though it was possible the dead roses were a onetime, random prank left by a bunch of drunk teenagers out for a night of fun, Mitch's gut told him someone was targeting Alison specifically. And unlike Erik, he was trying to scare her.

An image of the skull and crossbones on the bingo card flashed through his mind. Followed by a niggling sense that the perpetrator was planning to inflict a lot more than fear on Alison.

Unfortunately, safeguarding her from that kind of nebulous threat wouldn't be easy.

No matter how hard he or her two protective brothers tried.

7

"So whaddya gonna do, man?"

Irritated by the question, Daryl Barnes spared Chuck Warren no more than a quick, impatient glance as he paced in the dilapidated mobile home. There might not be any bars on the windows, nor armed guards at the door, but he felt trapped just the same. As if the walls were closing in on him and there was no escape. It was the same way he'd felt during his four long years in the maximum security prison in Potosi.

He hated it now as much as he'd hated it then.

"I don't know."

Chuck leaned back in an upholstered chair that looked as if it had been salvaged from someone's street-side garbage pile. Stuffing oozed through the rips in the stained fabric as he took a swig from his beer can. "You can stay here as long as you need to, man. Unless I get lucky some night. Then I might ask you to take a hike for a little while." His leering grin revealed several discolored, rotting teeth.

Pausing beside the battered TV set, Daryl looked over at Chuck. The years hadn't been kind to his onetime business partner, who looked fifty instead of thirty. His clothes hung on his gaunt frame, his hair had thinned, and his face sported what appeared to be a bad case of acne.

Thanks to meth.

Chuck wasn't just sampling anymore. He was using heavily—

and had been for a long time. Daryl had known that the instant he'd laid eyes on him, when Chuck had come to pick him up from the homeless shelter where he'd spent his first two nights of freedom while trying to track down his old buddy. He'd seen the classic signs of long-term addiction often enough in their customers to recognize them at a glance, and they turned his stomach. That's why he'd vowed never to let his own sampling get out of hand. A line now and then, that's all he'd ever done. Snorted, never injected.

Years ago, Chuck had kidded him about his delivery preference. Most people smoked—Chuck included. But the whole notion of putting toxic vapors into his lungs had freaked him out.

Now, from all indications, his onetime collaborator was way past smoking. He was slamming. Pumping the stuff right into his veins. Often. And Daryl didn't want to go down that road. Nor risk more time behind bars. If he'd had any other option, he wouldn't be here now. But he'd had no place else to go.

A rush of anger swept over him, and he clenched his fists at his sides. If Nicole had taken him in, given him another chance, he wouldn't have had to seek out his old partner in crime. But no. When he'd looked her up in the phone book and called after his release, she'd made it clear he wasn't welcome in her life—or her home. Even though he'd given her and her snot-nosed brat a place to live when he'd found her wandering the streets five years ago.

And who was to blame for her change of heart?

Goody two-shoes Alison Taylor.

His anger erupted into a white-hot blaze, and he slammed his fist against the cracked Formica counter. A piece splintered off, leaving a rough, dangerous edge.

"Hey! Chill, man." Chuck sat up straighter, his restless energy fueling Daryl's own edginess. "I'm just kidding. I owe you for keeping your mouth shut when the cops busted you. Otherwise, I'd have ended up in the slammer too. You can stay here anytime. Listen, you sure you don't want a line? It would make you feel better."

"No."

The other man jiggled his foot and scratched a sore on his arm. "Have it your way." He stood and headed for the fridge.

Daryl caught a rancid whiff as his host brushed past, and he took a step back. This was not how he'd envisioned his first few days of freedom.

Chuck rummaged through the collection of cans, selected one, and popped the top. He chugged several long swallows. Gave a small burp. "So whaddya think that social worker thought of our little present?"

Some of Daryl's anger ebbed as he considered the prank they'd cooked up between them, after he'd told Chuck how Nicole had credited Alison Taylor for helping her get a new start.

"I hope it scared her so bad she's afraid to go to the bathroom by herself."

Chuck cackled. "Yeah. The bingo card was a nice touch, if I do say so myself."

Edging past Chuck, Daryl took out a beer for himself. He hadn't been all that keen on the idea at first, but he was glad they'd done it. The thought of scaring Alison Taylor, of turning her world upside down, was sweet.

"You have an evil streak, you know that?" He popped the top, the whoosh of the carbonation sharpening his thirst.

"Don't I, though?" Chuck grinned and took another long swallow. "And I got more ideas, if you want to hear them. We can make her life real miserable. Might be fun."

As Daryl weighed the can of beer in his hand, he suddenly had the weirdest feeling. Almost like he was standing on the edge of a high cliff, and one move in the wrong direction would send him plummeting into the dark abyss below, while one move in the right direction would lead him to safety.

That was kind of how he'd felt as a kid, playing chicken on the railroad tracks. You were supposed to jump in front of the train, wait until the very last second, then jump aside and run for cover as the grinding brakes shrieked, metal on metal, sparks flying. He'd always broken out in a cold sweat as the train bore down on him. Hoping he'd make it to safety.

The same thing he was hoping for now.

He was tired of messing up his life.

Tired of proving his old man right.

Daryl took a swig of the cheap brew, trying to chase the bitter taste from his mouth. It wasn't as if Michael Barnes had had room to point fingers. Last time he'd seen him, the day he'd left home forever at fifteen, his father had been passed out on the couch, an empty bottle of Jack Daniels on the floor, oblivious to the squalls of the hungry toddler in the dirty playpen in the corner. Daryl remembered tossing his half sister a piece of bread before he left and whispering, "Good luck, kid."

He could use some luck himself now. Some guidance. Someone to tell him how to avoid the abyss. How to elude the train barreling down on him. But even if he didn't have any clear direction, he did know one thing.

Hanging around with Chuck wasn't the right step.

He slugged down the rest of the beer, crushed the fragile aluminum in his fingers, and tossed the can into the overflowing bag of garbage next to the sink.

"You know, I think I'm gonna pay Nicole a visit. Calling was a bad idea. I should have talked to her in person."

His host swigged his beer again. "You think she'll change her mind?"

"It can't hurt to try." He'd always been able to sweet-talk—or threaten—her into compliance. And she'd have a lot harder time saying no in person.

Chuck finished off his beer and tossed his can as well. "Guess not. Nicole always was a looker. It'd be a shame to lose her." He jiggled the change in his pocket and wiped the sleeve of his T-shirt across his forehead. "Hot night. Think I'll take a little walk. Maybe find me a chick of my own. Don't wait up." With a grin, he crossed to the front door, opened it, and clattered down the steps.

Through the window, Daryl watched a flash of lightning slash across the sky near the horizon, followed by a low, ominous rumble of distant thunder. Then he turned away from the emaciated figure disappearing into the deepening dusk and surveyed the rented dump Chuck called home. This wasn't where he'd expected to end up six years ago, when his drinking buddy had filled his head with grandiose dreams.

Dreams that had turned into a nightmare.

Shoving his hands in the pockets of his prison-issue pants, Daryl remembered the pitch as clearly as if it had happened yesterday. He and Chuck had struck up an acquaintance at a bar they'd both frequented in between their string of odd jobs. Chuck had been older and more street savvy. The kind of guy who understood how unfair the world could be. Who wanted more out of life—and had a plan to get it.

He knew how to make meth, Chuck had confided. And he knew of a secluded spot in Jefferson County, off the radar screen of cops, where they could set up a lab. He already had a network of people lined up who'd smurf pseudoephedrine for them in return for enough meth to feed their addiction. They could sell the remainder of the cook. Plus, he had a connection that would supply them with Mexican meth. Big profits there, Chuck had promised. They'd be living on easy street soon.

Daryl had fallen for the plan hook, line, and sinker.

But a dumpy trailer and four years in the joint was far from easy street.

He kicked the edge of the lopsided, lumpy sofa, creating a faint cloud of dust. Like most things that sounded too good to be true, Chuck's get-rich-quick scheme hadn't lived up to its promise.

Leaving him once more a victim of circumstances.

The abyss yawned at his feet again, sending a cold chill through him. He was on the edge, and he knew it. Desperation and despair could nudge a man into that precarious position. Force him to do things he didn't want to do.

But right now he was clean. There was still a chance he could dig himself out of the hole that was his life. All he needed was someone to believe in him. Encourage him. Trust him.

Someone like Nicole.

He'd come to that conclusion in Potosi, as he sat in his cell day after day with nothing else to think about.

The truth of it was, he needed her more than she'd ever needed him. The very woman he'd once rescued from the streets now held the key to his future. To his salvation.

Go figure.

His stomach growled, and he ambled back to the refrigerator. Rummaging through the beer cans, he came up empty except for a moldy pack of American cheese. Looked like it was peanut butter crackers again for dinner. Chuck had a drawerful of those. He grabbed two, ripped off the cellophane, and took a bite.

That was another thing he'd liked about Nicole. She'd fed him well.

Plus, as Chuck had noted, she was a looker. That was the reason he'd noticed her in the first place. The reason he'd been willing to take her kid, once she made it clear they were a package deal. And it had turned out okay. She'd worked hard, holding down two jobs. For the first time in his life, he'd eaten decent meals. Lived in a clean apartment. Experienced affection. It had been a sweet deal all around. The best life he'd ever known.

Until Alison Taylor had poked her nose in and destroyed it all.

Another surge of anger swept over him, but he tamped it down. He couldn't let his temper get out of hand. Not this time. He could end up shooting himself in the foot. Besides, if he could convince Nicole to take him back, why worry about the social worker? There'd be no need for revenge if life was good.

Tomorrow he'd pay Nicole a visit in that nice new place of hers. He and Chuck had driven by to check it out before they'd dropped off Alison Taylor's present, so he knew exactly where she lived. He'd even take a toy for the kid, if Chuck would loan him a few bucks. Maybe pick up some flowers for Nicole. She'd like that. There'd always been a salvaged flower of some kind stuck in a bud vase from Goodwill at their old place.

Once more, a rumble of thunder sounded in the distance, and a light rain began to fall. Chuck would be back soon. There were only a couple of other trailers along this stretch of road, tucked back in the woods, and he doubted his former partner was going to find a welcome reception in any of them.

Let alone romance.

After picking a path along the littered hall that led to the bedroom, Daryl pulled back the grimy blanket on the futon that had been his bed for the past few nights. If the gods were kind, this would be the last night he'd have to spend in a meth den.

He stretched out, doing his best to ignore the stench that permeated the trailer as he reviewed his plan. He was only going to have one more shot at this, and he needed to do it right.

Because his fate was in Nicole's hands.

When the knock sounded on her door a little before nine, Alison set down her knitting, gently toed a sleeping Bert off her foot, and stood. It was either Cole or Mitch.

Much as she loved her brother, she hoped it was Mitch.

Peeking through the peephole, she smiled. St. Louis County's newest detective stood on her threshold.

As she swung the door open, Mitch smiled back. "Sorry to come by so late. But I wanted to give you a firsthand account of what happened with Erik."

"Come in." She swept her arm toward the living room. "Would you like me to make you some coffee?"

"No, thanks. But I could use a soda."

He remained in the living room while she retrieved the drink from the kitchen. Bert stayed behind, and when she returned, she found Mitch sitting on the couch, scratching her pup's belly. Bert's eyes were half closed, his expression blissful.

She handed the soda to Mitch and sat in the wing chair she'd occupied earlier.

"What are you working on?" Mitch gestured to the mass of fluffy pink yarn peeking out of the knitting bag beside her chair.

"A baby blanket. I've been making them for years for the preemie ward at one of the local hospitals."

She couldn't quite decipher the emotion that flickered through his eyes, but she hoped it wasn't pity. She didn't need—or want—that. "So tell me about Erik. Is he okay?"

Mitch took another sip of soda and set it on the old trunk that functioned as a coffee table. "Yeah."

She listened as he gave her a recap, a pang of sympathy tightening her throat when he came to the part about Erik losing his home and his mother.

"Bottom line, I don't think he'll be bothering you anymore," Mitch concluded. "The house manager was going to have a talk with him."

Alison frowned. "I can understand the wilted flowers and the phone calls. They were just awkward attempts to express affection. But the dead roses and bingo card don't fit. Why would he send me those?"

"We don't think he did." Mitch leaned forward and clasped his hands between his knees. "He was completely taken aback when we showed them to him. We think someone else was behind those."

"You mean *two* people were targeting me?" A shiver of fear rippled through her.

"Weird as the coincidence is, that's our take."

Her spirits plummeted. So much for life getting back to normal.

"Alison, I know I've asked you this before, but are you sure you can't think of anyone who might have a motive to send you something like that?"

"No. I can't. But I've dealt with a lot of dicey family situations through the years, and not everyone is happy with the outcome. If this is work-related, it could be any one of thousands of people. It might even be a disgruntled child I placed in foster care a decade ago, who's now an adult. I wouldn't know where to start." Bert trotted her way, and she leaned down to pat the warm little body. "Maybe the roses are a random, onetime prank after all."

Even as she said the words, they didn't ring true. The macabre "gift" had an ominous quality that left her feeling unsettled and vulnerable.

It was clear from Mitch's reply that he concurred.

"Maybe. But as the old saying goes, better safe than sorry. We could have some outdoor security cameras installed here. Temporarily."

She blinked at him. "You're kidding."

"No. It was Cole's idea, but it's not a bad one. If this guy shows up again, we'd have a much better chance of identifying and catching him with that kind of security."

"It sounds like overkill to me. Not to mention expensive."

"Cole says he can get a deal on some equipment. And it's less intrusive than a bodyguard."

Her mouth dropped open. "Don't tell me he suggested that too?"

"No. Your other brother gets the credit for that one. Cole called him while I talked to Erik."

"Good grief." Bending down, Alison lifted Bert to her lap. "Talk about overreacting."

He regarded her, his expression difficult to decipher. "Your brothers love you."

"Yeah. I know." That was just it. She did know their concern was well-intentioned. But it was also smothering. "I'll tell you what. Why don't we wait and see if anything else shows up? In the meantime, I'll be extra careful. I'll hold off on resuming my evening walks with Bert, and I'll double-check all my locks every night. If there is another incident, we can think about adding some security. How does that sound?"

"Your brothers aren't going to like it, but I'll pass it on. I just hope they don't kill the messenger."

"You want me to call Cole?" Her offer was halfhearted, at best. Going a round with her brother tonight held no appeal.

"Thanks for the offer, but I can handle him." He stood and stretched. "You know, I seem to recall promising a pretty lady a trip to Ted Drewes tonight."

He smiled at her, but the fine fan of lines beside his eyes betrayed his weariness, reminding her it had been a long day for him too. He'd never changed out of his jacket and tie, so he must have gone straight from investigating the homicide to the quick shop.

After setting Bert down, she rose too. "Would you mind giving *me* a rain check this time? I'm beat."

"Are you sure?"

"Absolutely. Go home and get some sleep." She set off for the door.

He followed, pausing in the tiny foyer. "I like that plan. Unless my dad corrals me for another grout session." One side of his mouth hitched up.

"How's everything going on the home front?"

His grin faded. "He thinks I'm being overly protective."

"Are you?"

"Maybe."

"Well, speaking from the standpoint of the protectee, I can vouch for the fact it gets old very fast."

Mitch leaned a shoulder against the door frame and shoved his hands in the pockets of his slacks. "I realize it's a fine line to walk. And it's been kind of weird, stepping into the role of caregiver. To be the one watching out for him instead of vice versa. Frankly, I don't think I've been doing the best job of it."

"I bet your dad is struggling with the role reversal too. I know what it's like to go from being very independent to being forced to rely on people to do everything for you, and it's not fun. But you know what was worse? Having Cole and my mom—and Jake, after he got back from Iraq—hover. It drove me nuts. Still does. So I can sympathize with your dad. If you want my advice, give him some space to test his limits—and trust he'll respect them when he finds them."

"Sounds like excellent counsel." The last word ended with a yawn, and he gave her a sheepish smile. "Sorry about that."

She opened the door and gestured toward the porch, which was illuminated by the twin lanterns. "Go home, Mitch."

"Throwing me out, huh?"

"You need to get some rest."

"I need something else first."

He grasped the edge of the door and closed it again. Long enough to lean close and brush his lips over hers in a quick kiss.

Too quick.

"Sleep well. Call me if anything comes up."

His breath was warm against her cheek, and as she inhaled the scent that was uniquely his, she fought the temptation to pull him close.

Slow and easy, Alison.

As if he'd heard that admonition echoing in her mind, he straightened up. With one touch of her cheek, he eased through the door and pulled it shut behind him.

Through the peephole, she watched him disappear down the walk, into the shadows. A few moments later, the lights on his car flicked on. She stayed by the door until his taillights faded into the night.

Bert trotted over, and she looked down at him. He'd been a loyal and steadfast companion this past year, and his entertaining antics had helped cheer her and keep loneliness at bay through many a solitary evening as she battled pain, knitted afghans, and thought about babies she would never have.

But tonight, as she scooped up the little fur ball and accepted his slurping expression of affection, it was someone else's kiss that lingered on her mind and filled her heart with comfort—and hope.

8

"Mom, can we go to the Magic House sometime? Jeff said it's got really cool exhibits."

Nicole Larson turned into the entrance of the apartment complex she and Kyle had called home for the past two years and checked on her son in the rearview mirror. He'd been chattering nonstop since she'd picked him up from the after-care program at school, but her mind had only been half on the conversation. Just as it had been only half on her duties at work.

Thanks to Daryl's unexpected call last week.

The day he'd been released from prison.

After years of no contact, she couldn't believe he'd expected to waltz back into her life as if nothing had happened. She'd tossed every one of the few letters he'd sent directly into the trash. What had he expected her to do when he called out of the blue? Welcome him back with open arms?

Fat chance.

"Mom? Can we?"

Kyle's voice pulled her back to the present. "I don't know, honey. It's pretty expensive."

"Jeff says it's free sometimes on Friday night."

Was it? She'd scoured the city for kid-friendly things to do that didn't cost an arm and a leg. The Magic House had never popped up, but she knew he'd love it. From what she'd heard, it was filled with hands-on, interactive exhibits for the younger set. And Kyle was a hands-on kind of boy.

"I'll check into it, okay?"

"Okay. Thanks, Mom."

She smiled at him in the mirror as she pulled into a parking place. He was a good kid. Smart, polite, loving. She'd made a lot of bad mistakes in her life, but the baby she'd once considered aborting had turned out to be her greatest blessing.

Still smiling, she turned off the engine and spoke over her shoulder. "You hungry?"

"Yeah! What's for dinner?"

"How does spaghetti sound?"

"Cool!" He unbuckled his seat belt.

Nicole opened her door and swung her legs out. "I got some of that garlic bread you like too, and . . ."

The words died in her throat as she noticed a tall, thin man sliding from behind the wheel of a battered pickup truck a dozen cars down in the lot.

Daryl.

His long, shaggy hair was gone, but she had no problem identifying him.

She watched, shock rippling through her, as he reached back inside to withdraw a gift-wrapped object and a small bouquet of flowers.

When the back door started to open behind her, she jerked toward her son.

"Kyle, stay in the car. I have to talk to someone. Lock the door and don't open it until I tell you to, no matter what. Okay?"

As she issued the terse instructions, she checked to make sure the doors on the far side of the car were locked. Then she tucked the keys into the cup holder beside her and flipped down the cover. She wanted them locked in the car, not on her person.

"What's wrong, Mom?"

She heard the fear in his voice. Wanted to reassure him.

Didn't have the time. Daryl was closing his own door and turning toward her.

"Nothing." She fumbled through her purse for her cell phone and handed it to Kyle. "But if you get scared for any reason, I want you to dial 911. And stay put."

Without waiting for a response, she slid out of the car, locked her door, closed it, and marched toward the man she'd once viewed as a savior. She wanted to keep him as far away as possible from Kyle—and her life. She thought she'd been clear about that on the phone.

Obviously, he hadn't gotten the message.

She lengthened her stride, trying to ignore the shakiness in her legs. She'd always hated confrontation. In her old life, she'd avoided it at all costs. But as she'd learned in the past few years, her predisposition to give in under pressure was what had gotten her into trouble. Sometimes you had to stand up for yourself.

That's what she intended to do now.

Because the sooner she got rid of Daryl once and for all, the better off she—and Kyle—would be.

As Nicole approached him, Daryl's step faltered. She looked nothing like the meek, subservient woman he'd lived with for a year. Her entire demeanor had changed. Gone were the downcast eyes, the slumped posture. Her chin was up, her shoulders back. As if she was prepared to do battle.

He hadn't expected that.

Nor had he expected her polish. She'd cut her hair to chin length and wore it in a sleek, sophisticated style. Her makeup was subtle, the turquoise eye shadow she'd once applied with a heavy hand now absent. And her knee-length black skirt, silky green blouse, and silver necklace reeked of class. Especially in comparison to the cheap polyester pants and sport shirt he'd picked up at Walmart with the money Chuck had loaned him.

He came to a halt. On the phone, he'd gotten the feeling she thought she was too good for him now.

Maybe she was.

She stopped directly in front of him, blocking his view of Kyle.

Or was it the other way around?

"Hi, Nicole." He managed a smile.

She didn't return it.

"What are you doing here?" She pinned him with a glacial stare.

"I wanted to talk to you in person." He thrust the bouquet and present toward her. "These are for you and Kyle."

She ignored his offerings.

"I told you last week to leave us alone. Our relationship is over. I have a new life now."

He lowered the flowers and present, his smile fading. "I want to start a new life too."

"I'm glad to hear that. And I wish you luck. But stay away from us while you do it."

There was a hardness to her face he'd never seen before. Along with a deep resolve that told him he might be fighting a losing battle. That threats would work no better than sweet talk.

In desperation, he resorted to guilt.

"I want you back, Nicole. And after all I did for you, you owe me."

She tipped up her chin and glared at him. "The sympathy ploy isn't going to work. I paid that debt a long time ago. In fact, the way I see it, you owe *me* now. Thanks to you, I lost my son for a year. A year! Because you were doing drug deals out of our apartment! It doesn't get much lower than that."

His temper flared, and he struggled to contain it. Who did she think she was, anyway, acting all high and mighty? She'd done bad things too. That's why her old man had kicked her out. "You've changed."

"Yeah, I have. For the better. I have a good life now. And my head's finally on straight, thanks to a lot of counseling and the friendship of people who care."

He narrowed his eyes as a new possibility occurred to him. One that could explain why she'd never answered his letters. "Is there another guy?"

Her lips twisted into a bitter smile. "That's the last thing I need. For now, I'm happy to stick with the people who've helped me get my act together."

"Like Alison Taylor?" The social worker's name came out in a sneer.

"Yes. Like I told you on the phone, I owe her a lot. If she hadn't been in my corner, I might have lost Kyle to foster care forever. I've met other wonderful people along the way too. My counselor. My boss. My pastor."

He blinked, blindsided. "You go to church?"

"Yeah. I do."

"You always bad-mouthed God."

"That's because I blamed him for my problems instead of taking responsibility for my own life. I finally grew up. And found my way to God. Knowing he's on my side 24/7 has made a huge difference."

"I need *you* on my side." He hated the note of desperation that crept into his voice. But it did diffuse a tiny bit of the tension in her face—and stir the embers of hope in his soul back to life.

Then she frowned, snuffing them out.

"Look, I appreciate that you're trying to start over. I think that's great. But you don't need me to do that. You can do it on your own. Despite what your father said. What he did to you."

He stiffened. Very few people had seen the dozens of small round scars on his back, remnants of the cigarette burns his father had inflicted as punishment for the slightest transgressions—and sometimes just for fun. When Nicole had asked about them, he'd told her the basics in a dispassionate sentence or two. The horror in her eyes, however, had suggested she'd understood far more about the misery of his childhood than he'd intended to relay.

"This isn't about my father."

"Yes, it is. Because what he did had a big impact on you. But you can move beyond your past. All you have to do is stop finding excuses to do bad things. Stop being a victim, Daryl. Take charge of your life."

His anger bubbled closer to the surface, and he tightened his grip on the flowers, crushing their stems. "That sounds like a bunch of psycho jargon."

"Call it what you want, but it's true. Look, I'm sure my pastor would be happy to talk with you if you're serious about straightening out your life. Would you like his number?"

"No!" The word exploded from his mouth, and she recoiled as if she'd been struck. He dropped the gifts to the asphalt and grabbed her upper arms. "I want *you*."

The surprise on her face morphed into a taut anger. Her nostrils flared, but instead of bowing her head as she'd done in the past, she locked gazes with him.

And he knew he'd made a fatal mistake.

"Take your hands off me. Now." Her command came out low and forceful, without any trace of fear.

He didn't move.

"I said *now*, Daryl. Or I will scream and this place will be swarming with cops faster than you can put that beat-up truck into gear."

She didn't flinch. Didn't raise her voice. Didn't break eye contact. Yet she'd called his bluff, sending his anger ratcheting up another notch.

He dropped his hands.

"Let me make this clear." She leaned slightly toward him, her tone deliberate and measured. "If you come within fifty feet of me or Kyle again, I will ask for a restraining order. Since you've just been released from prison, that could have very bad consequences. I would suggest you get back in your truck and drive away. You have ten seconds."

Daryl considered his options.

Realized he had none.

Kicking the flowers as hard as he could, he sent blossoms

spewing over the pavement. Then he stomped on the wrapped package, shattering the cheap plastic robot he'd picked up for Kyle, and stalked back to Chuck's truck. As soon as he had it in gear, he spun out of the lot with a screech of tires.

When he reached the entrance, he cast one final look in the rearview mirror. Nicole was still standing there. Watching him. Waiting for him to disappear.

He pounded on the wheel with his fist, fighting the temptation to go back and smash her face, like he'd done a few times in the past after she'd defied him. But fear held him back. He couldn't risk an encounter with the cops. They'd throw him back in a cage. And he didn't intend to spend another night behind bars.

Gripping the wheel with unsteady fingers, he pulled into traffic, aimed the truck toward Chuck's trailer, and debated his next move.

He'd like to pay Nicole back for rejecting him. But if he did anything to her or Kyle, even something as simple and satisfying as slashing her tires, he knew she'd go straight to the cops and finger him as the likely suspect.

No, Nicole was off-limits.

Besides, the problem had begun elsewhere. With the woman who'd stuck her nose into his business in the first place, then turned Nicole against him.

Alison Taylor.

He dug through his pocket for the candy bar he'd pilfered in Walmart, ripped the paper off with his teeth, and took a bite. As he chewed, he thought back over his conversation with Chuck yesterday. The man had mentioned he had more ideas about how to make the social worker's life miserable.

That sounded real appealing. And fair.

After all, she'd made *his* life miserable.

Relaxing his grip on the wheel, Daryl savored the sweet taste of the melting chocolate on his tongue.

Chuck was right.

This could be a lot of fun.

As Daryl's truck disappeared from view, Nicole took a slow, deep breath.

He was gone.

Forever, she hoped.

But if he showed up again, she'd follow through on her threat—and she had a feeling he knew that.

Good thing he hadn't been privy to her shaky legs, though. Or the thunderous pounding of her heart. Or the tremors in her fingers that she'd disguised by keeping a tight grip on her purse.

"Mom?"

Swiveling toward the car, she saw that Kyle had cracked his window two inches. Some of the color had drained from his cheeks, and he was clutching her phone as if poised to tap in the three numbers that would summon help.

With one more glance toward the apartment complex entrance, Nicole pasted on a smile and returned to the car.

"You can open the door now, Kyle. And hand me my keys, okay? I want to get the groceries out of the trunk."

He passed them through the window, along with her phone. As she fitted the key into the trunk lock, he scrambled out of the car, toting his backpack, and joined her.

"Are you ready for that spaghetti?"

He studied her in solemn silence. Then responded with a question of his own. "Who was that man, Mom?"

She opened the trunk and snagged the three bags. "Someone I used to know."

"He looked mean."

No kidding.

"Well, he wasn't a very nice person a long time ago. But he told me he's going to try and be better."

"Is that why he brought that stuff?" He pointed to the scattered flowers and smashed package.

"Yes." She closed the trunk and urged him toward the front door.

"Was it for us?"

"Yes."

"How come he threw it on the ground?"

Nicole debated how to answer—and how to deal with the situation—as Kyle trotted along beside her. Daryl had always had a problem controlling his temper, and the sudden eruption of anger in his eyes when she'd held her ground told her he hadn't conquered it while he was in prison. Yet if he was truly trying to build a new life, raising an alarm with the authorities now could derail his efforts.

At the same time, she needed to be ready if he showed up again. As did Kyle.

"Mom? How come he threw it on the ground?" Kyle repeated the question as they climbed the two steps that led to her tiny porch.

She fitted her key in the front door and ushered Kyle in. With one more backward glance, she set the locks and started toward the back of the small two-bedroom apartment. "Come with me to the kitchen while I put away the groceries, and we'll talk about it."

He followed, maintaining a tight grip on his backpack, his eyes worried. More worried than a seven-year-old's should be. He had no specific memories of Daryl, which she considered a blessing. Nor did he remember his year in foster care. But their time apart had had a profound impact on both of them.

For her, it had been a wake-up call: get her act together or lose the child she'd tried so hard to protect and loved with an intensity she'd never known was possible. For Kyle, their separation had been equally traumatic, leaving him with insecurities that made him clingy at times. Even now, three years after they'd been reunited, he had occasional nightmares. Only after she tucked him close beside her and soothed him with comforting words or songs would he fall back asleep.

Putting him on alert without exacerbating any of his latent fears was going to be tricky.

Nicole set the bags on the counter that separated the galley kitchen from the combination living/dining room and prayed for guidance. "You want a cookie and some milk while we talk?"

His mouth dropped open. "Before dinner?"

"On second thought—I guess not." She grinned at him, took his hand, and led him toward the sofa she'd bought six months ago with money she'd saved specifically for the furnishings that graced the small living room of their home. The home she'd created.

She patted the cushion beside her, then pulled him close as he sat, tucking him into the crook of her arm while she searched for the right words.

"I knew that man a long time ago, honey. When you were really little. He wasn't a very nice person back then, but I didn't know that at first because he was nice to me in the beginning. He fooled me."

"Like Billy did with me?"

His manipulative classmate. Excellent analogy. The kid never had returned the video game he'd borrowed from Kyle. Her son's favorite.

"Yes. Just like Billy. That man was only nice until he got what he wanted. He also did some bad things and went to jail. Now he's out. He was hoping we could be friends again, but I told him he should make some new friends now."

"He looked mad."

"He was. That's why he threw those things on the ground." She brushed the fine brown hair on Kyle's forehead to one side. "I told him I didn't want to be his friend anymore and that he shouldn't come back again. I don't think he will, but I want you to promise you'll tell me right away if you ever see him again. And never, ever talk to him. Okay?"

"Do you think he might try to hurt us?"

A tremor of fear threaded through his question, and she had to wrestle her sudden anger—and hate—into submission. After four years of hard work getting their life in order, she didn't intend to let Daryl disrupt it again. Nor would she go back to living in fear.

But she wasn't as certain about *his* plans. That's why she intended to watch their backs and stick very close to her son for the next few weeks.

"I think he's smarter than that, honey." She hoped. "He knows if he does anything bad, he'll have to go back to jail, and I'm sure he doesn't want to do that. I don't think you or I will ever see him again. But in case you do, you know what to do, right?"

"Uh-huh. Tell you right away."

"You got it. Now, let's get to that spaghetti." She lightened her tone and summoned up a smile. "And maybe we'll go to DQ for dessert. Do you think you could handle an Oreo brownie earthquake?"

The mention of his favorite treat, reserved for special occasions, wiped most of the tension from his features.

"That would be cool!"

"I thought you might like that." Nicole gave him one more squeeze and rose. "Why don't you start your homework while I make the spaghetti? If you get it all done now, we might even have time for a video after our trip to DQ."

"Wow!" He popped up and jogged over to retrieve his backpack. "This is almost like my birthday!"

Nicole unpacked the groceries as Kyle tugged his math homework out of his backpack and began doing sums. Already he seemed to have put the earlier incident behind him.

But as she pulled out a pot and filled it with water for the spaghetti noodles, her unease didn't dissipate one iota. It was possible Daryl was sincere about wanting to stay clean and straighten out his life. People could change in four years. She had.

Yet doubt niggled at her mind. She'd gotten some bad vibes today.

And she knew that for the foreseeable future, she'd be looking over her shoulder.

A lot.

9

Alison pulled a box of oatmeal off the shelf at Schnucks, then checked the items in her cart against her grocery list. The only thing left to add was dog food.

As she traversed the store, she kept an eye out for Erik. He was often on duty when she did her Tuesday after-work shopping. Since hearing Mitch's story last night about the young man's distress, she'd been anxious to reassure him she wasn't angry. But she must have missed him.

No surprise, considering she'd worked later than usual, thanks to the Callahan case. The babysitting neighbor, Bev Parisi, still hadn't turned up—at her apartment or at the restaurant where she worked as a waitress—and Stan Orton was sticking to his claim that the mother often left the children at home unattended at night and on weekends. Unfortunately, Ellen had been unable to come up with anyone who could corroborate her story.

But logic told Alison that a woman who had reliable daycare arrangements in place with a reputable provider during work hours wasn't likely to leave her children unattended at other times. If she had to run out to get a leaky radiator checked, as she'd done on the night in question, she'd take them along. Unless her neighbor had offered to watch them, as Ellen maintained.

According to the young mother, the thirtysomething woman

down the hall had moved in about two months ago. They'd met while collecting their mail and chatted whenever they ran into each other. At some point, the neighbor had offered to watch the children if Ellen was ever in a bind. Ellen had never taken her up on that—until last week.

Now Bev seemed to have disappeared off the face of the earth.

As Alison grabbed a bag of Bert's favorite dog food, hefted it into the cart, and did a U-turn toward the checkout line, her phone began to ring. Digging through her purse, she smiled at the familiar number when her fingers closed over the phone.

"Hi, Mitch."

"You know my number by sight?" He sounded pleased.

"I memorized it when I was getting those suspicious calls, in case I needed to reach you quickly." She let a beat of silence pass. "But I don't intend to forget it."

He chuckled. "That's nice to know. I tried calling your house first, by the way."

She eased the cart into line and circled around to the front of it, setting a plastic divider on the conveyer belt. "I worked late. I'm at the grocery store as we speak."

"Burning the midnight oil on the Callahan case?"

"It's not quite midnight, but it feels like it." She began unloading her groceries, easing her weight off her injured leg, which had begun to throb. Not unexpected, in light of all the hours she'd spent on her feet today.

"Any progress?"

"Not yet."

"You'll get there. That family's lucky to have you on its side."

"I hope so." She tucked the phone against her shoulder, freeing her hands to hoist the bag of dog food to the conveyer.

"I know so."

The warmth in his voice sent a little trill along her nerve endings, but she hid her reaction under a teasing tone. "And to what do I owe the honor of this call?"

"I was hoping you might be interested in a Ted Drewes run. But if you're not even home yet, another night might be better."

A quick glance at her watch confirmed it was close to seven. Much as she'd love to spend an hour in his company, he was right. "To be honest, it would. I haven't had dinner yet, and I need to let Bert out and feed him too. Plus, I have to prep for a hearing tomorrow morning."

"Sounds like you have a busy evening ahead."

"Too busy."

"I'd offer to come over if I thought there was anything I could do to help."

She resisted the temptation to succumb to his hint, knowing his presence would be more distracting than helpful. "I appreciate the thought. Give me a rain check again, okay?"

"No problem."

As she tugged her cart forward, she caught sight of Erik several lanes away. He was bagging in his usual slow, methodical way, totally focused on his task.

"Hey . . . I just spotted Erik. I was hoping he'd be here tonight. I want to make sure he knows I'm not upset."

As her secret admirer deposited a filled bag in the customer's cart, she caught his eye and waved. Instead of responding with his usual open smile, however, he dipped his head and went back to work.

She lowered her hand. "He's ignoring me."

"The house manager said she was going to talk to him. Maybe he thinks he's not supposed to communicate with you at all."

"That's the impression I'm getting. I need to fix this."

"I'll let you go. Why don't I call you in a day or two? Or you can call me if you get any more suspicious packages."

"I'm hoping that's behind us."

"Me too. Good luck with Erik."

"Thanks."

As Alison ran her credit card through the machine, she kept tabs on Erik. No question about it. He was avoiding eye contact. She didn't want to undermine whatever the house manager had told him, but neither did she want him to think he could never talk to her again.

Without wasting time putting her credit card or sales slip away, she pushed her cart toward the door, a route that would take her past Erik. He was finishing up with his customer, and there was no one else in line. That should give them a minute or two to exchange a few words.

When she drew close, he ducked his head again and angled away, playing with the name badge on his shirt.

"Hi, Erik."

He didn't face her. "Hi."

Moving into his line of sight, she dropped her voice. "I'm not mad at you, you know."

He risked a peek at her. "That detective guy named Mitch . . . he said you were scared. I didn't mean . . . to scare you."

"I know that. It's okay."

"Ms. Walker told me not . . . to call you anymore. Or give you presents."

"She's right about that, but talking in the store is fine. I look forward to our chats whenever I come in. I hope we can still be friends."

His earnest gaze sought hers. "I hope so too." He gestured to her cart. "Do you want me to push that out for you?"

"I think I can do it tonight. But thank you." She set her shoulder purse in the basket and pulled out her wallet, intending to put away her credit card. But it slipped from her fingers, scattering plastic cards, her driver's license, photos, and change on the ground.

She surveyed the mess in dismay and eased herself to the ground. "I can't believe I did that."

Erik got down on his hands and knees, collecting the scattered contents alongside her. "I drop stuff all the time too. It's okay. I'll help you find everything."

As she rounded up the change, Erik dug out the family picture from her mom's birthday party that had wedged itself under a rack of candy. He also located her credit card among the plastic bags waiting to be filled.

With a wince, she pulled herself to her feet, using the edge of the counter for leverage. Her leg hadn't appreciated the unexpected exercise, but at least the incident had restored the easy give-and-take of her previous relationship with her favorite bagger.

Tossing the jumbled mess back in her purse to be sorted through later, Alison smiled at Erik. "Thanks. I don't think I would have found everything without you."

He beamed. "I like to help."

"I know. And I appreciate that." The checker had begun scanning another customer's items, and she started toward the door. "I'll see you next week, okay?"

"Okay. Bye, Alison." With a wave, he reached for the first item lumbering down the conveyer belt and went back to work.

Heading for her car, Alison found herself limping for the first time in weeks. Barring any unexpected occurrences, a long, hot bath was fast edging out dinner as her top priority once she got home.

As she loaded her groceries into the trunk, she kept her promise to Jake and surveyed the parking lot. Knowing how absorbed she could get in a case—to the point of being oblivious to her surroundings—he'd called last night to remind her to remain alert in public. She'd assured him she'd pay more attention until the black-roses/bingo-card incident was no longer a concern.

But all seemed quiet. Just the usual after-work crowd intent on wrapping up shopping chores after a long day.

Alison finished stowing her purchases, closed the trunk, and slid into the driver's seat. One button locked all the doors. Now that she was secure, she could focus on the Callahan case.

She backed out of the parking spot, her mind shifting gears to her meeting with Ellen today, and the woman's tearful visit to her children under Alison's supervision. She'd assured Ellen she was doing everything she could to validate her story, but there were no guarantees. The courts put the welfare of the children first, and until the judge was convinced Ellen was a fit mother, there would be no reunion. A statement from Bev Parisi about the incident that had precipitated the separation would help a lot. But if the woman was a user, as the evidence suggested, Alison knew she'd lay low. At least for a while.

Once again, she was reminded of the similarity between Ellen's situation and that of Nicole Larson four years ago. That young mother had been up to her neck in problems too. A child of the foster system herself, she'd been living with a drug dealer and working two jobs while trying to raise a child whose father had disappeared from her life.

Although the judge hadn't been convinced she'd be able to turn her life around, Nicole's determination to reclaim her son had impressed Alison. That's why she'd gone above and beyond to help her. And it had paid off, when the two had been reunited a year later.

She had a feeling her efforts would pay off in Ellen's case too. Preferably far sooner than a year. But the woman had a tough road ahead.

And in light of Ellen's thorny problems, a bouquet of dead roses and a bingo card didn't seem to merit a whole lot of worry.

"I don't know, Chuck." Daryl pulled a third beer from the fridge and popped the tab. "We could get caught."

"Not if we're careful." He held up a small jar of white powder and shook it. "You sure you don't want some? Gettin' close to the end of this batch."

Daryl took a swig of beer and eyed the meth. After his encounter with Nicole earlier tonight, he could use a rush—and beer wasn't cutting it.

"Come on, man." Chuck sidled closer and held the jar a few inches from his face. "Plenty here for both of us. It'll be like the old days."

Except the old days had led him to jail.

Daryl pushed the man's hand aside and took another chug of his beer. "Not tonight."

"Your loss." Chuck opened a drawer and pulled out his rig.

"When did you start slamming, anyway?"

"Two, three years ago. It's the only way to go, man." Chuck took a spoon out of the drawer and shook a small bump into the bowl. He added some tap water and mixed it with the cap of the syringe. "So getting back to your favorite social worker. I'm telling you, we can pull this off. If you want to hit her where it hurts, this is your ticket."

He did want to hurt her.

He just didn't like blood.

But he wasn't about to admit that to Chuck.

"We'd have to check the place out better. We weren't there long the night we dropped off the flowers." Daryl took another swig of beer.

"Yeah. We can be like private eyes. Do some surveillance." Chuck drew the meth water into the syringe. Sitting, he pulled off a shoe and sock. Daryl turned away as Chuck injected the stuff between his toes, where the prick mark would be hidden.

He'd never liked needles either.

"Bring it on, baby."

As Chuck spoke, Daryl looked back. The other man's eyes were half closed, pleasure smoothing out the lines in his face.

"You want to go over there tomorrow?" Daryl took a long swallow of his beer. It tasted flat.

"Yeah. Sounds like a plan. Give me a minute and we can talk about it some more."

Not likely. Once the rush passed, Chuck would be bouncing off the walls. He wouldn't be of any use for hours.

"Let's wait until tomorrow. I'm beat." Daryl took a final gulp of his beer and tossed the can in the trash.

"Whatever, man."

Heading down the hall, Daryl thought about Chuck's idea. The guy knew how to go for the jugular, no question about it.

114

Whether he had the stomach to follow his host's lead, however, was another question.

As he crossed the threshold into the bedroom and flipped on the light, a roach scuttled under the futon. Disgust churned his stomach as he surveyed the filthy, dismal surroundings. He didn't want to live the rest of his life like this. But what choice did he have? He'd never had a break, not once in his entire twenty-nine years—other than the day he'd crossed paths with Nicole. He'd told her earlier that she owed him, that he'd done her a favor. In truth, though, he was the one who'd gotten the most out of that deal.

And then Alison Taylor had ruined it.

Crossing to the futon, he kicked it, hoping the roaches would get the hint and exit. After shaking out the blanket, he lay down.

Alison Taylor probably had a nice, soft, clean bed. There wouldn't be any bugs in her house. She was one of the lucky ones. The kind of person who lived a charmed life in a perfect world.

But it was within his power to make her world less than perfect. All he had to do was go along with Chuck's idea.

As he stared at the dark ceiling, he could hear the other man beginning to prowl around the living room. He'd be roaming for hours, too energized to sit or sleep. Turning on his side, Daryl tried to tune out the noise and think about his future.

Except that was too depressing.

Once more, he felt as if he was teetering, off balance, on the edge of a precipice. Or trapped in front of a train. Worse, he felt powerless to affect the outcome. A victim of circumstances yet again.

Cold sweat beaded on his forehead, and he clenched the filthy blanket in his fist, crushing the fabric. Wishing he could take revenge on a world that had treated him unfairly.

That was beyond his power. But he could punish one person. Make her pay for ruining his life, then robbing him of his last chance to salvage it.

The black roses had been satisfying, and scaring Alison Taylor had been fun. But Chuck's new plan was even more diabolical. This one would make her suffer. And that outcome appealed to him. A lot.

A mirthless smile tugged at his lips as he punched the hard, lumpy pillow into submission and hoped sleep—and the escape it provided—would come quickly. Yeah, he'd have to talk more about the idea with Chuck.

As soon as he reconciled himself to the blood.

Juggling the cup of coffee he'd bought to go with his drive-through lunch, Mitch slid out of his car, set the locks, and scoped out the crime scene. The yellow police tape was already up around the run-down duplex in South County, and the Crime Scene Unit van was parked in front.

"You got tagged for this one too, huh?"

He turned to find Cole approaching from the other side of the street.

"Yeah. You know anything?"

"Not much. Sounds like it could be a drug overdose." He gestured toward the front door. "Let's take a look."

Without waiting for Mitch to respond, Cole gave his name and department service number to the responding patrol officer, ducked under the tape, and headed for the open front door.

Mitch gave the officer the same information and followed, pausing to examine the handle and lock. "No evidence of forced entry."

"Nope." Cole gave it a cursory once-over as a woman with short, curly ebony hair streaked with gray entered the living room from the hall. "Hey, Lacey. You done already?"

"For now."

Cole looked at Mitch. "Have you two met?"

"Not yet."

"Lacey, Mitch Morgan. New kid on the block." Cole shot him a grin. "Our block, anyway. Came from NYPD. Mitch,

Lacey Stephens. One of our best investigators from the medical examiner's office."

"Morning, Mitch. Welcome to the department." She didn't offer her hand, which was still encased in a latex glove.

"Thanks."

"So what do you think?" Cole inclined his head toward the hallway.

"Looks drug-related. From all appearances, the guy was a longtime meth user. Stroke or heart failure is my guess."

"What's your best estimate on time of death?"

"Based on the state of rigor, twelve to fifteen hours ago."

"Who called it in?"

"An anonymous tip, I think. I'll have more for you on cause of death later, once I get him to the morgue. Hank's with him now. In the bedroom." She peeled off her glove and hooked her thumb in the direction of the hall. "As soon as he's done in there, we'll remove the body. See you guys around." She lifted a hand in farewell and exited the house.

Mitch did a quick survey of the living room as they passed through. The place was cluttered, dust thick on top of the television. A gray T-shirt had been tossed over a lamp, and an empty, crumpled bag of chips lay on the coffee table.

It reminded him of a guy's dorm room.

They found Hank taking photos in the bedroom. As they entered, Mitch had the same thought he'd had when he'd been introduced to the crime scene investigator a week ago—the man looked more like an aging, absentminded professor than the media stereotype of a CSU technician.

Except he was sharp as the proverbial tack. And just as prickly.

"Hi, Hank."

The man finished his shot before responding to Cole's greeting.

"Cole. Mitch. I have a feeling there's not going to be a whole lot for you guys to do." He spared the dead man a quick glance. "I'm not seeing any evidence of foul play."

Mitch circled the bed to get a better view of the body. As Lacey had indicated, the man's appearance suggested heavy, long-term meth use. "Do we have an ID?"

"Yeah. Lon Samuels. The landlord gave the responding officers the name of the tenant, and this guy matches the photo on the driver's license we found in his wallet." He gestured toward the nightstand.

"Anybody run him for priors?" Cole leaned forward to inspect the body too.

Hank gave him a wry look. "I've been a little busy."

"I'll take care of it." Cole circled around to the nightstand, where the wallet lay open, dialed his cell phone, and relayed the pertinent data.

When he got to date of birth, Mitch checked out the dead man again. The guy was only twenty-eight, but he appeared to be in his late forties. What a waste.

"No priors." Cole ended the call and slipped the phone back into its holder on his belt. "Okay. We're going to do a walk-through. How long do you think you'll need, Hank?"

"Unless I find something that raises a red flag, I should be out of here in a couple of hours."

"We'll be around. After we finish in here, we'll talk to a few neighbors."

"Don't touch anything."

Cole shot him a peeved look. "How long do I have to be on the force before you stop treating me like a rookie?"

"Another ten years. Minimum. I don't want any slipups on my crime scenes."

"I'll try not to breathe too hard either." Sarcasm dripped from Cole's words.

"I appreciate that."

As Hank went back to work, Cole retraced his route down the hall. "He knows his stuff, but what a grump."

"You might be too if you had to do his job all day."

"Maybe. Why don't you take the bedroom and bathroom and I'll cover the kitchen and living room?"

"Works for me."

While Cole continued toward the main part of the house, Mitch detoured into the second bedroom. The furnishings were sparse—a double mattress and box spring on a frame, covered by a blanket. There was also a nicked chest of drawers. The indentation in one of the pillows and the open closet suggested recent occupancy and perhaps a hasty departure.

Mitch moved on to the bathroom. Some faint traces of white powder on the vanity caught his eye, as did a single strand of long blonde hair. He peeked around the edge of the shower curtain. Beads of water still clung to the chipped tile at the edge of the tub. Someone had used it in the past few hours.

And it hadn't been Lon Samuels.

Exiting the bathroom, he stuck his head back into the room where Hank was working. "There's a long blonde hair and some white powder on the vanity in the bathroom."

The man was on his knees, peering at the carpet. He didn't look up. "I'll check it out when I'm finished in here."

Heading down the hall, Mitch met Cole in the living room and shared his findings. "Did you come up with anything interesting?"

"There are traces of lipstick on a glass by the kitchen sink."

"Looks like Lon had company."

"Yeah. She might be our anonymous caller. The tip came from a phone booth not far from here, according to dispatch. Let's see if any of the neighbors can give us a description— just in case this is a homicide. But I'm betting it's not." Cole started for the front door.

"I'm with you. Lon's guest probably found him dead and freaked. Called 911 and took off rather than hang around and be linked to a drug incident." Mitch followed Cole out and shut the door behind him.

"Or she has something to hide."

"Also a possibility." He gestured toward the house on the right as they ducked under the police tape. "You want to go that way?"

"Sure. But I have a feeling this isn't going to lead anywhere."

Mitch scanned the run-down neighborhood, quiet on this Wednesday afternoon. Eerily quiet. No one stood outside the police tape, gawking. No groups of neighbors clustered on nearby lawns, talking in hushed, shocked voices. No one approached them, asking what had happened. Not in this part of town. Here, people disappeared at the first sign of trouble. Melted into the shadows. Nobody wanted to catch a cop's eyes. It was too risky.

Because a lot of them had something to hide.

But identifying Lon Samuels's blonde friend might be a moot point, anyway. If the death wasn't a homicide, he and Cole were off the hook. The drug unit might want to investigate further, but considering Missouri's dubious distinction as the nation's meth capital, one more dead druggie might not be worth adding to their caseload.

Thirty minutes later, as Mitch headed back toward his car, he was no closer to discovering the identity of the blonde than he had been when he'd started. Few doors had opened in response to his knock, and those that had been answered revealed stone-faced residents who claimed they'd seen nothing. No blonde, no unusual activity in the vicinity of the duplex, no visitors period.

Fortunately, Cole had fared better.

"An older woman two units down said she saw the blonde coming and going for the past few days," he reported when they regrouped by Mitch's car. "She couldn't offer much of a description, though. Said her eyesight was too bad. Last time she saw the woman was about two hours ago."

"Not long before the 911 call."

"Right. She said the blonde appeared to be in a hurry to leave. Bolted through the door, jumped in her car, and took off."

"I don't suppose there's any chance she saw the license plate."

"Nope. Best I could get was that the car was midsize and a dark color."

"That's not going to help a whole lot." Mitch surveyed the duplex again. "You see any reason for both of us to hang around?"

"No. You go ahead. I'll stick close until Hank is finished. If anything interesting turns up, I'll call you." With a mock salute, Cole strolled back toward the rental unit.

As Mitch climbed into his car, he took one more look at the seedy dwelling Lon Samuels had called home. Not the sort of place a man would choose to end his life. Yet that's what Samuels had done, indirectly. The choices he'd made in life had led him to this.

His choices.

Not God's.

God hadn't ordained his squalid end.

That unexpected conclusion furrowed Mitch's brow as he pulled out of the parallel parking spot. It had been years since he'd thought about God in connection with his work. Even then, it had been a rare occurrence. Prompted only by senseless carnage or a meaningless death. And it had usually been confined to flinging an agonized "Why?" toward the heavens, never expecting an answer.

Nor had he ever gotten one.

Easing his car into the flow of traffic, he assumed his unusual digression was related to the conversation he'd had with Alison on this topic last week. She'd acknowledged the existence of injustice but believed God could bring good out of it, if people let him.

Mitch wasn't certain he bought that. Not after all he'd seen during his SEAL missions and on the streets of New York. How did good come out of oppressive, totalitarian regimes and senseless killing of innocent people and brutal murders? Or out of a guy dying because he made bad choices and used drugs to escape his mistakes?

No answer suggested itself as he accelerated, blending into the traffic. But Alison had also said it could take time for a clear purpose to emerge. Or not. When it didn't, you had to trust in God's plan without understanding it.

That was a tough assignment. Tougher than a lot of the SEAL missions he'd been handed. Still, if Alison could do it, if his father could do it, maybe he could figure out how to do it too. If he didn't, he knew he'd never get right with God—a task that had skyrocketed in importance since Alison had entered his life. Because as a believer, she'd accept no less in a man with serious intentions.

And his intentions were getting more serious by the day.

Maybe that wasn't the most noble reason to seek God, but it was honest. And perhaps God didn't care why people came to him initially . . . as long as they came.

Unfortunately, he had a long way to go on the trust front. Today was a perfect example. While he'd seen far worse things than a drug addict who'd died in a sleazebag rental unit, it was sad nonetheless. How could there be a greater purpose in that?

It was hard to fathom.

Yet as Mitch flipped his turn signal and moved into the entrance lane for I-270, he couldn't help hoping there was.

10

At the sound of an approaching vehicle, Daryl froze, his hunger forgotten. Chuck had crashed on the couch an hour ago after prowling through the mobile home all night and all morning, and he was snoring up a storm, as oblivious to the heat that had been building steadily in the trailer as he was to their visitor.

Setting aside the jar of peanut butter he'd found wedged in the corner of one of the cabinets, Daryl backhanded the sweat off his brow and hurried to the front window. Through one of the broken slats in the blinds, he watched a dark blue car bounce up the driveway, moving far too fast across the rutted gravel. A blonde woman was behind the wheel. He didn't see any other passengers.

His tension ebbed slightly. It wasn't as daunting as a cop car showing up.

But for some reason the woman's arrival still gave him bad vibes.

Without slowing down, she circled around to the back of the trailer, past the odd collection of rusting animal cages Chuck had amassed, and disappeared from view.

Adrenaline surging, Daryl strode over to the sofa and shook his host's shoulder. "Chuck! Wake up. Somebody's here."

No response.

He shook harder. "Chuck. Come on, wake up!"

The other man muttered, opened his eyes, and squinted at him. "Whas wrong?"

"Someone just drove up. A blonde woman."

"Later, man." His eyelids drifted closed again.

A car door banged.

Daryl reached down and grabbed Chuck's shoulders, jerking him into a sitting position. The man's head lolled, and he spewed out a string of obscenities.

Someone jiggled the back door, then began banging on it. "Open up, Chuck. I know you're in there. I see your truck. Open the door!"

The note of hysteria in the woman's voice seemed to penetrate Chuck's fog. Rising to his feet, he stumbled toward the back door, unlatched it, and pulled it open. The blonde collapsed into his arms, sobbing, and he staggered back.

A cold knot of fear formed in Daryl's stomach, a reflex honed by years of living at the edge of danger, the fear of detection a constant companion. Every instinct in his body screamed at him to run. Far and fast.

But where would he go?

Chuck half dragged the woman to a kitchen chair and dumped her in it. She slumped, her shoulders heaving, as he barked out a question. "What's going on, Bev?"

The name clicked in Daryl's mind. Chuck had mentioned Bev several times. Some guy too. They were key members of his meth circle.

She turned a mascara-streaked face up to him, her puffy eyes distraught as she shoved back her tangled hair.

"Lon's dead."

As Alison pored over her notes for the Callahan protective custody hearing scheduled for nine o'clock the next morning, Bert trotted across the kitchen floor, stopped under the coat hook where his leash hung, and gave her an expectant look.

"Sorry, buddy. No can do. I'm still confined to quarters at night."

His ears drooped, and he padded halfheartedly to the back door.

Standing, she balanced herself, fingertips grazing the edge of the table as she gave her leg a moment to loosen up after two hours of immobility. She wouldn't mind the discomfort if she thought it was going to pay off. But while she'd give it her best shot tomorrow, she knew that without the testimony of Ellen's neighbor, the judge would most likely put the children in protective custody for at least thirty days. The drug paraphernalia found at the scene wasn't helping either, even though Ellen had disavowed any knowledge of it.

Bert gave an impatient yip, and she crossed to the door, checking the illuminated patio before unlatching the locks.

"Okay, big guy. Don't be long."

As he zipped through the door, a gust of hot, humid air slammed into her. If the calendar didn't say May, she'd peg it as August. The meteorologists were attributing the early heat wave to a stalled high pressure system, but whatever the cause, it was hot enough to have St. Louis air conditioners cranked up to full blast weeks sooner than usual.

Before Alison could retake her seat, the phone rang and she detoured toward the counter, checking caller ID as she picked it up.

Cole. No surprise there. He and Jake had been tag-teaming their phone calls, alternating nights. She picked up the phone and pressed the talk button.

"Hi, Cole."

"Hi. Am I catching you at a bad time?"

"Nope." She leaned back against the counter. "I'm just going over some notes for the Callahan hearing tomorrow."

"No trips to Ted Drewes tonight?"

"I'll go if you invite me." She knew that wasn't what he meant, and her lips twitched. She loved putting him on the spot.

"Uh, I was going to catch a Cardinals game on TV. I just

thought maybe . . . well, I know you've been going there with Mitch a lot."

"Twice is not a lot." She picked up her pencil and twirled it between her fingers.

Silence on the line. As if he was hoping she'd offer more.

Not a chance.

"You had lunch with him too."

She waited him out.

This time her silence was met with an exasperated sigh. "You think I'm being nosy, don't you?"

"Give the man a gold star. Besides, who are you to point fingers at me about a lackluster social life? When's the last time you had a serious date?"

"No comment."

"Ah . . . so when the shoe is on the other foot, it doesn't fit very well."

"Fine. I get the message. But for the record, I'm okay with you dating Mitch. He seems to have his head on straight."

"I'm so glad you approve."

Her sarcasm elicited another sigh. "Are all little sisters this difficult?"

"I guess it depends on how much their older brothers meddle." At a scratching sound from the back door, she pushed off from the counter. "Gotta run, Cole. Bert wants back in already. A solitary frolic in the backyard doesn't have the same appeal as our nightly walks."

"Give it a little more time. Let's make sure bingo man has lost interest."

"Yeah, yeah." She checked the back porch, flipped the lock, and pulled open the door. Bert brushed past her leg, intent on his water bowl.

"I'm serious, Alison."

"I know. All kidding aside, I am being careful. I want to make sure the guy's moved on too."

"Glad to hear it. Good luck on the hearing tomorrow."

"I'm going to need it."

126

"Any sign of the neighbor?"

"No. I checked with the superintendent. It was hard to be civil, after what Ellen's told me about him. Anyway, he hasn't heard from her either. I assume she'll show up eventually, if only to pick up her stuff. Some of your street cop buddies are swinging by there every hour. I'm hoping one of them catches sight of her. I was able to pass on a detailed description of her and her car, thanks to Ellen. And we have the plate number too."

"I wouldn't get my hopes up. If she left drug paraphernalia lying around, she has to know she's going to be questioned about that. She might also be trying to stay clean for a few days so if she's spotted and asked to do a urine drop, it'll be negative. Then there's the issue of leaving the kids alone. She might figure she's in trouble for that too. I wouldn't be surprised if she disappeared."

"Thanks for the encouragement."

"Just being a realist."

She took a deep breath and combed her fingers through her hair. "I know, but I'm trying to stay positive."

"I'll keep my fingers crossed, okay?"

"A prayer or two wouldn't hurt either."

"I'll leave those to you and Jake. I think they'd have a better chance of being heard. Let me know what happens with the case, okay?"

Alison had never understood why Cole's faith had lapsed a few years ago. At one time, he'd been the most devout of the three siblings. She'd tried to ask a few discreet questions now and then, but whenever the conversation turned to God, he changed the subject. Like now.

She decided to let it go for tonight. "Sure."

Bert stretched out on his rug, tucking his chin between his paws as he looked up at her. Once he had her attention, he rolled over and waved one paw in her direction. As always, his antics brought a smile to her lips.

"I think Bert is angling for a belly rub. Thanks for checking in, Cole. And I mean that."

"Hey, what are big brothers for? Let me know if you need anything, okay? Unless you'd rather call Mitch."

"Good-bye, Cole."

The rumble of his chuckle came over the line. "Bye."

Replacing the phone in the holder, she smiled at Bert. He squirmed happily when she approached, then went limp while she scratched him.

"You are so easy to please, my friend."

He looked up at her with his big brown eyes and gave her a doggy smile.

She smiled back. This house would be a lonely place without her loyal little buddy. He'd been a godsend over the past year, keeping her company without asking a lot of questions or giving her advice. If only all relationships could be this uncomplicated, the sole agenda being to love and be loved.

Instead, she had to deal with superintendents out for revenge, neighbors who turned out not to be very neighborly, and weirdos who got their jollies by sending dead roses and threatening bingo cards.

With a final pat, Alison returned to the table to finish outlining her comments for the judge. Superintendents and neighbors she could deal with. Weirdos with twisted agendas were another matter entirely.

But if she was lucky, whoever had targeted her for a practical joke had moved on to other things.

At least she could hope.

Daryl slouched in the shadow of a tree in the common ground behind Alison's house, craving a cigarette. Not that he'd had one in years. The whole lung cancer thing scared him. But a shot of nicotine would help settle his nerves. And a line of meth would be even better. He wasn't going there, though. Not after the story Bev Parisi had told earlier in the afternoon, once she'd calmed down enough to form a coherent sentence.

Leaning a shoulder against the rough bark, he shoved his

hands into the pockets of his slacks and studied Alison's house. She'd let her dog out a few minutes ago, and after a few sniffs, the little yipper had barreled straight toward the far corner of the yard, barking like crazy. Daryl had scuttled deeper into the underbrush, tempted to beat a hasty retreat and hightail it back to Chuck's truck a block away. But the dog had lost interest when the wind shifted. Besides, Alison's windows were closed, insulating her from outside noise.

Funny. He'd been griping about the hot weather all day, lamenting the busted air-conditioning in the trailer that had turned the tin can into a sweatbox. Yet the heat wave might have saved his hide tonight.

His reconnaissance outing had been worthwhile, although he hadn't planned to play private eye alone. This was Chuck's idea, after all. But Chuck was scrambling to keep his meth circle intact now that he'd lost a key member—and trying to console Bev, who was beyond freaked. Who wouldn't be? First she almost gets caught with a chrome taco while watching her neighbor's kids. Too afraid to sneak back to her apartment to collect her stuff, she crashes at Lon's place. Then she wakes up a few days later and finds him dead. Now that was a string of bad luck.

Daryl could relate.

But Chuck wasn't happy. Bev had violated one of his cardinal rules: if you're in trouble, don't get me involved. Stay away.

How they were going to resolve their problem, Daryl had no idea. But he'd decided not to hang around while they hashed it out. The farther he removed himself from the situation, the safer he'd feel.

Though safety was a relative term.

A sudden gust of wind whipped through the trees, and a cloud scuttled across the moon, darkening the night. The thunder and lightning a few nights ago hadn't amounted to anything, but this time he caught the scent of rain in the air and sensed the approach of unsettled weather. He didn't like storms, but at least a downpour might offer a reprieve from the intense heat.

Once more, he scanned the back of Alison's house, where a glow shone behind a drawn shade.

She was alone, except for her dog.

He knew that because his hiding place gave him a view of the street in front of her house too, and no one had come or gone all evening.

She was also vulnerable—despite the security system stickers he'd spotted the night they'd delivered the roses.

Not even the most elaborate alarms would protect her from the revenge he had in mind. Tonight's reconnaissance mission had convinced him Chuck's plan was very doable, with minimal risk of detection. It would just be a matter of waiting for the right moment, doing the job, and getting out. Fast.

Tomorrow was the night. With or without Chuck.

A sudden splash of rain against his forehead startled him, and he jerked back. Or tried to. But his ankle was stuck. For an instant, panic suffocated him, like it always did when he thought he was trapped. One sharp tug, however, freed him, and he let out his breath in a long whoosh. He must have gotten caught in a tangle of vines as he'd backed away from the dog. Some of them were still wrapped around his leg.

Weaving through the dense underbrush, he jerked them off. And hoped they weren't poison ivy.

As he cautiously exited the thicket on the far side and hurried toward Chuck's truck, he took one last look back toward Alison's house. Only a very faint glimpse of the light in her window was visible through the trees. The thicket itself was pitch-black.

Perfect.

The rain intensified, and he picked up his pace. He wasn't in any hurry to get back to the trailer, but if he kept the truck out too long, Chuck might not loan it to him again. And he needed it—for one more night, anyway. After that . . . he didn't know.

About anything.

The future loomed like a black, empty void.

All he knew for sure was that hanging around Chuck wasn't an option. Not unless he wanted to end up back in Potosi.

Back at the truck, he swung into the driver's seat, started the engine, and drove toward the entrance to Alison's small, dead-end street. As he approached, he spotted a cop car coming from the other direction. He slowed, watching as it turned down her street.

Could the timing have been any worse?

He slumped lower in his seat and kept his chin down.

But as he drove past the street, he risked a quick glance toward her house. The cop appeared to be doing a normal patrol circuit. He didn't slow down, just cruised down to the end, turned around, and circled back to the entrance.

Still spooked, Daryl accelerated.

It had to be a fluke, though. A tiny street like that probably only saw a patrol car once a week, if that.

Besides, it didn't matter. By the time his handiwork was discovered, he'd be long gone.

And there would be no witnesses.

He'd make certain of that.

"It's only for thirty days, Ellen. Don't give up."

Alison sat beside the distraught dark-haired mother as the woman sank into one of the hard plastic chairs in the hallway of the Family Court building. But her consoling words did nothing to stem the flow of Ellen's tears.

"I've tried so hard to do right by my kids." She choked out the words, groping for a handkerchief in the pocket of the beige uniform slacks she wore for her job as a receptionist at a health club. "After Danny took off, I was determined to keep the rest of my family together. I work hard, I have reputable daycare, I pay my rent—why can't the judge see that?"

"We've been over this before, Ellen." Alison kept her voice gentle but firm. "The children were alone when the police arrived, and there was evidence of drug use outside your back door. The court's main objective is to protect the welfare of the children."

"That's my main objective too." She swiped the tissue across her eyes. "I'm not surprised by the stunt Stan pulled. He's scum." She spat out the word. "But I can't believe Bev would do this. She seemed like such a nice person."

"She may come back at some point to claim her stuff."

"Unless she doesn't care about it."

Or doesn't want to get caught.

Cole's words echoed in Alison's mind. There'd been little of material value when the superintendent had let the police in, but they'd found enough incriminating evidence of drug use to cause her serious problems . . . giving her a strong incentive to stay away.

Alison's only hope was that a few of the personal items they'd noted might have sentimental value. Like the antique locket with faded, yellow photos inside. Or the small collection of Precious Moments figurines. Or an old teddy bear, frayed around the edges.

Still, Bev might never show. And considering their overwhelming caseload, the drug unit wasn't going to spend a lot of time looking for her. They'd already placed a phone call to the sole relative they'd tracked down, a sister who lived in Idaho. But she hadn't heard from her sibling in more than eight years. Nor had the BOLO alert they'd issued on her car yielded any results.

"Let's assume she's not coming back, Ellen." Alison touched her hand to emphasize the importance of her next statement. "You need to demonstrate to the judge that you're doing everything you can to provide a safe and healthy home for your children."

"What else can I do?" The last word caught on a sob.

"I have some ideas, but right now you need to get to work. Losing your job won't help your case."

The younger woman glanced at her watch. Eyes widening, she shoved the tissue back in her pocket and jumped to her feet. "I had no idea it was this late!"

Alison rose too. "I'll tell you what. I'll jot down a few

thoughts and drop them off at your place this afternoon, along with some material to look over. I have to be out in that area, anyway. After you review it, give me a call."

The woman gripped her hand. "Thank you for everything. Most of all, for believing in me." With one final squeeze, she hurried down the hall.

As Ellen disappeared around a corner, Alison followed more slowly. It was going to take a lot of perseverance to convince the judge Ellen was ready to reclaim her children. Plus a lot of hard work on the young mother's part. If Ellen was willing to do the work, however, Alison intended to be her cheerleader.

After the ruling this morning, though, she could use a cheerleader herself.

Someone like Mitch.

She hadn't heard from him yesterday, but she knew he'd been busy. Cole had told her the homicide division had been hopping all week. Busy or not, though, he did have to eat. It was possible he'd be available for lunch.

Alison started to reach into her purse for her phone. Hesitated. She wasn't accustomed to initiating dates. But what did she have to lose? Worst case, he'd say no.

Decision made, she pulled out her phone and tapped in his number. Much to her disgust, her heart tripped into a staccato beat as she waited for him to pick up. How ridiculous was that? She was thirty-four years old, not some schoolgirl with a crush.

Even if she felt like one.

He answered on the third ring. "Alison? Is everything okay?"

At the sharp edge of concern in his voice, she rushed to reassure him. "Yes. Sorry. I didn't mean to alarm you. This is a social call."

"Okay." Relief smoothed the tension from his words. "What's up?"

She moistened her lips. "Well, I was just wondering . . . since we never have made it to Ted Drewes, and our last get-together was a little rushed, I thought . . ." She sucked in a sharp breath. *Just spit it out, Alison.* "I wondered if you might be free for lunch today."

When silence greeted her suggestion, a warm flush crept over her cheeks. Time to backpedal. "Look, I know it's short notice. Don't worry about—"

"Whoa. Wait a minute. I'm not letting you off the hook that fast. Give me a second to think about how I can juggle things to make this work."

Did he want to go? Or was he simply trying to be polite, to think of some excuse that would allow her to save face?

"We can do it another day, if that's better for you."

"No. I'd like to have lunch with you today. In fact, I was planning to call you in about an hour to see how the Callahan hearing went. Is it over?"

"Yeah. And it went the way I expected. The children will stay in foster care until the next hearing in thirty days."

"I'm sorry to hear that. You put in a lot of hours on that case."

"But I couldn't change the circumstances. Maybe I'll have more to offer the next time we meet. I'm still hoping the neighbor shows up."

"Hang on to that thought. Okay—about lunch. I have to run my father to a doctor's appointment at St. Luke's at eleven, and I promised to take him out to eat afterward. Why don't you join us?"

"I wouldn't want to intrude on your time with your dad. We can do this another—"

"Alison." He cut her off firmly. "We live in the same house. I see him every day. Besides, he likes you."

"He's only met me once. For a minute or two."

"Trust me. You made an impression. So where will you be about twelve thirty?"

Wherever you are.

That was the response that popped to mind. But she didn't voice it.

"I have to do a home visit this morning. Then I have to stop at my office to pick up some GED material for Ellen. I could meet you somewhere halfway, if that works. Do you have a place in mind?"

He named a chain restaurant. "I know it's not gourmet fare, but my dad likes it, and I let him pick the place today. Is that okay?"

"Sure. Why don't you call me after you're finished at the doctor's office?"

"That works. And Alison . . . I'm glad you called."

The warmth of his tone dispelled her lingering second thoughts. "I am too. See you soon."

The line went dead, and Alison found herself smiling as she slipped her phone back in her purse and picked up her pace down the hallway. While the hearing hadn't turned out as well as she'd hoped, lunch with Mitch would go a long way toward restoring her spirits.

The trailer felt like a morgue.

As Daryl sharpened the hunting knife Chuck had loaned him, he checked out the two occupants of the living room, visible over the pass-through counter in the kitchen. His host was sitting on the lumpy couch, ankle crossed over knee, jiggling his foot as he stared into space. Bev was slouched in the chair that oozed stuffing, her expression vacant.

They hadn't said more than a few words to each other all morning. Bev had tried to start a couple of conversations, but Chuck had told her to shut up and let him think.

Suddenly Bev blinked, zoned in, and turned her head to look at him, her gaze lingering on the knife in his hands.

"Is there any food in this place? All I've had to eat since I left Lon's yesterday is a candy bar."

"Peanut butter crackers." Daryl tested the edge of the knife with the pad of his thumb. Nice and sharp. Excellent. That would make it go quicker. "I picked up some soup and cereal in town yesterday too."

She pushed herself to her feet. "I gotta eat something."

Chuck focused on her. "You need to go to town. I have to cook up another batch tomorrow, and I need the stuff Lon was gonna get. We got customers waiting."

She stared at him. "Are you nuts? The cops are looking for me. I left those kids alone, and you can bet they found the broken pipe. They've probably been through my apartment too."

"You should've cleaned up the glass and gotten rid of all that stuff in your place before you left. That was stupid."

Color surged in her cheeks. "Don't call me stupid! I didn't have time to get rid of anything! When Stan called to tell me the cops were on their way over to talk to Ellen, I got out as fast as I could."

"How did you get roped into that babysitting gig, anyway?"

She lifted one shoulder. "When my neighbor called, she sounded desperate. Car trouble. She said she'd have taken the kids with her to the garage, but the baby had an ear infection. It was only going to be for a couple of hours."

"And you had to have a fix while she was gone?"

She glared at Chuck. "That wasn't in my plans. But I ran into Stan on my way to her place, and half an hour later he showed up with some ice. Extra good, he said. He was willing to give it to me, but he didn't want it lying around. If I wanted it, I had to smoke it then. I wasn't about to turn down a freebie. So I ran next door to get my pipe and some foil, then lit up outside Ellen's back door. Things were just fine until the phone rang and Stan said cops were there, asking questions about her."

"What'd she do to get the cops interested in her, anyway?"

"Beats me. She seemed like the real straight type. She works hard, and she sure loves her kids. I guess you never can tell about people, though." She shrugged. "Anyway, I freaked. Dropped the pipe. I started to clean it up, but next thing I know, the cops are knocking on the door. I grabbed my purse, ran around the building, and headed for Lon's. I thought I'd be safe there." A grimace twisted her mouth.

"So who's gonna get the stuff I need?"

Chuck stared at her in silence. She stared back. Then, in unison, they turned toward Daryl.

His heart stumbled, and he stopped sharpening the knife. "No way."

"Come on, man. One time. That's all I'm asking. I'll line up somebody else before the next batch. We're in a tight spot here." Chuck walked into the kitchen.

Bev followed.

"If I get caught with anything connected to drugs, I'll be back in Potosi faster than you can cook a batch. And I'll never get out."

"Look, we got everything covered except the cold pills. You just need to go to a few stores and pick some up. It's no big deal."

"It is if somebody gets suspicious."

Chuck grabbed his shirt, bunched it in his fist, and moved in close. Too close. "It's not against the law to buy cold medicine. I'll give you a fake ID. Besides, you're clean. Even if they stopped you, what could they prove?" Chuck invaded his personal space, and Daryl took an involuntary step back. "You owe me, man. I gave you a place to stay when your woman wouldn't have anything to do with you. I also gave you that idea about how to deal with your social worker friend." He gestured to the hunting knife. "Even bought the bingo cards. Where you gonna go if I throw you out?"

He hadn't considered that. Most likely, he'd end up back at the homeless shelter. And maybe that wasn't such a bad idea. Maybe . . .

"I thought we were friends."

The man's fetid breath made his skin crawl, and as he looked into Chuck's dilated pupils, Daryl tasted fear for the first time in their acquaintance. His onetime partner's mean streak had widened considerably through the years, and Daryl didn't doubt the man was capable of violence. He'd discovered weapons hidden all over the trailer, suggesting paranoia and a leaning toward aggression that had been absent five years ago when they'd started slinging meth.

"We are."

"Then do this. One time."

It wasn't a request. Daryl's fingers clenched on the knife in his hand, and he held on tight. "Okay. I have to go into town anyway." He lifted the gleaming blade of the knife. "For this."

"There you go. Just add this to your agenda." Chuck grinned at him, revealing a mouthful of rotting teeth no dentist could save. "You can use Bev's car. I changed the plates and the VIN." He released his grip on Daryl's shirt.

"What's a VIN?" Bev sidled in.

"Vehicle identification number," Chuck supplied. "Just don't get stopped, since you don't have a license."

"Maybe you could pick some things up for me from my apartment too." Bev edged closer.

"That's not part of the deal." Daryl slipped the knife back into its sheath. "Besides, the cops may be watching for you."

"They've got enough to do without worrying about one druggie. Look, all I want is my mother's locket. It's on my dresser. Gold, with real pretty filigree around the edge. You can't miss it. It would take you less than two minutes."

"Forget the locket, Bev." Chuck paced the living room, jiggling the change in his pocket. "It's not worth the risk."

"It is to me."

"Then you go get it!"

Tears welled in her eyes. "I can't. They're looking for me. But they're not looking for him." A tear rolled down her cheek. "Chuck, you know how much it means to me. And I've done favors for you for years. Personal favors."

He gave her an impatient perusal. Daryl saw him waver. Capitulate.

The bottom fell out of his stomach.

"Okay. Fine. Daryl, stop by the apartment and get her locket. She's right. No one's looking for you, and they don't have the manpower to plant some cop at her place 24/7 anyway. You'll be okay."

Chuck started fooling with some TV remote device he was

taking apart with obsessive fascination, piece by piece, on the kitchen table. Bev rummaged through the cabinet next to him, foraging for lunch.

The matter was settled.

And Daryl was in the hot seat.

Again.

11

"There she is, son. Looking mighty pretty too."

Following the direction of his father's gaze, Mitch caught sight of Alison. She was on her cell phone, focused on the wall in front of her, in a far corner of the restaurant's foyer. And she did look pretty. She had on that sleek pinstripe suit with the sexy slit in the skirt again. A smile tugged at his lips as he gave the exposed length of her leg a leisurely perusal.

"Lucky you aren't hooked up to one of those blood pressure machines, like I was at the doctor's office. It'd be off the scale."

At his father's comment, heat surged on Mitch's neck. He did his best to keep it below his collar as he turned to the older man, who was several inches shorter than his own six-foot frame.

"Dad . . ." He put a stern warning note in his voice. They'd had a long conversation en route to the restaurant, and his father had promised to keep the lunchtime discussion light and impersonal. No hints about a romance between his son and the lovely Children's Service worker.

Things were not getting off to a promising start.

"This is just you and me talking, Mitch. I'll behave when the young lady joins us." He slashed his finger in an X shape on his chest. "Cross this rejuvenated ticker of mine."

Before Mitch could pursue the subject, Alison saw them. Lifting her hand in greeting, she ended the call, slipped the phone back in her purse, and walked across the foyer.

He picked up on her slight limp at once.

Touching her arm as she joined them, he scrutinized her face. "Everything okay?" He flicked his gaze toward her legs.

Her cheeks pinkened and she adjusted the strap of her shoulder purse. "Too many hours in heels." Smiling, she transferred her attention to his father. "It's nice to see you again, Mr. Morgan."

"Please call me Walt." He gave her extended hand a vigorous shake. "And the pleasure is all mine—and Mitch's. Right, son?"

Mitch shot his father another warning look. This was exactly why he'd hesitated when Alison had called about lunch. At some point since he'd returned to St. Louis, his father had decided his son's social life was lacking. And he seemed to think Alison might be the solution.

Truth be told, so did Mitch. But he preferred to deal with this relationship at his own pace—doing his best to match it to Alison's. The last thing she needed was pressure to get serious too quickly, and he didn't want his dad scaring her off.

"So tell me, Alison, why isn't a beautiful young woman like you married by now?" His father took her arm as they followed the hostess to the table.

Relegated to the rear, Mitch rolled his eyes and stuck close. It was going to be a long lunch.

As Alison gave her order and handed her menu back to the waitress, she snuck a peek at Mitch. He was studying the oversized bill of fare, faint parallel grooves creasing his brow.

"I'll have the burger with everything on it." Walt started to close his menu.

"Dad." There was a warning note in Mitch's voice. "Think healthy. No more artery-clogging fat."

Sending his son a disgusted look, Walt opened the menu again, gave it a quick scan, and passed it to the waitress. "The grilled chicken sandwich."

"Fruit cup, slaw, or fries?" Pencil poised, the young woman waited while the older man considered his options.

At last, he gave a long-suffering sigh. "Fruit."

"And you, sir?" She smiled at Mitch. Not just a polite, be-nice-to-the-customer smile. A real smile. Warm. Personal. Inviting.

If Mitch noticed, he gave no indication.

"Turkey club. With slaw." He handed her the menu without making eye contact.

Alison watched the waitress's smile fade. Understandable. A woman would have to be dead not to hope a tall, dark, and handsome man like Mitch would notice her.

He caught her watching him, and the slow smile he sent her way—the one that produced the hint of a dimple in his cheek—made her wish they'd crank up the air-conditioning in the restaurant. She picked up her glass of ice water and took a long drink.

"It sure is a hot one." Walt hoisted his glass too. "I'm glad the doc gave me the okay to start swimming again."

Setting her glass back on the table, Alison turned her attention to the older man. "You like to swim?"

"Yes. Until the old ticker acted up, I went to the Y and did laps three times a week. Been doing that for years. Swimming is great exercise, you know—and good for the waistline." He patted his trim midsection. "Of course, even in my prime, I was never in Mitch's league. I still have a roomful of awards from his swim meet days."

"That was a long time ago, Dad." Mitch reached for a package of crackers from a basket on the table and ripped open the cellophane.

"You're as good as you ever were. Maybe better. You don't get to be a SEAL unless you can swim like a fish."

"That was a long time ago too."

"Four years ago isn't that long. And you still swim laps every day."

Alison looked over at him. Yeah, that made sense. His lean,

muscular build belonged to a swimmer. As did the broad shoulders and powerful chest. "How do you manage to fit that in?"

"Usually goes before the sun gets up," Walt supplied without giving Mitch a chance to respond. "Sometimes he waits till after dinner, though. Me, I like to swim before lunch. Nice way to break up the day. I'll be able to drive myself too, now that the doctor gave me the green light to get behind the wheel."

"No need to rush things, Dad."

Alison studied Mitch. He was playing with his crackers, not eating them. And he was keeping a keen eye on his father. There was some dynamic here she couldn't identify. Nothing bad. But interesting.

"I'm not rushing things. Surgeon said it was fine. I'll be able to drive myself to church now too, but I hope you'll keep coming, anyway. It's nice to have you back in the pew beside me."

Alison stared at him. "You're going to church?"

"Yes, isn't that great?" Walt grinned at her. "He started attending again not long after he met you. Interesting coincidence, isn't it?"

Clearing his throat, Mitch crumbled a cracker, then brushed all the fragments into a neat pile. "So how is your mom doing since her bout with the flu, Alison?"

Not the smoothest segue she'd ever heard, but she got the message. Mitch didn't want to talk about going back to church. And that was okay. The important thing was that he'd taken a first step back toward his faith.

And that was the best news she'd had all day.

Daryl pulled into a parking spot in the lot at Bev's apartment building and surveyed the three-story structure of peeling white stucco. The concrete sidewalk was cracked in several places, the downspout was dangling, and the lawn was more mud than grass. He doubted it looked any better inside. Still, it couldn't be as bad as Chuck's trailer.

Settling his sunglasses on his nose, he inspected the area. It seemed quiet on this early Thursday afternoon. The lot was half empty, none of the cars were occupied, and there wasn't a soul in sight. If the cops were anywhere around, they were keeping a very low profile.

Time to go in.

He palmed Bev's keys, pulled the borrowed baseball cap lower on his forehead, and opened the door. If all went well, he should be in and out in less than five minutes.

As he slid from the car and skulked toward the entrance, he kept an eye out for anything that looked suspicious. But nothing raised a red alert. Good. The simpler this detour was, the better.

After unlocking the front door with the key Bev had specified, he draped the hem of his T-shirt over the knob, twisted it, and slipped inside. All appeared to be normal here too. A worn beige carpet, frayed along the edges, ran the length of the hall, and from the far end the muffled sound of rap music seeped through a door.

He didn't linger by the entrance. Once outside of 1E, he inserted the other key and used his T-shirt again to turn the handle.

The door didn't give.

Daryl frowned. Had Bev given him the wrong key?

He tried again.

Nothing.

Maybe, by chance, the key for the main door worked for her unit too. It was worth a shot.

Switching keys, he tried to insert the one he'd used out front. It didn't fit.

Stymied, he examined the two keys in his hands. Only one explanation came to mind.

After the visit from the police, the landlord had changed the locks.

Pocketing the keys, Daryl started back down the hall toward the front door. No sense wasting time here. If Bev wanted the locket that badly, she'd have to call the superintendent she was so chummy with and see if he could get it out for her. That was a better plan all around, anyway. As far as he was concerned, this little side trip had been far too risky.

Relieved to be on his way out, he pushed through the door—and almost knocked over the woman who was reaching up to press the bell for the superintendent.

The woman who had ruined his life.

Alison Taylor.

His heart slammed against his rib cage and he dipped his chin, pulling the brim of his cap even lower. How bizarre was this?

He brushed past her, averting his head. Not that there was much chance she'd recognize him. It had been years since she'd seen him, and his hair had been much longer in those days. But her presence unnerved him nonetheless.

Mumbling a muffled "Sorry," he kept walking. And didn't look back until he was safely behind the wheel of Bev's car.

Alison was still standing by the door. Dressed in a classy business suit. Paying no attention to him as she waited for the superintendent to answer her ring. If she had any clue who he was, she gave no indication of it.

He put the car in gear, backed out of the spot, and pulled away. Glancing in the rearview mirror, he saw that a guy had answered the door. Fortysomething, with a paunch his white undershirt did nothing to disguise. He was staring after the car—as if he recognized it.

Assuming the man was the superintendent, that was a definite possibility.

A cold trickle of sweat inched down between Daryl's shoulder blades, and he tightened his grip on the wheel. At least Chuck had changed the plates. If the superintendent alerted the police that Bev's car was in the area, the cops would be looking for the wrong plates.

As for his own appearance, he could alter that. With one hand, he whipped off the glasses and cap. Then, despite the heat, he shrugged into the black jacket on the seat beside him, covering his tan T-shirt.

The sooner he got away from the area, however, the better. Because he still had a lot of things to do before he returned to the trailer. First, smurf some cold pills for Chuck. While he was making a circuit of stores taking care of that, he also intended to pick up a few supplies he needed. Latex gloves. Plastic sheeting. A burger too, while he was at it.

Then—tonight—he'd pay another visit to Alison.

He checked the rearview mirror. No sign of the cops.

The tension in his shoulders eased, and he let his thoughts return to Alison. He'd only seen her up close once before, the day she'd refused to turn Kyle over to him after calling the cops. The day he'd been busted. He'd been too angry to notice details then. But today he'd gotten a better look at her. She had a pretty face—and big blue eyes. The kind that could turn a man to mush if she smiled at him.

But she wouldn't be smiling later.

Daryl's lips twisted into a smirk, and he bent down to finger the knife sheath hidden under the seat.

He couldn't wait.

"That was a mighty tasty piece of salmon, son." Walt wiped his lips on a paper napkin and sat back in his chair. "You sure have given that grill a workout since you've been home."

"You need to learn to use it too. It's a very healthy way to cook." Mitch rose and picked up their empty plates. So far, getting his father interested in the culinary arts had been a losing battle. "Would you like some more iced tea?"

"Yes, thanks. But if you keep waiting on me, I'm going to get lazy."

"How come I don't think that will happen?" Mitch retrieved the pitcher of tea. "Case in point: I noticed the freshly turned earth in the garden as I pulled in tonight. You were busy after our lunch."

146

"The doc said it was okay."

"It's too hot to be out in the sun."

"It'll only get hotter. Wait till July."

"Why don't you forego the garden this year?" Mitch refilled his father's glass, then cut them each a slice of angel food cake, ladling sliced strawberries over the top.

"I've had a garden every year of my adult life, and I'm not about to quit now. But I might scale it back a little." Walt dug into the cake the instant Mitch set it in front of him.

There was nothing wrong with his dad's appetite, that was for sure. Another positive sign. The older man's rising energy level was also encouraging. He should be grateful his father was making such a speedy recovery.

He took his own seat again and used the edge of his fork to slice through his cake. "I guess you know what's best."

His father stopped eating and stared at him. "Well, that's quite a change from the mollycoddling you've been dishing out up to now. What happened?"

Mitch lifted one shoulder and continued to eat. "Alison suggested that I trust you to test your limits—and assume you have the common sense to respect them."

"Did she, now." His father grinned and speared a strawberry, waving it to punctuate his next comment. "I knew I liked that girl. She has a first-rate head on her shoulders and a warm heart. That's a winning combination. So when are you going to take her out on a real date?"

After spending the entire dinner listening to his father effuse about today's lunch—and sidestepping the older man's queries about his intentions with Alison—he should have known better than to bring her up again.

"When life slows down." He took a sip of his iced tea and stirred in some more sugar.

"Trust me, son. That'll never happen. Life just gets busier and busier until you're my age. And then there's not much left of it to enjoy. You have to go for the gusto when the opportunity presents itself. What's holding you back, anyway? Don't you like her?"

"Of course I like her. What's not to like?"

"My point exactly."

"I need to take it slowly, Dad. She was involved in a serious relationship a year ago that didn't work out. That's why she brushed off your question today about why she wasn't married. Now she's a little gun-shy." Mitch kept his explanation spare, careful not to reveal too much of the personal information she'd shared in confidence. "I don't want to rush her. That could backfire."

Walt speared another strawberry and twirled it on his fork. "You want my opinion?"

"Do I have a choice?"

"No. Your mother always said I was too outspoken, and she was right. But as one Musketeer to another, I can tell you the lady is interested. You pussyfoot around too long, she'll find somebody else."

Mitch took a sip of tea. "I'm not pussyfooting around."

"Yeah?" His father gave him a skeptical look. "You haven't even taken her on a real date."

"I'll get around to that."

"Hmph. He who hesitates . . ."

"If it makes you feel any better, I'm planning to call her after I get back from swimming and ask her out for Saturday night."

His father's face brightened. "That's the best news I've had all day. At least she'll know you're interested."

Smiling, Mitch finished off his cake and rose. "Trust me. She knows I'm interested." He winked and reached for his father's empty plate too.

Walt smiled back. "Well now. Maybe there's hope for you yet." He stood and shooed Mitch away from the sink. "You go on and swim. I'll clean up in here. It'll help me get the blood moving. Besides, the sooner you get home, the sooner you can call that pretty little lady."

"No argument from me." Mitch draped the dishcloth over the sink and headed for the hall to collect his duffel bag.

"And son . . ."

At his father's words, he turned in the doorway.

"If I haven't told you lately, it's good to have you home again."

Mitch tried to swallow past the sudden pressure in his throat. "It's good to be home."

As he continued toward his room, Mitch realized that affirmation was true on many levels. Although he'd liked the NYPD, he loved his dad more. Since the bypass scare, spending time with him had become a top priority.

And as it had turned out, his new job was proving to be every bit as interesting as the NYPD gig.

Plus, he'd met Alison. That had been a huge—and unexpected—bonus.

Grabbing his duffel bag from the corner of his childhood bedroom, he glanced around at the dozens of swimming ribbons, medals, and trophies that decorated the walls and shelves. The ones his father had told Alison about at lunch. He'd sweated blood to win most of them. Pushed himself to the limit. Been harder on himself than any coach had ever been.

As a result, he'd had his fleeting moments of glory. And he'd enjoyed them.

But he was prouder of what the awards represented at a deeper level—perseverance, determination, and commitment. The ability to establish a goal and go after it with single-minded determination.

Those skills had served him well in every endeavor he'd undertaken. In college, in the navy, as a SEAL, on the NYPD.

And he hoped they'd continue to serve him well now as he wooed a lovely Children's Service worker with amazing blue eyes and a warm, caring heart.

From his hiding place at the edge of the wooded common ground behind Alison's house, Daryl kept vigil. Night had fallen, and there was a subtle glow through the drawn shade in what he assumed was her kitchen. Not as bright as last night, so she must be in a different part of the house. But he'd seen her come home. Knew she was inside. Knew, also, that she was alone. There had been no visitors.

Soon he would make his move.

After wiping his palms on his slacks, he pulled on the latex gloves. Then, using the knife he'd withdrawn from its sheath, he opened the pouch of plastic sheeting. He removed one piece, cut a hole in the center, and pulled it over his head. The second piece he laid on the ground, securing it in place with two large rocks. After a couple more simple preparations, he was ready.

Now all he had to do was wait.

This was the hardest part.

With nothing to do but think about the blood to come, he had difficulty keeping his queasiness at bay. But the two whiskeys he'd downed at a tavern on the way had smoothed out his nerves and helped him focus on the outcome, not the act.

He thought again about the glimpse he'd had earlier today of Alison's clear blue eyes. Eyes that didn't seem to have a care in the world.

Once again, his lips twisted as he balanced the knife in his hands.

In less than twenty minutes, if all went well, she'd have plenty to worry about.

And those eyes would be awash with terror.

The baby afghan she'd been knitting slid from Alison's lap, rousing her. Blinking, she glanced at her grandfather's antique clock on the mantel. She'd actually fallen asleep for ten minutes while sitting upright. That was a rarity.

Then again, she'd had a busy day—the Callahan hearing this morning, lunch with Mitch and his father, plus a full afternoon of paperwork that had kept her at the office later than usual. She'd been too tired when she got home to do anything more than reheat a piece of the lasagna she'd made a couple of weeks ago and feed Bert.

Bert.

She'd let him out just before dozing off. Had he been trying to signal her he was ready to come back in?

Rising, she deposited the afghan on the seat of the chair. She didn't hear any scratching at the back door, which meant one of two things. Bert had given up summoning her and was waiting patiently on the stoop for her to let him in. Or he'd found some dead creature in a far corner of the yard and was dragging it back for her to see. He'd done that with a rabbit a few weeks ago.

Her less-than-enthusiastic response to his find hadn't seemed to faze him.

She flipped on the light in the kitchen as she entered, crossing to the back door to crack the blinds on the window above the knob.

He wasn't on the steps.

Not a positive sign.

She opened the door a few inches, stuck her head out, and looked around. The pool of illumination from her security lighting only extended to the edge of her patio, and he was nowhere in sight.

"Bert! Here, boy! Time to come in!"

In general, Bert would bound to the back door at her call, often yipping with excitement the whole way.

Tonight, an eerie silence met her summons.

Alison frowned and tried again. "Come on, Bert! I have a doggie biscuit for you!"

The phrase "doggie biscuit" never failed to catch his attention. Any second now he'd come dashing across the stone patio and careen past her legs into the kitchen in search of the promised treat.

But Bert remained mute. And absent. Only the whisper of the wind in the trees at the far dark edge of her lawn broke the silence.

Despite the heat, a shiver ran through her.

Something wasn't right.

Yet he had to be in the yard. The electric fence she'd installed last year was on. Perhaps he'd tangled with some larger critter. One that had gotten the upper hand. Mr. Harrison next door had mentioned seeing a coyote a few weeks ago. Maybe Bert was hurt.

Heart hammering, Alison retreated to the kitchen, grabbed a flashlight from under the sink, and pulled the broom out of her utility closet. The latter wasn't much of a weapon, but it would shoo away a coyote. She hoped. As she passed the counter, she snagged the portable phone as well and slipped it in the pocket of her shorts.

At the door, she hesitated. Should she call Cole or Jake? They wouldn't be happy about her wandering around the dark yard on her own, not with the specter of bingo man still hovering over her. Nor was she all that thrilled with the idea.

But this could be a false alarm. It was possible Bert was just ignoring her. He'd done that a time or two, when he'd gotten really engrossed in some interesting find. He always came, though, if she ventured out into the yard after him.

Surely it would be safe to go as far as the edge of the patio. She could aim the beam of the flashlight around the yard and call him again from there. If that didn't yield any result, she'd enlist the help of one of her brothers. She'd rather call Mitch, but she'd feel guilty bothering him with a mundane matter like this.

Stepping onto the stoop, she tried calling Bert once more from there. When that didn't produce a response, she eased to the edge of the patio, scanning the perimeter of light as she went. One suspicious shadow, and she'd bolt for the kitchen mere steps behind her.

But nothing moved. Nor did Bert respond to another round of calls.

With a flick of the switch, she turned on the flashlight and moved the beam across the yard. Although it didn't reach to the far corners, it extended her range of vision quite a bit. However, she saw nothing suspicious as she slowly swung it in a wide arc. It was as if Bert had disappeared without . . .

152

The beam of light caught the edge of an unfamiliar object. Less than five yards in front of her.

She swung it back.

Took a few steps closer.

Froze.

A scream clawed its way past her lips, ripping through the night, shattering the stillness.

And as denial warred with reality, a single agonized word roared through her mind.

No!

12

Mitch sliced through the water in the Y pool, staying dead center in his lane, counting laps—six more to go—and thinking about the call he was going to make to Alison in a few minutes about a date for Saturday night.

He was so focused on debating the merits of one of the higher-end Italian restaurants on The Hill versus a sidewalk café in the Central West End that the ringing of his phone didn't immediately register.

By the time it did, he was at the far end of the pool. No way could he get back to the other side before it rolled to voice mail.

After executing a flip turn, he used the combat sidestroke he'd mastered as a SEAL to propel him back toward the phone. In light of the demands of his job and his father's recent health issues, he tried to stay within arm's reach of it at all times. Since that wasn't possible in the pool, he'd grown accustomed to leaving it on his towel, set to audible. But it rarely rang at the hours he swam.

When it did, there was usually a problem.

At the end of the pool, he pulled himself out of the water as another call came in. He grabbed the phone with one hand, his towel with the other, and wiped the water off his face as he checked caller ID.

Alison.

He'd memorized her number too.

Maybe this wasn't a problem call, after all.

His lips tipping into a smile, he pressed the talk button. "Hi, Alison. I was just going to call you."

He waited for her to toss back some pert reply. Instead, an odd noise came over the line.

One that sounded a lot like a strangled sob.

Adrenaline surging, he shot to his feet and took off at a jog for the dressing room, wet feet slapping against the cement surface, a drip line marking his path.

"Alison, what's wrong?"

"S-somebody k-killed Bert."

As she choked out the words, Mitch felt as if someone had kicked him in the stomach.

"Where are you?" He put the phone on speaker, set it on a bench in the dressing room, and grabbed his clothes out of the locker. No time for his customary shower to rinse the chlorine from his skin.

"In m-my backyard."

"Okay. Listen to me." He shoved his legs into his jeans. "I want you to go in the house right now. Lock the door behind you. I'll wait while you do it."

"I c-can't leave B-Bert." Once more she began to sob.

"I'm on my way. But I need to know you're safe. Go in now. Please."

No response.

His pulse kicked into overdrive, and his fingers fumbled the laces on his shoes. "Alison? Are you still there?"

"Y-yes."

"Please . . . go in the house. Now. I'm waiting." He slammed the locker shut, pulled his keys out of his pocket, and charged toward the exit. If he floored it, he should be able to get from the Y in Kirkwood to her house in Fenton in less than fifteen minutes.

He heard some shuffling on the line, then the sound of a door opening and closing.

"I'm in."

"Is everything locked?"

"Yes."

Pushing through the main door of the Y, he sprinted toward his car, hitting the button on his key chain to release the door locks as he approached.

"I'm getting in my car. I'll be there in a few minutes. Sit tight."

"Okay."

Severing the connection, Mitch called dispatch and requested that a patrol car be sent to Alison's house. Then he pulled up Cole's number and used autodial to connect. Alison's brother answered on the second ring. Mitch didn't waste words.

"Cole, it's Mitch. Alison just called me. Someone got to her dog. I notified dispatch and I'm on my way."

The other man uttered a word that wasn't pretty. "I'm right behind you."

The line went dead.

As Mitch merged into the westbound traffic on I-44 and accelerated, he wasn't certain what he'd find at Alison's house. But one thing was very clear.

Bingo man was back.

Twelve minutes later, as he slammed on his brakes behind one of the two patrol cars parked in front of Alison's house, an officer appeared from around the side of the attached garage, following the beam of a flashlight.

Mitch met him in the middle of the front yard and flashed his badge. "What do we have?"

"Somebody sure did a number on that dog." The man looked a little green. "He's in the back. I'll show you."

He retraced his steps, pausing at the edge of the patio, where the other officer stood. "About fifteen feet straight ahead." He pinpointed the spot with his flashlight.

Mitch understood at once why the man's complexion had taken on a sickly hue.

Clicking on his own light, he approached the mound of fur. Two feet away, he stopped.

Bert lay on a small square of plastic. One side of his head had been smashed in, and his body had been slashed in several places. A bingo card had been propped against him. Two of the squares were marked off with a skull-and-crossbones stamp.

The whole thing was beyond sick.

And the small pile of vomit off to one side told him more eloquently than words what Alison's reaction had been to the scene. He'd heard the shock and horror and terror in her voice. But the sadistic cruelty startled even him—and he'd seen a lot.

He turned to the two officers, who were conversing in low tones behind him. "Stick close while I talk to Ms. Taylor."

Without waiting for a response, he took the three steps to the back door in one leap and knocked. "Alison. It's Mitch."

He heard a chair scrape, and a few moments later the lock was flipped.

When she opened the door, a second shock wave rocked him. Her face was colorless. Ravaged. And the numb blankness in her eyes reminded him of how he and his fellow SEAL wannabes had looked during the Hell Week training segment, after they'd gone five days with a mere four hours of sleep while being pushed to their physical and psychological limits. The trauma had been so great that the only way he could get through it was to distance himself. Withdraw to a place where he couldn't feel the pain.

That's what Alison had done.

But when she saw him, that shaky defense shattered. Her face crumpled, the horror returned to her eyes, and she swayed.

He'd intended to lead her to the kitchen table, get her some clear soda, and calm her enough so she could run through the events of the evening. Now, he scrapped that plan.

After crossing the threshold, he shoved the door shut with his foot and pulled her into his arms.

She clung to him, clutching his shirt in her fists. Shaking

157

and silent as tears trailed down her cheeks and soaked into his T-shirt.

He held her, searching for words of comfort and consolation. But all he could come up with was the old standard that was never adequate.

"I'm so sorry." He rested his chin on top of her bowed head and pulled her closer, rage roiling in his gut. If he ever got his hands on the guy who'd done this, he'd . . .

"Why?" Her whispered word, filled with anguish, interrupted his vengeful thoughts and tore at his heart.

"I wish I knew." He stroked her back, the fierce feelings of protectiveness that swept over him reinforcing what he'd already suspected—Alison Taylor was fast laying claim to his heart.

All at once the door banged into his back, and he shot an irritated look over his shoulder. Cole peered back at him through the six-inch opening. He assumed the tall, dark-haired guy behind his colleague was the brother he hadn't met, Deputy U.S. Marshal Jake Taylor.

"You want to let us in?" Cole's expression was grim, and anger flared in the depths of his eyes. The same anger Mitch was struggling to contain.

Moving to one side, Mitch kept an arm around Alison as she shifted to face her brothers.

Based on the simultaneous narrowing of their eyes as they entered, neither missed his proprietary gesture. And Mitch sensed they had mixed feelings about it.

Tough.

Still holding on to Alison, he offered his hand to Jake. "Mitch Morgan."

There was an infinitesimal hesitation before the other man took it in a firm grip. "Jake. The other brother."

"That's what I figured."

Jake edged around Cole, touched Alison's cheek, and gentled his voice. "You okay, Twig?"

"I guess."

Cole moved closer to his sister and pulled a handkerchief out of his pocket. "It's clean." The words came out husky as he dabbed at her tears, and he cleared his throat.

She took the handkerchief from him and squeezed his hand. Rising on tiptoe, she kissed Jake's cheek. "Thanks for coming."

"We're going to find this guy, Alison." Cole's jaw settled into a hard line.

"I hope so."

"Will you be okay in here alone for a few minutes while Cole and Mitch and I do a quick sweep of the area? There are two officers outside too." Jake touched her shoulder again, as if reassuring himself she was okay.

Mitch could relate.

"Yeah."

"Let me get you something to drink first." Mitch guided her over to the kitchen table, removed a clear soda from the fridge, and pulled the tab. Keeping his back to her brothers, he set it in front of her and leaned close, speaking in a voice only she could hear.

"Remember, you've got three able-bodied men dedicated to keeping you safe and tracking this guy down."

She took a shuddering breath. "You have enough on your plate already. You don't need to add me to your list of responsibilities."

"Maybe I want to." He locked gazes with her, and only after the barest hint of color seeped back into her cheeks, telling him his message had been received, did he straighten up. "We'll be back in a few minutes."

Jake and Cole were waiting for him by the back door. As they exited and walked over to where Bert lay, he half expected Cole to comment on the cozy scene with his sister. But for once, his colleague had more pressing matters than Alison's love life on his mind.

Namely, her safety.

Mitch was glad Cole had his priorities straight.

As they gathered about three feet from the dog, Jake flashed his light along the lawn from the square of plastic toward the back of the yard. A subtle path of crushed grass was discernible. "The guy took care of the dog farther back and dragged him closer to the house."

There was a hard edge to Cole's voice when he responded. "He must have hidden in the common ground, waiting for Alison to let Bert out for his nightly run."

The implication was obvious. Someone had been watching Alison's house. Knew her habits.

That didn't sit well with Mitch. Or with her brothers, judging from their somber demeanors.

Mitch spoke to the two officers at the edge of the patio. "Did you guys see anything when you got here?"

"Just the dog," one of them replied.

"Okay. Hang tight for a few more minutes. We're going to check out the back of the property."

He took off for the woods, and Alison's brothers fell in behind him.

Much to his surprise, the perpetrator hadn't made any attempt to erase evidence of his presence. A large, bloodstained rock had been left at the edge of the property. A half-eaten hamburger patty lay on the ground beside it. A bribe for Bert, no doubt.

"Over there." Cole trained his flashlight on a bloody sheet of plastic that appeared to have a hole cut in the middle. It lay in the center of the thicket, as if it had been discarded on the run.

Jake moved into the underbrush, staying wide of the bloody plastic as he swept the beam of his light toward the far side of the common ground. "I can see a trail of broken branches. He must have exited on the other side."

"I think it's time to call in the Crime Scene Unit." Cole's voice was somber. "I didn't want to overreact to the dead roses, but there's a pattern of threats now. Plus an act of violence." He turned to Mitch. "Let's get some patrol officers canvassing the neighborhood. Alison's street, and the one behind us."

"Okay. But then we need to address another issue."

"I'm with you." Jake shot him a look that told Mitch they

were on the same page. "Our guy's been here twice. This incident was far worse than the first one. And the fact he left another bingo card with a second square marked off tells me he's not through yet. That this has become a game to him, and he won't stop until he hits bingo—which is just two squares away."

"That leaves us with one critical question." Mitch looked at the two men beside him and cut to the chase. "How are we going to keep Alison safe?"

There was blood everywhere.

How could one little mutt bleed so much?

His stomach still heaving, Daryl stared in the mirror at the gas station restroom and scrubbed at the maroon flecks on his cheeks. Covering himself with plastic had been a smart move, considering how the blood had spurted. Otherwise, his clothes would be a disaster. As it was, they'd escaped unscathed.

He couldn't say the same about his face. Or the hair that hadn't been protected by his baseball cap.

Dipping his head in the sink, he jabbed at the hand-soap dispenser and worked up a lather. It would have been a lot tougher to get rid of the evidence if he'd still had the long hair he'd once favored. At least fate worked to his advantage once in a while. On small things, anyway.

When he finished, he blotted out as much water as he could with paper towels, ran a plastic comb through his hair, and checked himself in the mirror. Not bad.

For the first time in hours, he relaxed. His mission had been a success, and he'd emerged unscathed. All traces of blood had been removed from his person. He'd disposed of the bloody latex gloves and baseball cap in a dumpster outside, hidden in his McDonald's bag. He'd seen no one in the vicinity of the thicket, so there couldn't be any witnesses.

And Alison Taylor had been hurt.

He knew that, because as he'd driven past her street with his windows down, he'd heard her piercing scream.

That moment alone had made the outing worthwhile. It had been far more gratifying than simply imagining her reaction.

Smiling, he unlocked the door and strolled into the small quick shop every gas station seemed to have these days. A Hershey bar caught his eye, and he hesitated. When he was a kid, chocolate candy had been reserved for special occasions, like Christmas. But today felt a lot like a holiday. Except for failing to retrieve Bev's locket, it had gone well. Why not indulge? He'd even pay for it, generous soul that he was.

With Chuck's money.

After plucking it off the rack, Daryl moseyed over to the counter and fished a couple of singles out of his pocket.

The long-haired guy behind the register rang up the purchase, took his money, handed over the change. "Enjoy the treat, man."

"Yeah. I will." Daryl picked up the candy bar and exited.

Once outside, he ripped the paper off and took a bite. As the chocolate dissolved on his tongue, he slid behind the wheel, put the car in gear, and pointed it south.

Back to reality.

Back to Chuck's trailer.

A bitter taste overpowered the sweet flavor of the candy, and his breath stuck in his lungs. He sucked in air, but he couldn't dispel the suffocating feeling of being trapped. Helpless. Caught in front of a fast-moving train, with an abyss on both sides.

He clenched his fingers on the wheel and forced himself to keep breathing.

He hated this feeling.

But he'd vanquished it tonight, when he'd been exacting his revenge on Alison Taylor. For a brief interlude, he'd felt powerful. In control. It had been an exhilarating feeling. The kind of feeling he wanted to have all the time. But he wasn't going to get it hanging around Chuck.

Unless he went back to the meth.

Flipping his blinker, he signaled a move into the fast lane and toyed with the idea of snorting a line. Just one. For old time's sake. He didn't want to end up addicted, like Chuck, but a little rush would be real nice.

Or maybe he'd think of some other way to torture the woman who'd ruined his life. That had given him just as big a rush as meth had.

Better yet, why not do both?

A smile tugged at the corners of his mouth. Yeah. That sounded real fine. Chuck had said he had some more ideas for Alison. They could talk about them tonight.

Over a line.

Two hours after Alison had discovered Bert, Mitch joined the three Taylor siblings at her kitchen table to discuss a game plan while Hank processed the crime scene and patrol officers questioned neighbors.

He sat across from her, which gave him a straight-on view of her face. She'd regained very little color, and before she folded her hands on the table in front of her, he noted they were still trembling.

More than anything, he wanted to circle the table, pull her to her feet, and enfold her in his arms. To assure her they had the situation under control and it was only a matter of time until they found bingo man and brought him to justice.

But he doubted her brothers would appreciate any further displays of affection. Nor was there any guarantee they'd find her stalker soon—or ever.

The truth was, the guy represented a serious threat for the foreseeable future.

That's why they were having this powwow.

Cole took a long drink of the soda he'd retrieved from Alison's refrigerator, then set it on the table, his expression grave. "We need to talk about some defensive measures."

"I have an excellent security system. You picked it out." A tremor ran through Alison's voice, her usual independent manner subdued.

"It wouldn't have helped you tonight. What were you thinking, anyway, going outside in the dark? That guy could have
been waiting for you instead of Bert!"

What minimal color had crept back into her cheeks seeped
out at Cole's heated censure. "I checked before I went out. The
whole patio was lit up, and I didn't go far from the door. I was
going to phone you or Jake if Bert didn't come when I called
from out there." Her eyes filled with tears again.

Mitch was about to step in, but Jake beat him to it—after
casting a reproving glance at his younger brother.

"I'm sure you were careful." His tone was calm. Measured.
"What Cole is trying to communicate with his inimitable tact
and diplomacy is that despite your caution tonight, this guy
could have gotten to you if he'd wanted to. All he would have
had to do was hide around the side of the house, block the
door as you started back toward it, and drag you inside."

She moistened her lips. "Okay. You're right. I shouldn't
have gone out. But up to this point, all we had were some dead
roses. I wasn't convinced he'd ever come back."

"Well, he did. And now we need to make some plans." Cole
shoved his soda aside and leaned closer to her, forearms on the
table. "Until this thing is resolved, you need to stay with either
me or Jake. We don't want you here at night alone, despite
the security system."

"Leave my house?" She frowned and stared at her clasped
hands. Mitch watched her knuckles whiten. "But this is my
home. Besides, it's too much of an imposition. You guys have
your own lives."

"You're part of our lives." Jake touched her clenched hands.
"And we want to keep it that way."

She looked from Jake to Cole. Then to Mitch. Although
this was a family matter and Mitch had intended to keep a
low profile, the uncertainty in her eyes convinced him to join
the discussion.

"What Jake and Cole are suggesting makes sense. I think
we'd all breathe easier knowing you were safe at night."

After a few beats of silence, she gave a brief nod. "Okay."

Her brothers looked at him, wary—or impressed—by his influence. Mitch wasn't sure which.

Cole opened his mouth, but Jake spoke first. "Wise decision. Now let's talk about your daily routine."

"I don't have one. Every day is different."

"That's a plus." Cole jumped back in.

"Yeah, but I don't like some of the areas you go to for home visits." Parallel grooves dented Jake's brow. "Cole, could you pass on Alison's schedule to the patrol division and have them ask the officers to do a few extra runs in the areas where she'll be working?"

"No problem."

Jake turned his attention back to Alison. "Your building has a security guard, right? And swipe cards for access?"

"Yes."

"Good. Go straight to and from work. No stops. In terms of any other errands you have to run, tap one of us for escort duty."

"Me included," Mitch chimed in.

"Are you with us on this?" Cole cocked an eyebrow at her, as if daring her to argue.

She didn't. Telling Mitch her terror ran deep.

"Yes. I just hope you catch this guy fast."

"We do too." Jake stood. "Why don't you pack whatever you need while we see what's going on outside?"

"Okay."

She rose, holding on to the edge of the table for support. Giving her injured leg a chance to adjust to the new position. Mitch was beginning to recognize the subtle aftereffects of her accident.

As her brothers started toward the door, she called after them. "Wait. What about B-Bert?"

Mitch glanced at the two men, then rounded the table to stand beside her. Raw grief and pain had dulled the vivid blue of her eyes, and he touched her cheek, swallowing past the lump in his throat. "When I was ten, our border terrier was killed by a car. Her name was Patsy, and she'd been part of our family my whole life. I was devastated. My dad had a pair of small wooden chests, and we buried her in the garden in one of them. If you'd like to use the other one, I know he'd be glad to let me have it. I could take Bert home with me tonight, then come back in the morning before work and bury him in the backyard."

Her eyes filled with tears. In their depths, he saw gratitude and tenderness . . . and a deeper emotion that caused his heart to skip a beat—then accelerate.

"Thank you. I'd like that."

He nodded. "I'll be here at seven. Wait in your car if you get here first."

Turning toward the door, he found her brothers still watching him. This time he had no trouble reading the emotions in their eyes—respect in Jake's, approval in Cole's.

"Get your stuff together, Twig." Jake broke the poignant mood by leaning around him to direct his comment to his sister.

"Okay."

Mitch heard her exit the room behind him as he joined her brothers at the door.

"Nice job, Galahad." Cole smirked at him, stepping aside with a sweep of his arm to let him pass.

Jake shook his head. "Ignore him."

"Who? Is there someone else here?" Mitch walked right past Cole.

One side of Jake's mouth hitched up. "I think my brother has finally met his match."

Mitch's own mouth twitched. "More than. Now let's see what Hank and the patrol officers have discovered. One solid clue may be all we need to wrap this thing up."

13

"I'm glad you finally got with the program, man."

As Chuck pulled out his rig and Bev prepared to light up, Daryl rolled his line of meth in a dollar bill. He was having some second thoughts about snorting, but admitting that to Chuck wasn't an option. Besides, this was a onetime deal. A quick escape to brighten up his life for a few hours. Nothing more.

"I figure I ought to celebrate after my successful day."

"Yeah, well, you didn't get my locket." Bev's expression was glum as she focused on her task.

"I told you, they must have changed the locks."

"Stan would have had a key."

"And you think he'd give it to some stranger who happened to waltz in and ask for it?" He shot her a disgusted look as he finished rolling the line. A buzz of anticipation was already building inside him, and his fingers began to tremble.

"Forget the locket, Bev." Chuck drew the meth water into the syringe.

"It's the only thing I have of my mom's."

"Like she was so good to you." His mouth curled into a sneer.

"Hey, don't bad-mouth my mom! She did her best. Can she help it if she married a drunk who beat her? What did you expect her to do, stick around and maybe get killed?"

"So she left you and your sister to get killed."

"My dad never hit us."

"Whatever."

Ending the discussion, Chuck moved to the living room and sat on the lumpy couch.

Daryl followed him, lowering his voice. "I still can't believe how smooth your idea worked. The greedy little mutt was so busy gobbling down the hamburger he never even saw the rock coming."

"I told you it would be easy." He pulled off his shoe and sock. "Too bad you couldn't have hung around and watched her reaction."

"I know. But I did hear her scream as I was driving away."

His host looked up. "Yeah? That would have been cool. It's always nice when people get what they deserve."

"Who got what they deserved?" Bev entered the living room, scanned the littered space, and tugged her purse from beneath a pile of clothes.

"The broad who ruined Daryl's life." Chuck lined up the syringe.

"What'd you do to her?"

At Bev's question, Daryl turned away from the needle and positioned the rolled-up dollar bill. He took his time, savoring the thrill of anticipation. "That's not important. What matters is what I'm gonna do next. You still have some other ideas, Chuck?"

The man grinned and leaned back against the couch. "Oh yeah. I got lots of ideas. We can talk about them all night, if you want."

That sounded better than sleeping on the roach-infested futon. Daryl snorted the meth and prepared for the rush.

"A slumber party, huh?" He was feeling it already.

Daryl chortled. "Slumber party. I like that. Why don't you join us, Bev? We're gonna have some fun—and make some plans."

168

"In other words, we don't have a lot."

Hank stowed the last of his equipment before responding to Cole's comment.

"Not much. I didn't pick up any prints on the plastic tarp, the rock, or the bingo cards. Nothing on the roses either." He picked up his case. "I followed the trail through the woods, but I didn't see much of anything. If you want to keep the area restricted, I'll check it over again tomorrow in the daylight. There might be a footprint or two, with all the rain we've had. Then again, there are a lot of leaves on the ground."

"It can't hurt to take one more look. Thanks, Hank." Cole let out a frustrated breath. The lines between his eyebrows were growing deeper by the hour, Mitch noted.

He knew his were doing the same, now that Hank had given them no leads to follow up on.

"No problem. Sorry about your sister's dog." He gave the pup another look. "If the media jumps on this, they'll have a field day. A lot of people get more excited about cruelty to animals than they do about violence directed at people."

"I hear you. Have any reporters shown up?"

"No. I think they're all covering that bomb situation on the North Side."

"That works in our favor. I'd rather not give this a lot of media play."

"Like you'll have any choice if they pounce on it." Hank hefted his case and trudged toward his van.

"Yeah. I know." Cole sighed and called after him. "Thanks for coming out."

Lifting his hand in acknowledgment, Hank kept walking.

"Okay." Cole raked his fingers through his hair. "As far as I can see, we're . . ." He stopped and pulled his phone off his belt. "Taylor."

Mitch exchanged a look with Jake as they waited for Cole to complete the call. Based on what Mitch was picking up from the brief, one-sided conversation, one of the patrol officers canvassing the area had come up with some information.

"Thanks, Wes. That's more than we had a few minutes ago." After pushing the off button, he slipped the phone back on his belt.

"This sounds promising." Mitch tried not to get his hopes up, but sometimes tips from citizens were the key to solving cases.

If they were lucky, this might be one of those times.

"Maybe. A Neighborhood Watch coordinator lives on the street behind us, and she saw an unfamiliar, dark-colored car parked in front of an empty lot earlier tonight. Last night, she saw a dark-colored truck there. They caught her attention because no one ever parks in that spot.

"About the time we estimate Bert was killed, she saw a person with a lanky build walk down the street from this direction toward the car. The bad news is he or she had a baseball cap pulled low and it was dark, so she couldn't offer much of a description. As the person drove away, though, she managed to get three numbers off the license when a streetlight illuminated it. She said if either vehicle had come again, she was going to notify the police. The officer who took the statement checked for tire tracks. No luck."

The back door cracked open behind them, and Mitch turned to find Alison silhouetted in the sliver of light.

"I'm ready to leave whenever you guys are."

Her voice was still too unsteady for his liking, and she was holding on to the door frame as if she needed it for support. Mitch's stomach clenched, and he had to fight down the urge to pull her into another consoling hug.

"Okay. We're about done here." Jake approached the door. Mitch followed, Cole on his heels.

"Did you find anything helpful?" Alison stepped aside as they entered.

"A woman on the street behind you saw a suspicious vehicle. A midsize dark-colored car. A lanky figure wearing a baseball cap got in it, but she couldn't ID age or gender."

As they all regrouped in Alison's kitchen, she frowned. "That's odd."

Mitch narrowed his eyes. "What do you mean?"

"When I stopped by Ellen Callahan's apartment today to drop off some information, I literally ran into a lanky guy in a baseball cap who was driving a car that fits that description. He was—"

"Who's Ellen Callahan?" Jake interrupted.

She gave her brothers a quick recap of the case and the players. "Anyway, this guy was leaving as I was going in. The strange thing was, I had a feeling I'd seen him somewhere before, even though I didn't get a clear view of him. He seemed startled by me too. But I'm sure it was just a weird coincidence."

Mitch exchanged a look with her brothers and saw his own thoughts reflected in their faces.

There were very few coincidences in their business.

"Are you sure you can't place him?" Cole pressed.

"Yes. It was just a fleeting impression. Maybe his body build reminded me of someone. Who knows? But I'll think about it. If I make a connection, I'll let you know."

"Did anyone else see him?" Mitch kept his tone conversational. No sense building false hopes—or raising unfounded alarms.

"The superintendent came out to answer my ring, but the guy was already driving away. He did seem interested in the car, though." Her expression grew speculative. "You know, that car fits the description of Bev Parisi's vehicle. I didn't think about that until now, since a guy was driving it."

"We might want to have a little talk with the superintendent." Mitch directed the comment to Cole.

"Not a bad idea. Do you have the name and address handy, Alison?"

"Yes." She lifted her briefcase to the table and began riffling through it.

"I've got a seven o'clock meeting in the morning. Why don't I meet you there at eight?" Cole directed the question to Mitch.

"Let's make it eight thirty." He tipped his head toward the backyard and made a digging motion.

"Oh. Yeah. Okay."

Alison jotted down a name and address, handed it to Cole, and repeated the process for Mitch. "Don't expect much. This guy's a real sleazeball, just like Ellen said."

Catching her slight shudder, Mitch's eyes narrowed as he tucked the piece of paper in his pocket. "He hit on you, didn't he?"

She stared at him in surprise, her lips parting slightly. Then she shot a quick glance at her brothers, whose attention was now focused on her.

"Did he, Twig?" This from Jake. In a low, ominous tone.

"That's his modus operandi." She wrinkled her nose in distaste and lifted one shoulder in dismissal. "He's exactly the way Ellen described him. But trust me, I can handle guys like him."

"Or we could handle him for you," Cole said, his expression stormy.

"I'd rather you focus on my stalker. He's a lot scarier. I do love you guys for caring, though." She rose on tiptoe and gave Cole a hug. "So who's putting me up tonight?"

"I won the toss." Jake bent down to pick up her overnight bag and briefcase. "Keep me in the loop." He included Mitch in that directive.

"If you all want to go out, I'll arm the system and meet you in front."

Jake and Cole complied. Mitch hung back, closing the door firmly behind them. Then he moved to Alison.

Resting his hands on her shoulders, he examined her face. She had a little more color now, and some of the shock had faded from her eyes. But it had been replaced by deep sadness. And grief.

"Could you use another hug?" The question came out husky, but he didn't care.

Her eyes filled, and without a word she took shelter in his arms.

When she spoke at last, her words came out broken. "I don't know what I-I'll do without him."

172

He swallowed past the tightness in his throat. "I felt like that when Patsy died. It's hard to lose a companion you love. Human or animal."

Silence fell. She stayed in his arms for another minute, letting him stroke her hair. At last she eased back slightly. "My brothers are waiting."

"I know."

Had she attempted to step out of his arms, he would have let her go. But she didn't. She just looked at him, her eyes still shimmering with tears. "I appreciate all you did tonight. Having you here helped a lot."

He brushed a stray strand of hair off her forehead, letting his fingertips graze her soft skin. "I'm glad you called me."

"You were the first one I thought of."

Her words warmed him, and he tugged her close for one last hug. "That means a lot to me."

A discreet tap sounded on the front door, and he released her reluctantly. "Jake's waiting."

She stepped back and shoved her hands in the pockets of her khaki shorts. "How do you know it's Jake?"

"Because Cole would have banged on the door and hollered for you to come out."

The faintest smile kissed the corners of her mouth. "You pegged the two of them pretty fast."

"It pays to be a detective."

"Or an insightful judge of character."

He tried not to let her compliment inflate his ego. "Or lucky."

"No." She walked over to the security system control panel, waited for the green light, then punched in her code. "Luck has nothing to do with it." Rejoining him by the table, she picked up her purse, took his hand, and gave him a look that sent a bolt of warmth straight to his heart.

And as they walked toward the front door, her fingers clasped in his, Mitch redoubled his vow to find the guy who was wreaking havoc on her life. The sooner the better.

Because he knew she wouldn't rest easy until the guy was caught.

And neither would he.

"Here it is." Chuck pulled a glossy brochure out of the mound of junk mail piled in the corner of the living room. "I knew I remembered seeing this." He examined the cover, then tossed it onto the couch where Bev was sprawled. It hit her leg and fell to the floor. She was too zoned out to notice. "Weird thing to advertise through the mail, if you ask me."

Daryl picked up the direct mail piece. It was weird, all right. Spooky, even. But it would work very well for phase three of Operation Alison, as he and Chuck had named it during the early hours of the morning. He'd already moved on to formulating plans for the final phase, but Chuck was right. They'd started this bingo thing. They needed to send one more bingo card first, and this was a great way to do it.

"I think I'm gonna make a trip to the woods, check things out before the sun comes up. I'm starting a new cook tomorrow." Chuck jiggled the change in his pocket and grinned. "You wanna come? It'd be like old times."

"No. I have things to do." He waved the brochure.

"Oh yeah. Right."

"Hey, Bev, can I borrow your car to go mail this when I'm done?"

No response. She just kept humming some tuneless song and gyrating like she was on a dance floor, even though she was prone.

"Take it. She won't be using it for a while." Chuck spared her another quick, disgusted look. "Mixing booze and meth. Not smart. Anyway, find a box far away from here. Don't forget to wear gloves. And don't lick the stamp."

"Yeah. I got it covered."

"We'll work on the finale when I get back." Still jiggling the coins in his pocket, Chuck pushed through the back door, letting it slam behind him.

Once Chuck disappeared, Daryl retrieved another pair of latex gloves from the box he'd left next to the futon where he slept, slipped them on, and began paging through the catalogue. It didn't take him long to find the perfect image.

A quick search through the drawers in the kitchen didn't produce any scissors, so he ripped the page out. He did find a ballpoint pen, and it took him less than a minute to write his cryptic message on the page. Then he selected another bingo card from the pack on the counter, inked the skull-and-crossbones stamp, and marked off three numbers straight across. As an afterthought, he also marked off the free spot in the center, leaving one open square. He wanted the message to be crystal clear.

The next time—the final time—was bingo.

Satisfied with the results, he dug through Chuck's drawers until he found a crumpled kraft-colored envelope. Stuffing the page from the catalogue and the bingo card inside, he moistened the flap with water from the faucet. He hadn't needed Chuck to tell him not to lick it. He wasn't that dumb. In fact, he was a lot smarter than most people gave him credit for. Only an idiot would leave a trail the cops could follow. He'd rather live in this dump than end up behind bars again.

And really, the trailer wasn't bad once you got used to it. Maybe he'd hang out here for a while, after all. Do a little smurfing for Chuck until he figured out the master plan for his life. He hadn't had any trouble picking up the stuff yesterday. No reason he'd have trouble for a few weeks, as long as he kept hitting different stores.

Yeah, he might think about that. It wasn't like he had anyone waiting to welcome him with open arms. Nicole had been his best hope. But thanks to Alison Taylor, that hope had died.

Well, Miss Do-Gooder was paying a price for that. A big price.

As her scream reechoed in his mind, he smiled. That had been sweet.

But he had bigger plans than that for her. Plans he hadn't

even told Chuck about. Phase four had begun jelling in his mind last night. He was still working out the details, but when it all came together, she'd pay a far worse price than finding her beloved dog dead and mutilated.

Mitch was already here.

As Alison turned down her street at 6:55 on Friday morning, she spotted his car parked in front of her house. The Accord, not his Taurus. He'd come straight from home instead of stopping at the precinct station to pick up his duty vehicle.

As she pulled into her driveway, she was glad she'd declined Jake's offer to come with her. The moral support had touched her, but she knew he had a busy schedule today. And based on snippets of conversation she'd overheard during the many calls he'd fielded this morning alone, it sounded like the U.S. Marshals Special Operations Group was about to be summoned for duty. He had enough on his plate without attending a dog's funeral.

Besides, in all honesty, she preferred to hold Mitch's hand.

By the time she got out of her car, Mitch was removing a small wooden chest from his trunk. She'd spent most of the night crying in Jake's bed while he slept on the couch, and she thought she'd used up all her tears. Yet as he carried the chest toward her, she felt her throat closing again, and her vision blurred.

When Mitch stopped in front of her, she rested her hand on the burnished walnut wood. It was a beautiful piece, and all at once she had qualms about accepting the generous gesture.

"Mitch . . . this is lovely. Are you sure your dad is okay with me using it for Bert?"

"More than okay. A woodworking friend of his gave him the pair decades ago and kiddingly told my dad he should put his treasures inside and bury them in the backyard. They stayed in our basement for years, gathering dust. But when Patsy died, Dad pulled out one of them. I remember exactly what he said. 'A faithful, loving dog is one of life's greatest treasures. This was meant for Patsy.' I knew, once he heard about Bert, he'd want you to have the other one."

A tear spilled out of Alison's eye, and she bit her trembling lower lip. "Please thank him for me."

"I will. Are you ready?"

No. She'd never be ready to say good-bye to Bert. But Mitch needed to get to work, and so did she.

Without responding, she reached in her car and pressed the automatic garage door opener. "I'll get the shovel."

He waited for her, holding the chest in his arms. Then he followed her around the garage, across the spring grass fresh with dew, to a garden just beyond the patio.

She pointed to a bare spot in the center of the stone-rimmed patch. "I'm planning to put a rosebush there. I'd like Bert to be underneath it."

With a nod, Mitch set the chest on the green carpet of grass. He'd left his jacket in the car, and now he rolled up his sleeves. She noted he'd worn work boots too, rather than his usual dress shoes.

Moving into the center of the garden, he dug in silence while she watched, the rising sun casting a golden glow over the world. She caught the scent of peonies in the air. A bird trilled overhead. The soft breeze was warm on her face. It was a beautiful day.

Bert would have loved it.

Dropping down to one knee, she rested her hand on top of the box as she grappled with the malicious cruelty that had robbed her of her loyal little companion. She hadn't been able to make any sense of it last night. Nor had the light of day brought clarity.

Why, God?

She'd asked that question during the long, dark night too. Prayed for an answer. But none had come.

As she stroked the lid of the box, she recalled telling Mitch once that in times like this, when you didn't understand, you had to trust in the Lord. And she was trying. But it was very, very hard. Even for her, despite her strong faith.

How much harder it would be for someone like Mitch, whose faith was shaky at best, to take that leap.

As that thought flashed through her mind, he came down on one knee beside her, his hand on her shoulder as he searched her face.

"Would you like to see him first?"

She stared at him in shock, picturing Bert as he'd been last night, bloody, mangled, and . . .

"Alison . . . it's okay. He looks like you remember."

She squinted at him, not comprehending. "What do you mean?"

He lifted one shoulder. "I learned rudimentary first aid in my SEAL days. I know how to take care of wounds. And I cleaned him up."

Even as she processed his generous, altruistic act, fear held her back. Yes, she wanted to see Bert. But how could Mitch possibly have erased all evidence of last night's trauma?

"Trust me on this."

She looked into his caring eyes, eyes filled with compassion and tenderness, and knew she could, indeed, trust him. With this. Or with anything.

"All right."

He held her gaze for another moment, his own reassuring. Fortifying. Then he opened the lid on the box.

Summoning up her courage, Alison looked down—and saw the little fluff ball who'd stolen her heart at the pound with his winsome face and the endearing cock of his head, as if he was listening to everything she said. The box was lined with brown velvet, and he was on his stomach. His paws were in front of him, his head resting on top and tipped toward her, just as it had often been in real life. His fur was fluffy and clean and had obviously been brushed.

Reaching out, Alison touched the familiar soft fur, closed her eyes, and tried to process the incredible gift Mitch had given her: a final peaceful image to hold in her heart, to replace the brutal one from last night.

Alison had received many treasured gifts in her life, but none compared to this in terms of selfless generosity. She'd seen Bert last night. She knew the task Mitch had set for himself couldn't have been easy or pleasant to accomplish. Yet he'd done it for her.

Her heart melted.

Blinking back her tears, she looked up to find him watching her. "Thank you doesn't even begin to capture my gratitude."

He touched her cheek. "I'm just sorry it came to this."

She covered his hand with hers. "Me too."

Once more she looked at Bert. "Good-bye, big guy." Her quiet farewell came out choked. "Thanks for being my friend."

Slowly she closed the lid and turned the catch.

Mitch rose first and held out a hand to her. She was glad for the strength of his touch, because it wasn't only her injured leg that was shaky.

He waited until she had her footing, then bent and picked up the chest. After settling it in the bottom of the hole, he began replacing the ground. It took less than three minutes.

Rolling down the sleeves of his shirt, he rejoined her. "I'll plant that rosebush for you too, whenever you're ready."

"Thank you." With one final look at the small mound of dirt, she turned away and started toward the front of the house. "We both need to get going."

He replaced her shovel in the garage and joined her beside her car. "Will you be okay at work today?"

"Yes. There's always a lot going on, and the distraction will help." A smudge of dirt on his shirtsleeve caught her eye, and she brushed it off. "Sorry about that."

"I've been dirtier."

She didn't doubt that. Navy SEALS saw tough action. As did NYPD detectives. Getting dirty was part of the job. But the messy job he'd tackled with Bert had been by choice. For her.

It blew her away.

"You know, if I was living in my house, I'd invite you to dinner Saturday." She cast a regretful look at her small bungalow. "It's the only concrete way I can think of to say thank you for all you did last night . . . and this morning."

"It seems to me I'm the one who owes *you* a dinner. We never did reschedule after the homicide nixed our date last Friday. In fact, I'd intended to call you yesterday and see if tomorrow would work. Then everything went south."

Without hesitation, she reached for his hand. "If the invitation is still open, I accept."

His eyes darkened as his lean, strong fingers enfolded hers, and a slow smile tugged at the corners of his lips. "You're on. I'll call you later to work out the details."

She managed a small smile in return. "I'll look forward to it."

As she began to turn away, he tightened his grip. Surprised, she looked up at him—just in time to feel his warm lips cover hers in a brief, tender, toe-tingling kiss.

"I'll wait to watch you drive away."

His breath was warm on her cheek, and she could manage no more than a single word. "Okay."

He opened her door, and she slid in. After using the remote to close the garage door, she started the car and backed out—feeling as if *she* was on remote. The tingle of his kiss continued to linger on her lips, muddling her mind.

Once on the street, she checked on him in her rearview mirror. He was still standing in her driveway, hands in pockets. When she waved, he responded in kind.

And as she accelerated, leaving behind the new man in her life, it occurred to her that despite the sorrow of this day, there was joy too. For while she'd lost one dear friend, she'd gained another.

A man who was strong and smart and skilled but whose well of kindness and compassion ran deep.

A man perhaps destined to be far more than a friend.

God did, indeed, work in mysterious ways.

14

"Man. Alison had that guy pegged." Cole leaned against the hood of Mitch's Taurus and turned his back on the seedy apartment building, disgust tugging down the corners of his lips. "Sleazeball is an understatement."

"Yeah." The very thought of Stan Orton hitting on Alison was enough to nudge Mitch's blood pressure into the danger zone. And he now had even more sympathy for Ellen Callahan. Having spent the past fifteen minutes watching Orton slime his way through their questions, he had no doubt the man was capable of the sort of retribution Ellen claimed had been directed against her after she'd rebuffed his advances.

"What's your take on his comments about the car?"

Right. They were here about the car. Mitch refocused. "I think he suspects it was Bev Parisi's, even though he managed to avoid giving us a direct answer."

"I agree. But I also think he was telling the truth about not recognizing the driver."

"I do too."

"So where does this leave us?"

Mitch checked out the parking lot again. "I say we beef up the patrols around here. If that was Bev's car, she must have sent someone to clean out her apartment. Since the locks were changed by the owner, he couldn't get in. If Orton's not-so-subtle insinuation that he and Bev have—or had—some kind of relationship beyond superintendent/tenant is true, she may come back herself and try to convince him to open the door."

"I agree." Cole pulled out his sunglasses and slid them over his nose as the early morning sun topped the nearby buildings. "What do you think about Alison's impression that she'd seen the guy before?"

"I'm not discounting it, but I don't see how it helps us much unless she remembers more."

"Me neither. I have a feeling it's relevant, though, considering the car she saw here sounds very similar to the one spotted by the Neighborhood Watch coordinator. The three numbers don't match Bev Parisi's car, but it's not hard to change out plates."

"True. And here's another interesting thing. That car also sounds like the one the neighbor saw with a blonde behind the wheel at Lon Samuels's place."

Cole squinted at him. "When did you make that connection?"

"Last night. About two in the morning." *While I was lying there wide awake, thinking about your sister.* "Bev's blonde, according to the police report. I assume she's into drugs because of her fast exit here when the police showed up after Orton's call to the child abuse hotline—not to mention the evidence of meth use that was found outside Ellen Callahan's back door and in Bev's apartment. Lon Samuels died of complications from meth use. A blonde in a midsized dark car was seen fleeing his apartment shortly before the 911 call came in."

"There are a lot of blondes—and a lot of dark-colored midsized cars." Skepticism narrowed Cole's eyes.

"My gut tells me there's a connection."

"And you trust your gut?"

Mitch pinned Cole with an intent look. "Always. It's saved my life more than once."

After appraising him for a moment, Cole lifted one shoulder. "Okay. So what do you suggest we do next?"

"There's already a BOLO alert on Bev's car, but I'm guessing she's changed plates. I think the best plan is to beef up the patrols here. I have a feeling if we can get our hands on Bev, she could be a gold mine of information. If the car Alison saw here is the same car spotted by the Neighborhood Watch coordinator and the witness in the Samuels death situation, and if the guy she thought she recognized was the same guy spotted in her neighborhood last night, Bev could lead us right to Alison's stalker."

"That's a lot of ifs."

"You have anything better?"

"I wish I did." Cole let out a long breath. "Okay. Let's talk to patrol and hope Ms. Parisi wants her stuff badly enough to send our guy back—or come get it herself."

"I've been thinking about your idea." Chuck was rummaging around for his rig again in the trailer kitchen. "Man, that is really far out."

Yeah, it was. Maybe too far out. Daryl slumped against the cushion of the lumpy sofa and took a swig from the can of cheap beer. The plan he'd concocted for Alison Taylor after snorting the line of meth last night sounded a lot more intimidating now than it had a few hours ago, when he'd first shared it with Chuck. When he'd still been high and feeling invincible.

Now, fifteen hours later, he was coming down. Fast. And not liking it. Nor the plan, which was beginning to get fuzzy around the edges. Odd, since it had been crystal clear last night. The meth had made it seem easy. Perfect.

"You want some more? I'm starting another cook tomorrow night. Might as well use up what's left." Chuck shook the small jar of white powder at him.

Daryl was tempted. He wasn't looking forward to bottoming out. That had been the worst part of snorting. But he'd only planned to indulge once. Using more meth to stave off withdrawal led to addiction, and he didn't want to end up like Chuck.

"No. I'm gonna work on my plan some more."

"Yeah, let's talk about that." Chuck stopped assembling his rig and began prowling around the living room. Daryl was beginning to think the man never slept. But that wasn't unusual for tweakers. He'd seen people who used heavily—and often—go almost two weeks with no sleep. "Where'd you come up with the idea, anyway?"

"From those cages on the side of the trailer. Where'd you get them?"

"Had a dog for a while. Three dogs, actually. Including a pit bull. I thought they'd be a cheap alarm system, let me know if the cops were nosing around. They ended up being more trouble than they were worth."

"So what'd you do with them?" Daryl took a long swallow of beer.

"Got bored one night. Decided to practice my gutting skills in case I ever got a hankering to go hunting again. That's what gave me the idea for your friend's dog."

Daryl choked on his beer.

His reaction was met with a leer from Chuck. "Don't worry, I put them out of their misery before I started carving them up. Buried them out back. So how you gonna get Miss Do-Gooder to go along with your plan? She sure ain't gonna do it willingly."

It took Daryl a few seconds to refocus. "I have an idea about that, but I'll need Bev to help me."

"Get her high enough, she'll do anything. Just don't tell her the gory details. She's got a soft spot that surfaces every now and then. That's why I never told her about the dogs. She'd throw a hissy fit if she knew what I did. When do you plan to do this, anyway?"

"Monday or Tuesday. I'll need your truck, though."

"Wait till Tuesday, then. I'll be back from the cook sometime Monday night." He poked around at the TV remote on the kitchen table, which he was still in the process of dismantling. "What're you gonna do with her once you have her?"

184

"I haven't thought this through to the end yet. I'm not even sure I'll do it, anyway."

"Why not? She wronged you. Seems like she oughta pay."

"Yeah, but I gotta plan this just right. Otherwise, I'll end up back in Potosi." The very thought sent a chill snaking through him.

"As long as you blindfold her, she won't be able to identify you. After you get tired of the game, you can dump her on some back road. It's foolproof."

Daryl wasn't as certain of that as Chuck was. And even though the idea of playing out the bingo game to the end had appealed to him last night, he was beginning to think the risk wasn't worth the satisfaction it would give him. It might be better to end the game with the envelope he'd mailed earlier today. That would keep her looking over her shoulder for a very long time. She'd probably be so scared she'd have to sleep with the light on for years.

Maybe that would be enough to satisfy his need for revenge.

"So what are you gonna do?"

At Chuck's question, Daryl rose to toss his beer can in the overflowing waste can. "I think I'll sleep on it."

"Okay." His host returned to the task he'd abandoned a few minutes earlier. Smiling, he tucked the bottle of white powder in the drawer next to the sink. "If you need some inspiration—or courage—you know where to look. Tell Bev it's here too. There'll be plenty more in a couple of days. No rationing with this stuff, like they had to do with that flu shot a few years ago."

"Where is Bev, anyway?" He hadn't seen her since he'd come back from mailing the envelope to Alison and doing some scouting.

"She took the truck as soon as I got back and went out to buy olives and anchovies."

Daryl shot him a puzzled look. "Why?"

He gave an indifferent shrug. "When she's crashing, she gets these cravings. Eats the weirdest stuff. One time she wanted corn curls dipped in chocolate sauce. Disgusting, isn't it? And not too healthy either. My solution to crashing is simple. Don't do it!" He cackled, pulled out the syringe, and went to work.

Daryl suppressed a shudder and turned away. Needles and blood were disgusting. That's why neither were in his plans for Alison. There were other ways to hurt someone. Lots of other ways.

And as he headed down the hall to his roach-infested room, he intended to consider every one of them.

After the previous traumatic thirty-six hours, Alison had planned to sleep in on Saturday. Except Jake's phone kept ringing. She ignored the first call. And the second. But when it rang a third time, she hauled herself out of bed and yawned her way to the kitchen.

Shoving her sleep-tangled hair back from her face, she picked up the remote from its cradle. "Hello."

"Where have you been?"

At Cole's irritated question, her hackles rose. "In bed. It's Saturday, remember? What time is it, anyway?" She peered at the clock on the far side of the room, but the numbers were too small to make out and she'd left her watch on the nightstand.

"Nine thirty."

"Oh." Okay, that was on the late side. "So sue me. I was tired. If you're looking for Jake, I'll try to find him."

"He's not there. The SOG was tapped for a most-wanted arrest. He called me en route to the airport about seven."

Trying to tamp down her worry, she slid onto a stool at the counter that separated the galley kitchen from the small dining area. Since the U.S. Marshals select tactical Special Operations Group only handled the most hazardous missions, Jake was directly in the line of fire every time he was called up. It wasn't quite as dangerous as when he'd been in Iraq—but close.

"I figured something was up yesterday. His ear was glued to the phone while he inhaled a bowl of cereal at breakfast. I wonder if he's going to stay in the group once he and Liz are married." She hoped not—and she had a feeling Liz preferred that he give up the ancillary duty too.

"That's their decision. Anyway, he said you were out cold and he'd leave you a note to call me. When I didn't hear from you, I started to worry."

Her gaze fell on said note, lying on the counter, six inches from her elbow.

"Yeah, I see it."

"Okay, I'll be by in half an hour. I already changed the sheets on my bed in your honor."

"Look, Cole, we can't do this forever. Eventually I have to go back to my house."

"We've only been doing this for two days. That's not forever. And bingo man is still out there. Be ready when I show up."

The line went dead.

As she stared at the phone, Alison was annoyed on one hand, touched on the other. She knew she was lucky to have two brothers who cared so much for her, but Cole could use a few lessons in diplomacy. He was much too bossy. Which could very well be the reason he'd never married, she decided, sliding off the stool. It would be fun to watch someday if he met his match, though. That could be a fireworks show worthy of a front-row seat.

Amused by that thought, she traipsed back to the bedroom. Before she left, she intended to shower, change Jake's sheets, and throw in a load of laundry. If that took more than the thirty minutes her brother had allotted her, tough.

Cole Taylor might be a daunting figure on the job, but he didn't intimidate her one little bit. She could remember him as a skinny ten-year-old who'd decided his Superman cape gave him the power to fly from the garage roof to the deck—ten feet away. Eight stitches later, he'd learned otherwise.

Talk about a dumb stunt.

And if he got huffy with her today, she'd be sure to remind him of that.

"Do you have a hot date or something?" Alison checked on Cole over her shoulder as she pushed the grocery cart through Schnucks. He was trailing behind her, his expression peeved.

"No, I don't have a hot date. But wandering through the aisles of a grocery store isn't my idea of a great Saturday morning. Tell me why we're here again?"

"We've been over this already. When I asked what you had in your refrigerator, all you could come up with was ketchup, American cheese, pickles, and a bag of English muffins. I rest my case."

"I've got plenty of canned and frozen stuff."

She wrinkled her nose. "You, dear brother, need to improve your diet. What about salad and fresh vegetables and fruit and eggs?" She selected a bag of grapes and waved them in his direction before depositing them in the cart.

"I eat on the run most of the time. Do I look unhealthy?"

He had her there. Both of her brothers could be poster boys for a health club, despite their spotty diets. She ignored the question.

"Say . . ." His demeanor grew hopeful as he followed her toward the front of the store. "Does this mean you might cook a few meals while you're at my place?"

"I might. But not tonight. I have plans this evening."

He frowned. "I thought we agreed you'd have an escort for the next few days whenever you went out?"

"I'll have an escort." She jockeyed her cart into a checkout lane and circled around to the front to begin unloading the groceries. "Mitch is taking me to dinner."

"Yeah?" Leaning forward, he grabbed some containers of yogurt from the cart and placed them on the conveyor belt. "Where are you going?"

"I didn't ask."

"When did this come up?"

She shot him an annoyed glance. "What is this, the third degree?"

"Hi, Alison."

Grateful for the interruption, she turned to find Erik smiling at her from the end of the checkout lane.

She smiled back. "Hi, Erik. I didn't know you worked on Saturday."

"Sometimes." He began bagging the groceries. "But you usually come at night. After work."

"That's right."

He peered past her, to where Cole was emptying the last of the items from the cart, his head averted. "Is that your boyfriend?"

Alison stifled a laugh. "No. That's my brother."

"Oh. I guess you have a boyfriend, though, don't you?"

An image of Mitch came to mind, but their relationship was too new to categorize that way. "Not right now." She dug out her wallet, determined to keep a firm grip on it this time. No more chasing credit cards and photos and change on her hands and knees.

Erik set a filled bag in her cart. "I bet you will soon."

As he went back to his bagging, Cole leaned toward her and spoke close to her ear. "I'm going to cut out before Erik recognizes me. He was really stressed the night Mitch and I visited him in the group home, and I don't want to upset him again. I'll meet you in front."

Without waiting for her to respond, he melted back into the store.

Well, how about that? She watched him disappear, impressed for once by his discretion and sensitivity.

Maybe there was hope for him yet.

His plan wasn't jelling.

As Daryl slammed his hand against the kitchen counter, Bev fumbled the bottle of meth she'd just removed from the drawer.

"Watch it, dude! What's with you, anyway?"

He jammed his shaky hands into his pockets. "Nothing."

"Yeah?" She squinted at him, clearly not buying his denial. "Look, if you got a problem, I got an answer." She waved the bottle at him.

He wavered. His brain had been fuzzy since he'd started bottoming out from his high. It was possible one more line would help him finish his plan.

Or send him down a road that offered no U-turns.

The old panicked feeling of being caught in front of a train overwhelmed him yet again. What was with that, anyway? He'd hardly ever had it in the slammer, and now it was slapping him in the face every day. Sometimes several times a day.

Grabbing Bev's keys from the counter, he headed for the door. "I need to take a ride."

"You want some company?" She wandered after him. "I don't know where Chuck went, and it's kinda lonely here."

"No." He motioned to the jar in her hand. "Save me some, okay?" Just in case.

"Sure."

As he stepped out into the late afternoon sunshine, he blinked against the glare. He'd been holed up in the trailer all day, and the dirty, shaded windows hadn't even hinted at the brightness outside.

Shoving on his sunglasses, he trudged toward Bev's car, no destination in mind. All he knew was that he had to get away from this place for a while. Before he succumbed to the lure of the meth. He'd come too close a few minutes ago.

He knew why too. The plan he'd concocted for Alison Taylor when he'd been high had buoyed him up. Made him feel powerful and in charge. But as he'd begun to crash, his confidence had wavered. Doubt had begun to undermine his conviction that he could pull it off. He'd messed up everything he'd ever tried. Why should this be any different?

If he didn't try, though, she'd win.

That didn't sit well with him either.

He slid into the car. What he needed to do was get himself all riled up again. That would boost his determination.

And all at once he knew exactly how to do that.

Shifting into gear, he bumped down the rutted, gravel driveway and aimed the car toward St. Louis.

"That was a fabulous dinner. Thank you."

As Alison smiled at him across the snowy expanse of white linen, Mitch was glad he'd opted for the high-end Italian restaurant on The Hill. It was quiet, elegant—and far safer than a sidewalk café in the Central West End, charming as those were. From his seat, he had an excellent view of the entire room and the doorway to the lobby. They were steps away from a fire exit. They could be out of here in seconds, if necessary. The favorable setup allowed him to focus on his lovely companion rather than security concerns.

"Would you like some dessert?"

She groaned. "I can't eat another bite."

"Coffee?"

"I usually drink tea, but coffee does sound appealing tonight."

He signaled to the waiter, and two minutes later they both had steaming cups in front of them. When Alison added two packets of sugar and a very generous dollop of cream to hers, Mitch's lips twitched.

She caught his reaction and stopped stirring. "What?"

"Maybe you should have ordered a mocha."

"Very funny." She wrinkled her nose at him. "You sound like my brothers again."

After her trauma with Bert, he hadn't expected her to be in the best of moods tonight. But she'd surprised him. While she was more subdued than usual, she'd responded to his light banter throughout the meal. He'd even managed to elicit a few quiet laughs.

"I thought we'd gotten past the brother thing."

She smiled at him over the rim of her cup as she brought it to her lips. "We have." Setting the cup back in its saucer, she grew more serious. "I appreciate all the effort you went to tonight to give me a pleasant evening."

"It was no effort." He reached across the table and captured her fingers in his. They felt small and delicate and vulnerable—an impression that did nothing for his peace of mind, considering bingo man was still on the loose. "I hope we can have a lot more evenings like this in the future."

"I hope so too."

She met his gaze, responding to his comment with a sweet, simple honesty that touched his heart. He was quickly learning that unlike many of the women who'd sought his attention through the years, Alison Taylor didn't play games. You knew where you stood with her at every moment. He found that refreshing. And very, very appealing.

Stroking his thumb over the back of her hand, he decided to be just as candid. "You know, you're different from any woman I've ever met."

She studied him, a flicker of uncertainty shadowing her blue irises. "Is that good or bad?"

"Good. In every way."

The shadow vanished, and she looked down at their entwined hands, a smile tugging at the corners of her mouth. "I ran into Erik Campbell today at the grocery store."

"Did you?" It was an odd subject to introduce, but Mitch knew Alison had a reason for bringing it up. She wasn't given to non sequiturs. He waited while she ran her fingernail around the base of her stemmed water glass.

"He asked me if I had a boyfriend."

Now he got the connection. "What did you tell him?"

She transferred her attention to him again. "I said no."

His spirits nose-dived.

"I figured it was too soon to say yes, since we've only known each other for a couple of weeks. But can I tell you something? Even in this short time, I've realized that what I had with David would never have led to the connection I already feel with you." She moistened her lips, telling him she was nervous. Yet she didn't break eye contact. "I hope this doesn't scare you off, because I'm not suggesting we speed things up. But I'm hopeful at some point down the road, *boyfriend* might be the perfect way to describe you."

His mood took a decided uptick.

"Can I tell *you* something? That doesn't scare me off in the least. Just the opposite."

Soft color suffused her cheeks, and she lifted her cup of coffee in a salute. "Given all the rough spots we've encountered in our short acquaintance, shall we toast to happier tomorrows?"

He picked up his cup and clinked it against her. "I'll drink to that."

And as he sipped his coffee, his fingers still entwined with hers, he realized that despite the trauma that had marred their relationship so far, his life was already happier than it had been in a long, long time.

But it would be even happier once they got rid of the stalker who was tormenting Alison and giving him a chronic case of insomnia.

"Mom!"

At Kyle's frightened summons from the other side of the bathroom door, Nicole's pulse vaulted into double time. She twisted off the shower and lurched out of the tub.

"What is it, honey?" After toweling herself dry as fast as she could, she grabbed her robe off the hook on the back of the door and shoved her arms into the sleeves.

"I think that man is in the parking lot." His muffled voice quivered with alarm.

She didn't have to ask who "that man" was. Since Daryl had shown up last Tuesday, she'd found herself constantly looking over her shoulder. She'd also kept Kyle on a short leash. He had strict orders to stay with his group during aftercare at school and not to wander into remote corners of the playground during recess. They'd gone to the park yesterday, but again, she'd stuck close. And she'd asked him on several occasions, doing her best to keep her tone casual, whether he'd seen Daryl anywhere. The answer had always been no, but she could tell the question upset him.

Now this.

Pulse accelerating, she opened the door. Kyle's eyes were too big in his solemn face as he grabbed her hand.

"Come on, I'll show you. I heard a noise in front. That's why I looked out. I saw him right away."

He started back toward the living room, but she tugged him to a stop. Although she kept the blinds closed at night, the lights were on in there. If she cracked them, it would be apparent from the outside.

"Let's look from your bedroom."

Keeping a firm grip on his hand, she led him to the darkened room and shut the door behind them. Then she felt her way across the carpet. Once her toe connected with the toy chest that rested on the floor under the window, she helped him climb up. "Okay, honey, where is he?"

She cracked one of the slats in the blinds so they could peer out. Two seconds later, she felt his shoulders droop.

"He's not there anymore. I guess he left while I came to get you."

She exhaled slowly. Now what? If Kyle had seen Daryl, she'd have no compunction about calling the police. She'd warned him away twice, and he had no business hanging around her parking lot. That was stalking, and it was against the law. But if she lodged a complaint and Kyle was mistaken, she'd be bringing more trouble down on a man who'd already had plenty and who might be trying to build a new life.

"What was the man doing, Kyle?"

"Sitting in his car. Right there." He pointed to an empty parking spot a few doors down from the entrance to their building. "And he was looking up at our apartment."

"Are you sure it was the same man, honey? It's really dark out there."

"I'm pretty sure." He scrunched up his face. "Somebody had a flashlight or something down there, and it shined into his window. He kind of ducked down when that happened, but I saw his face for a minute."

Nicole knew her son had keen observation skills. He often surprised her by noticing things most kids would never spot. An unusual pattern of lighted windows in an office building. A tiny flower growing in the cracks of an old wall. A small scar on a passerby's forehead. She was certain he'd taken note of Daryl's features the day she'd talked to her former boyfriend.

Still . . . with the darkness and the quick glimpse he'd had, he could be wrong.

"Was he driving that same truck, Kyle?"

"No. It was a dark-colored car."

A different vehicle. That shot a few holes in Kyle's story. She'd been surprised Daryl had access to one vehicle, let alone two.

Torn, Nicole helped her son down from the toy chest. Then she crossed to the wall switch and flipped on the light, bathing the room in a warm glow from the bedside lamp.

"So what are you gonna do, Mom?" He looked up at her, his features taut.

"I don't know, honey. I need to think about it. And we'll both keep watching for him until I decide, okay?"

"Okay." He poked at the corner of his mattress, eyes downcast. "Could I sleep with you tonight?"

At his plaintive request, a pang echoed in her heart. She'd tried so hard to give Kyle a sense of security and safety. Now, Daryl had undermined that. Even if it hadn't been him outside tonight, his reappearance in their lives had been disruptive. She fought down a rising tide of anger, determined not to further upset her son.

"I think that would be fun." She summoned up a smile, hoping he wouldn't notice it was strained around the edges, and pulled him into a tight hug. "We haven't done that in a long time."

She could feel the tension ease in his body.

"I'll get my stuff."

As he scrambled for his pajamas, Nicole was still undecided about how to handle the situation. So she did what she'd learned to do over the past three years whenever she'd been confronted by a difficult problem.

She put it in God's hands, with a plea for guidance.

That had been close. Too close.

Lifting his arm, Daryl tipped his head and wiped the film of sweat off his upper lip with the sleeve of his T-shirt as he pulled onto I-55 south. Nicole's brat had seen him. No question about it. The way his eyes had widened had been a dead giveaway.

He should have left when he'd spotted those kids playing with that flashlight.

Well, it was too late for second thoughts. If he was lucky, Nicole would tell her son he was imagining things. If he wasn't . . . no one knew where he was staying. And they couldn't prove he'd been in the lot even if they did find him. No one else had seen him. He was safe.

The good news was his visit had done the trick. As he'd sat there looking at Nicole's apartment and envisioning himself living there instead of in Chuck's hovel, his anger had returned. Hot enough to convince him he needed to put the finishing touches on his plan and then carry it out.

Alison Taylor deserved to suffer for sticking her neck in where it didn't belong and ruining his life.

Tonight, after he got back, he'd do one more line of meth to clear up his thinking so he could nail down all the details. He wanted to be ready to move by Tuesday.

In the meantime, he'd enjoy thinking about how he'd been making her life miserable. If she hadn't gotten his love letter today, it would be waiting in her mailbox when she got home from work on Monday. While she spent a sleepless night worrying, he'd be going over his plans. Everything had to be in place before he made his move. There couldn't be any slipups.

And if he was lucky, if he did this right, for once in his life he'd prove his old man wrong and not mess up.

196

15

"Good night, Rog."

"'Night, Alison. I'll watch from the window until you get to your car."

Alison gave the uniformed, middle-aged security guard in the lobby of her building a resigned look. "My brother called you, didn't he?"

He grinned back at her. "Can't blame a guy for wanting to take care of his sister."

She sighed. "I guess not. See you tomorrow."

With a wave, Alison exited the South County strip mall office space that was shared by multiple state agencies, then set off across the parking lot. It had been a busy Monday—but not as productive as she'd hoped. Her thoughts had kept wandering to the dinner she'd shared with Mitch on Saturday . . . and the Sunday service she'd attended with him and his father yesterday.

Mitch had suggested the latter when he'd dropped her off at Cole's, after he'd asked about her plans for the next day and she'd mentioned church. Although Cole had already offered to take her and pick her up, he hadn't been in the least disappointed to hear she'd made other arrangements.

One of these days, she'd get to the bottom of his faith crisis.

But at the moment, she had too many other issues to deal with.

Once in her car, she locked the doors, pulled out her cell phone, and dialed her brother's number. He answered on the first ring.

"Hi, Alison. What's up?"

"When did you talk to Rog?"

"Who?"

"The security guard at my building."

She heard him expel a frustrated breath. "Don't make an issue of it, okay?"

"I'm not making an issue of it. I just asked a simple question."

"I called him last Friday."

"Okay. Thank you."

There was a brief hesitation, as if he was debating whether her expression of gratitude was sincere. "You're welcome."

She put her key in the ignition and smiled at his cautious inflection. "I need to stop by my house and pick up three days' worth of mail. It's probably falling out of the box."

"Could you ask a neighbor to get it?"

"Yes, but I'm sure there are a couple of bills in there that need attention. I can reach it without getting out of my car. I've done that in rainy weather. Then I'll come straight to your place."

"I guess that will work. Promise to stay in the car, though. No matter what."

"You have my word." She pulled her seat belt across her lap and clicked it into place.

"Are you planning to cook tonight?"

She smiled at his hopeful tone. "Yes. Baked chicken, mashed potatoes, broccoli au gratin. I might even whip up some choco- late chip cookies."

"Wow." His response came out hushed. Reverent. "Look, I'll be home as soon as I can, okay?"

"I had a feeling that menu might light a fire under you."

"Hey, you can't blame a guy for looking forward to a home- cooked meal. Since Mom moved to Chicago, I've been relying on takeout and nuking."

"You could learn to cook."

"Not likely. See you later."

As Alison tucked the phone back in her purse and started toward her house, her thoughts shifted to the encouraging conversation she'd had with Ellen Callahan today. The woman had seemed receptive to all the ideas Alison had suggested, and she'd already reviewed the GED information Alison had dropped off at her apartment on Thursday.

With each day that passed, Alison was more confident her assessment of the woman was accurate. Like Nicole Larson four years ago, Ellen was determined to get her children back and build a better life for herself. Now she just had to demonstrate that commitment to the judge.

Twenty minutes later, when she turned onto her street, she remembered her promise to Cole and pulled close to the mailbox. As she'd feared, it was packed. She had to twist in her seat and tug at the envelopes and circulars with both hands to dislodge them. Mostly ads and junk mail, she confirmed with a quick glance.

After dumping the first batch on the seat beside her, she pulled out the rest and tossed it on top of the pile, eyeing the mess in disgust. Sorting through it would be a welcome, mindless task for after dinner. Followed by some nice, relaxing knitting.

And if Mitch happened to call, maybe she could round out her evening with a trip to Ted Drewes.

Smiling at that thought, she closed the mailbox and headed for her brother's.

She wasn't staying at her house.

Slowly making a second run past Alison's street, Daryl watched her pull away from her mailbox. He'd followed her here from her office, which had been a breeze to track down. There were only four locations for the Children's Division of Social Services, and he'd guessed right on the second call. He'd simply asked for her, then hung up while the call was being transferred. It hadn't been hard to blend in at the strip mall parking lot while he'd waited for her to get off work either.

It was tougher to be inconspicuous here, but he doubted a moving car would attract much notice. After she exited her street, he'd follow her to wherever she was staying. He didn't think that information would be important to his plan, but you never knew when some nugget might be useful.

Once she was en route to the main road, Daryl fell in behind her, maintaining a safe distance. Feeling smart. And in control. Maybe he shouldn't have caved over the weekend and done two more lines, but they'd bolstered his courage—and confidence. Plus, they'd helped clarify his thinking.

As Alison pulled into the eastbound entrance ramp for I-44, he edged over a lane to do the same, going over his final plan in his mind. After a lot of thought, he'd decided not to blindfold her, as Chuck had suggested. Why go to all that effort if he couldn't see the fear in her eyes? That was the payoff.

That change had also given him a great idea for the abduction. A lot of women these days knew better than to get in a car with a kidnapper—even an armed one. They just stood their ground and screamed bloody murder. Took their chances. But Alison Taylor was a do-gooder. A woman who cared about others. No way would she put her own interests above those of someone else. She would do whatever it took to protect another life.

Even if it meant putting her own on the line.

His idea was pure genius.

Unfortunately, dispensing with the blindfold did create a problem. She'd be able to identify him. So if he let her go after he was through with her, she'd lead the cops straight to him—and he'd end up back in Potosi. Forever, this time.

He couldn't allow that to happen.

And that left him only one option.

Alison Taylor had to die.

He knew just how he was going to do it too. It had come

to him after he'd snorted the second line, and the sweet irony of it had appealed to him. Not only would his chosen method get rid of her, it would also allow him to triumph over—and vanquish—the old fears that had haunted him since childhood.

It was perfect.

And once this was over, once he was avenged and feeling upbeat about finally pulling something off without making a mess of it, he'd be ready to move on and start a new life. One that didn't include Chuck and his fleabag trailer.

The blink of Alison's turn signal pulled him back to reality, and he exited at Elm, keeping her in sight. In less than five minutes, she swung into the parking lot of an older, tree-shaded apartment building. She must be staying with a friend. For safety's sake.

A smirk twisted his lips.

Good luck on that, sweetie.

He watched her exit the car, her arms bulging with mail. His love letter had to be in that pile. Too bad he couldn't watch her reaction.

But he'd soon see plenty of reaction firsthand.

Starting tomorrow night.

Smiling, Daryl stepped on the gas. Operation Alison was about to hit bingo.

"Can I have a drink of water, Mom?"

Nicole paused at the door of Kyle's bedroom, her hand on the light switch. The water-delay ploy must be a universal bedtime trick among children. But at least his fears had diminished to the point he felt comfortable in his own room again.

"Sure, honey. I'll be right back."

Leaving the light on, she walked down the short hall to the kitchen. As she filled a plastic cup with tap water, the tattered slip of paper with Alison's home number caught her eye. She'd set it on the counter earlier, and she'd been debating all evening about whether to bother the Children's Service worker with her dilemma. So far, she hadn't made a decision.

Nicole fingered the slip of paper and thought back to the time four years ago when her problems had been on the verge of crushing her. They would have too, if Alison hadn't thrown her a lifeline by offering her home number and assuring her it was okay to call anytime. That had been her salvation. Just knowing she had someone in her corner had given her the strength to tackle her problems. She'd only felt desperate enough to call the number twice, and she hated to intrude now on Alison's personal time. The woman had already done far more for her than her job required.

Yet she was stymied about how to address the situation with Daryl. Or even if she should.

"Mom? Are you coming?"

She hesitated, then set the piece of paper back on the counter and returned to Kyle's room.

"You must be really thirsty."

"Yeah." He took the glass, but after a few small sips he handed it back.

She wasn't surprised.

"Feel better now?"

"Uh-huh. Thanks."

He wiggled down into the bed, and Nicole used her free hand to settle the light blanket over his shoulders. Then she bent low and kissed his cheek.

"'Night, honey."

"Good night, Mom. I love you."

Her throat constricted at his innocent, heartfelt declaration, and she had to swallow before she could respond. "Love you too."

At the door, she stopped on the threshold and looked back at the little boy who meant more to her than life itself. A little boy she'd do anything to protect. No matter the cost.

And as that affirmation echoed deep in her soul, she suddenly knew what she had to do.

After flipping off the light, she returned to the kitchen, picked up the slip of paper, and dialed the phone.

"What is all this stuff?"

Alison turned from the oven, a tray of fresh-baked chocolate chip cookies in hand. Cole was sifting through the pile of mail she'd dumped on his coffee table, sipping the strong brew he favored from a mug. Though he'd wandered out of the kitchen once the cookie-making began, he did get points for clearing the table and stacking the dishwasher.

"The contents of my mailbox." She slid the tray onto a cooling rack. "I'll go through it as soon as we have our dessert."

"You get this much mail in three days?" He continued to riffle through the stack.

"Not always. And most of it is junk."

As he straightened up, the pile began to slide toward the floor. He grabbed for it, but several pieces got past him— including a kraft-colored envelope.

"Who's that from?" She peeked at him through the pass-through that separated his tiny kitchen from the eating area and living room.

He picked it up. Flipped it over. "There's no return address. But it has a Manchester postmark."

"Must be an ad."

Moving to the lamp beside the couch, he scrutinized it under the light. "No, it's hand lettered."

Some nuance in his voice put her on alert. Wiping her hands on a dish towel, she joined him in the living room. "Let me see."

She held out her hand, but instead of giving it to her, he backed away, keeping the envelope out of reach. "Before you touch it, tell me if you recognize the lettering."

"Why?"

"Humor me, okay?"

Based on his sober expression, she guessed that humor didn't come close to describing his feelings.

Leaning closer, she examined her printed name and address.

The sender had used basic block letters. Nothing about the style was familiar.

"I've never gotten anything like that."

Without a word, Cole walked toward the eating nook.

She trailed behind. "What are you doing?"

After setting the envelope on the table, he started down the hall. "Don't touch it until I get back."

"You want to tell me what's going on?" She raised her volume as he disappeared, trying not to sound worried. But she was fairly certain she knew the reason for his sudden serious mood.

When he rejoined her, he was pulling on a pair of latex gloves. Confirming her suspicion even before he spoke.

"This may be from bingo man. On the slim chance he left fingerprints this time, I don't want to obscure them any more than I already have."

He continued toward the kitchen, where he withdrew a letter opener from a drawer. Moving to the table, he slipped it under the flap and slit the envelope.

Alison gripped the back of a chair, watching his face as he bowed the envelope and peered inside.

When his mouth flattened into a taut line, her breath hitched in her throat.

"It's from him, isn't it?"

"Yes."

"W-what is it?" She hated the catch in her voice. It made her sound wimpy and weak and scared. That wasn't how she saw herself, and she didn't want her brothers to see her that way either.

"Another bingo card. And what looks like a page from a catalogue."

"What kind of catalogue?"

His hesitation told her he didn't want her to know.

"It was sent to me, Cole." She tried her best to sound forceful. "I have a right to know what it is."

Without responding, he set the envelope on the table and returned to the kitchen. Once more he rummaged around in a drawer and extracted a pair of long-handled tweezers. Still silent, he inserted them into the envelope, pulled out a single sheet of thin paper, and laid it on the table.

Alison's heart skipped a beat. Staring back at her was a photograph of a tombstone. In the same block letters used to address the envelope, the sender had written her name across the top of the granite monument.

While she digested that, Cole removed the bingo card and laid it beside the catalogue page. All but one square in the center line had been marked off with a skull-and-crossbones stamp.

"Wow." The faint word was all she could manage.

"My reaction is a little stronger than that."

At his terse tone, she lifted her chin and looked at him. His fingers were clenched, and he was glowering at the items on the table.

"This guy is sick."

She wrapped her arms around her middle and held on. "No kidding."

"I wish you'd taken that concealed carry training, like I pushed you to do last year."

A shiver ran through her as she eyed the Sig Sauer in the holster on his belt. "I don't want to carry a gun. Besides, even if I had one, I'm not sure I could shoot someone."

"I bet you could if your life depended on it."

"You think it could come to that?"

His unrelenting gaze locked onto her. "Yes. This guy is playing a deadly game."

"Maybe I could just go away for a few days."

"What's to keep him from tracking you down?"

Her stomach bottomed out. "What's your solution, then?"

"You need a bodyguard."

"A bodyguard." The concept was surreal. "That seems extreme."

"No more extreme than what he did to Bert."

She sucked in a sharp breath. His comeback was harsh, but true. "I have you and Jake. Mitch said he'd pitch in too."

"We can't be with you 24/7. And Jake's out of town."

Alison sank into the chair in front of her, on the pretense of studying the monument and bingo card. But in truth, her legs were threatening to give out. The notion of a bodyguard was beginning to become more palatable. There was no telling how long it might take to find this guy, and she couldn't impose on her brothers and Mitch indefinitely. Besides, no matter what kind of fearless front she might manage to put up, she was more scared than she'd ever been in her life.

Apparently interpreting her silence as resistance, Cole sat beside her and touched her shoulder. She braced for a brow-beating—but he surprised her.

"I don't want to smother you. Believe it or not, despite the grief I give you about your I-can-handle-it-on-my-own attitude, I like your self-sufficiency and spunk." His voice roughened, and he cleared his throat. "So how about this for a compromise? Instead of hiring a bodyguard, I'll take you to and from work. Cancel your home visits for the next few days. Stay in the office and get caught up on paperwork and case files. This guy seems to be on a fast track. If he's going to make another move, I expect he'll do it soon. And once we catch him, I promise to toss you out of my apartment on your ear so you can go back to being Miss Independent. Okay?"

Alison blinked as moisture pooled in her eyes. Just when she thought Cole was hopeless, he pulled a stunt like this. Paid her a compliment instead of complaining. Took her feelings into consideration instead of steamrolling over them. Compromised instead of pushing his own preferences.

"Okay. Thanks." She sniffed. "And in case I've forgotten to tell you lately, thanks for being such a good brother."

"Hey." He gave her an alarmed look. "You're not going to go all sappy on me, are you? Because that would . . ." He reached for his phone and shot her a relieved grin. "Saved by the bell."

As he took the call, she poked him in the shoulder and rose. He grinned, then waved her off so he could focus on the conversation.

She returned to the kitchen and began removing the cookies from the baking sheet, unfazed by the tempting aroma that usually pushed her salivary glands into overdrive. Her appetite had vanished.

Seeing your name on a tombstone could do that to a person.

"I'm on my way." Cole ended the call and came around to join her, grabbing a cookie to go with his coffee. "Duty calls." He finished off the cookie in two bites.

"Another homicide?"

"*Possible* homicide." His response came out garbled as he took another cookie. "These are great."

"How can you eat when someone just died?"

He paused with the cookie halfway to his mouth. "The same way you can eat despite the child abuse you witness. By seeking justice for the victim. By knowing you're going to do your best to find the perpetrator or fix the problem."

She conceded his point with a lift of her shoulders. Battered children, dead bodies . . . neither was pretty.

"Will you be late?"

"Probably." Popping the cookie in his mouth, he grabbed two more before returning to the living room, where he snagged his jacket off the back of the couch. "Don't open the door for anyone. I'll lock the dead bolt when I leave."

She leaned against the edge of the wall that divided the living room and kitchen, watching as he carefully slipped the bingo card and monument photo back in the envelope, then slid the whole thing in a larger plastic bag he retrieved from a drawer in the kitchen.

"I'll drop this off at the lab before I head home." He tucked it under his arm.

"Be careful, okay?"

"I'm always careful."

"Right, Superman."

He huffed out a breath and shot her an annoyed look. "I'm never going to live that down, am I?"

"Nope."

"I was only ten, you know. People do grow up."

"Yeah, they do. Remember to keep that in mind once we get past this stalker thing, okay?"

Shaking his head, he opened the door. "Good night, Alison."

"Good night, Superman."

As the door clicked shut behind him and she heard the dead bolt slide into position, she wandered back to the kitchen and removed the remaining cookies from the pan. So much for her plans for the evening. Sorting through the mail held no appeal, knitting felt too passive, and Ted Drewes was out. If Cole had been called in on a possible homicide investigation, there was a strong possibility Mitch had been too. Maybe she'd scrub the bathroom after she finished cleaning up the cookie mess. That might expend enough of her nervous energy to allow her to fall asleep later.

The only problem with sleeping, though, was that she couldn't control her dreams. The past few nights they'd jolted her awake with a parade of macabre images that included dead roses, bingo cards, and Bert. Now she could add tombstones bearing her name to that lineup.

The worst thing was, she felt totally helpless. She didn't have the remotest clue who her tormentor was.

Yet he was out there. Planning his next move.

And according to Cole, he wouldn't wait long to make it.

A floor creaked in the apartment above her, and the cookie she'd been transferring to a plate flew off the spatula as her hand jerked. It broke in half when it hit the floor, leaving a dark swath of melted chocolate as it slid across the light-colored vinyl.

It almost looked like blood.

A shudder rippled through her, and she bent to pick it up, wiping the chocolate away with a paper towel. Wishing she could wipe away her anxiety as easily.

With a weary sigh, Alison leaned against the counter and thought about the reading from yesterday's service. The familiar story of the Lord walking on water had resonated with her as never before. She felt like Peter, who'd begun to sink when fear had overwhelmed him and his trust in the Lord had faltered.

In these past few days, fear had overwhelmed her too. But she had to do her best to let it go. To put it in the Lord's hands. Trust in his goodness.

And pray he would give her strength and fortitude to weather whatever turbulent seas might lie ahead.

"I found it!"

Daryl looked up from the jar of meth as Bev waved a short-haired black wig in his direction.

She waltzed through the living room, dancing to music only she could hear, and tugged it on. "Whaddya think?" Striking a pose, she fluttered her eyelashes.

If he ignored the ends of her long blonde hair sticking out underneath, he had to admit it changed her appearance a lot. "Not bad. Where'd you find it?"

"In the closet. Chuck keeps a bunch of this stuff for the smurfers. He won't care if I use it. So tell me the plan again."

They'd been over it three times already, and Daryl was beginning to get nervous. If Bev blew her small but critical role, they'd both be busted in a heartbeat. But he needed someone, and she was the sole volunteer.

She leaned in close to his face and put her hand on his arm. Her eyes weren't quite focused, and he tried not to flinch.

"Hey, chill, man. I used to do a lot of acting. That's what I wanted to be when I grew up, you know? An actress. I was good too. My high school acting coach, Mr. Montesi, said so. That's why I got the lead in *Our Town*. You ever see that show? It's a downer, let me tell you. I played this girl who dies and then comes back as a ghost. But I liked being onstage."

She dropped her hand, and her expression grew dreamy. "When the lights are on, you can't see the audience. It's like nothing exists except this made-up world, where you can be somebody else. That's what I wanted to do all the time. Be somebody else."

Daryl edged away. "If you help me with my plan, you won't be on a stage with lights shining in your eyes."

Blinking, she refocused on him. "Yeah, I know that. But acting is acting. I'll pretend like I'm on a stage. It would be fun to be somebody else for a while again. I'll be great. You'll see."

"Okay. Fine." Like he had a choice. "Be ready to leave tomorrow at two o'clock."

"You can count on me." She twirled the wig again and sashayed back down the hall.

As he watched her disappear, Daryl tried not to worry. Bev's job was simple. There was no reason to think she couldn't pull it off.

Still, they'd have a rehearsal before they left. To be sure she had the part down.

And in the meantime, he knew how to chase away the worry.

Resuming the task he'd been performing when Bev interrupted him, he shook a line of meth onto a dollar bill, started rolling it up—and quashed a fleeting qualm. He wasn't going to get addicted. He just needed a boost of confidence to help him get through the next couple of days.

After that . . . after Alison Taylor paid the price for ruining his life . . . he'd move on. Away from this filthy trailer. Away from Chuck and Bev. Away from meth. To . . .

That's where his vision faded.

He knew what he wanted to run away from. He just didn't know what he wanted to run *to*.

But he'd figure it out. Later. Right now he had more important things to do.

Smiling, he picked up the dollar bill and got ready to rock.

16

Someone was in Cole's apartment.

As a surge of adrenaline kick-started her brain, vanquishing sleep, Alison rose on one elbow to check the digital dial on the bedside clock.

Four fifteen.

Heart pounding, muscles quivering, she cocked her head and listened for another sound that would confirm she had company.

All was quiet.

But she hadn't imagined the muffled thump. It had been loud enough to penetrate the mind-numbing slumber that had finally sucked away her consciousness at two thirty. And it had come from inside her brother's apartment. The prickle on her skin told her someone else was close by.

It had to be Cole, though. He'd said he'd be late, and no one else could have gotten past the dead bolt.

Could they?

Doubt lingering in her mind, she swung her feet to the floor and crept toward the closed door. She'd noticed Cole's old hockey stick in the corner of the bedroom, and now she felt for it in the dark. It wasn't much of a weapon, but it was better than nothing.

She held her breath and eased the door back, relieved when

it didn't creak. Peering through the crack, she looked down the hall.

Empty.

Was it possible she'd imagined the noise, after all? Had it been part of some vague dream that . . .

She froze as a ragged sound emerged from the stillness. One she recognized instantly from the anonymous phone calls she'd received.

Labored breathing.

The person in the apartment wasn't Cole.

A wave of panic surged through her, and her fingers tightened on the hockey stick. She needed to call 911.

Except . . . her cell was in her purse in the kitchen. On the counter next to Cole's remote phone.

Her stomach clenched as her panic ratcheted up another notch.

She tried to think rationally, run through her options. But only one came to mind. And while waking the neighbors wouldn't win her any popularity contests, she wasn't about to take chances with her life.

As she prepared to shut and lock the bedroom door before banging on the ceiling with the hockey stick and yelling for help at the top of her lungs, a dark figure started down the hall.

With a gasp, she jerked back and opened her mouth to scream.

"Sorry for waking you. I tripped over your briefcase in the entry."

She closed her mouth and peeked into the hall.

"Cole?" The slightly slurred voice sounded like him, but why were his words garbled? If she didn't know better, she'd say he'd been drinking.

"Yeah."

He stopped in front of the bathroom and reached in to flip on the switch. Light spilled into the hall, illuminating his pasty face and the bulky white bandage that encased the upper part of his left arm. An arm that now rested in a sling. A blood-spattered shirt was draped around his shoulders.

"Cole! What happened?" Shock ricocheted through her as she barreled down the hall toward him.

"Tangled with a punk who didn't like our questions and decided to demonstrate his displeasure with a knife."

"He cut you?" She stared at him, appalled by his pallor.

"He was more into stabbing than cutting." Cole leaned against the edge of the door, looking like he was about to keel over.

"How bad is it?"

"I'm okay. Nothing hurts. Arm's still numb. But that pain-killer did a number on my brain."

"How many stitches did you get?"

"I don't know. Fourteen, maybe. I'm fine."

"You don't look fine. You're pale as a ghost."

"Guy nicked an artery. I lost a little blood."

The bottom fell out of her stomach. Taking his uninjured arm in a gentle but firm grip, she guided him back to the bedroom she'd just vacated. "You need to lie down before you fall down."

"I'm okay." He staggered as he muttered the reassurance, and she tucked her shoulder under his arm to steady him.

"Yeah, yeah. You're in great shape. How'd you get home?"

"Mitch drove me. He's a good guy."

She already knew that.

After guiding him through the door, she pulled his cell phone and his gun from his belt and set them on the nightstand. Keeping an arm around him, she eased down beside him as he sat heavily on the bed. Once he was settled, she stood, removed the bloody shirt from around his shoulders, and draped it over a chair on the other side of the room.

"Lie down."

"You sure are bossy."

Despite his complaint, she noticed he didn't argue. Once he was on his back, she tugged off his shoes and covered him with the sheet. Snagging the extra pillow, she tucked it under his injured arm.

"Do you need anything else?"

"No. Sorry I woke you."

"Go to sleep, Cole."

"Yeah." His eyes were already drifting closed. "Thanks, Alison. You're a good sister."

Before she even reached the door, she heard the slight snuffle in his rhythmic breathing that told her he'd already caved.

As she stood in the hall, her pulse galloping, Alison debated the merits of trying to catch a bit more shut-eye on the couch. But that was a lost cause. By the time her adrenaline spike subsided enough to let her drift off, it would be time to get up.

Knitting. That would help pass the next hour. It had often been her solace during the long, pain-filled nights after her accident, as she'd waited for dawn to signal the start of a new day. The rhythmic clack of the needles would soothe and calm her—although it would never again have quite the same consoling effect without Bert cuddled up at her feet.

Fighting back a pang of sorrow, Alison extracted the mass of pink yarn from her knitting bag and settled into Cole's recliner. She wasn't going to give in to grief. Instead, she would focus on gratitude and say a few prayers of thanks. Cole could have been killed tonight. But he was okay. And she would be too.

She'd knit for a while. Check on Cole. Grab a quick breakfast. Then she'd go to work a lot earlier than usual. No way was she going to let Cole drive her—if he was even allowed to get behind the wheel in his condition. As long as she was careful, she'd be fine. She'd wait until she saw some other residents walking toward their cars. Safety in numbers and all that. The coffee shop near her office was always busy in the morning. There'd be plenty of people coming and going in the strip mall parking lot, too, at an early hour.

And if Cole wasn't happy about her solo trek, too bad.

At 7:10, Alison's cell rang. Closing the case file she'd been reading, she swiveled in her desk chair, pulled the phone out of her purse, and checked caller ID.

Mitch.

Smiling, she pressed the talk button. "Good morning."

"Hi. Did I wake you?"

"Hardly. I've been up for hours—and that's no exaggeration."

"I take it you heard Cole coming in?"

"Yeah. He tripped over my briefcase and scared me to death. I was about to scream and start banging on the ceiling with his hockey stick when I realized it was him."

"How is he?"

"Last time I checked, he was sleeping. What happened? I didn't get much out of him last night."

"We were following up on a lead in the homicide and the guy didn't like our questions. He pulled the knife before either of us had a chance to react. I'm happy to say he's now resting not so comfortably in the county jail. In case Cole didn't tell you, the guy nicked an artery. The doctor said he should take it easy for a few days."

"I knew about the artery. He didn't say anything about taking it easy. Not that he'll follow that advice, anyway. Thanks for driving him home."

"No problem. And speaking of driving, he told me about the latest communication from bingo man—which I just delivered to the lab. I'll be relieving him of chauffeur duty for the next few days. What time would you like me to pick you up for work?"

She took a deep breath. Mitch wasn't going to be happy about her decision either. "I, uh, decided to come in early. I got here about six thirty."

Several beats of silence ticked by.

"Look, I'm fine." She jumped back in, feeling the need to defend her actions. "I waited until there were people around before I left the apartment and also before I got out of my car in the parking lot here. I locked my doors. It was very safe."

"Why didn't you call me?"

"You were up all night too. You have to be beat."

"It will be hours yet before I have a chance to go home and crash."

"All the more reason not to bother you."

"It's not a bother. Until we catch this guy, I'd prefer you not take any chances. What time are you planning to leave work tonight?"

"My normal quitting time is 4:45."

"I'll swing by, walk you out, and follow you home."

She tapped her finger on the desk, debating how best to respond. Firm, but conciliatory, she decided. "I appreciate the offer, but that's really not necessary. We have a guard in the lobby who can walk me out, and once I'm in my car, I'll lock the door. I'll be fine."

"You know . . . I'm beginning to see why your brothers get frustrated with you."

His tone was mild and half-teasing, but Alison also heard a faint touch of exasperation. Her heart thudded. Okay, time to regroup.

"Goodness. The last thing I want to do is force you into my brothers' corner." She hoped her joking response would ease the sudden tension. Mitch was exhausted after a long night, and he didn't need push back from her when he was only trying to help. "You win. What time works for you?"

He released a breath, telling her he was relieved she'd capitulated without further argument. "Sometime between 4:45 and 5:00. I'm hoping to get home by noon, clean up, and grab a couple hours of shut-eye. I'll call you when I'm ready to leave the house. How's that?"

"Fine. And thank you."

"It's my pleasure." The warmth in his response sent a little tingle through her. "Maybe we can pick up some Chinese take-out to share with Cole. I saw his arm before it got stitched up, and I'd be willing to bet he'd appreciate a little distraction by tonight, once the high-powered painkillers have worn off."

Touched by his thoughtfulness, she smiled. "That's very kind of you."

"Hey, I figure I owe him. He introduced me to a very special woman."

She could get used to having this man around, no question about it. "I think I'm in his debt too. But if you ever tell him I said that, I'll disavow any knowledge of this conversation."

Mitch's deep chuckle came over the line. "Understood. I'll call you later."

As they said their good-byes and Alison dropped her cell back in her purse, she checked the clock. Nine hours and forty minutes to fill until she saw Mitch.

It was going to be a long day.

Chuck tossed Daryl the keys for the truck and grinned at him. "Good luck, man."

Clenching the ring in his hand, Daryl smiled back. He'd snorted another line an hour ago, and he was pumped for the finale of Operation Alison. "This is gonna be a piece of cake."

Bev sauntered into the living room from the back of the trailer, and he gave her a quick inspection. She must have raided the prop closet Chuck kept for his smurfers again. In addition to the short black wig, she'd dug out a pair of glasses, a white schoolgirl-style blouse, and a gray, knee-length skirt. She looked like a conservative, decent, law-abiding citizen. In other words, perfect for the part. There was nothing in her demeanor to arouse suspicion.

Maybe that theater stuff she'd done would come in handy, after all.

Chuck hooted as she came into view. "Hey, Bev, are you in there somewhere?"

"Bev?" She gave him a guileless smile. "I'm sorry, sir, you must have mistaken me for someone else. My name is Caroline. But have a nice day."

Not bad. She might pull this off after all. "Are you about ready to go?"

She turned to him with a smile and lifted the oversized purse she'd scavenged from the closet. "All my props are in order. My lines are down. Just point me to the stage."

"Okay." He rubbed his hands together, once more running over his own prop list. Yeah, he had everything. It was all stashed in the truck. He was set. "Let's get this show on the road."

Bev started for the back door, and he followed.

"So when do you think you'll be back?" Chuck sat at the kitchen table to fiddle with the latest electronic device he'd begun disassembling. A VCR.

"When do you need your truck?"

He shrugged. "Whenever. I'll probably stick close. I got everything here I need." He jerked his head toward the kitchen drawer where he kept the meth stash and grinned. "Did you take some for yourself?"

"Yeah." Daryl didn't plan to use it all, but he wanted plenty on hand if his confidence—or courage—began to waver.

"Happy hunting." With a wave, Chuck bent to his task.

Pushing through the door, he found Bev already in her car, the engine running. Anxious to step onto the stage again. She was getting a real kick out of this.

But he doubted she'd be as gung ho to help him if she knew the full extent of his plans. Even Chuck wasn't privy to the fine points. It was safer this way. The fewer people who knew details, the fewer chance there was for anything to go wrong.

Jiggling the keys in his hand, Daryl double-checked the tarp-covered cage in the bed of Chuck's truck. Once upon a time, it had housed a doomed dog.

And very soon, for a brief time, it would house a doomed social worker.

"What were you thinking!"

At Cole's explosive question, Alison cringed and drew her

office phone back from her ear. "Hello, Cole." She did her best to keep her voice neutral. "How are you feeling?"

"Lousy. Worse, since I found out you drove to work without an escort."

"My escort was in no condition to get behind the wheel of a car. I take it you talked to Mitch."

"Yes. I am not happy about this, Alison."

"No kidding."

"We had an agreement."

Her injured leg suddenly cramped, and she rose to stretch it. Long hours in one position—and stress—could do that to her, and today had been filled with both. She hadn't budged from her desk in the past four hours. Not since she'd grabbed her container of yogurt from the fridge at eleven o'clock. Worrying about Cole's impending sure-to-be-furious reaction to her morning commute hadn't helped either.

"I know we did, but an emergency arose. I handled it the way I thought best. As I told Mitch, I didn't take any chances. I only left your apartment and my car when there were a lot of people around. I was perfectly safe. I was in public places, with plenty of witnesses around if someone tried to pull a fast one."

"That doesn't make me feel any better. You're going to let him escort you home tonight, right?"

"That's the plan."

He blew out a breath. "Okay. Stick to it."

"So how's the arm?"

"It's been better."

"Did you just get up?"

"No. I ate some soup at lunch, and a few of your cookies. But I'm about ready to pop another couple of the painkillers they gave me at the hospital and crash again. I wanted to make sure you were covered first, because these knock me out."

"Everything is copasetic. Don't worry. By the way, we're going to stop on the way back and grab some Chinese. Any preferences?"

"Mongolian beef. Plus a few egg rolls."

She smiled at his predictability. That had been his standard Chinese restaurant order for as long as she could remember. "Okay. Now go get some rest. I'll see you around six."

"Yeah." He stifled a yawn. "I'd rest better if you'd stick with the plan."

"Mitch and I have it all arranged. Don't worry. You're the one who was in the line of fire last night." She gentled her voice. "Just take care of yourself, okay? I want you to be around for a very long time."

"Likewise. And trust me. I'll be bugging you for many, many years. See you tonight."

As she replaced the receiver in its cradle, Alison prayed that was true. Both of her brothers were in very dangerous professions. Bingo man's threats notwithstanding, she was the least likely of the Taylor siblings to find herself in a perilous predicament, as last night proved.

But she had an advantage. She knew someone was after her, and the old cliché about forewarned being forearmed was true. Until her stalker was found, she intended to be very, very careful.

And as long as she did that, she'd be safe.

Standing under the hot spray, Mitch tipped his head back and let the water sluice down his body. He'd planned to shower as soon as he got home around noon, but his eyes had been gritty with fatigue. Instead, he'd fallen across the bed—and into an instant deep sleep.

When he'd awakened a few minutes ago, he'd been in the exact same position as when he'd conked out. He doubted he'd moved a single muscle in the four hours he'd slept.

Much as he wanted to stay under the relaxing stream of water, he twisted the knob off and stepped out, toweling his hair dry. He needed to get an update on the homicide, throw on some clothes, and head to Alison's office.

He padded barefoot to his room, then pulled on jeans and

a black T-shirt, tucking his off-duty compact Glock into the concealed holster on his waistband.

As he ran a comb through his damp hair, a shuffling noise in the hall caught his attention and he crossed to the doorway. His father was slowly walking toward him, one hand braced against the wall. He was slightly bent, as if in pain, and his complexion was an alarming shade of gray. Beads of sweat stood out on his upper lip.

"Dad?" He tossed the comb on the dresser and started toward his father. "What's wrong?"

Walt stopped, grimacing, as he rubbed a hand over his chest. "I'm not sure. Must be that frozen Mexican dinner I ate at lunchtime. It was a lot spicier than I expected. I just want to lie down for a while. It'll pass."

He made an attempt to continue down the hall toward his bedroom, but Mitch stopped him with a firm hand on his arm. "Tell me what hurts."

"My chest. Like a real bad case of indigestion. And my arm. But I was working in the garden earlier, and my muscles are out of shape."

Mitch tried to rein in his panic. "We need to get this checked out."

"I know what you're thinking." He propped a shoulder against the wall, breathing heavily. "But it can't be a heart attack. I just had bypass. They fixed all my clogged arteries."

"I know that, but we're not taking any chances. Did you take an aspirin?"

"No. There's a bottle on the counter in the kitchen."

"Okay. I'll get one for you. Sit here." He tried to ease his father to the floor, but Walt shook him off.

"I'll sit in a chair."

Before Mitch could stop him, he pushed off from the wall and retreated six steps to his favorite easy chair in the living room.

Expelling a frustrated breath, Mitch strode to the kitchen and grabbed the portable phone. After punching in 911, he propped it against his shoulder, shook an aspirin out of the bottle, and filled a glass with water. He gave the dispatcher all the particulars, then returned to the living room.

"Here. Take this. Drink all the water."

His father's hand was shaking, and as Mitch bent down and cupped his own around the gnarled fingers that had taught him how to wield a saw and tenderly plant seedlings and bait a fishhook, tears pricked at his eyes.

Please, God, don't take him yet. Give us some more time together. Please!

The plea to the Almighty came unbidden, surprising Mitch as much as he suspected it surprised God. It had been years since he'd prayed. Years since he'd felt the need for divine intervention in his life. But back in the familiar home of his youth, where the seeds of his faith had been planted and nurtured, it seemed the most natural thing in the world to direct a request to God.

Or perhaps observing the powerful, fortifying faith that was so important to his father and Alison was making him take a second look at the possibility of a relationship with the Lord.

Now wasn't the time to mull that over, however. As his ears picked up the distant wail of an ambulance, he refocused on his father. The only thing that mattered at the moment was getting him through this crisis.

The two paramedics had the same priority. After asking Mitch a couple of questions, they gave the older man their full attention. But Mitch did step in when his father began protesting about a trip to the hospital.

"Dad . . . don't fight us on this, okay? The paramedics think you need to go, and I agree."

"Look at it this way, Mr. Morgan. If everything checks out, you can say I told you so to your son." The paramedic grinned at his patient and continued to ready him for transport without missing a beat.

Walt aimed a peeved look at the three of them. "I'm telling you all, it's a lot of fuss about a bad case of indigestion. I know better than to eat that spicy Mexican food. But fine, I'll go. Waste of time and money, when a few Tums would take care of the problem."

As Mitch followed the paramedics out, locked up, and slid behind the wheel of his car, he hoped his father was right. He'd like nothing better than for this to be a false alarm—but he wanted that verified by medical professionals. He'd come home to spend time with his father. And he intended to do everything he could to ensure that time wasn't cut short.

Daryl wiped his palms on his slacks and looked toward Alison's office building from the passenger seat of Bev's car. In fifteen minutes the nosy social worker would walk out that door.

And they were ready for her.

Bev had followed him to the deserted storage-unit facility he'd found on his scouting expedition. He'd left Chuck's truck in an isolated corner of the parking lot, and they'd continued to Alison's South County office.

Although Alison had left at quarter to five the day he'd followed her home from here, white-collar types didn't punch a time clock. She could cut out early if she wanted to. That's how life worked for the lucky people. He and Bev needed to be set to move the second she appeared at the door.

"You ready?" He shot a quick glance at the woman beside him.

Bev examined her makeup in the mirror and patted her wig. "As soon as you say the word." She rubbed at a smudge of lipstick with her finger. "You know, you never did tell me exactly what this woman did to you."

"She got me sent to prison."

"Yeah?" She stopped rubbing and slanted a glance at him. "How'd she do that?"

"By sticking her nose in where it didn't belong."

"A busybody, huh?" Bev sniffed and tucked a stray strand of hair back into the wig. "I don't like snoops either. There was a brownnoser in high school who was always ratting on her classmates to the principal. Got me busted once for smoking in the girl's john. And it was just a plain old cigarette. Like that was some huge crime." She rolled her eyes. "You point her out and I'll be ready to give the performance of my life. What're you gonna do with her, anyway?"

"Teach her a lesson."

"We did that with the brownnoser in high school too. Some of the kids broke into her locker and trashed it. The rest of us spray painted a message on her car. She stopped being such a jerk after that. I guess we scared her. Is that sort of what you have in mind for this woman?"

"Sort of." Daryl grinned, his gaze fixed on Alison's office. "And I can guarantee that when I'm finished with her, she'll never stick her nose in where it doesn't belong again."

Or anywhere else.

17

Alison had expected Mitch to call no later than 4:30 with his ETA.

It was now 5:15.

And he wasn't answering his cell phone.

Frowning, she drummed her fingers on her desk. It was possible some new development in the homicide had diverted his attention. But he didn't seem like the type to forget a promise, no matter how distracted he might be.

She considered driving herself home . . . but she wasn't keen on incurring Cole's anger—or Mitch's displeasure—again.

With a sigh, she pulled out a phone book and scanned the listings, searching for his father's number. Mitch had sounded exhausted earlier; maybe he'd fallen into such a deep sleep he hadn't heard his cell phone ring.

After locating Walt's number, she tapped it in. Once again, the phone rolled to voice mail. She left a message there, as she had on his cell.

Stymied, Alison replaced the handset in its cradle. She hated to call Cole, but she'd rather disturb his rest than face a dressing-down later. Maybe if she offered to talk to him on her cell from the time she left the building until she was safely locked into her car, he'd be okay with her driving home alone.

It was worth a try.

But calls to both his cell and apartment numbers produced the same result.

No response.

Again she left messages.

Alison was less worried about Cole's lack of response than she was about Mitch's. If the painkillers were as high-powered as she suspected, Cole could be down for the count. A ringing phone might not rouse him.

On all the messages, she'd said she'd wait fifteen minutes for a callback. To pass the time, she answered email and refiled some case folders. All the while hoping the phone would ring.

By quarter to six, it hadn't.

So now what?

As far as Alison could see, there wasn't much choice, unless she wanted to hang around the office until someone finally got her message. But who knew when that might be? She'd already been waiting an hour.

And cooling her heels in her office was not the way she wanted to spend her evening.

Time to go to Plan B—a repeat of her morning ritual. She'd wait until she saw other people in the parking lot, then hurry to her car. Once she was locked inside, she'd be safe.

Cole and Mitch might not like it, but short of calling a cab and leaving her car in the parking lot all night—not an appealing option—she didn't know what else they expected her to do. She was the last one in the office, and Rog had left for the day. There was no one to walk her out.

Gathering up her purse and briefcase, Alison stood and flipped off the light in her office. As long as she kept a sharp lookout in the parking lot, what could happen between the door and her car?

And in less than thirty minutes, she'd be safe and sound in Cole's apartment.

Employing the best-defense-is-a-good-offense tactic by giving her brother grief for not answering his phone.

226

"So how much longer are we gonna wait?" Bev shot Daryl an impatient look and tapped her finger against the steering wheel.

Good question.

Daryl squinted at the entrance to Alison's office, located in the corner of the L-shaped mall and partly shielded from view by a planting area of trees and shrubs. The social worker should have come out an hour ago. Why was she running so late?

This delay hadn't been part of his plan. If they sat around in the parking lot much longer, they might start to arouse suspicion. That kid on the skateboard had already given them a couple of curious looks.

On the other hand, the delay could work to their advantage. The later Alison left, the less chance other occupants of the building would be leaving at the same time. As it was, no one had exited in the past ten or fifteen minutes. The building was probably deserted by now.

Except for Alison.

"Chill out, Bev. Her car's still here. She has to leave eventually." He gestured toward the older model white Civic, parked farther down the row, closer to her office. The cars in this part of the mall lot had thinned out, but there were still three between theirs and hers.

"Yeah, well, I'm getting hungry."

He was too. And thirsty. But there would be time to eat and drink later.

"She's not going to spend the night. You can eat when the show is over. All artists have to suffer for the sake of their art. Why don't you run over your lines again?"

Crossing her arms over her chest, she glared at him.

Although he ignored her irritated look, he, too, was getting restless. Maybe this thing wasn't going to go down tonight after all. What if Alison intended to stay until seven or eight? There was no way Bev would hang around that long. She was already beyond edgy. They might have to try again another day.

A muffled rumble of thunder suddenly reverberated through

the hot, muggy air, adding to his jitters. Dark clouds were beginning to mass on the horizon, suggesting a storm would soon be rolling through.

He hadn't counted on bad weather either.

Just when he was on the verge of chucking the whole thing, a movement in the doorway of the building caught his eye.

Alison.

A rush of adrenaline jerked him upright from his slouched position, and his heart slammed into overdrive.

This was it.

"Bev . . ." He elbowed her, keeping Alison in sight through the branches of the trees in the planting area. "Here she comes. Are you still with me?"

His partner blinked and peered at the front of the building. Alison was hovering outside the door now, scanning the parking lot.

"She seems nervous." Bev leaned forward, one hand resting on the wheel, the other shading her eyes against the glare of the setting sun.

"Yeah." Daryl grinned. "She does."

The exact effect he'd intended to achieve with acts one, two, and three.

Now it was time for the finale.

He slumped in the seat again, tucking the cowboy hat he'd salvaged from Chuck's prop closet low over his forehead. "You remember the plan, right?"

"Of course." She adjusted her wig and grabbed her purse. "Don't worry. I've never forgotten a line onstage. Mr. Montesi said I was a real pro."

The opinion of her high school acting coach was of no interest to Daryl. All he cared about was her performance tonight.

Because if it wasn't flawless, they were both in big trouble.

Alison remained by the door for several minutes. But at last she crossed in front of the building, following the walkway that led around the planting area. Daryl did a quick survey of the parking lot. There were a few people down by Home

Depot, all focused on the carts they were pushing or busy stowing their purchases in their car. None were close enough to cause a problem.

Perfect.

"Okay, Bev. Go!"

Taking the cue, she opened the door and slid from the car.

And as he watched her walk in the direction of Alison's Civic, making a pretense of digging through her purse, he flexed his fingers and took a deep breath to steady his pounding pulse.

The curtain was going up.

"Hey, Dr. Lampke. Sorry to delay your dinner."

While his father greeted his cardiologist, Mitch pushed off with his shoulder from the wall in the corner of the ER treatment room where he'd spent the past hour and twenty minutes. There'd been nonstop action since they'd arrived— constant monitoring of vitals, blood tests, an EKG, an echocardiogram. They'd given his father oxygen, hooked him up to a heart monitor, administered nitroglycerin, and fed him more aspirin.

The whole experience had freaked Mitch out. A fact he'd tried to hide under a placid demeanor. If his father *was* having a heart attack, the last thing the older man needed was more tension and anxiety in the room.

"Not a problem, Walt." The midfiftyish man ran a hand over his salt-and-pepper hair and smiled at his patient. Mitch hoped the doctor's upbeat manner was a positive sign. "I never get home before seven. I'll be there in plenty of time." Turning toward the corner, he held out his hand. "Hello, Mitch."

The man's pleasant expression and firm handshake were comforting, but Mitch wasn't going to assume anything. "So what's the word?"

"All positive news." The doctor addressed both Mitch and his father. "Your vitals are all sound, Walt. Blood enzymes are fine. Heart rhythm is normal. All the vessels are pumping nicely. But I want to take a quick listen." He fitted his stethoscope in his ears and proceeded to do just that. When he finished, he pulled out the earpiece and smiled. "You want my diagnosis? Indigestion."

Thank you, God. Mitch sagged against the wall.

"I told you it was that Mexican food." Walt wagged a finger at Mitch. "Wasted everybody's time."

"On the contrary. You did exactly the right thing," Dr. Lampke interjected. "Never, ever take a chance with chest pain. A small percentage of patients do have heart attacks not long after by-pass surgery. For some reason, their coronary arteries go into spasms. A lot of research is being done on that phenomenon, as a matter of fact. Bottom line, though, you didn't make a mistake by coming in. I'm just glad to report that salsa, not spasms, was the cause of your chest pain and discomfort."

"So I can go home?"

"Yes. As soon as they get your paperwork in order. One piece of advice—stay away from the Mexican food for a while, okay?"

"Trust me. If I never see a refried bean again, it will be too soon."

The doctor chuckled and once more shook their hands. "Call me if you need anything. Otherwise, I'll see you in my office for your next routine visit."

Once he exited, Walt scrutinized Mitch. "You don't look so hot."

"I've had calmer days."

"Maybe you'll feel better after you have some dinner."

Dinner.

Angling his wrist, he checked his watch—and muttered a word he rarely used.

Walt raised his eyebrows. "What's wrong?"

"I was supposed to meet Alison at her office. We were going to pick up some Chinese food and eat at her brother's." Even as he spoke, he was reaching for his cell phone.

230

Except it wasn't there.

And he knew why. In the midst of the emergency, he'd left it sitting in the charger in his room.

He switched to the phone on the wall. Tried several times to dial out. Failed.

"That one's out of service." A nurse pushed through the door and motioned behind her. "There's one at the desk you can use while I unhook your father from all this equipment."

"Thanks." He hung up and looked toward his dad. "I'll be back in a few minutes."

"No problem. You tell that pretty little lady it's my fault you stood her up."

His father increased his volume as Mitch pushed through the door and it swung shut behind him.

But he wasn't worried about Alison being mad. She'd understand his oversight in light of the emergency.

What worried him was her safety.

The last missive from bingo man had been overtly threatening. Even now, picturing her name written on that tombstone sent a cold chill through him. Cole had felt the same way. That's why they'd agreed to stick close to her in public. No way did they intend to give the guy any opportunity to check off the last box on his bingo card.

But in the past fifteen hours, their plans to provide constant coverage had crumbled.

Leaving Alison on her own.

And as he strode down the ER corridor in search of a phone, Mitch prayed she'd played it safe and either waited him out at her office or called Cole.

As Bev walked away from the car, Daryl tugged on a pair of latex gloves. Patted his pocket to reassure himself the 9mm Smith & Wesson handgun he'd borrowed from Chuck's stash was in place. Picked up the folded newspaper from the seat beside him.

Resettling the sunglasses on his nose, he grasped the door handle, preparing to move. Timing was critical at this stage. Every second counted—and he didn't intend to waste a single one.

Her attention still focused on the contents of her handbag, Bev slowed a bit as she passed the back of Alison's car. That delay gave Alison a chance to get closer to the small island containing a single tree, which separated the row of parking spots from the drive that ran in front of the mall.

Then, just as Alison passed the tree, Bev picked up her pace. Feigned a stumble. And scattered the contents of her purse behind the social worker, all over the mulch-covered island.

Daryl was impressed. Bev's timing had been impeccable.

"Oh, goodness!"

Through his cracked door, he could hear Bev's expression of dismay as she surveyed the items littering the island. As he'd expected, Alison hesitated and looked toward her. The social worker was a do-gooder, after all. She wouldn't walk away from someone who needed help.

"My heel must have gotten caught in the pavement." Bev threw the comment over her shoulder as she bent and began to retrieve the items. "What a mess!"

Turning her back to Daryl, Alison set her briefcase beside her and began to help Bev gather up the contents of the overloaded purse.

This was his cue.

Easing the door open, he slid out, quietly clicked it shut, and headed toward the two women.

"I did this not long ago myself, at the grocery store." Alison's voice floated his direction as he approached them. "I had to practically crawl under the checkout stand to find half my stuff."

Bev laughed. "That sounds like the kind of thing I'd do." She cast a quick sidelong glance toward him as he approached. "Did we miss something over there?" She pointed to a spot in the center of the small island, distracting Alison as he drew close.

Give the lady a gold star.

Feeling more confident by the minute, Daryl retrieved the gun from his pocket, concealing it behind the newspaper as he did a final sweep of the parking lot. For once, the gods had smiled on him. No one was close enough to hear their conversation or suspect anything out of the ordinary was happening. From a distance, it was going to look like nothing more than a pleasant conversation. As long as Bev continued her great acting job.

And if she did, in less than five minutes they'd be out of here.

"I don't see anything else. I think we got it all." Alison readjusted her shoulder purse, picked up her car keys from the curb around the island, and used the concrete edge to help leverage herself to her feet. She'd definitely sat too many hours in one position today. It would take awhile for the stiffness in her left leg to dissipate.

The other woman stood too—just as a lanky man in a cowboy hat and sunglasses joined them.

"Do you ladies need some assistance?"

Alison lifted her briefcase and took an involuntary step back. There was an odd, nervous energy radiating from the man.

"No, thanks. I dropped my purse, but we got everything." The brunette gave him a perky smile.

The man moved close. Too close. Before Alison could react, he flipped the newspaper aside so she and the other woman could see his hand.

It held a gun.

And it was pointed at them.

The breath lodged in Alison's throat.

Grabbing the other woman's arm, the man shoved the gun into her side. Near her heart. It was hidden behind the newspaper again, but Alison knew it was there.

"If either of you does anything to attract attention, this little lady will die." He tugged the brunette closer. "Are we clear on that?"

The brunette nodded. Her eyes had gone glassy, and she was shaking.

"Do you understand me too?"

As he stared at her, Alison nodded as well.

"Okay. You do what you're told, no one gets hurt." He gestured toward the keys in Alison's hand. "Open your car."

When she didn't comply at once, he jabbed the gun harder into the brunette's side. The woman gasped and sent her a pleading look.

Alison pressed the automatic door opener. The muffled but distinctive click of doors unlocking came from her car, one empty spot away.

"Let's all get in, nice and easy. I want you behind the wheel. Your friend and I will sit in the backseat. You do one thing wrong—one thing—and she dies. Let's move."

"Look . . . if you want money, or my car, why don't you just take them and leave us here?" Alison held her ground, clenching her keys in her fist. She knew what she was supposed to do in a situation like this. Her brothers had drummed it into her head since her college days. Scream. Attract attention. Take your chances out in the open. Do not, under any circumstances, get in a car. Even under gunpoint.

But what were you supposed to do when the gun was aimed at someone else?

"Why don't you just keep your mouth shut and do what I say?"

Alison couldn't see the man's eyes behind the dark glasses, but she heard the anger nipping at his words. Watched his fingers crimp the newspaper. Sensed he was getting more jittery.

None of that was reassuring, considering he was holding a gun next to the other woman's heart.

Hard as she tried to think of some way out of this, she couldn't come up with one that wouldn't put the brunette's life at risk. If the man had accosted her, she'd have followed her brothers' advice. But how could she endanger someone else?

Slowly she circled toward the driver's side of her car,

favoring her leg. Opening the door, she slid in and set her purse and briefcase on the seat beside her. Behind her, she heard the woman and their abductor join her from the passenger side.

"Close your door." The man barked out the order as he pulled his own shut.

She complied.

"Now, start the car and go south on Lindbergh."

It took her two tries to fit the key into the ignition. As she turned it and the engine sprang to life, her cell phone began to ring inside her purse.

"Ignore that."

The order came from the backseat.

Alison glanced in the rearview mirror. The man had his left arm linked with the woman's right arm. The gun was now visible. He was holding it low, and it was still aimed at her side.

The phone continued to ring.

It had to be Mitch or Cole, returning her call.

Alison choked back a sob, berating herself for her lack of patience. If only she'd waited a few more minutes.

But there was irony here too.

For while her brothers and Mitch had been focused on protecting her from a stalker, this situation didn't seem to have a thing to do with bingo man.

As Alison's cell phone rolled to voice mail, Mitch frowned. He'd gotten the same result when he'd tried her office number.

Why wasn't she answering?

Turning his back on the bustle at the ER desk behind him, he called his unit supervisor. Cole's cell and home numbers were stored on his phone, but that did him a fat lot of good. His boss would have both numbers on hand, though.

As Paul answered, Mitch reached for a pen and paper from the desk.

"Sarge, it's Mitch. Sorry to bother you, but I need a couple of phone numbers." He gave the man a cursory briefing, then jotted down the numbers as the man dictated them.

"If you need the department to get involved, let me know."

"Thanks. I hope it doesn't come to that."

Severing the connection, he waited for the dial tone and tapped in Cole's home number. Maybe Alison had gotten tired of waiting and gone on ahead. If she'd left her purse in a different room, she might not hear her cell ringing.

But no one answered at the apartment either.

Doing his best to quell his burgeoning worry, Mitch punched in Cole's cell number. If the man was like him, he kept his phone close at hand.

Usually.

Disgusted, Mitch blew out a breath. He could count on one hand the occasions in the past few years when he'd been without his cell phone.

Too bad tonight was one of them.

Just when he thought he was going to strike out again, Cole answered. Still sounding a bit out of it.

"Cole, it's Mitch."

"Sorry it took me so long to pick up. I've been in the bathroom trying to clean up. Man, I've got blood all over me. Not a pretty sight to accompany Chinese food, let me—"

"Cole." Mitch cut him off. The pain meds must be powerful to make a cut-to-the-chase kind of guy garrulous. "Is Alison there?"

His question was met with dead silence.

"Cole?"

"Yeah." He cleared his throat, and Mitch suspected he was also trying to clear his head. "What do you mean, is Alison here? I thought you were going to follow her home. What time is it?"

"It's seven minutes after six. And that was the plan. But my father was rushed to the ER this afternoon with chest pains and I lost track of time. I've called her office and cell, but she's not answering. I thought she might have gotten tired of waiting for me and gone to your place."

"She's not here." All traces of grogginess had vanished from Cole's voice. "I did a circuit of the apartment and checked through the window for her car while we've been talking. Is your dad okay?"

"Yeah. He's fine."

"Okay. Let me see if she left a message on my home phone."

Mitch could hear the sound of movement as Cole walked through the apartment.

"The light's blinking. Hold on while I replay it."

A disembodied voice announced, "Tuesday, 5:26 p.m." And then Alison spoke.

"Hi, Cole. I guess you're still knocked out from the pain meds, and I'm sorry to bother you. But Mitch hasn't called or shown up. I've left messages on his cell and home phones, but I haven't heard back. I assume something major distracted him. I know you're not in any condition to drive, and I'm not crazy about taking a cab and leaving my car here all night. So I was going to suggest I call you on my cell as I leave and talk to you while I walk to my car. That way you'd know I was safely locked in and I could drive home. I'll wait until quarter to six to see if either of you calls. If not, I'll follow the same routine I did this morning. Don't worry. I'll be fine. See you soon."

The line went dead.

"How come you didn't answer your cell?" Cole was back in his normal get-to-the-point mode.

"In all the excitement, I left my phone at the house. In the charger."

Two paramedics pushing a gurney brushed past him. A young woman lay on the stretcher. Her eyes were closed. She looked dead.

Mitch turned away. Took a steadying breath. "I'm not liking this whole situation. If she was in her car, she'd have answered my call."

"Agreed. Where are you?"

"Still at the hospital, but getting ready to leave."

"I'll call dispatch and have them send a couple of patrol

officers to cruise through Alison's parking lot. See if they can spot her car."

"I'm going to drop my father at home and pick up my phone. I'll call you as soon as I get there. Less than thirty minutes."

"If her car isn't in the lot, I'll have a BOLO alert issued. There could be a simple explanation—like maybe her cell phone battery died—but I'm not taking any chances."

"I'm with you. I'll be back in touch ASAP."

The line clicked, and Mitch headed back to the treatment room, prepared to hustle his father out the door—and use his badge to light a fire under hospital personnel, if necessary, to make that happen.

Because much as he hoped this was a false alarm, his gut told him Alison was in danger.

And to make matters worse, it was his fault.

18

The ten-minute ride had been silent, except when their kidnapper issued directions. As he did now.

"Make a right at the next driveway."

Alison scanned the dilapidated—and seemingly deserted—storage-unit facility to her right. A cold band of fear squeezed the breath from her lungs, and she eased back on the accelerator.

"Why are you slowing down?" The sharp question held more than a hint of agitation. "You want your friend to die?"

The woman behind her gasped, and Alison looked in the rearview mirror. Their abductor still had the gun pointed at her, and as the brunette's frightened gaze connected with hers, a tear trickled down her cheek.

"Please."

The woman's terrified plea, no more than a broken whisper, left Alison with no choice.

She turned into the entrance.

"Drive around the back."

Doing her best to avoid the potholes that pockmarked the crumbling asphalt, Alison followed his directions, her panic escalating. The facility was on a road spur in an industrial/wholesale area of South County. She hadn't seen a single car since they'd turned onto the narrow access lane. And it was well past normal quitting time.

But the main road was only a couple of blocks away. Close

enough for the traffic to be audible. That road was also lined with retail businesses, where customers would still be shopping. Surely a few of them would hear two women screaming as they worked together to try and overpower an abductor.

And that's what she and the brunette had to do.

Even if one of them got shot.

Once they were out of the car, Alison would try to communicate that plan to the other woman through body language. Or with her eyes.

Because if they didn't attempt to get free, Alison had a feeling neither of them would live to see another morning.

The phone was ringing in his father's house as Mitch ushered the older man in. He'd made far better time than he'd expected—thanks to a heavy foot on the gas pedal.

"You go get that, son. I'm fine. You need to find that young lady."

His father shooed him toward the phone, but Mitch didn't need any urging. He snatched it off the hook on the third ring, an instant before the answering machine would have kicked in.

"Hello."

"I thought you were going to call me as soon as you got back?"

At the grim undertones in Cole's accusatory question, Mitch's pulse accelerated. "I just walked in the door. What do you have?"

"The patrol officers did a sweep of the lot. There's no sign of Alison's car."

"Did anybody see her leave?" Mitch jogged for his bedroom.

"They're canvassing the adjacent businesses as we speak."

He yanked his cell phone out of its holder and slid it onto his belt. "What about security video at her office? That would establish her time of departure."

"I checked. The building doesn't have any outdoor video."

"Great." Mitch put his father's remote phone on speaker and set it on top of his dresser as he exchanged the compact

Glock for his duty weapon. "Okay. Alison said in her message to you that she'd hang around until 5:45. I think we can assume she did. Can anyone in her office corroborate that?"

"The office manager is making some calls. You want to head down there? He said he'd meet us on-site in case we have any questions."

"Yeah. I'll run by the precinct to get my duty car and pick you up in fifteen minutes."

"I can meet you there."

"The doctor said no driving for twenty-four hours."

"I'm fine."

Mitch blew out an annoyed breath. "And you claim Alison is stubborn? Just sit tight, okay? It's not going to help anyone if you get lightheaded from blood loss or pain meds and run into a tree."

"Fine." The acquiescence came through gritted teeth. "I'll be waiting."

The phone slammed in Mitch's ear.

Cringing, he hit the off button and carried the portable back to the kitchen. Cole had given in too fast. Leading Mitch to the obvious conclusion: his colleague was feeling a lot worse than he'd let on.

But he wasn't going to convince Alison's brother to sit back and let him handle this. Protective as he and Jake were about their kid sister, they'd have to be on their deathbed not to throw themselves into any effort to find her.

Not that he blamed them. If he was the one injured, he'd react the same way Cole had. And he'd be motivated by the same emotion.

Except the kind of love he was beginning to feel for the lovely social worker could by no stretch of the imagination be called brotherly.

A fact he intended to make very clear to Alison as soon as they found her.

And they would find her.

Failure wasn't an option.

"Park next to the truck."

Hands trembling, Alison eased the car beside the dark pickup.

"Turn off the engine."

She twisted the key.

"Now sit tight while we get out of the car. And remember
. . . I have a gun in your friend's ribs. You make one wrong
move, she's history."

Alison's heart began to thump harder as the two people in
the backseat exited. Time was running out. She didn't know
what their abductor had in mind, but she had to assume it was
far worse than robbery. If all he'd wanted was their money,
he'd have taken that back in the parking lot.

They had to make a move.

Now.

The man stopped beside her door and motioned her to get
out.

She wiped her palms on her Capri slacks, leaving a damp
swath on the beige material. Then she opened the door and
stood, steadying herself on the side of the car as her bad leg
protested the sudden weight.

For the first time, she took a close look at the man who'd
abducted them. Despite the dark glasses and cowboy hat, he
seemed familiar. Why?

As her brain struggled to place him, he jerked his head
toward the back of the truck. "Move."

For a brief second, Alison locked gazes with the woman
beside him, grasping at an idea that had just occurred to her.

"I have a bad leg. It's hard for me to walk after I've been
sitting."

Twin furrows appeared on his brow. "You're lying."

"No, I'm not. I was in a car accident a year ago." She hated
the tremor that shook her words, but she couldn't control it. "I
had to have a metal rod put in my leg." She inched her pants
leg higher, revealing the end of her long scar.

After a cursory inspection, the man shoved the brunette her direction. "Lean on her."

The other woman joined her, and Alison put her arm around her shoulders. Feigning more of a limp than necessity demanded, Alison leaned into the woman and breathed, more than spoke, her plan, never turning her head.

"We have to rush him. It's our only chance. I'll figure out a way to distract him."

"No. He'll shoot us."

"He'll shoot us anyway. Work with me."

"Are you two talking?" The man erased the gap between them. He was close enough for Alison to feel the heat of his body.

She repressed a shudder.

"No." The brunette aimed the response over her shoulder.

"You better not be. Stand behind the truck."

As they shuffled into position, Alison took another surreptitious peek at the woman beside her, hoping to see agreement in her eyes—and conviction. But the brunette refused to look at her. Out of fear? Or opposition to the plan? Alison hoped it was the former. She needed her fellow victim to join forces with her when the time came. If she took the initiative, maybe the other woman would find the courage to join her. She hoped.

Because it would take both of them to pull this off.

"You." Their abductor motioned to the brunette. "Get the rope out of the back of the truck."

He was going to tie them up.

Alison's pulse skittered. They couldn't let that happen. Once trussed up, they'd be totally at his mercy.

As the woman started to turn toward the truck, Alison went with the first idea that occurred to her.

Feigning a startled gasp, she looked over his shoulder as if she'd seen something frightening. Praying he'd fall for the bait.

He did.

As he jerked his head around to check out the scene behind him, the gun shifted. It was no longer pointing straight at them.

Grabbing the brunette's hand, she pulled her along and rushed their abductor. "You take his left side."

The man was only six feet away, and she was on him in four steps. Alison launched herself at his chest with her right shoulder, grabbing his wrist with both hands, shoving the gun back.

With a muttered curse, the man swung toward them. Staggered back at the impact.

But he didn't fall.

Alison kneed him in the groin, hoping the other woman was doing her part to topple him too.

The man doubled over but remained upright.

Then, all at once, Alison felt her hair being grabbed. Her head was yanked back. She lost her grip on the man's wrist.

The next thing she knew she was lying flat on the ground, her elbow scraped raw from a slide across the coarse asphalt.

Panting, she stared up at the man looming over her—and into the barrel of the gun.

"That wasn't smart at all, Alison. You'll be sorry you did that."

Alison.

He knew her name.

Turning her head slightly, she searched for the brunette. She was standing off to the side, watching the scene. The man was paying no attention to her.

The hard truth slammed into Alison.

The other woman was in on this. This whole scenario in the parking lot had been a setup.

She'd been duped.

A wave of nausea rolled over her. But close on its heels came questions. Was this bingo man? If so, how was the other woman involved? *Why* was she involved?

None of it made sense.

"Who are you?"

Instead of responding to her shaky question, the man leaned down, grabbed her arm below her short-sleeved blouse, and yanked her to her feet. When she swayed, he tightened his grip, squeezing hard. Harder. Harder still.

She gasped in pain, and he jerked her close to his face, shaking her until her teeth rattled.

"You and me are about to have some real fun, baby. It's beach time."

Alison had no idea what that meant. But she knew it was something bad. She also knew her chances of getting away had plummeted. Though the man was lanky, his grip was like a vise. Plus, he still had a gun—and a partner who would back him up.

But if she couldn't physically overpower her captors, she could at least use her lungs to try and send a plea for help. He might shoot her—but she suspected he was going to do that anyway, and she'd rather die now, before he carried out whatever else he had in store for her.

Praying for courage, she stamped hard on his foot. He cursed, loosening his grip just enough for her to jerk away. She took off for the front of the building as fast as her limp would allow, screaming all the way.

She didn't expect to get far. All she wanted to do was buy herself a few seconds to send a loud signal for help.

And that was all she got. Within moments, he was on her. Grabbing her arm, he jerked her toward him.

The last thing she remembered was a fist heading directly for her face.

As Mitch swung into the parking lot at the strip mall that housed Alison's office, Cole grunted from the passenger seat and grabbed his arm.

"Sorry about that."

What little color had been in the man's face when he'd picked him up fifteen minutes ago had evaporated during the drive, thanks to the bouncing of the car and the waning effect of the pain medication.

"I'll live." Cole grimaced and slipped his phone back on his belt. "Jake's not answering. Those most-wanted arrests can get hot and heavy. He's probably too busy staying alive to take calls."

"Maybe this will all be over before we have to freak out any other family members."

"I hope so. That's why I haven't called our mom yet. If this turns out to be nothing, Alison will read me the riot act for worrying her."

Mitch didn't think it was nothing. And he doubted Cole did either. But he let the comment pass.

As he pulled into a spot beside a patrol car, he gestured toward the entrance to Alison's building. "The lights are on. The manager must be here."

He set the brake, shut off the motor, and got out of the car. Cole was still struggling out of his seat when he circled the hood.

Mitch didn't mention the other man's sluggishness. Neither did Cole. But they both knew he wasn't anywhere close to fighting form.

Hopefully, that wouldn't matter. Mitch much preferred to resolve this situation without a fight.

Gesturing to a patrol officer, Mitch started toward him. "Let's get an update."

After introducing themselves and flashing their credentials, Mitch took the lead. "Any new information?"

"No. We've talked to every business that's still open. No one saw anything suspicious. We also checked to see if there were any security cameras covering the parking lot. No luck there either. The office manager arrived about ten minutes ago, along with the security guard. They're inside."

"Thanks." Mitch did a 360 of the parking lot. Most of the activity was at the other end, near Home Depot. This side of the mall contained offices that operated during normal business hours—insurance, brokerage, a career assessment center. There wouldn't have been a lot of traffic—pedestrian or vehicle—at the time Alison left.

Finding any witnesses would be tough.

"You coming?"

Cole had started toward the office building but paused to look back at him.

"Yeah." In a few long strides he caught up to the other man and indicated the single-story offices on their right. "We need to contact the managers of these places and find out if anyone worked late. The windows look directly onto the parking lot, and since Alison came in so early this morning, it should be safe to assume she got one of the first spots. These offices have a perfect view."

"I agree."

Mitch pulled out his phone. "I'll call Sarge and get some of our people on this."

"And I'll try Alison's cell again. Just in case."

Mitch didn't respond as he punched in Paul's number. He'd like nothing better than to have Alison answer her phone and berate them all for overreacting.

But even as Cole put the phone to his ear and waited, Mitch knew that wasn't going to happen.

Because wherever Alison was, she was in big trouble.

At the sudden jangle of the phone from inside the social worker's purse, Daryl's hands jerked on the wheel of the truck. The guy in the lane next to him honked, swerving out of the way as he aimed an irate look his direction.

Daryl ignored him.

And wished he could ignore the phone.

But it had been ringing every few minutes.

Keeping one hand on the wheel, he opened the purse and groped for her cell. When his fingers closed over it, he flicked a glance at the face, searching for the off button. Depressing it, he held it down until the display went dark and the ringer was silenced.

Better.

He didn't want any distractions for the next few hours.

Settling back in his seat, he smiled. Things had gone well so far. Like clockwork, in fact. The scene in the parking lot had played out just as he'd planned. And the abandoned storage facility had worked out great. They hadn't seen one person or one car during their brief stay. The single glitch had been Alison's scream. But he'd cut that off real quick.

In a few minutes, about the time he'd be merging onto I-44 to head for his next stop, Bev would be back at the strip mall. The plan called for her to park Alison's car at the other end of the lot, retrieve her own, and drive back to Chuck's.

That would be the end of the show for her.

And he hoped she stuck with the script. She'd done great up until he decked the social worker. Then she'd gotten squeamish on him. She hadn't liked seeing the other woman prostrate on the asphalt, nose and lip bleeding, lying still as death.

His hands flexed on the wheel, and his smile faded. He hadn't liked that either. Physical violence that produced blood hadn't been part of his plan. But what else could he have done when she started screaming? Still, a punch in the face shouldn't have knocked her out. She must have hit her head when she'd fallen.

To assuage Bev, he'd checked Alison's pulse. Pointed out that she was breathing. Assured the other woman she'd be okay.

His partner hadn't been convinced. Instead, she'd gone hyper on him. Started pacing the parking lot, agitated, jumpy, second-guessing what they'd done. Her anxiety had begun to make him nervous too.

Like he needed that.

Finally, he'd offered her some of his meth. She didn't usually snort, but it was the best he could do under the circumstances.

She'd taken it.

And she'd been a lot happier when she left.

He just hoped the stuff didn't muddle her brain. With him, it had the opposite effect. But Bev was kind of a space cadet under normal circumstances. He wasn't certain how snorting would affect her. Not that he cared, as long as she returned

Alison's car and left his little present inside. After that, she could do whatever she pleased.

As he approached a traffic light, Daryl eased back on the accelerator. Given his cargo in the back, it was important to drive with extra care. The last thing he needed was to be stopped by a cop. If he was, the lack of a driver's license would be the least of his problems.

Waiting for the light to change, he tapped his left foot on the floor and studied the sky. The black clouds continued to mass in the west, blocking the setting sun. Might not be a bad idea to turn on his lights. Him being such a conscientious driver and all.

As he searched for the headlight switch, the smirk faded from his lips.

According to the fuel gauge, there was less than an eighth of a tank of gas in the truck.

A surge of panic swept over him. Chuck had told him he'd filled it up on his way back from his cook, and Daryl hadn't bothered to verify that.

Now, he had a glitch. A major glitch.

He'd only brought a few bucks with him.

A honk alerted him that the light had changed, and he accelerated, sorting through his dilemma. If he filled up and drove away without paying, the cops would be on his tail in minutes.

He needed some cash.

Checking the passenger side mirror as he switched lanes, his gaze fell on Alison's purse—and the tension in his shoulders dissolved.

Problem solved.

Keeping a firm grip on the wheel with one hand, he rummaged through her purse with the other until his fingers closed over a wallet. He pulled it out, unsnapped it, and flipped it open.

Oh yeah.

His lips curled into a smile as he fingered the bills. There was plenty of money here. For gas. And cigarettes. One pack wouldn't give him lung cancer. Maybe he'd get a few beers too. Not that cheap generic stuff Chuck bought either. There was enough cash here to buy a first-class brand like Budweiser.

A gas station came into view on his right, one he'd stopped at on his last foray into town, and he set the wallet on the seat beside him.

Things were gonna be just fine.

"That was a bust."

Cole's comment followed Mitch as they exited the state offices into the twilight. He held the door for his colleague, whose complexion was looking more and more like his dad's had in the ER.

"Yeah. But it makes sense that Alison was the last to leave. Otherwise, she would have asked someone to walk out with her."

And none of this would have happened.

Mitch didn't voice that thought, but it echoed between them as if it had been spoken.

As they walked toward his car, Mitch slowing his pace to match Cole's, the same patrol officer waved them over.

"Looks like he might have something." Mitch elbowed Cole and motioned toward the man, who was standing next to a kid with a skateboard.

Switching directions, they walked over to the duo.

"Guys, this is Shawn Riley. I saw him skateboarding a few aisles over. He's awesome." The kid, who appeared to be about twelve, reddened. "Anyway, I asked him how often he practiced, and he said before and after dinner. Every day. Shawn was here from about 4:45 until 5:15, and he noticed an interesting situation. He was just telling me about it. Shawn, why don't you start over so the detectives can hear the story from the beginning?"

The boy shrugged and flipped his too-long bangs out of his eyes. "Yeah, sure. It was just kind of weird, you know? That car over there"—he gestured to a dark-colored sedan backed into a spot about halfway up the first row—"was parked here the whole time I was practicing. I noticed it because there was a dude in the passenger seat wearing a cowboy hat. You don't see a whole lot of cowboy hats around here, you know? There was a woman behind the wheel, and they were just sitting there. They didn't seem to be talking much. I mean, I kinda got the feeling they were waiting for something, you know?"

"I'm Detective Morgan, Shawn." Mitch held out his hand, and the kid fumbled with his skateboard to take it, reddening again. "This may be very helpful." He turned to the patrol officer. "Run the plates."

As the man took off at a trot, Cole stepped in. "I'm Detective Taylor, Shawn. Can you describe the two people in the car?"

The boy eyed Cole's sling and bandaged arm. "The dude was wearing sunglasses and the hat. I couldn't see much of his face. The lady had short black hair."

"How old would you say she was?"

The kid frowned. "I don't know."

"Was she a teenager?" Mitch pressed. "Or more like your mom's age? Or your grandmother?"

"More like my mom, I guess. She didn't look like a teenager, but she wasn't real old either."

Mitch took out a notebook, jotted the boy's name down, and asked for his phone number and address. Then he handed him a business card. "If you think of anything else later, that's my cell number. Call me anytime, okay?"

The boy examined the card. "Did something bad happen here?"

"That's what we're trying to find out."

Fingering the card, Shawn shoved it in the pocket of his cargo shorts and took another look at Cole. "So did you get shot or what?"

"Stabbed."

"Whoa." The kid's eyes widened.

"Remember to call us if you think of anything else, okay?" Mitch slipped his notebook back into his pocket.

"Sure. Listen . . . good luck."

"Thanks."

The twentysomething cop rejoined them. "Plates on the car are stolen. You want me to check the VIN?"

Mitch doubted the vehicle identification number would be much help. Whoever had changed the plates had probably changed that too. If that was the case, the National Crime Information Center would only be able to tell them if it was stolen, not who currently had possession. But he wasn't about to leave any stone unturned.

"Yeah. Let's see what we get."

The young officer took off again, and Mitch looked at Cole. "What do you make of this?"

"If these two were involved in abducting Alison, it plays havoc with our stalker theory. Most of those guys work alone."

"I know." Mitch massaged the back of his neck. The clock was ticking, and they were getting nowhere. "But their presence is suspicious. Could someone else have been after Alison?"

"That seems far-fetched." Puzzlement deepened the lines of pain etched on Cole's face. "Maybe it was a random robbery. But what I don't get is why Alison would go with them. Jake and I have drummed it into her since she was a teenager never to let anyone force her into a car. This doesn't make sense."

Cole didn't appear to expect a response, and Mitch was just as clueless about Alison's motivations. So he focused on what he did know. Procedures.

"If the NCIC doesn't give us anything on the VIN, we need to get a CSU technician out here. Check for prints."

"Agreed. But what are we supposed to do in the meantime?" Cole sounded as frustrated as Mitch felt.

"Trust that the BOLO alert on Alison's car will pay off. Hope someone calls in a tip that gives us a great lead. And say a few prayers."

19

Daryl topped off the tank in Chuck's truck, hung the nozzle back on the pump, and replaced the gas cap.

On the pretense of adjusting the tarp that covered the large, square object in the bed of the truck, he climbed up on the bumper. Bending down, he lifted the bottom edge of the heavy canvas.

Behind the bars of the cage, Alison was still out cold. The bruising on her cheek was spreading, but the blood around her nose and mouth had dried. That was an improvement over fresh stuff, but it still made him queasy. With a quick tuck of the tarp, he blocked out the stomach-churning view.

After jumping down from the bumper, he wiped his hands on his pants and surveyed the gas station. Only two other cars were parked at pumps, neither near him. It should be safe to run into the store long enough to pay the gas bill, grab a six-pack and some cigarettes, and scrounge up some food. Lady luck was smiling on him today, after all. Besides, bound at ankles and wrists, with a rag tied around her mouth, Alison wouldn't be able to move or call for help even if she did come to.

Satisfied the risk was minimal, Daryl circled back to the driver's side. Leaning across the seat, he snagged Alison's wallet. And as he hefted it in his hand and walked toward the quick shop, he grinned.

Today, the drinks were on her.

Erik studied the selection of candy bars beside the checkout counter in the quick shop. It was always hard to pick. The trouble was, he liked them all. Well, all except the ones with caramel. That stuck in his teeth, as he'd found out the hard way. Yuck.

"What'll it be today, Erik?"

He looked over at the grinning clerk and smiled back. Daniel was nice. He never ignored him, like a lot of people did. And he talked to him like he was a grown-up, not some dumb kid. The same way his friend Alison did.

"Maybe the Three Musketeers." Erik reached for it.

"Those are good."

He pulled his hand back. "But I like Hershey bars too."

"Yeah. Those are my personal all-time favorite."

A customer came up to the counter, and Daniel moved back to the cash register. "Take your time, Erik. I'll be with you in a minute."

The customer put some beer and a packaged sandwich on the counter. He glanced at Erik, then quickly looked away. Like most people did.

Erik went back to his selection. The Hershey bar, he decided, taking one from the display. Next time he'd get a Three Musketeers.

Edging closer to the register, he waited while Daniel put a package of cigarettes on the counter, rang up the man's items, and gave him the total.

As the customer unsnapped his wallet and flipped it open, Erik stared.

It was just like Alison's.

Erik remembered hers real well. He'd seen it up close the night she'd dropped it on the floor in the grocery store. It was pretty, with a butterfly on one corner and a coin purse that snapped open.

Funny that this guy would have the same kind.

As the man riffled through the bills, a photo slipped out of its plastic sleeve and fell to the counter. The man grabbed it and put it back in the wallet real fast, but Erik saw it long enough to recognize Alison in the picture.

His heart did a funny flip-flop and he straightened up, easing closer. "Where did you get that?"

The man's head jerked toward him, and his eyes narrowed. Then they got real squinty and mean. He snapped the wallet closed, shoved it in the pocket of his pants, and turned back to Daniel.

The guy was going to ignore his question.

Usually, Erik walked away when people did that. And tried not to let it bother him. But Alison was his friend, and he didn't understand why this man had her wallet.

"Mister . . . Where did you get Alison's wallet?"

The man's face got kind of red, like he was mad. "Mind your own business, kid."

"I'm not a kid! And that's Alison's wallet!"

"Hey, Erik, take it easy." Daniel joined the conversation. "Maybe it just looks like Alison's wallet."

"Yeah." The man shoved the pack of cigarettes into his pocket and picked up his beer and sandwich. "It belongs to my girlfriend."

"Alison doesn't have a boyfriend. She told me that. And if that's not her wallet, why is her picture inside?"

The man laughed. But his face didn't seem happy, like it was a real laugh. It looked like something hurt. "I think you need to get your eyes checked." He held out his hand to Daniel. "Can I have my change?"

"Yeah. Sure." Daniel counted it out.

"Thanks."

The man brushed past him, like he was some pesky dog, as he left.

Erik watched through the window as the mean guy crossed to a big pickup truck. His stomach was doing a funny jumpy thing. "Daniel . . . that man shouldn't have Alison's wallet."

"Maybe it's not hers."

"Yes, it is." He turned back to the clerk. "Can I have a piece of paper and a pencil?"

"What for?" Daniel pulled a tablet and pen from under the counter and handed them over.

"I'll tell you in a minute."

Pen in hand, Erik walked to the plate glass window that ran the length of the storefront. Watched the man get into the pickup truck. Waited until he pulled out. The man had to stop to let another car go by, and Erik squinted at the license plate. He had just enough time to copy down the letters and numbers before the man gunned the engine and drove away.

Erik tore off the top sheet of paper, walked back to the counter, and set the tablet and pen down. "That man wasn't very nice."

"No, he wasn't. He was in here once before, and he wasn't all that friendly then either." Daniel stowed the paper and pen back under the counter. "What did you write down?" He motioned to the piece of paper in Erik's hands.

"His license number." That's what you were supposed to do if you thought a person was bad. He knew that from TV shows.

"What are you going to do with it?"

"I might give it to the police."

Daniel rested both elbows on the counter and leaned toward him. "I know you think that man had your friend's wallet, but you could be wrong. Do you really want to have any more trouble with the police?"

Erik frowned. Was he wrong? He'd only gotten a quick glimpse of the picture. Maybe it hadn't been Alison. Maybe it had just looked a lot like her. And Daniel was right about the police. He didn't want them coming around again. The ones wearing uniforms hadn't been nice to him. At first, anyway. That detective named Mitch had been okay, though. But he didn't know how to find him.

"Erik?"

He refocused on Daniel. The clerk was his friend. If Daniel

thought it was better not to give that man's license number to the police, he was probably right.

Erik folded the sheet of paper and shoved it in his pocket. "I guess I could have made a mistake."

"Hey, buddy, that's okay. We all make mistakes." Daniel smiled and straightened up. "So what candy bar won the contest?"

After giving the Hershey bar in his hand a disinterested scan, Erik wrinkled his nose and put it back on the display. He wasn't hungry anymore. "I think I'll skip tonight." He turned and walked toward the door.

"You sure? You always get one."

"Yeah." He aimed the response over his shoulder. "I'll see you tomorrow."

As he walked back to the group home, a route he'd followed so often he didn't even have to think about it anymore, the scary feeling in his stomach got worse. It was like . . . like when his mom died. Like something really bad had happened, and things would never be the same again.

All because that man had Alison's wallet.

But who would believe him? Even Daniel, his friend, thought he'd made a mistake.

What if he hadn't, though? What if Alison was in trouble?

Erik kicked at a rock and shoved his hands in his pockets. The paper he'd written the letters and numbers on crinkled under his fingers, and he pulled it out and stared at it.

He hated not knowing what to do.

Heaving a sigh, he trudged over to the bench at the bus stop and sat down. He wished his mom was here. She'd listen if he told her someone was in trouble. But she was in heaven now. Far away.

All of a sudden, his eyes got watery. Sniffing, he wiped his sleeve across them and tried to think about happy things. Like how he and his mom used to take picnics to the park, until she got sick. And how she used to read him stories about Jesus. He'd always liked the one where Jesus told the grown-ups to

let the children come to him. Jesus had listened to everybody.
Especially people who were in trouble or didn't know what
to do.

He wished Jesus were here now. He would listen to his story.
But Erik had a feeling no one else would.

Talk about bad timing.

A trickle of sweat inched down the middle of Daryl's back
and his hands shook on the wheel as he turned onto the entrance ramp for I-270. That had been a close call.

But he had to stay cool. It was too easy to make mistakes
when you panicked.

Maybe a smoke would help him calm down.

He pulled the pack out of his pocket, ripped off the cellophane with his teeth, and shook one out. He'd seen a lighter
in Chuck's glove compartment the last time he'd borrowed
the truck, and he leaned over and rummaged for it. When his
fingers closed over it, he flicked on the flame and lit up. Inhaled.

Yeah. That was better. Years ago, smoking had made him
feel like a big shot. Like he was in control. It had been a long
stretch between cigarettes, but already he was feeling more
confident.

Okay. So what was the real risk here? Some kid with Down
syndrome claimed the wallet belonged to Alison. But if the
clerk, who seemed to know him, hadn't taken the claim seri-
ously, there was very little chance anyone else would either.
Right? After all, who was going to believe the rantings of a
retard?

He took another deep drag, feeling more upbeat by the
minute. So he'd run into a small glitch. Nothing had come
of it. In a few minutes, he'd be tooling west on I-44. Twenty
minutes after that, he'd be off the radar screen. Safe until he
ventured out for the final scene.

And at that hour, no one would be around to watch the
finale. Not where he was going.

Daryl cracked his window, flicked out some ash, and fiddled with the radio dial, settling on a hard-driving rock station. One with the kind of music that got your heart beating fast. Pumped you up.

As he cranked up the volume, another bolt of lightning slashed through the dark, western sky. He grinned. It was almost like a rock concert, complete with loud music and special effects.

This was gonna be a great night.

Bev felt good.

Really good.

Just like she'd felt during the curtain calls after *Our Town*.

She smiled. High school might be ancient history, but she still had the magic. Still knew how to play a part.

Mr. Montesi would be proud.

She flipped on her turn signal and changed lanes, her smile broadening as she headed back to the strip mall parking lot to switch cars. She'd even managed a tear when that Alison woman had looked at her in the rearview mirror. That had been masterful. In fact, everything had been flawless.

Until the end.

Bev's lips flattened. The last part had been off script. And messy. She didn't like improv. So she'd moved offstage and let Daryl handle the staging problem. Not that she'd agreed with his fix after Alison had gone ballistic, but hey—it was his show. He was the director. And it wasn't as if Alison was dead or anything. She'd be fine once she woke up. Daryl had promised her that. He just wanted to teach Alison a lesson. Then he'd let her go.

At least Bev thought that was the plan. He'd never gotten too specific about the details. But what else could he do? He couldn't keep her prisoner forever. Chuck needed his truck back.

The bingo card Daryl had put on the seat beside her, face-down, didn't give her a warm and fuzzy feeling, though. That skull-and-crossbones stuff was creepy. He'd told her to leave it in the driver's seat after she got out of the car, as kind of a practical joke. Except she didn't think it was very funny.

But someone else might—and Daryl was the director. Like Mr. Montesi had always said, you have to trust the director. So she would.

Tapping her latex-encased finger on the wheel in time with the tune on the radio, she hummed along. She'd never snorted before, but wow! It had been awesome. She might have to switch from smoking.

Too bad she had to go back to reality already. Playing a part again had been fun. It had given her almost as big a rush as chasing the white dragon. And it was a whole lot healthier. She sure didn't want to end up like Chuck. He was a mess.

She glanced in the rearview mirror to check out her appearance, reassure herself the meth wasn't messing with her looks yet. But the reflection caught her off guard. It was amazing what a wig could do. She hardly recognized herself.

And no one else would recognize her either.

Or the car she was driving.

Hmm. Maybe this was her chance to visit her old digs and sweet-talk Stan into unlocking her apartment so she could get her stuff. No one would be looking for a brunette driving a Honda Civic. Breezing in and out ought to be a cinch. The whole thing shouldn't take more than a few minutes. Then she could exchange the cars and go back to Chuck's dump.

That prospect still didn't thrill her, but at least she'd have a consolation prize. Her mother's locket.

And didn't she deserve a reward after giving such a stellar performance?

Spotting a gas station up ahead, Bev signaled another lane change. After pulling in, she drove past the pumps and waited for a break in traffic that would allow her to reverse course.

This was one of the best ideas she'd had in a long time.

Why was it so dark?

Why did she hurt so much?

What was that odd vibration?

As she struggled to engage her mind and process those questions, Alison felt herself tilting. Her head exploded and she tried to scream . . . but no sound emerged.

Something was wrapped around her mouth.

She tried to reach up to remove it, but her arms wouldn't move.

They were tied behind her back. And her ankles were bound too.

Then she remembered.

She'd been kidnapped.

Now she was gagged, tied up, and—based on the rocking motion and road noise—in the back of some kind of vehicle.

She was also hurt. She remembered the fist coming toward her, and the side of her face ached. But why did the back of her head hurt too? Had she hit it when she'd fallen?

As the vehicle jolted again, she groaned and fought back a wave of nausea. She couldn't throw up! With the gag across her mouth, she'd choke to death if she did.

Tears pricked her eyes, and she blinked them away. Crying wouldn't solve anything. In fact, it might be just what her tormentor wanted. And she wouldn't give him that satisfaction. No matter what he did to her.

A shudder rippled through her and she closed her eyes. If her abductor and bingo man were one and the same, she knew what he was capable of doing. He'd shown no mercy to Bert. There was no reason to think he'd show any to her. But why had he put her in his sights? Was he a former client who'd been unhappy with the outcome? Could she reason with him? Bargain with him? Somehow convince him he was making a huge mistake?

Alison wasn't optimistic about any of those possibilities, but neither was she willing to give up. Mitch and Cole would be looking for her by now. Perhaps the entire St. Louis County

PD was assisting with the search. Through Cole, she knew a lot of the officers and detectives, and they were pros. They'd find her—given enough time.

So that was her job.

She had to buy them time.

Ending his call to the unit supervisor, Mitch checked on Cole in the passenger seat. The other man was also slipping his phone back onto his belt.

"I just reached Jake. The arrest went down twenty minutes ago. He'll catch the next plane back, but Phoenix isn't exactly close." Cole wiped a hand down his face. "He won't get here until the early morning hours."

"I hope this is over long before that."

"Yeah. Did our people have any luck finding anyone who worked late in the offices near Alison?"

"So far, everyone left on time."

"That figures."

"The CSU unit is there, though. We may have some prints soon."

Mitch pulled onto Alison's street. A K-9 unit was on the way to the mall, and Alison's house was a closer source of her personal items than Cole's apartment. Once they gathered a few things, they planned to let the dog track her movements on the parking lot. Mitch wasn't sure that would yield much—but you never knew.

As he pulled to a stop in the driveway, Cole fished out his keys. "This won't take long. You want to come in or wait here?"

"I'll come in."

Mitch followed Cole in. As Alison's brother focused on his task, Mitch went into the kitchen for a glass of water. The blinking red light on Alison's answering machine caught his eye, and he detoured toward it.

In all probability, the message or messages would be innocuous. A donation solicitation. Or a friend setting up a lunch date. Why would her abductor call? But it was worth checking.

The standard mechanical voice kicked in. "You have one message. Monday, 8:47 p.m."

A woman's voice followed.

"Hi, Alison. It's Nicole Larson. I'm sorry to bother you, especially at home, but a troubling situation has come up and I wanted to get your advice. I'll give you the details when we talk, but Daryl is out of prison and Kyle spotted him sitting outside our apartment the other night. He's also called and come by, trying to convince me to take him back. Thanks to you, I've learned a lot over the past four years, and I turned him down flat. He wasn't happy, though, and I'm concerned. Can you call when you have a minute? Sorry again about bothering you. Everything else is going well."

As the woman recited her number, Cole entered the kitchen with a bag of Alison's personal items.

"Who's on the phone?"

"A woman named Nicole Larson. Sounds like she's one of Alison's former clients."

"Yeah. I remember Alison talking about her. She was living with some meth dealer but claimed she didn't know about his business. The state took her son for a while until she got her act together. Alison went to bat for her, though. I think the woman still sends her Christmas cards. Why'd she call?"

Mitch furrowed his brow. "Her ex-boyfriend is out of prison and trying to get her to take him back. She wants Alison's advice."

"Sounds messy. You ready to roll?"

"Yeah. Look . . . let me jot down her number." He hit the play button again and pulled a notebook out of his pocket.

"Why?"

"Doesn't the timing of this call strike you as odd?"

Cole squinted at him. "You think it's connected to Alison's disappearance?"

"I don't know. But I want to follow up with her. Get a few more details on this Daryl guy." Mitch waited as the message played, then wrote down the number and tucked the notebook back in his pocket. "Okay. Let's go."

Cole's color had gone from pale to pasty, and Mitch thought about offering to carry the bag of Alison's things. Decided against it. Cole didn't strike him as the type of guy who was comfortable accepting help.

Kind of like his sister.

As they secured the door behind them and started toward the car, Mitch's phone began to vibrate. He pulled it off his belt, answered, and slid behind the wheel.

"Mitch, it's Paul. I've got some information you and Cole may want to check out. Two patrol cars were dispatched a little while ago to investigate a report of a woman's screams coming from an abandoned storage facility in an industrial park not too far from Alison Taylor's office. The officers found two sets of tire prints—a car and a truck—and a small amount of fresh blood at the scene."

His pulse kicked up a notch. The incident could be unrelated to Alison's disappearance, but the timing was too fluky for his taste. This might be the lead they'd been hoping for. That was the good news.

The bad news was the blood.

"Give me an address." Mitch pulled the notebook from his pocket again and scribbled down the information as the unit supervisor dictated it. "We had a K-9 unit dispatched to the mall parking lot. Can you redirect it to this location? We just collected some of Alison's things from her house."

"No problem. Stay in touch."

"What's going on?" Cole shifted toward him, twin grooves etched on his forehead.

Mitch started the engine and put the car in gear as he gave him a recap.

"It could be a coincidence, but I thought it was worth diverting the K-9 unit."

"I agree. And I think we feel the same way about coincidences in this business."

264

They did. True coincidences happened, but they were rare. Most weren't coincidences at all. Mitch had a feeling this one fell into the latter category.

And they'd know soon enough.

The sun was starting to set. If he didn't get back soon, Ms. Walker would worry about him. And Erik didn't like to cause problems.

He looked at his watch. Twenty-five minutes had passed since he'd sat on this bench by the bus stop, and he'd been thinking hard the whole time. About that man in the quick shop. About what Daniel had said. About Alison.

Mostly about Alison.

He kept trying to picture the photo of her with her family that he'd dug out from under the rack of candy the day she'd dropped her purse in the grocery store. It had taken him a few tries to coax it from under the metal rack, and he'd gotten a long look at it. Everyone had been wearing those pointy hats, like it was a birthday party, and . . .

Erik blinked. The people in the picture in that man's wallet had been wearing pointy hats too.

And the woman he'd thought was Alison had been standing between two men, all of them clustered behind an older woman.

The same way they'd been in Alison's picture.

That wallet *had* been Alison's. He was sure of it now.

He stood abruptly. That man shouldn't have had Alison's wallet! She wouldn't be friends with someone who had mean eyes. He must have stolen it from her. Maybe he'd even hurt her to get it. A lot of people did bad things. That's why Ms. Walker was always telling him and the other people he lived with to be careful.

Erik's heart began to beat really hard. Maybe he should call Alison's house. Ms. Walker and that detective and Alison herself had told him not to, but it would be okay one time, if he was trying to help, wouldn't it? He still had her number.

He kept it in his pocket, even though he hadn't called her since the night the police had scared him. But having it with him made him feel good.

And if she didn't answer, he could call 911 and ask for that detective named Mitch. He'd been nice. Maybe he'd be able to find Alison and make sure she was okay.

He started to retrace his route to the quick shop. Stopped. He couldn't call from there. That was the phone he'd used to make those calls to Alison, and those policemen had found him somehow.

There was another phone inside the restaurant on the corner of the street where he lived, though. He'd seen it once, right inside the door, when someone was leaving as he passed. But it was noisy in there, with loud music, and he'd heard Ms. Walker call it a biker bar once. He didn't know what that meant, but from the way she'd said the words, he knew it wasn't the kind of place she'd want him to go into.

Still, that would be a better phone to use. In case the police were still watching the other one. He didn't want to cause any trouble. He just wanted to find that detective named Mitch.

Switching directions, he trudged toward the biker bar.

As he approached, he could hear the music through the walls. And the instant he opened the front door, it blasted him in the face. It also hurt his ears, and he almost changed his mind. Then he thought about Alison being in trouble, and he made himself go in. After digging some coins out of his pocket, he slipped them in the phone and carefully dialed Alison's number. After three rings, her answering machine kicked in.

He hung up.

As he felt around in his pocket for some more quarters, his heart began to pound again. He didn't want to call 911. The police might get mad. Or make fun of him.

But what if that man had done something bad to Alison when he took her wallet? You were supposed to help people who were in trouble. That's what his mother had always told him. Jesus had said that too.

He had to call. Even if he was scared.

Heart still hammering, he put the coins in the slot and dialed the three digits.

"St. Louis County 911. What is your emergency?"

He tried to talk, but nothing came out.

"St. Louis County 911. Please state the nature of your emergency."

Erik took a deep breath. "I think my friend is in trouble."

"Can you describe the problem?"

"I think she might be hurt. That man had her wallet."

"Okay." The lady's voice got nicer. More friendly. "Can you give me your name?"

"Erik."

"Where are you, Erik?"

He couldn't tell her that. She might send the police again. He squeezed the phone tighter. "I need to talk to that detective. His name is Mitch. He knows her. Can you give me his number?"

"I'm sorry, we don't give out that information. But we'll dispatch a patrol car to your location and you can—"

Erik didn't wait for the rest. He hung up and stumbled through the door, half running down the street toward his house. They must have some magic way to figure out where people were. And he wasn't waiting around for the police. The last time they'd scared him. Bad.

"I'm sorry, Alison." He whispered the words as he hurried down the street. To safety. "I tried."

20

"The K-9 unit beat us." Mitch swung into the abandoned storage facility and indicated the officer in combat boots and cargo pants, a golden retriever on a leash beside him. He was standing off to one side of the building.

"Let's not keep them waiting." Cole tightened his grip on the bag containing Alison's things.

Mitch pulled up beside the two patrol cars parked in front of the building and slid out of his seat. An officer approached, lifting a hand in greeting when he recognized the other detective.

"Sorry to hear about your sister, Cole."

"Thanks." Cole heaved himself out of the car.

Noting the other man's white-knuckled grip on the bag and his subtle attempt to steady himself against the side of the car, Mitch bought him a moment by introducing himself to the officer.

Once they'd shaken hands, the man guided them to the back of the building. "Your boss pulled in another CSU van. Hank's been here about five minutes."

As they passed the K-9 unit, Cole gave the bag of Alison's items to the handler. "Hold on a minute while we make sure Hank's got whatever photos he needs."

"No problem." The man patted the dog. "Callie's ready to go anytime. You're just trying to verify the presence of your sister, right?"

"Right."

As they rounded the corner of the building, Hank was on his knees studying the asphalt while the other patrol officer watched from a few feet away. When the technician caught sight of them, he waved them over as he bent to retrieve a sample.

Mitch had no trouble identifying the small maroon globs that had caught Hank's attention. He'd never been squeamish, but this blood did a number on his stomach. Swallowing past the lump in his throat, he took a deep breath.

"I got excellent photos of the two sets of tire tracks. Very clear patterns. Lucky thing we had that heavy rain a few days ago. Washed some dirt onto the parking lot." Hank continued to work as he spoke. "One larger vehicle, pickup truck size. And a smaller compact car."

"Like a Honda Civic?"

At Cole's terse question, Hank looked up. "Could be. That what your sister drives?"

"Yes."

"If she keeps decent car records, we should be able to determine if we have a match."

"We have a faster way. We've got a K-9 team standing by in front as soon as you're finished here."

Rising, Hank sealed the sample. "I've got the preliminary stuff done. Let's bring the dog back. See what we have."

"I'll get them." The officer who'd greeted them took off at a jog.

Half a minute later, the K-9 team appeared. The handler set the bag of Alison's items on the pavement, sorted through it, then extracted a lacy camisole.

Mitch's pulse stumbled. It looked a lot like the one that had peeked through the V-neck jacket of her business suit the day they'd met for lunch.

This was getting more difficult by the minute.

"Did she wear this recently?" The K-9 officer held up the delicate garment.

269

"I think so. It was on top of her clothes hamper." Cole's voice roughened, and he cleared his throat.

"That should work." The man bent and had the dog take a whiff before letting her get to work.

Callie sniffed around the asphalt, straining at the leash. Within seconds she led the handler straight for the globs of blood, sat down, and perked up her ears.

The passive alert stance answered their question.

Alison had been here.

The blood was hers.

Mitch looked at Cole. The hard set of the man's jaw and the dread tightening his features mirrored his own reaction.

"Do you want me to see how far Callie can follow the scent?"

At the handler's question, Mitch transferred his attention to him. "Yes. But they may have switched vehicles here, so Alison would have been in a truck."

"Callie's trained to trail. If the victim's scent blew out of a window or through a vent, we might be able to track it for a while. Far enough to give you a direction, if we're lucky. Or would you rather I head over to the mall parking lot?"

"Stay here." Cole dug a card out of his pocket. "And call me on my cell if you have anything worth reporting."

"Will do." The man pocketed the card and urged the dog back to work.

Taking Cole's arm, Mitch pulled him aside. "At least we have more information now than we did a few minutes ago."

"Yeah. We know Alison's hurt and that she's been abducted." Cole's expression was bleak. "What we don't know is the important stuff—who took her and where she is."

And whether she's alive.

Mitch didn't voice that. He didn't have to. He saw the same thought reflected in Cole's eyes.

"We will." Mitch watched the K-9 team disappear back around the side of the building, toward the road. Following Alison's scent. "We're going to get a break soon."

"I hope so."

So did he.

The vehicle stopped.

The vibration of the engine ceased.

Alison's pulse accelerated.

Wherever her abductor's destination, they'd arrived.

Although the jouncing had been painful, she was sorry it had come to an end. As long as her abductor was driving, he couldn't carry out the next part of his plan. Whatever it was.

A car door banged shut behind her, and she stiffened. Since regaining consciousness, she'd worked herself into a sitting position, knees drawn up slightly due to the confined space. She'd also explored as much as she could—enough to know she was in some kind of metal-mesh cage. After working her fingers through the bars, she'd also determined the cage was draped in canvas.

A noise sounded in front of her, and she braced herself. In the darkness, she heard a latch releasing. Hinges squeaked. The vehicle shifted, as if accommodating extra weight.

In the next instant, the canvas was whipped off the cage.

And in the deepening dusk she found herself face-to-face with the man who'd abducted her.

Two things registered at once.

He'd removed his hat and sunglasses, giving her a clear view of his face. His lack of concern about her ability to identify him could mean only one thing.

He intended to kill her.

And the nagging sense of familiarity returned. She knew this man from somewhere. But she still couldn't place him.

"You're awake. Good." He tossed the tarp into a corner of the bed of what she now realized was a pickup truck. Lowering himself beside her, he rested his back against the side and crossed his legs at the ankles. After retrieving a pack of cigarettes from his shirt pocket, he lit up and took a long drag. Then he leaned close and blew the smoke in her face.

When she averted her head, he laughed.

"Not a smoker, Alison? No, I guess not. You're too busy arranging people's lives to have any bad habits like that." He took another drag. Blew the smoke her direction again.

This time she didn't flinch.

That seemed to amuse him. "Used to my smoking already? I guess I'll have to find some other way to annoy you."

Sliding to the rear of the truck, he lifted the lid on a small toolbox and withdrew a knife. With a long blade.

Alison stopped breathing.

Scooting close to her, he stuck the blade through the cage. She cringed and tucked herself into the farthest corner.

"Now that's the kind of reaction I like to see." He grinned and slowly twisted the knife. "I want you scared, honey. Real scared." Withdrawing the blade, he ran a finger down the edge, his gaze locked on hers. "This worked so well on that mutt of yours, I just might have to test it out on something bigger."

She stared at him, her suspicions confirmed.

Her abductor and bingo man were one and the same.

As the image of Bert's mutilated body flashed through her mind, her stomach heaved. Bile rose in her throat, blocking her windpipe. Her fingers clenched and her body went rigid as she gasped for air. What little light remained in the evening sky began to fade as blackness sucked her down, down, down.

All at once, the gag was ripped from her mouth. She was pulled forward, and the man began to beat on her back. The bile loosened, and she began coughing and choking it up, still trying to breathe.

When the man released her at last, she fell sideways. Chest heaving, head pounding, she finally managed to draw some air into her lungs.

Totally spent, she lay on the bottom of the cage as tremors shook her whole body. She could sense the man looming over her, but she didn't have the strength to look up at him.

"This party is just getting started, honey." He rattled the

cage, and she groaned. "I'm not going to let you die on me. Yet. You catch your breath while I get ready for round two."

The bed of the truck jiggled. He'd moved away. For now.

From her prone position, she examined the surrounding area. From what she could tell in the fading light, they were in the middle of nowhere. Tall, dense trees and shrubby brush lined the rutted, barely discernible road where he'd parked the truck. No light penetrated the gloom. There was no sign of human habitation.

It was just the two of them.

And he'd be back soon.

For round two.

In a macabre game that was destined to only get worse.

Bev turned into her apartment complex and drove slowly through the lot. With the dusk deepening, she should have no problem getting in and out undetected. There were no cop cars around, and even if the police were still looking for her, they thought she was a blonde. This would be a piece of cake.

Parking in a spot close to the entrance, Bev did one more scan, then slid out of the car and removed the latex gloves Daryl had insisted she wear, tucking them into her purse. He'd said her outside key worked, so she slipped it in the lock and let herself in.

As the familiar musty odor assailed her nostrils, she wrinkled her nose. She'd always hated that smell. But after spending the past few days in Chuck's stinking trailer, it didn't seem as bad. Not that she'd ever be moving back here. She'd have to start over again somewhere else, with nothing. So what else was new? She'd never had much to begin with. All she wanted to keep were a few personal items in the apartment.

And Stan could help her get them.

After making her way down the hall, she took the steps in the dank stairwell to his second floor corner apartment, where he spent most of his time planted in front of the boob tube.

She'd been up there often enough, exchanging favors for a break on her rent, and knew his patterns. Right about now he'd be watching ESPN. Probably a boxing match, if he could find one.

As she approached his door, she heard what sounded like a sportscaster on TV. Stan never changed.

Smoothing her hair with one hand, she knocked with the other.

No response.

She knocked again.

"Yeah, yeah. I'm comin'."

A few seconds later, Stan pulled the door open. As usual, he was wearing a white undershirt that accentuated his paunch.

He looked her up and down, making no attempt to hide the lascivious gleam in his eyes. "Can I help you?"

Bev tried to suppress her grin. Even Stan didn't recognize her, thanks to her great costume. Patting her hair, she fluttered her eyelashes at him. "I came to inquire about an apartment."

He cocked his head and squinted as he scrutinized her. "Bev?"

She chuckled. "It took you long enough."

Leaning past her, he checked the hall. Then he grabbed her arm and pulled her inside, shutting the door behind him.

"What are you doing here? The cops have been crawling all over this place." He scuttled to the window that overlooked the parking lot and peered through one of the broken slats in the miniblinds.

"Chill out, Stan. You didn't recognize me, did you? Why should they?" She sauntered into the living room. As usual, the place was a sty. Empty pizza boxes were stacked in one corner, a pile of newspapers covered the top of the dinette table, and the sink was full of dishes encrusted with dried food.

It reminded her of Chuck's trailer.

He turned back to her. "They might not recognize *you*, but they'll recognize your car. I don't need any trouble around here."

"I didn't bring my car. I . . . borrowed someone else's. You don't think I'd be stupid enough to come back if I thought I was going to get caught, do you?"

His dubious expression irritated her.

"Look, I'll get out of your hair in a minute. I just want a few personal things from my apartment, and my key doesn't work."

"The landlord changed the locks after the police and Social Services started nosing around."

She sashayed over to him. "But you have a key, don't you?"

"I might." His gaze raked over her appraisingly. "What's it worth to you to get it?"

That was the response Bev had expected. And she was willing to barter. Her mother's locket was worth it.

Smiling, she ran a finger down his arm. "I think we could come up with a fair price, don't you?"

He belched, and she tried not to cringe.

"Yeah, baby, I think we can. Come on. Let's discuss it." He grabbed her hand.

As he tugged her toward the back of the apartment, she peeked at her watch: 8:15.

In twenty minutes, tops, she'd be out of here.

Treasures in hand.

"Did you miss me?"

At bingo man's question, Alison worked herself back into a sitting position, wincing as her left leg spasmed. She needed to stretch it out. But that wasn't going to happen anytime soon.

The light had faded, and the man's features were fuzzy. But as he sat on the tailgate and began whittling a sharp point on a long stick, the acrid taste in her mouth turned her stomach. Again.

She retched, and he shot her a disinterested look.

"Still feeling sick, huh? At least you're done throwing up. Must have emptied your stomach on the last round."

He swung his legs into the bed of the truck and stood. Pulling a strip of cloth out of his pocket, he unlatched the top of the cage and reached down.

"No." The word came out raspy, and she tried to twist away.

Grabbing her hair in his fist, he pulled upward. Hard enough to lift her off the floor. The tender spot on the back of her scalp felt like it was splitting open, and bright lights strobed across her field of vision.

After dangling her for a moment, he let her fall. As she sagged sideways he whipped the cloth across her mouth and tied it in the back. Then he closed the top of the cage, relatched it, and once more sat with his back against the side panel of the truck. He picked up a beer can. Released the tab. Took a long swallow. All the while watching her.

At last he set the can down and went back to work on the stick, testing the point with his finger as he continued to sharpen it.

"I think it's about time you and me had a talk, Alison." He smiled at her. "It's okay if I call you that, isn't it? Nicole does."

Nicole.

With that single word, all the pieces suddenly fell into place. Her stalker was Daryl Barnes, Nicole's onetime boyfriend. A meth dealer. The man who had caused Nicole to lose her son for a year. A convicted criminal who'd gone to prison.

He was also the man she'd seen exiting Ellen Callahan's apartment building the day she'd gone there to drop off some GED material.

"So you finally figured out who I am?" He grinned at her. "I knew you would. You're a smart lady. Too bad you're also a busybody."

He scooted closer, his smile fading, his dark irises glittering with hate. Alison tried to ignore the point on the stick he was holding.

"Here's the deal, Alison. Because of you, I spent four years behind bars. Locked up like an animal. I thought it was only fair for you to see firsthand what that felt like. It's not a lot of fun, is it?"

When she ignored him, he stuck the stick through the bars and pressed the point against her thigh. "Is it, Alison?"

She tried to move away, but there was nowhere to go. He pressed harder, twisting the point until it broke through the fabric and bit into her flesh.

Although she did her best to contain it, a tear escaped and trailed down her cheek.

"Oh." He gave a mock sigh. "Did I make you cry? What a shame. Not." He leered at her and jabbed harder, the malevolent gleam in his eyes sending a shaft of terror through her. "And that's just the warm-up."

He glanced at her Capri pants, and a muscle twitched in his cheek. She followed his line of sight. A dark circle was spreading around the tip of the stick, staining the beige fabric.

The next instant he yanked it out of her leg. After tossing it aside he grabbed the knife and stood. She began to shake harder as he unlatched the cage and lifted the lid.

"You know, I tried to convince Nicole to give me another chance when I got out of prison. But I wasn't good enough for her anymore. She said she had a new life now. One you helped her build. One that didn't include me. She also said she owed you a lot. And you know what? So do I. Tonight I plan to repay that debt."

Alison's heart slammed against her rib cage, and she struggled to breathe.

God, please help me! I don't want to die!

The silent cry came from the depths of her soul as she stared up at Daryl Barnes. A man who took no responsibility for the mess he'd made of his life. A man who was looking for someone to blame for all the misfortunes that had plagued him. A man who needed a scapegoat.

And he'd found one in her.

When he bent toward the cage, she shrank away, closed her eyes, and tried to prepare herself for the searing pain she would feel as the blade of the knife plunged into her.

Instead, he grabbed one of her feet. Startled, she opened

her eyes and watched as he cut through the rope around her ankles, freeing her legs.

Locking gazes with her again, his face mere inches from hers, he brushed his hand up the outside of her leg. Fingered her hair. Touched her cheek.

"I think it's payback time, don't you, Alison?"

As his intent registered, icy fingers of dread clawed at her throat and she began to shake.

Maybe it would have been better if he'd killed her after all.

Police officer Sarah Kaufmann pulled into the apartment building parking lot and guided her patrol car down the row of cars, processing the latest report on the Alison Taylor situation that had just come over the radio. After ten years with the County PD, you got to know almost everyone on the force, and she'd run into Cole on a number of occasions. She'd met his sister too, when he'd brought her to a department-wide picnic a couple of years ago. Nice woman.

This whole thing that was happening to her stunk.

On the other side of the spectrum, you had people like Bev Parisi. A real loser. County had been patrolling this lot for days hoping to spot her, but she'd never shown up. Probably never would. She'd disappear into the woodwork and find somewhere else to nurse her meth habit.

That stunk too.

But a lot of things did, as she'd learned during her decade in law enforcement. Innocent people got hurt. Bad guys got away. Sometimes it was hard not to get discouraged.

Sarah turned up the next row. No sign of Bev's car—though she'd most likely changed the plates by now, anyway. But a white Civic did catch her attention. It was parked close to the entrance, angled into the spot crooked, as if the driver had been in a hurry. Or drunk.

Since it was a slow night, she keyed in the license plate.

When a BOLO alert flashed up, her eyes widened.

No way.

She checked the license number again against the Civic, letter by letter, digit by digit.

Yes!

Reaching for her radio, she prepared to pass on the good news.

She'd just found Alison Taylor's car.

"The lab got a positive ID on one set of prints from the car at the mall." Cole slid his phone back into its holder. "A guy just released from Potosi, who served four years for dealing meth. Daryl Barnes."

Cutting off his tire-tread question midsentence, Mitch jerked away from Hank and stared at Cole. His colleague must really be out of it if the connection had failed to register.

As he yanked his own phone off his belt and punched in the number he'd copied from Alison's answering machine, he clued Cole in. "Nicole Larson said her boyfriend's name was Daryl."

A muscle in his colleague's jaw clenched. "I can't believe I missed that."

"You shouldn't even be on your feet, let alone working a case, after an injury like that." Mitch motioned toward the sling.

The other man glared at him. "What do you expect me to do? Sit at home and twiddle my thumbs?"

Settling the phone against his ear, Mitch ignored the anger he knew was prompted by frustration and instead focused on the latest break. The only other new information they'd received had come from the K-9 unit, which had been able to follow Alison's scent as far as Lindbergh Blvd. But that had been of little help.

This, however, could be big.

Nicole answered on the second ring, and Mitch gave her a cursory explanation of the situation.

"We're pretty certain Daryl is our man, Ms. Larson," he concluded. "Do you know where he's staying?"

"No. I'm sorry. I wish I could help." The distress in her voice was almost palpable. "But I think you're right to suspect him. When he stopped by after his release, I mentioned how much Alison has done for me. I could see he wasn't happy about that. I should have called her sooner, I guess, but I never expected him to resort to violence. Or kidnapping."

"Do you have any idea where he might have taken her?"

"No. None."

Mitch's surge of hope waned. They might have a prime suspect, but they had no idea how to find him. "Let me give you my number. If you think of any information that might be useful, please call me. No matter the time."

As Mitch recited his number, he saw Cole pull out his own phone. The sudden tense line of the other man's shoulders after he answered put him on alert and he tuned in.

"Okay. We're on our way. Tell the officer to stay out of sight until we get there. Our ETA is about twenty minutes. Have her watch for us at the entrance to the parking lot about then. And send enough patrol officers to cover all the exits. They should be watching for a woman about thirty with long blonde hair or short black hair. If anyone answering that description attempts to leave, they need to be stopped and held for questioning."

Ending the call, Cole cradled the sling with his good arm and took off at a trot for the front of the building. "We've got Alison's car."

Mitch's hope swelled again, and he fell in beside the other man. "Where?"

"The parking lot of Bev Parisi's apartment building."

His brain clicking into analytical mode, Mitch pulled out his keys and took the driver's seat. "This isn't a coincidence. Remember, that Neighborhood Watch coordinator on the street behind Alison spotted a car that matched the description of Bev's. The next night, when Bert was killed, she saw a pickup truck in the same spot."

Cole eased into the passenger seat as Mitch started the engine. "You know, when you suggested a connection between Bev and Alison's stalker, I wasn't convinced. Now I am."

"It makes sense. Barnes served time for dealing meth. Bev is a user. So was Lon Samuels—where a blonde matching Bev's description was also seen. Meth is the connection among all these players."

As Mitch turned on the flashing light bars mounted on the front and back windows and sped out of the storage unit lot, Cole grabbed the dash to steady himself. "You think Bev was the one in the car with Barnes in the mall parking lot?"

"Yes."

"But she has long blonde hair."

"A wig can change that. So can dye and a haircut."

Cole tucked his injured arm closer to his body as Mitch took a sharp corner. "Why would she go along with a scheme like this? Doing drugs is one thing; kidnapping is a whole different ball game."

"We'll have to ask her that when we find her." Mitch hit the siren as they swung onto the main road, clearing the path for them as he floored the gas pedal.

"It's possible she just dumped the car there."

"True. But if she's in disguise, she might have figured this was her chance to clear out her stuff without being noticed." Swerving around a car that didn't get out of the way fast enough to suit him, Mitch pressed harder on the accelerator. Trying to eke a few more rpms out of his Taurus.

"That would be stupid."

"No more stupid than participating in a kidnapping. Or using meth."

"Good point. But even if she was involved, it doesn't mean she knows where Barnes took Alison."

That was also true.

But as they sped toward Bev Parisi's apartment, Mitch was resolute on one point. If they did get their hands on the elusive blonde, he was going to pull out all the stops to persuade her to tell them every single thing she knew about Daryl Barnes and his plans for Alison.

21

A distant rumble of thunder shook the ground, and Daryl grinned as he popped another beer and watched Alison, cowered below him in the open cage, her eyes wide with terror. She'd been shaking like a leaf since he cut the rope around her ankles. Hard enough to rattle the cage.

That was what he'd been after.

Taking a swig of beer, he prowled around her like a stalking animal. Knowing she was thinking exactly what he wanted her to think gave him almost as much of a rush as the meth did. It made him feel powerful. In control. Invincible.

And very, very good.

The truth was, he had no intention of touching her in the way she feared. She repulsed him, with all that blood smeared across her face. But she didn't know that. And he intended to keep it that way. Right up to the end.

In the meantime, though, he was going to have a lot of fun.

He set the beer on the bed of the truck and moved over to the cage. "Stand up."

She burrowed deeper into the corner.

Leaning down, he grabbed her arm and yanked her up. She swayed, and he kept a firm grip on her until she steadied. Maybe she did have a bad leg. That scar had been for real. A smile twitched at his lips as he considered that nice bonus. Limited mobility would work to his advantage.

In one swift movement, he bent and slung her over his shoulder. She was a little thing. Couldn't weigh much more than 110, 115. Kind of like Nicole. But she was a lot more feisty. Even trussed up and injured, she was wiggling like a worm on a hook.

He liked that. There wasn't much thrill in subduing someone docile.

Carefully, he lowered himself to the tailgate. Still holding her, he slid off and walked a few steps away from the truck, where he dumped her onto a clear patch in the overgrown two-track path that had once been a road.

Her muffled groan was satisfying.

He watched as she tried to right herself, aiming a few kicks her direction to thwart her. Finally, panting, she quit struggling. He smiled as he stood over her. Shoving Nicole around had always given him a sense of power.

This did too.

And this was the perfect place to do it. He knew rural Jefferson County from his younger days. He and his friends had spent some wild times in this neck of the woods. Drinking, partying, causing trouble. The area had built up a lot, but he hadn't had any problem finding a spot that suited his needs during his scouting expedition. Posted with a no trespassing sign, the overgrown lane had been blocked off with a rusted chain that had quickly succumbed to Chuck's metal cutters. Most of these places were unoccupied. Probably owned by rich guys who were holding the land, waiting to make a profit.

Daryl didn't know if the owner of this piece of property would profit from it.

But he intended to.

Taking his time, he crossed to Alison, then crouched beside her. She tried to push herself away, but he grabbed her good leg. The other one didn't seem to be working too well, and he doubted it would cause him any trouble.

The daylight was gone now, the sky faded from ominous gray to black. Most of the stars were hidden, but the full moon hadn't yet been obscured by the dark clouds that were beginning to mass overhead. Only the sound of Alison's ragged breathing broke the stillness as he unclasped one of her open-toed sandals.

"Nice polish." He ran his fingers across her toes. "Pink suits you."

A distressed sound came from deep in her throat, and she tried to tug her foot free. He tightened his grip and continued to work the shoe off.

Once he had it unclasped, he let it drop to the ground and stroked a finger over her instep.

"Nice feet too."

He continued to play with her toes for a few minutes, enjoying her struggle and obvious distress.

Tiring of that game, he slid his hand up her leg, to the hem of her Capri pants. For an instant she stiffened. Then she redoubled her efforts to pull out of his grasp. This time using both legs.

So there was some life in the bad leg after all. Not a problem.

Grasping both her ankles, he straddled her in one quick movement and sat on the lower half of her legs. Pinning her in place. Rendering her helpless. The moonlight illuminated her face just enough for him to see her fear.

Yeah. This felt real good.

Now to ratchet up the terror a notch.

Reaching forward, he slid a finger inside the waistband of her slacks.

Once again, she reacted exactly as he'd hoped.

She writhed beneath him. Tried to buck him off. And was incapable of doing either.

"Are you liking this, Alison?" Slowly he ran his finger back and forth.

She made a sound in her throat. Like a growl.

It was too bad she looked so bloody and busted up. Otherwise, he might have been tempted to take this further. But he didn't have the stomach for gore. Never had. He'd have to content himself with tormenting her.

And that was okay. Because terrifying someone, having them completely helpless and in your power, was about the biggest rush he could imagine.

Mitch cut the siren and the light bars half a mile from Bev's apartment. Taking her by surprise would work to their advantage.

After parking a block away, he slid out of the car and waited for Cole to join him. His colleague was moving even slower now, and his face was pinched with pain.

Officer Sarah Kaufmann was waiting for them at the entrance to the parking lot, materializing out of the shadows as they approached.

"Any activity?" Mitch looked past her toward the front door of the building.

"No. Are you thinking the person who dropped the car is still in the area?"

"That's a strong possibility. She has an apartment here, and we think she might have returned to . . ."

The door of the building opened, and a woman with short black hair, carrying a shopping bag and a purse, cast a furtive glance around. Apparently reassured by the quiet parking lot, she hurried down the walk.

Heading straight for Alison's car.

"This is it." Mitch's pulse took a leap, and he pulled out his Sig Sauer as he spoke to Sarah. "Circle around behind her. And alert the rest of the officers we have a suspect."

With a nod, the woman ducked behind some cars, pulled out her radio, and disappeared into the night.

Beside him, Cole drew his gun as well.

The man wasn't in any shape to take part in this arrest. But Mitch wasn't about to tell him that.

"Let me take the lead, okay?" He hoped Cole would concede that much, at least.

"Okay."

Relieved, Mitch worked his way closer, using other cars for cover as the woman fumbled with Alison's key chain. When the automatic locks clicked open, he stood, pointed his gun at her, and chose a position that gave him a clear line of sight.

"St. Louis County Police. Drop the purse and bag and raise your hands out from your sides, palms back."

Startled by the command, the woman swung toward Mitch. He repeated the command.

She turned again, as if contemplating flight. But then Sarah stepped into view, her gun also raised. Three other officers also materialized out of the darkness.

Slowly she swiveled back to Mitch. Dropped the bag and purse. Raised her hands.

Sarah moved in and cuffed her hands behind her.

Holstering his gun, Mitch closed the distance between them in a few long strides, Cole on his heels. The other man retrieved the keys from her hand.

"You are Bev Parisi, correct?"

The woman lifted her chin and stared him down. "I'm afraid you have the wrong person."

"Is that right?" Mitch snagged her purse off the ground. Pulled out the woman's wallet. Flipped through to the driver's license. "If you're not Bev Parisi, why do you have her license?"

"Do I look like the woman in that picture?"

Mitch wasn't in the mood to play games. Leaning forward, he yanked the wig off.

She gasped as blonde hair spilled down her shoulders.

"Now you do. So tell us where Alison Taylor is."

She glared at him and clamped her lips shut.

Behind him, Mitch heard Cole pop the trunk on Alison's car. He'd done the same many times, never knowing what he'd find. A stash of dope, stolen electronic equipment . . . a body.

Holding his breath, he called over his shoulder. "Anything?"

"Not unless you count the decrepit spare I told Alison to replace six months ago." Cole slammed the trunk with more force than necessary.

As Cole circled around the car to the passenger doors, Mitch turned his attention back to Bev. Her lips were still pressed together, her stance defiant.

"Okay. Let's try one more time. Where is Alison Taylor?"

"Mitch."

At Cole's hoarse summons, Mitch motioned for Sarah to keep watch on Bev and circled the car. Cole's gaze was riveted on the front passenger seat.

As Mitch approached, he understood the man's reaction. A square piece of cardboard lay facedown on the upholstery.

And the size and shape were all too familiar.

Stomach clenching, he dug a quarter out of his pocket, inserted it under the edge of the cardboard, and flipped it over.

All the squares in the center row of the bingo card were marked off with a skull-and-crossbones stamp.

Mitch exchanged a look with Cole. "We need answers. Now."

"Agreed."

He strode back to Bev, Cole on his heels.

"She's asking for a lawyer," Sarah informed him when they rejoined the duo.

"She's going to need one."

Mitch leaned close, invading her personal space. He noticed two things immediately—the distinctive smell of her breath and her dilated pupils.

She'd been using. Very recently. Maybe even tweaking.

"Still on the meth, I see."

She lifted her chin. "I don't know what you're talking about."

"Think you could pass a drug test?"

"I want to talk to a lawyer."

"Yeah. I'll bet you do. I would too if I were in your shoes. You have quite a list of charges against you." Mitch folded his arms across his chest. "Auto theft, possession of an illegal substance, kidnapping. Not to mention murder."

Bev narrowed her eyes. "What are you talking about? I didn't kill anyone."

"No? Then what's the bingo card on the front seat all about?"

She lifted one shoulder. "It's not mine."

"Did Daryl give it to you?"

"Daryl who?"

Fighting to control his anger, Mitch took a deep breath and spoke in a cold, terse voice. "Okay, Bev. Let me give this to you straight. We know you and Daryl abducted Alison Taylor. We found your car in the parking lot at her office. Daryl's prints were inside, and a witness saw you both there. We also investigated a report of a woman screaming at an abandoned storage-unit facility. Two sets of tire tracks were identified— one of which I guarantee will match Ms. Taylor's car. A K-9 unit dog verified her presence there.

"What we don't know is where Daryl took her. And time is running out. If he kills her, you will be charged as an accessory to murder and spend the rest of your life in prison. I will personally see to that." He enunciated each word. "If, however, you tell us what you know, I will be sure the appropriate authorities are aware of your cooperation."

Once more he leaned in, his eyes inches from hers. "So here's the deal. You can tell us what you know now, and maybe we'll find Ms. Taylor in time to rescue her. Or you can wait until we take you in and book you and find you a lawyer. By then, Ms. Taylor could be dead—and I won't be able to do a thing to help you. It's your choice."

For several long seconds, Bev searched his eyes while he held his breath. He'd done everything he could do to convince her to talk, and he prayed it was enough.

As he watched, some of the light went out of the woman's face. Her posture also underwent a subtle shift, her shoulders rounding, her stance transitioning from confident to defeated.

"I guess the show's over."

Mitch didn't understand her comment, but he'd learned to read nuances. And Bev had caved.

Thank you, God.

"Do you know where Daryl took Alison?"

"No, but he promised he'd let her go. He said he just wanted to teach her a lesson."

"There was blood on the ground at the storage facility."

"Yeah." She frowned and tossed her head as a sudden gust of wind whipped her hair across her face. "See, I pretended like I was being kidnapped too. That's how Daryl got her to go with us. He said he'd kill me if she didn't. So at that warehouse place, she asked me to help her rush him and get the gun away. When she tried, Daryl hit her. What else could he do?"

Cole had let him handle the questioning so far, but now he joined in.

"How badly was she hurt?"

Transferring her attention to him, Bev inspected his bandaged arm.

"I don't know. She fell backward, and I guess she hit her head. I thought she was dead, but Daryl showed me she was breathing. He said she'd be okay."

Mitch exchanged another glance with Cole, feeling as grim as the other man looked. A head injury with loss of consciousness was bad news.

And there was no telling what Daryl had done to her since.

Fighting back a wave of panic, Mitch drew a steadying breath. "Do you have any idea where he took her?"

"No."

"Is there anyone else who might?"

She hesitated. "I don't think so."

"Whose truck was he driving?" Cole asked.

Biting her lip, she gave them an uncertain look. "I can't tell you. I'll get in big trouble if I do."

"Trust me. You'll be in bigger trouble if you don't." Mitch pinned her with the most intimidating scowl he could muster.

She studied him for a moment. Moistened her lips. Gave a sigh of capitulation. "Chuck Warren. Me and Daryl have been staying with him."

"Where does he live?"

Cole jotted down the address as she dictated it, then spoke to Sarah over her shoulder. "Have one of the guys do an NCIC search on Warren. And get his plates."

"They won't match the ones on the truck."

At Bev's comment, Mitch refocused on her. "What do you mean?"

She lifted one shoulder. "Chuck changes plates all the time. He put different ones on the truck again yesterday."

"Run them anyway," Mitch told Sarah. "Okay, Bev. Back to Daryl. Is he using meth?"

"Not at first. But he is now."

"How recently?"

"About noon, I guess. He had more with him too."

Bad news. If the guy was tweaking, he'd be even more volatile.

Leaning closer, Mitch invaded Bev's personal space again. "Before we take you to the station, I want you to think once more about anything Daryl said while you were with him that might give us a clue about where he was going."

He didn't expect her to offer anything more. Most likely Daryl hadn't revealed his destination. All he could hope was that this Chuck Warren knew something Bev didn't.

But she surprised him.

"You know . . . he did make one comment that was kind of weird." She pursed her lips, and parallel creases appeared on her brow. "I didn't understand it. He said he and Alison were going to have some beach time."

Perplexed, Mitch checked with Cole. The term meant nothing to him, referred to no slang he was aware of. Cole appeared to be equally at a loss.

"Is that all he said?" Mitch tried once more.

"Yeah."

"Okay. But if you remember anything else—anything—tell someone to get in touch with me." He made sure Sarah and the other officers heard that instruction as well. "The more you help us, the better the outcome will be for you." He motioned toward Sarah. "Mirandize her, then take her in and book her."

As Sarah approached, Bev indicated the shopping bag at her feet. "What about my stuff?"

Mitch picked it up and glanced inside. A worn teddy bear lay on top.

"My mother's locket is in there. I don't want anything to happen to it." The woman's voice caught, and her eyes grew moist. It was the first real emotion she'd shown.

"I'll see it's taken care of."

With a nod, she let Sarah lead her toward the squad car.

Tipping the bag toward Cole, Mitch shook his head as the other man looked in. "She cares about a locket and a teddy bear but helps a guy kidnap a woman and stands by while he beats her up."

Disgust contorted Cole's features. "Don't even try to figure it out."

"Yeah." Motioning to one of the officers, Mitch handed the bag over to him. "She was high as a kite too."

"I noticed."

"We need to assume Daryl is tweaking." A muscle clenched in Mitch's jaw as he exchanged glances with Cole. They both knew that was the most dangerous state of meth use. While a tweaker needed little provocation to behave aggressively, confrontation increased the chances of a violent reaction—the very outcome liable to occur if they got a lead on Daryl's location.

"I agree. Unfortunately." Cole held up the notebook with Chuck's address. "You want to pay this guy a visit?"

"Yeah. And let's get a couple of the drug guys to go with us. I think they might find it worthwhile."

As Alison stared up at the night sky from her prone position on the ground, choking back fear and revulsion, she tried not to hyperventilate. Daryl had finally risen and left her for a moment. To light up another cigarette or open another beer or think up some other torture to add to her nightmare, she assumed. She'd run if she could, but he'd sat on her legs for so long, pinning them to the ground with his weight, that she could no longer feel them.

Maybe that was why he'd left her alone. He knew she wouldn't be able to move.

Tears welled in her eyes. Never had she felt this helpless. This vulnerable. This powerless.

And she was certain that was the precise effect Daryl had been after.

He'd said as much as he'd touched her. As he watched her thrash. As he threatened her with the glowing tip of his cigarette, bringing it so close to her cheek she could feel the heat.

But he hadn't burned her. And even though he'd opened her blouse—one button at a time, sipping beer or smoking between each one, stretching it out until her nerves were taut as a bowstring—his touches hadn't escalated to anything worse.

Yet.

She knew it was only a matter of time before they did, though. When he tired of tormenting her, he'd—

Alison jerked at a sudden, cold tap on her forehead. Followed by a similar tap on her bare midriff. Then more, in rapid succession, beating a tattoo against her skin.

It was raining.

A dark shadow loomed over her, and behind the glow from his cigarette, Alison saw Daryl's face. He took a long drag and flicked the ash her direction, laughing when she recoiled.

The rain intensified.

Tossing his cigarette aside, he leaned over and yanked her upright. But she had no feeling in her legs and collapsed against him.

With a grunt, he bent and once more slung her over his shoulders. Striding back to the truck, he sat on the tailgate and swung around, leveraging himself to a standing position. After lowering her into the cage, he secured the top and tucked the canvas around himself, creating a makeshift tent.

Once settled against the side of the truck, he popped another beer tab and lifted the can in mock salute.

"Rain delay, honey. But don't worry. We're gonna finish this game. Sooner or later."

As the drops pummeled her and began to run down her face in rivulets, Alison prayed it was later. Because every minute Daryl put off finishing his game was another minute Mitch and her brothers would have to find her.

And she had a feeling they'd need every one they could get.

Trying to rein in a sneeze, Officer Jeff McIntyre retreated farther under the shelter of the dripping carport of the house where they'd been summoned to investigate a potential break-in.

The sneeze won.

"Getting a cold?" Rob Nelson tucked his radio on his belt after notifying dispatch that the break-in had been a false alarm, triggered by miscommunication between a husband and wife about whether the home alarm system had been activated.

"Allergies."

"St. Louis is the wrong place to live if you have those."

"Tell me about it." He sneezed again and peered into the torrential rain. "I'm going to wait this out for five more minutes. It can't stay this intense for very long."

"I'm with you." Rob perused the sky. He'd rather not spend the rest of his shift in wet clothes either, if he could avoid it. "You deal with anything interesting tonight yet?"

"Yeah. Julie and I responded to a weird 911 call from a biker bar."

Jeff mentioned the name, and Rob nodded. "I know the place. What was the problem?"

"Not a thing, as far as we could see. The guy told dispatch his friend was in trouble and might be hurt, then hung up when the operator tried to get a location. Communications traced the call to a public phone in the foyer. We asked around when we got there, but no one saw anything."

"Maybe it was just a prank." Rob lifted a shoulder. He might be one of the newer officers on the force, but he'd already run into plenty of those.

"That's what I thought too. But we called dispatch for a few more details, and the operator said the guy had sounded sincere. Here's another odd thing. She said he had an adult voice, but he spoke more like a child."

"He might have been drunk. The patrons ingest some high-octane stuff at that place."

"No. He was coherent. And clearly concerned. He even asked to talk to a detective named Mitch." The other man hitched up his shoulders. "But what can you do? This Erik guy was long gone by the time we arrived."

Rob frowned. "His name was Erik? And he asked to talk to Mitch?"

"Yeah. Why?"

"I had a run-in with an Erik at a convenience store not far from there. He was making calls to Cole Taylor's sister. Mitch Morgan, that new detective from the NYPD, handled it after we caught the guy."

"You think there's a connection to Cole's missing sister?"

"I think I'm not going to take a chance." He pulled his radio back off his belt. "It might be nothing, but I'm going to tell dispatch to pass on the information about the call to Morgan and Taylor and let them decide if they want to pursue it."

As Cole conferred on his cell phone with the drug unit detectives who were en route to Chuck Warren's trailer, Mitch's own phone began to vibrate.

Keeping a firm grip on the wheel with one hand as the rain slashed across his windshield and gusts of wind buffeted the car, he pulled the cell off his belt.

"Morgan."

"Detective Morgan, this is Amy Knight with dispatch. Officer Rob Nelson asked me to call you. We have a situation he thinks you might want to investigate."

Thirty seconds into her explanation, Mitch began signaling Cole to end his call. "Can you play the audio transcript for me?"

"Sure."

There were a few clicks, and Mitch listened to the replay of the 911 call. After only a few words, he recognized Erik Campbell's voice. Though Erik hadn't offered a lot of information before hanging up, it was enough to send a surge of adrenaline pumping through Mitch's veins.

"Okay, Amy. That's excellent information. Thank you."

Ending the call, he cut across two lanes of traffic.

"What's going on?" Cole gripped the dash at the sudden move.

Mitch gave Cole a rapid-fire briefing as he aimed for the exit ramp, concluding with his take on the situation. "The caller was Erik Campbell. I recognized his voice, and the location fits. The biker bar is between the convenience store where he placed his calls to Alison and the group home. He mentioned that a female friend was in trouble. That a man had her wallet. He asked for me and said I knew her. The only connection there is Alison."

"You think he's a credible source?" Cole didn't sound convinced.

Mitch topped the exit ramp and pulled off to the side of the road as the rain continued to beat against the car.

"I don't know."

"And even if he is, what could he possibly know that would help us find Alison?"

"I don't know that either."

"We could send one of our people to the home to talk to him."

"He freaked the last time the police showed up."

"A detective wouldn't be in uniform."

Mitch stared into the night, tapping a finger against the wheel. Hating that they were losing even one minute to indecision. "No, but he'd be a stranger. Erik asked for me by name. He may not talk to anyone else."

"You could call him."

"I don't think that will be as effective."

A few beats of silence passed before Cole responded.

"Talking to Chuck Warren may be more productive, and we're closer to his place."

"Yeah." Mitch wiped a hand down his face. "But the drug unit guys could do that for us if we brief them."

"Maybe not with the same . . . passion."

He couldn't argue with that. Both he and Cole had a vested interest in getting Warren to cooperate. And they wouldn't hesitate to let him know that if he balked.

Yet some instinct was pushing him toward giving Erik top priority.

"My gut tells me Erik has information we need."

A flash of lightning lit up the sky, and in that brief illumination Mitch got an unsettling glimpse of his colleague's conflicted expression. They both knew the wrong decision could be deadly, and he felt the pressure as heavily as Alison's brother.

"I don't feel a strong pull either way, but I can see you do." Cole blew out a breath. "Okay. Let's go with your gut."

With Cole behind him, Mitch put the car back into gear and pulled into traffic. "Why don't you call Dorothy Walker at the home and alert her we're on our way? If you give her some background, she can prep Erik for our arrival."

"Good idea."

After crossing the highway overpass, Mitch sped down the entrance ramp, heading back the way they'd come. At the end of the ramp, he flipped on the flashing light bars and hit the siren.

Hoping he'd made the right decision.

Because if he hadn't, they'd be wasting a lot of time.

And Alison could die.

22

Daryl readjusted the tarp around his shoulders and took a long drag on his last cigarette. A quick inventory told him he was down to his last beer too.

The game was starting to lose its luster.

And the beating rain was dampening his enthusiasm as well. It was beginning to seep through the folds in the canvas.

He picked up the stick he'd sharpened earlier and poked it through the cage again. When it encountered soft resistance, he pressed harder. Let up. Repeated that routine a few times. Sometimes he stopped there. Left Alison hanging, wondering if he was going to jab it into her flesh. Sometimes he did, with a sharp thrust and a twist.

Like this time.

A small moan followed.

Tormenting her had amused him for a while, and the dark hid any blood that might be a by-product. But he was growing tired of this diversion too.

If the weather had cooperated, he'd have found plenty of other ways to make her suffer, dragging out her torture into the wee hours of the morning. But the rain was beginning to annoy him.

A flash of lightning strobed through the sky, and he flinched. The ominous rumble of thunder that followed close on its heels added to his unease.

It was time to get this show on the road.

Flicking the stub of his cigarette over the edge of the truck, he stood, using the tarp as a cape. Another bolt of lightning slashed across the sky, this one much closer. He heard a splintering sound, and the pungent smell of sulphur assaulted his nostrils.

Yeah. It was definitely time to get out of here. Electrocution wasn't in his plans. For either of them.

Bending down beside the cage, he peered at Alison, who was huddled in one corner, her knees drawn up close to her chest. She wasn't moving much now, but the next round of lightning told him she was wide awake. Her eyes might have dulled, but they were registering his presence. Excellent. He wanted her fully conscious and aware for the ending.

"You look a little wet, honey. But that doesn't matter. You'll be even wetter soon."

Standing, he draped the canvas over the cage, tucked it in, and jumped off the back of the truck. Once the tailgate was secure, he climbed into the cab. He might be damp, but Alison was drenched. She looked like a drowned rat.

As he started the motor, he grinned at the analogy. Rat . . . social worker. One and the same, to his way of thinking. And drowning was a fitting end for vermin.

That's why it was beach time.

Dorothy Walker was waiting for them when they arrived at the group home a few minutes after ten. She opened the door as they approached and ushered them into the dimly lit foyer.

Mitch took the lead. "I'm sorry we had to disturb you at this hour, Ms. Walker. But as Cole explained, we think Erik may have information that could save Alison Taylor's life."

"I did have to wake him, but he's dressed and waiting for you in the kitchen. I gave him some milk and a cookie and tried to reassure him he wasn't in trouble, but his last encounter with the police has left him a bit gun-shy."

"I understand. We'll do our best to put him at ease. Detective Taylor is going to wait out here so Erik doesn't feel as if we're ganging up on him."

They'd discussed this on the drive over, and though Mitch knew Cole wanted to be part of the interview, he'd bowed to Mitch's logic.

She dipped her head. "Good idea. Make yourself comfortable, Detective."

Turning, she led the way through the darkened house. Mitch followed as she opened a door in the back that led to a brightly lit room. Erik sat at a large dinette table, his untouched cookie on a plate in front of him, his eyes filled with trepidation as he cast a nervous glance toward the two people who had entered.

"Here's Detective Morgan, Erik. He came all the way over here on this rainy night to talk to you."

Reaching deep for a smile, Mitch crossed the room and pulled out a chair next to the young man. "Hi, Erik. I'm sorry we had to wake you up, but from what you told the 911 operator, it sounded like you had something important to tell me."

Erik fiddled with the paper napkin next to his plate and cast a sidelong look at Mitch. "She wouldn't give me your number."

"But she told a policeman about you, and he told her to call me." Mitch tried to keep his tone conversational. "I listened to a recording of your call. You said a friend was in trouble. Was that friend Alison?"

Distress tightened the young man's features. "Yes. A mean man had her wallet. He said he was her boyfriend, but Alison told me she didn't have a boyfriend. I was afraid he might have hurt her to get the wallet. Is she okay?"

"Right now, we don't know where she is. We're trying to find her, and we're hoping you can help us do that. Where did you see this man, Erik?"

"At the quick shop. Where I used to call Alison from. I walk there every day to get a candy bar."

"Are you certain it was her wallet?"

He nodded vigorously. "Yes. When he opened it, a picture

299

fell out. The same one that fell out the day Alison dropped her wallet at the store. She was in it, and everybody was wearing pointy hats, like it was a birthday or something."

Mitch's heart skipped a beat. He'd seen the same picture. Cole had a copy in his wallet too. It was the one his colleague had shown him the day he'd asked him to take Alison to the family wedding.

Their first date.

He cleared the sudden tightness from his throat. "What did he look like, Erik?"

The young man scrunched up his face. "He was skinny. And he was wearing a cowboy hat."

The guy from Alison's parking lot.

"Did you see what he bought?"

"Yeah. Some cigarettes and a sandwich and beer."

Alcohol and meth. Dangerous combination.

"What about his car. Did you notice that?"

"Uh-huh. It was a black pickup truck. There was some big square thing in the back, covered with a sheet or something."

Mitch had no doubt the man Erik had encountered was Daryl Barnes. He was equally certain Alison had been inside that big square thing in the back of the truck.

But none of the information Erik had passed on would help them locate her.

This may have been a fruitless trip after all.

His spirits nose-diving, he folded his hands on the table, frowning at the slight tremor in his fingers. That was an anomaly. He was always steady under pressure. "Erik, did the man say anything at all that gave you an idea about where he might be going?"

The young man across from him slowly shook his head. Then he reached into his pocket and withdrew a small, crumpled piece of paper. "No. But before he drove out of the gas station, I copied this down." He held out the sheet.

Curious, Mitch took it. Scanned the letters and numbers. Blinked. Sucked in a sharp breath as his pulse took a leap.

"Sometimes on TV shows people copy down license numbers," Erik added. "I thought it might be important."

Casting a quick glance at Dorothy Walker, Mitch rose. "It's very important, Erik. It may be the thing that helps us find Alison. And we're going to go look for her right now. Thank you, Ms. Walker." He started toward the door.

"Will you let me know as soon as you find her, please?"

At the question from Erik, Mitch paused on the threshold and turned. "It could be very late." He cast a glance at Dorothy Walker. She gave a slight nod. "But I promise, you'll be the first to know."

And as he rejoined Cole in the foyer and prepared to call in another BOLO alert, Mitch prayed he'd be disrupting Erik's sleep again in the very near future.

As Daryl wound along the dark, narrow road, he shut off his windshield wipers. The wind was still gusty, but the rain had stopped. That was a plus.

But there was bad news too.

He was getting nervous. The plan that had seemed so perfect in theory was freaking him out in reality.

He needed some more meth. For courage—and confidence.

When he drew close to his destination, he flipped off the headlights and eased back on the accelerator. There were a few houses tucked into the trees, and he didn't want to alert anyone to his presence. At ten thirty, he hoped most people were in bed—or tuned into a late-night talk show. And there should be minimal traffic on this dead-end road.

Approaching the gravel turnoff that paralleled the railroad tracks, he slowed even more. The wind should mask the crunch of his tires, but no sense taking chances. He was in no hurry at this point.

As Bev would say, they were in the final scene of the final act.

His fingers tensed on the wheel as he drove to the end of the turnoff, well out of sight of any nearby houses. He couldn't see very far ahead in the pitch darkness, but he knew what lay ahead of him.

A long railroad bridge that spanned the Meramec River.

Beads of moisture formed on his upper lip, and he backhanded them away. He hadn't been here in years, and his last visit had been painful. His friends had known he'd never liked playing chicken. So one day, they'd brought him here. Frankie, the leader, had told him it was a test. Had dared him to walk to the middle of the bridge and wait for a train. And when it approached, Frankie hadn't wanted him to run, as usual. He'd wanted him to lay on the narrow walkway that extended on each side of the tracks and wait high over the river as the train rumbled by, inches away.

A trickle of sweat inched down Daryl's back. He remembered staring at the long trestle—and the long drop to the water—and imagining the train thundering by. Recalled the goading faces of his friends as they'd urged him on. Tasted again the terror that had left his legs wobbly.

Most of all, he remembered the ridicule that had followed after he'd refused not only to take the test but even to set foot on the menacing bridge.

It had been one more dismal failure in a series of failures stretching back to his childhood.

Well, he wasn't going to fail tonight. He was going to walk right out to the center of that bridge. Face his dragon and triumph over it. Vanquish his old fears forever.

And in the process, he was going to get rid of the woman whose meddling had robbed him of his future.

He fumbled for the meth he'd stashed under his seat and pulled out the small jar. Withdrew a dollar bill from his pocket. Shook out a line.

Less than half a minute later, he snorted it and settled back in his seat to enjoy the brief rush.

And then, bolstered by his courage-in-a-jar, he'd raise the curtain on the finale.

As Mitch hung up after doing his best to expedite the BOLO alert on Daryl's truck, Cole ended his call with one of the drug unit detectives who'd paid Chuck Warren a visit.

"What did they get?" Mitch tucked his phone back on his belt as they sat in his car outside the group home.

"Enough meth paraphernalia to book the guy. They think he's cooking and has a steady clientele. He's not admitting anything on that score yet, but he did acknowledge that Barnes has his truck. However, he claims he doesn't know anything about the kidnapping. Nor where Daryl went. He was also high. Surprise, surprise."

Sarcasm dripped from Cole's voice. But a tremor also ran through it. Telling Mitch the other man was beginning to succumb to both stress and pain.

"You want to check and see if Sarge has any news from the CSU folks?"

"Sure." Cole weighed his phone in his hand. "They should have Warren in Clayton within half an hour. You want to pay him a visit? See if we can dig a little deeper?"

"Yeah. I guess."

They didn't have anything else to do, since there were no other leads to follow up on. Taking a deep breath, he started the engine and put the car in gear.

"You know, you made a smart call about where to focus our energies. This visit to Erik paid off big-time."

Mitch blew off Cole's praise with a dismissive gesture as he pulled into traffic. "Not unless someone spots the license plate. Right now, we're no closer than we were before to finding Alison."

"Yes, we are. Every law enforcement officer in a fifty-mile radius will be looking for that plate. Unless he's left the area, which I doubt, someone's going to spot it."

That was true. Mitch knew the truck would turn up eventually.

The real question was, would it be in time?

Denver Jackson punched the remote, silencing the late-night talk show on TV and plunging the living room into darkness. None of these new guys could hold a candle to Johnny Carson. Now *there* was a talk-show host. He'd been funny too. That Carnac the Magnificent mind-reading routine had always left him in stitches. Laughs like that were hard to come by these days.

Yawning, he heaved himself out of the armchair, cursing the arthritis that stiffened his knees whenever he sat too long. But his evening glass of wine would ease the discomfort and help him sleep. It always did.

After hobbling to the kitchen, he uncorked the bottle of red wine on the counter and poured four ounces. He knew precisely how much that was, because he'd measured it last year and put a mark on the side of the wine glass. It was too easy to succumb to the lure of alcohol when you were hurting and alone, especially late at night.

With a sigh, he walked over to the window that overlooked the river. How he missed Margie. But she was in a better place now, just like Reverend Sheldon had said at the funeral two years ago. It had almost been a blessing when God had called her home. For both of them. Watching the cancer eat her away to nothing, helpless to alleviate her pain, he'd ended up with an ulcer himself as his stomach twisted into knots day after day.

Sipping his wine, he did his best to block out thoughts from that sad time. Giving in to melancholy wouldn't change the past. The key to happiness was counting your blessings in the present, and he had a lot of them. A house that was his, free and clear. A steady pension from his railroad job. Decent health, good enough to live on his own at seventy-nine. A nice river close by where he could spend his days fishing when he wasn't volunteering at the World Bird Sanctuary down the road.

All in all, he couldn't complain. A lot of folks had it much tougher.

Denver did a circuit of the house, checking all the locks as he finished off his wine. He liked this secluded spot. It was woodsy and felt remote, but it wasn't too far removed from civilization. You had to be careful, though. The news was full of stories of addicts who would slit your throat for ten bucks to feed a drug habit, and thieves out to make a fast buck from stolen merchandise. That's why he had double locks on some doors and a first-class security system, even if he didn't have much worth stealing.

Pausing by the back door, he checked the sky. Looked like the rain had finally stopped. It sure had been a gully-washer tonight. River would be running high. But at least the storm might have broken the heat wave.

He opened the back door and exited onto the screened-in deck. Yep. It was a lot cooler now. Low seventies, maybe. Almost cool enough to turn off the air-conditioning. Except tomorrow could be ninety again. That was St. Louis for you.

If he could take the heat, he'd do without air-conditioning and open the windows to let in the peaceful sounds of the night. A gentle breeze rustling the leaves, the call of an owl, the croak of a frog, the . . .

A sudden loud squeaking noise closer to the river intruded on the stillness, jolting him. It sounded like the door of a car opening.

Odd. There weren't any houses down there.

He peered toward the river, but with all the trees and bushes leafed out, it was tough to see very far. Especially at night. It got pretty dark out in this neck of the woods, away from city lights.

Denver waited a couple of minutes. He didn't hear any more noise, but someone was over by the railroad tracks. And whoever it was didn't belong there.

It could be a couple of kids necking, like the time he'd called the police a few months ago, after he'd heard suspicious noises in the same area. The two teens had sure been surprised—and embarrassed—when the cops showed up.

But that had been a nice night. Balmy. Full moon. Romantic, he supposed, if you were young and feisty. Kids looking for fun and games wouldn't show up on the heels of a raging storm, with thunder rumbling in the background and the threat of another downpour hovering in the moisture-laden air.

No. Whoever was down there was up to no good.

He reentered the house, set his wine glass on the counter, and grabbed the binoculars he used for his bird work. Then he began the slow ascent of the steps that led to the second floor, grateful his knees were cooperating now. He could see part of that gravel road from his bedroom. It might be worth a look.

Three minutes later, wedged into a corner of his room, he aimed the binoculars sideways out his window and focused on the dead-end gravel lane that paralleled the railroad tracks. Trees obscured most of the view, but he could see a dark pickup truck. There was a big, covered box of some kind in the bed. A person stood by the driver's-side door, upending a can against his lips.

Beer, Denver assumed. Nobody drove out to an isolated place like that to stand around and drink Coke. Alone.

The alone part bothered him. It didn't feel right.

When the moon suddenly peeked out of the clouds, Denver focused in on the bottom of the tailgate, where the license was. The binoculars had excellent magnification, but the truck was a couple hundred yards away and his eyes weren't as sharp as they'd once been. Nevertheless, he managed to make out a letter and two numbers before another cloud snuffed out the moonlight.

The person by the truck was still drinking his beer. And pacing. Looking jittery and nervous. Like he was waiting for someone. Or something.

All of which added up to trouble.

Setting the binoculars on his nightstand, Denver picked up his portable phone. This might turn out to be a bust, but as a police buddy of his had once told him, a lot of their tips came from observant citizens who weren't afraid to get involved.

And as he'd also pointed out, it was better to be safe than sorry.

As Mitch moved into the right lane of I-270, heading for I-64 east, his BlackBerry began to vibrate. He took one hand off the wheel and pulled it from his belt, glancing at Cole in the seat beside him. They'd spoken little since leaving Erik's house twenty minutes ago. There hadn't been much to say.

"Morgan."

"It's Paul. We may have a break."

A shot of adrenaline ratcheted up his pulse. "Tell me."

"A guy on a dead-end spur off Lewis Road spotted suspicious activity and called 911. A dark pickup pulled down a gravel lane next to some railroad tracks near his house. There's a large, covered square object in the back. The caller got part of the license number, and the 911 operator checked it against the BOLO alert for Chuck Warren's truck. It looks like we may have a match."

As he listened to his boss, Mitch maneuvered out of the eastbound I-64 lane. It would be easier to reverse directions if he took the next exit.

"What's up?" Cole's terse voice broke the silence in the car as he straightened up.

"Hold on a second, Sarge. Cole's still with me. I'm going to brief him and put you on speaker." As he removed the phone from his ear, he brought Cole up to speed.

"He sounds like our guy."

"I agree." Mitch hit the speaker button. "Sarge, you're on. We need to get a helicopter in the air and paramedics standing by."

"We also need a couple of snipers from the SWAT team on-site," Cole added, his tone grim.

"All three are already in the works. How fast can you get there?"

Mitch pressed harder on the accelerator and flipped on the lights and siren. "Fifteen minutes." If he floored it all the way. As he intended to.

"We've got some patrol cars ten minutes away. I'm going to have them get in as close as they can on foot without alerting the subject. If he's our man, he's likely volatile. I'd rather have all our ducks in a row before we move. Unless he forces our hand."

"Agreed. Give me some directions from Lewis Road."

"Just follow it to Deicke. Stay straight ahead when Lewis curves right. The guy's parked by the Meramec River, next to the Times Beach railroad trestle."

Beach time.

As the words echoed in Mitch's mind, he looked at Cole— and saw his own thoughts reflected on the other man's face.

The beach time reference now made sense. And they both wished it didn't.

Because when you put together a railroad trestle, a river, and a tweaking meth addict bent on vengeance, it was a recipe for tragedy.

23

Daryl took a final swallow of his beer. Tossed the can to the gravel. Crushed it under his foot.

It was time.

And he felt ready.

Pumped.

Powerful.

Poised for victory.

Tonight, he'd play the game of chicken and win.

Bending, he grabbed the crushed can and sailed it into the woods that ran in a steep slope down to the river. Then he lowered the tailgate, swung into the bed of the truck, and whipped the canvas off the cage in the back. Jiggling the change in his pockets, he grinned at Alison.

"It's beach time, honey. Ready to go for a swim?"

As Alison stared up at the man looming over her, his face moved in and out of focus. After the bouncing ride in the back of the truck, her head was pounding and she felt nauseous again. It was hard to think. But the word *swim* set off a new wave of panic, and the rush of adrenaline helped clear her mind.

With her hands cuffed and her left leg of little use after hours in the cramped cage, an encounter with water would be deadly.

Daryl was fiddling with the top of the cage, and a moment

later he swung it open. Leaning down, he grasped her under her arms and pulled her to a standing position.

Once more the world tilted and she listed to one side as her unbuttoned blouse gapped open.

He grabbed her shoulders. "A little unsteady, are we? I guess that means I'll just have to keep a tight grip on you." He squeezed until his fingers bit into her upper arms, waiting until she winced before he released her. Then he bent and hefted her over his shoulder again.

The blood rushed to her head, setting off an explosion of pain, and she moaned low in her throat.

Moving to the back of the truck, he set her on the edge of the tailgate, her legs dangling over the side as he jumped to the ground and positioned himself in front of her.

"My, my, such immodesty." He reached over and stroked a finger along her collarbone. Dipped lower. When she shrank back, he chuckled. "Don't like that? Well, I do. Guess you'll just have to get used to it. Or not." He chuckled again.

As his fingers continued their unhurried exploration, Alison tried to shut him out, tried to ignore his repugnant touch. She made herself stay absolutely still, refusing to give him the satisfaction of any further reaction. Instead, she focused on her surroundings. They were on a gravel drive. Beside them was a railroad track. Ahead of her, a few hundred feet away, was a small road. In the distance, she could see faint lights through the trees on the hills. Houses? Close enough to help her if she could draw attention to her plight?

At Daryl's sudden, painful squeeze, she swallowed a gasp. Then he drew his hand back and began to button her blouse.

"Let me help you with this, Alison. After all, you'll want to look presentable when you meet your maker."

An icy chill swept over her.

Please, Lord, not yet! I need more time to think of a way out. And Mitch and Cole need more time to find me. Please! Help me!

"There. Much better." After adjusting her blouse, he inspected her. It was too dark to see his features, but she could

310

sense his growing excitement, feel a burgeoning anticipatory energy. He was like an athlete preparing for a sprint to the finish line, his goal in sight.

Pulling her off the tailgate, he kept a grip on her arms until she was steady. Her leg was stiff and cramping, but it was holding her weight now. In another couple of minutes it might be strong enough for her to run.

But Daryl didn't wait for that to happen. Taking her arm, he started walking toward the railroad tracks. As he stepped onto them, pulling her after him, the moon suddenly peeked through the clouds and bathed the world in silver light.

And Alison stopped breathing.

Stretching ahead was a railroad trestle high above a river. *No!*

Reacting on instinct, she pulled back and tried to jerk away.

Her sudden resistance must have taken him off guard, because he loosened his hold long enough for her to give him a hard kick with her uninjured leg and take off as fast as she could toward the road—and the lights beyond. Desperately praying a car would appear.

She heard the muttered oath behind her, and less than fifteen feet into her frantic dash, her arm was taken in a fierce grip. He yanked it, jerking her back against his chest, and his putrid breath warmed her temple as a cold metal cylinder jabbed into her neck.

"Not a smart move, Alison. Maybe I'll just finish you off right here." He pressed the gun harder, and she closed her eyes.

For several eternal seconds, he remained unmoving. But at last he eased off on the pressure.

"No. I think I'll stick with the original plan. It's more dramatic—and much less messy. Come on." Turning, he propelled her back toward the tracks.

She tried to slow him down by limping, stumbling, dragging her feet. But he kept pulling her forward. Onto the tracks. Out toward the river. Leading her to her death.

And short of a miracle, Alison knew her time had run out.

311

As Mitch barreled down Lewis Road, his flashers and siren now off, his cell phone began to vibrate. He yanked it off his belt and tossed it to Cole. "Put it on speaker."

Cole complied.

"Morgan," he barked.

"Detective Morgan, this is Officer Hunter." The urgency in the man's voice came through loud and clear, even though he was speaking softly. "Two of us just arrived at the scene on foot and we have a problem. The suspect is on the railroad tracks, heading out onto the trestle. He has a woman with him, who's resisting. He appears to be armed."

For the second time that day, Mitch uttered a word he rarely used and pressed harder on the accelerator. They weren't ready for this confrontation.

"Okay. Move in and alert him to your presence. We'll be there in less than two minutes."

He hit the flashers and siren again as Cole punched in Paul's number and gave their boss a status report in two sentences before issuing clipped instructions.

"Send in the helicopter. Tell the pilot we need a spotlight on the guy. What's the status of the SWAT snipers?" There was silence for a few seconds. "Okay." Cole ended the call and briefed Mitch. "The helicopter's three minutes away. One of our snipers lives in this area and will be here in five. The other won't arrive for fifteen. He's going to find a position on the far side of the bridge. More patrol cars have been diverted here and to the other side."

"If this guy freaks, it's over." Mitch's voice rasped on the last word.

"I know. We're going to have to try and talk him out of this."

Mitch didn't respond. They both knew that was a long shot.

As he veered onto Diecke and raced down the narrow road, he saw flashing lights in his rearview mirror. Reinforcements were on the way. But numbers didn't matter. The meth addict on the tracks held all the cards.

Namely, Alison.

The railroad tracks appeared ahead, and Mitch swung into the gravel drive that ran beside them. His headlights illuminated the pickup truck—and two figures partway out on the trestle, over the water.

His heart stuttered.

Daryl had a death grip on Alison, and he was jerking from side to side, using her as a shield. Her hands were bound behind her back, she was gagged, and one side of her face was bruised.

But she was alive.

So far.

And Mitch intended to do everything in his power to keep it that way.

As they exited the car, crouching beside it for cover, an officer joined them from behind the truck.

"He knows we're here. But he keeps moving farther out and we can't get a shot without risking hitting the woman."

The patrol car that had followed him down Diecke pulled in, spewing gravel. Still crouching, Mitch ran toward the car as the whump, whump, whump of rotor blades grew louder. Cole followed.

"Open a communications line to the helicopter," he instructed the patrol officer.

An unmarked vehicle swung in. Fast. A man got out, carrying a sniper rifle.

"That's Alan. One of our SWAT team snipers." Cole waved the man over.

As soon as he was within hearing distance, Mitch spoke. "Can you get a line of sight on him?"

The man studied the scene, narrowing his eyes as he peered at the two people on the bridge, faintly illuminated by Mitch's headlights. "The way he's twitching and twisting back and forth, it could be dicey."

All of a sudden, a spotlight pinned the two figures in a

megawatt glare. Mitch issued one clipped instruction to the sniper as he grabbed the PA mike in the patrol car. "Do the best you can. If he doesn't let her go, and you get a shot, take it."

With a curt nod, the sniper melted into the night as Mitch flipped on the PA system.

"This is Detective Mitch Morgan." He said that more for Alison's benefit than her kidnapper's. He wanted her to know he was close by. "We have people on both sides of the river, Daryl. There's no way off that bridge. Don't add murder to your list of charges. Just drop your weapon and let Alison walk away." It was a struggle to maintain a calm, neutral tone when his pulse was edging into the danger zone. "Things will go a lot easier for you if you do. No one will hurt you, and—"

The distant whistle of a train sounded in the night air, cutting off his air supply midsentence.

No!

Panic clawed at his gut, and he struggled to fill his lungs.

"Get me some binoculars. Now! And someone see if we can make contact with that train."

Fifteen seconds later, the patrol officer thrust a pair of binoculars into his hands and grabbed his radio to call dispatch.

Mitch fitted the binoculars to his eyes and scrutinized the trestle, trying to ignore Alison's battered face and fear-filled eyes. He focused instead on the three-foot-wide walkway on either side of the tracks.

"Is there room to stand there while a train goes by?" Cole's question came out tight and tense from behind him.

"Yes. If you have nerves of steel."

They both knew a guy who'd been tweaking didn't.

Mitch thrust the mike into his colleague's hand. "Keep trying to talk him into giving up."

"Where are you going?"

"Down there." He gestured to the base of the wooded hill, on the far side of the trestle. "If Alison goes over the edge, instruct the helicopter to follow her with the spotlight. And tell them not to lose her!"

Without waiting for a response, Mitch crouched and sprinted across the tracks. At the edge of the woods, he charged down the hill and through the underbrush. Toward the rain-swollen river.

Praying he wouldn't have to put his SEAL training into practice.

His perfect plan had failed.

As Daryl clutched Alison in front of him, changing position constantly so none of the cops could get a shot at him, the whistle sounded again. Louder this time.

He tried to breathe. Tried to rein in his fear. But it was hard not to panic. He was well out onto the trestle. The river was far below. A train was approaching. And cops had guns trained on him. Waiting to kill him. Or send him back to prison.

Neither option was acceptable.

A faint vibration in the rails told him the train was getting close.

He had to make a decision.

Now.

Keeping a tight grip on Alison, he eased to the edge of the platform and looked over.

His stomach lurched.

The river was a long way down.

But it was his only chance of escape. Under cover of darkness, he might be able to ride the current downstream, swim ashore, and slip away.

It was a long shot, though, and the odds had never worked in his favor. But what choice did he have?

The vibration in the trestle intensified.

Daryl tightened his grip on Alison and tucked the gun against her rib cage. She stiffened. Perfect. He needed her close and upright for another few seconds. She was his cover.

But just before he hit the water, he'd do what he came to do.

Finish her off.

And he wouldn't even have to see the blood. The river would wash it away.

"Time for a swim, honey." His heart began to thump, and he took a deep breath.

She tried to twist away, but he jerked her closer.

Then he stepped to the edge.

He was going to jump.

Mitch couldn't see what was happening above him, but he could hear Cole's voice over the PA. His colleague's urgent tone clearly communicated the desperate situation.

"Don't try it, Daryl. It's too far down. Just walk over here, and you'll be safe."

As the train whistle blew again, Mitch stripped off his gun and phone and kicked free of his shoes, his gaze never leaving the arc of light spilling over the bridge. With each passing second, the rumble in the trestle grew louder, echoing in his ears as he stood poised at the edge of the river, every nerve vibrating, every muscle taut.

It was possible Daryl would try to wait out the passing train on the edge of the trestle, but he doubted he'd be able to hold on. Not in his hyper state. And Daryl probably knew that too. Chances were he'd ditch and take his human shield with him—all the way down.

As the silence following Cole's plea lengthened, Mitch called out, loud enough to be heard on the trestle. "Take a deep breath, Alison."

In the next instant, two bodies plummeted toward the river on the other side of the bridge, upstream.

A heartbeat later, he was in the water, moving toward the center of the river as fast as the current allowed.

Swimming as he'd never swum before.

As Alison fell, the only thing that kept total panic at bay was the knowledge that Mitch was waiting for her. His voice had come from below, by the river.

And her fate couldn't be in better hands.

If a Navy SEAL couldn't save her, no one could.

So she did what he'd said to do. She took a deep breath. She also kicked out at Daryl. His grip had loosened as he'd pulled her over the edge, and the gun was no longer pressed against her side.

She heard a shot. But she had no time to focus on that. Because as she hit the water, a blunt shock wave ricocheted through her, so intense she almost sucked in a fatal mouthful of water.

At least the force of hitting the water had broken Daryl's hold on her.

But with her arms tied behind her, she couldn't use them to push herself back to the surface. And her bad leg wouldn't be much help either.

Her plunge into the depths of the river seemed to go on forever, but when at last it slowed, she kicked as hard as she could, trying her best to propel herself upward.

The powerful current worked against her, however, foiling her efforts to make any headway.

Though she had excellent breath control and had been a strong swimmer before the accident, Alison knew the situation would have been desperate even if she was in top form.

In her present condition, it was deadly.

She held her breath as long as she could. Kicking. Metering out tiny puffs of air. Praying she'd suddenly feel Mitch's strong arms pulling her to the surface. To safety.

But as the seconds ticked by and her lungs began to deflate, she knew time was running out.

In less than a dozen heartbeats, her life would be over.

With the swift, relentless current tugging him downstream, Mitch surfaced to find himself mere yards from the spotlighted section of river.

Alison must be close.

But a quick sweep revealed only a piece of driftwood floating under the glare.

Arms slicing through the water, Mitch propelled himself toward the center of the light, then treaded water, letting the current carry him downstream. If Alison was below the surface, the river would be carrying her along at the same pace.

All at once, a head bobbed up six feet upstream.

The wrong one.

Daryl flailed when their gazes met, his eyes widening in panic.

But Mitch had no interest in the man at the moment. His total focus was on finding Alison.

Since the two had fallen into the river at the same spot, Mitch assumed she was nearby and trying her best to reach the surface. But as she'd told him a few weeks ago, she hadn't been able to keep her swimming skills in top form, thanks to the accident. And with bound arms and a bad leg, the odds were stacked against her.

Time was also running out. Fast. Even if she'd been able to take a deep breath, even if she had strong lungs, she had to be reaching the end of her air supply.

Mitch scanned the river again. Despite the spotlight, visibility in the murky water would be close to zero. Searching below the surface would have to be done by feel rather than sight. The chances for success weren't just small. They were miniscule.

But he had no choice. That was his only hope.

Filling his lungs with air, he sent two words heavenward: *Guide me!*

Then he dove.

Daryl watched the other man disappear under the water and struck out as fast as he could downriver, fear driving him forward. If the guy was aiming for his legs, he wasn't going to make it easy for him.

Arms splashing in the current, he pushed himself as hard as he could. It had been years since he'd gone swimming, but the skill came back to him, like riding a bicycle. He'd been a strong swimmer, once upon a time. His gym teacher in high school had even approached him on several occasions about trying out for the swim team.

He might have, if he hadn't decided to drop out.

Casting a look behind him, he saw nothing but empty river. Best of all, he'd floated out of the range of that spotlight now too. The cops must be more interested in finding the social worker than nabbing him.

Good luck on that. She was probably already fish bait, and—

His hand connected with a solid surface, and he lifted his head. It was dark here, but he seemed to have met up with a dead tree bobbing along in the water. Convenient. He could cling to it for a few minutes, get his breath.

Grabbing hold of the stump of a branch, he smiled. Maybe his luck was about to change, after all. If he could float along for a mile or two, he'd—

All at once, the tree swept sideways, across the current, then jolted to a stop as if one end had gotten wedged against something and was stuck. Daryl let go of the branch and kicked away from it, but the current was stronger now, the rushing water funneling along the edge of the obstacle in its path. It sucked him in and slammed him against the solid wood, knocking the breath from his lungs.

Gasping, he found himself being propelled along next to the trunk, toward the center of the river.

Okay. No problem. Once this vortex of rushing water pushed him back into the main channel, he'd be able to drift along again. He'd be fine. In another few seconds he'd be clear and—

Something grabbed his ankles and held fast.

The rest of his body kept moving.

Suddenly Daryl found himself facedown in the water, his legs locked in place, as the relentless water swept over yet another obstacle.

His body.

Panic clawed at him, but he tried to think past it. His legs must have gotten tangled up in some branches. Yeah. That had to be it. Maybe he could kick himself free.

He tried. Frantically. But the tree refused to relinquish its grip.

Summoning up all his strength, he attempted to reach back and use his hands to free himself. Except the current kept pulling his upper body forward. Away from his ankles. And the resistance was too strong to overcome.

His lungs began to burn.

He clutched at the trunk, trying to raise his head above the rushing water so he could suck in some air.

But the smooth, slippery surface offered no handholds.

With desperation providing one final spurt of adrenaline, he made one last attempt to fight the current and reach back for his ankles.

Failed.

The water closed over him, dragging him down. And as he succumbed to the dark abyss, one final thought echoed in his mind.

He'd just played his last game of chicken.

And lost.

24

Six seconds after diving beneath the murky water, Mitch's fingers made contact with a leg.

Yes!

Working his way up Alison's body, he slid his arms under hers, pulled her close, and propelled both of them to the surface with several powerful kicks.

She came without offering any resistance—or assistance.

Meaning she was unconscious.

But assuming she hadn't blacked out on impact . . . assuming she'd held her breath as long as possible . . . assuming her airway was still sealed from the reflexive laryngospasm that always kicked in for drowning victims . . . she'd make it.

He wasn't even going to think about the possibility that some of his assumptions could be wrong.

As they surfaced, her head lolled to one side, her cheek against his chest. Keeping her face above water, he eased her onto her back, locked his arm under her chin, and began towing her toward the bank, using the combat sidestroke he'd mastered in SEAL training. The spotlight followed them as he fought the current, swimming as fast as he could. Every second counted if she'd stopped breathing.

When he hit bottom, he slipped his arms under her knees and shoulders, then struggled to his feet in the swirling water.

Cradling her against his chest, he waded to shore and scrambled up a few large, slippery rocks to a level area. As he laid her on the ground, he gave her a swift sweep while he dug out the pocketknife he'd carried since his Boy Scout days. The spotlight from the helicopter wasn't as effective here, thanks to the dense woods. But enough illumination got through for him to conclude she'd been through hell—even before she'd plunged into the water.

As his unsteady fingers eased the blade of the knife under the sodden cloth around her mouth and he disposed of the gag, he did his best to ignore her multiple abrasions. None of that would matter if she wasn't breathing.

And a quick check told him she wasn't.

On the plus side, the pulse in her carotid artery was steady, if weak, under his fingertips.

The paramedics would be on their way, but the dense woods would slow their progress down to the river from where the road dead-ended.

It was up to him to convince Alison's lungs to reengage.

Mitch hadn't had to use much of his water-based rescue training for several years, but the knowledge was ingrained, allowing him to switch to autopilot.

Tilting her head back, he pinched her nose, took a deep breath, and covered her mouth with his. Then he blew. Long and hard. Praying she'd ingested most of the water into her stomach rather than her lungs. Laryngospasm should have constricted her throat and sealed her air tube. Only after she'd been unconscious for a while would the muscles relax and allow water into her lungs.

He hoped there hadn't been time for that.

Removing his mouth from hers, he waited five seconds.

Breathe, Alison! Breathe!

Nothing.

Once more he covered her mouth with his, trying not to panic. Trying to remain optimistic. In such a high-stress situation, she'd have been hyperventilating. That would have flushed carbon dioxide out of her blood and suppressed her breathing reflex, buying her some time before nature kicked in and forced her to take a breath. Though it wasn't recommended, some of his SEAL buddies had hyperventilated on purpose before drown-proofing exercises so they could hold their breath longer.

Mitch backed off again, waiting for Alison's chest to rise on its own.

It didn't.

Leaning down, he tried again, a desperate plea echoing in his heart.

God, please let her live!

He backed off. Waited.

Still nothing.

Just as he prepared to repeat the procedure, he heard a small, sharp intake of breath. Then her chest rose, her eyes flickered open, and she began to cough.

It was the most beautiful sound he'd ever heard.

"You're okay, Alison. You're okay." Hardly recognizing the shaky voice as his own, he rolled her onto her side. Fingers trembling, he inserted the blade of the pocketknife under the rope that bound her wrists and cut through it with a gentle, careful sawing motion.

She coughed up some water, and he stroked her back, murmuring encouraging words. Trying to reassure her. And himself.

In the distance, he could hear thrashing in the underbrush. Help was getting closer.

Alison continued to cough and regurgitate water. She also began to shake. Badly.

So did he.

When her coughing subsided, she gasped for air and groped for his hand, clinging to it as if she never wanted to let go.

And that was fine with him. He didn't want her to.

As the voices of the approaching paramedics drifted through the woods, she looked up at him. "Thank you."

Her teeth were chattering, and the words came out raspy. Wobbly. Barely there. But the emotion in her eyes was strong. Solid. And far deeper than mere gratitude.

It was the same emotion that filled his heart.

Leaning close, he pressed a kiss to her forehead and stroked her temple.

"Stay with me?" Her question whispered against his neck.

"Count on it."

And as the paramedics pushed through the brush with Cole on their heels, Mitch vowed to keep that promise.

For a lot longer than just tonight.

Two hours later, as Mitch paced in the ER waiting room and Cole nursed his third cup of coffee, the outside door whooshed open to admit Jake, a duffel bag slung over his shoulder.

Scanning the otherwise empty room, he was beside them in a few long strides. "Any news since I called from the airport?"

Mitch doubted Cole was up to an interrogation. But he waited, giving the other man a chance to respond. When he didn't, Mitch spoke.

"She's stable, but we haven't seen her for a while. We came out here after they took her to X-ray. The doctor hasn't given us a prognosis yet."

A frown darkened Jake's stubbled face and his jaw hardened. No telling when he'd last slept. Given the smudges under his eyes, Mitch assumed it had been awhile.

"Why not?"

"They've been running tests. They're still—"

The door from the treatment area opened, and a forty-something man in scrubs appeared. "Are you with Alison Taylor?"

"Yes." Mitch answered in unison with her brothers.

Cole vaulted to his feet. Swayed. Mitch grabbed his good arm as Jake eyed the white dressing and sling on the other, his frown deepening. "What happened to you?"

"Long story." Cole took a deep breath and straightened up, extricating his arm.

The man approached them and extended his hand. "I'm

Dr. Matthews. Let's sit for a minute. It's been a long night."
He sized up the three of them. "For all of us, I assume." He
gestured toward a grouping of chairs off to one side, and they
followed him over.

Once seated, the doctor didn't keep them in suspense.

"Ms. Taylor is a very lucky young woman, considering all
the trauma she's experienced in the past few hours. In addition to assorted cuts and bruises, she's suffering from a slight
concussion. Despite her near drowning, however, there's no
water in her lungs. That's positive news. I understand one of
you is to be commended for an exceptional water rescue and
some first-class artificial respiration."

Mitch felt heat creep up his neck as Alison's brothers looked
at him.

"He was a Navy SEAL," Cole offered.

"You were the right man to have on hand, then." The doctor acknowledged him with a nod. "We'll keep her overnight
for observation, but barring some unforeseen complication, I
expect we'll release her tomorrow morning."

"What about the leg she injured in the accident last year?"
Cole spoke up.

"We've talked with her surgeon and done some additional
X-rays. He'll check them out, but I see nothing to suggest this
experience has further damaged that leg nor undermined her
recovery. She does have small puncture wounds on that leg,
and eight or nine others in the trunk area, but none required
stitching."

Mitch exchanged a look with Cole. One of the patrol officers
had called their attention to the stick with the bloody point in
the back of the pickup truck before they'd left for the hospital.

Now they knew how it had been used.

"Was she sexually assaulted, Doctor?"

The grim question from Jake jolted Mitch back to the present, and he braced himself. It was the same question that had
ripped at his gut since he'd learned of her abduction. And one
he would have asked if her brothers hadn't.

"No."

He closed his eyes. Exhaled.

Thank you, God.

"She's on her way back from X-ray now. Would you like to come back to the treatment room?"

"Yes." Mitch answered for all of them.

The doctor rose, and they fell in behind him. Mitch thought about letting her brothers take the lead. They were family, after all.

But in the end, he claimed the prime spot. Because while he might not be family yet, if all went as he hoped, there was a very strong possibility he would have his own family ties to the Taylor clan in the not-too-distant future.

As the murmur of voices penetrated Alison's sleep-fogged brain, she tried to rouse herself. She hadn't planned to doze off, but lethargy had overcome her mind and limbs as they'd wheeled her back from X-ray, and she'd faded into oblivion. They must be giving her some heavy-duty pain meds through her IV.

"She's really pale." Cole's comment.

"Her body has been through a lot. She'll regain her color soon." She recognized the doctor's voice.

"Is there any damage to her eye?" That question came from Jake. So he was back from his mission. Because of her?

"No."

All at once, she felt her hand taken in a gentle, warm clasp. "I think she looks great."

Mitch. She'd know that tender, husky baritone anywhere.

Forcing her heavy eyelids open, she smiled up at the man beside her. After the paramedics had taken over by the river, he'd hovered an arm's reach away while they'd worked on her. Ridden with her in the ambulance. Stayed within speaking distance, just on the other side of the curtain in the ER treatment room while the doctor had examined her. Only when

326

they'd wheeled her away for X-rays had he been forced to leave her side.

And while his hair was disheveled, his clothes were as rumpled as if he'd slept in them for a week, and the five o'clock shadow on his cheeks had burgeoned into full-blown stubble, he looked great to her too.

She squeezed his hand. "Hi."

He returned the smile and squeezed back. "Hi yourself."

At the sudden clearing of a throat from the corner of the treatment room, she turned toward her brothers. Jake raised an eyebrow, and she felt warmth steal over her cheeks.

Her older brother's lips quirked as he addressed Cole. "Her color is coming back."

The doctor chuckled and edged out the door. "Even faster than I expected."

As the man disappeared, Jake's demeanor grew more serious and he took up a position on the other side of the bed, reaching down to touch her shoulder. "You okay, Twig?"

The hoarse question from her big brother, along with the suspicious glint in his eyes, tightened her throat. Jake was the rock in the family. The one who kept his emotions on the tightest leash. She'd rarely seen his control falter; only when someone he loved was hurting or in serious trouble did he reveal his softer side.

"Yeah. I'm fine. How can I not be, with all you guys watching out for me?"

Truth be told, she wasn't fine. Every inch of her body ached. But they didn't need to know that. Besides, as her gaze swept over the three men clustered around her bed, she realized Cole looked worse than she felt. "You need to go home and get some rest. What time is it, anyway?"

"It's 1:15. And Mom will be here in eight hours."

"You called Mom?" Alison regarded Cole in dismay.

"The story's all over the news. I wanted her to hear it from me, not some reporter."

She grimaced. "I've given her enough worry over the past couple of years. Now this."

327

Jake tugged gently on a strand of her hair. "Don't start that routine again. When people care, they worry. Live with it."

"Yeah, I'm not covering for you anymore. If you . . ." Cole stopped and pulled the phone off his belt, checking caller ID. "I need to take this."

As he turned away, Alison lowered her voice. "Take him home, Jake. He's about to fold."

"What happened to him, anyway?"

While she brought him up to speed, Cole finished his call. He swapped looks with Mitch, and she narrowed her eyes. "What's going on?"

"Nothing you need to be concerned about."

"Cole Taylor, don't you dare treat me like a kid sister! If that call was related to what happened tonight, I want to hear about it."

After squinting at her for a moment, he lifted one shoulder. "Fine. They found Barnes's body fifty yards downstream. He got tangled up in some limbs from a dead tree."

Jake and Mitch didn't respond in words. But she could read their reaction to the news on their faces.

Good riddance.

She couldn't disagree. Someday, with God's help, maybe she'd be able to forgive the man who'd blamed her for all his problems. Who'd tortured her and tried to take her life.

But it wasn't going to be a swift or easy journey.

Swallowing, she motioned Jake and Cole toward the door. "Go home. Get some rest. And after you pick up Mom in the morning, swing by my house and grab some clean clothes for me, okay?"

"She must be feeling better. Did you notice she's getting bossy again?" Cole directed the comment to Jake and Mitch but sent a smirk her direction.

"I noticed." Mitch winked at her, then turned to Jake. "You took a cab from the airport, right?"

"Yeah."

He dug through his pocket, withdrew his keys, and tossed

them to her older brother. "I'm staying. Take my car. I'll get a ride from you in the morning."

"You don't have to stay, Mitch." Alison's eyelids were growing heavy again, and she struggled to prop them open. "I'm just going to fall asleep anyway."

Her fingers were swallowed in a firm, warm grip. "And I'll be here when you wake up."

She thought about protesting. Thought about insisting Mitch go home too. That would be the considerate thing to do.

But as she drifted to sleep, her hand tucked in his, she didn't say a word. Because selfish or not, she knew she'd sleep better if he was by her side.

As sunlight began to peek through the slats in the blinds in Alison's hospital room, Mitch took a sip of the coffee the nurse had offered him. It wasn't much better than the stuff Alison brewed—lucky thing she had no aspirations to be a barista—but he needed the caffeine. Although he'd drifted to sleep a few times during the waning hours of the night, he'd always jolted awake after a few minutes, muscles taut, adrenaline pumping, pulse pounding.

Fortunately, Alison had had a far more peaceful slumber.

He rose and moved beside the bed to assess her, his stomach knotting as he took in her discolored cheek and eye, her swollen lip, the bruises on her arms where Barnes had squeezed her, the abrasions on her wrists. And those were just the visible signs of trauma. There were many other physical—and psychological—wounds he couldn't see.

She might have slept well in the past few hours, thanks to all the pain meds. But there would be difficult nights ahead. Nights when she'd awake in a cold sweat, trembling with fear. Nights when she'd be alone, with no one to comfort her.

That's why he intended to extract a promise from her to call him when that happened. No matter the hour.

She stirred, and he sat on the bed beside her as her eyelashes flickered open. Weaving his fingers through hers, he summoned up a smile. "Good morning."

For a moment, she seemed disoriented. Then her beautiful blue eyes cleared. "You stayed."

"You asked me to. At the river."

"That was selfish. I'm sorry."

"Don't be. Spending the night with a beautiful woman is no hardship."

She blushed, as he'd expected. "Is anyone else here?"

"Not yet." He checked his watch. "Jake's picking up your mom about now. Then they're going to swing by and get Cole, stop at your place for some clothes, and come out here. So we have plenty of time for this." Without releasing her hand, without giving her a chance to realize his intent, he bent and claimed her lips in a tender, lingering kiss.

When he drew back at last, she let out a shaky breath. "Wow. I hope I'm not still hooked up to a heart monitor."

He chuckled. "You're safe."

Squeezing his hand, she locked gazes with him, her expression suddenly serious. "I know. That's how I always feel with you. Safe and protected. You're the real deal. True hero material."

His lips tightened. "No, I'm not. I failed you last night. I didn't show up at your office when I was supposed to. If I had, none of this would have happened."

"I suspect there was a very valid reason for that."

"Yeah. I guess." He explained what had happened with his father, then stared down into his coffee. "But I should have remembered to call."

"Hey." She tightened her grip on his hand. "It was an emergency—and people get distracted in emergencies. It's called being human. And it's okay. I'm just glad it turned out to be a false alarm. Now tell me how you found me. It couldn't have been easy."

Mitch wasn't as ready as Alison to forgive his lapse, but he

330

did his best to switch gears, relating the story of the skate-boarder, Nicole's phone message, and the observant citizen's 911 call about odd activity at the railroad bridge. But most of all he focused on Erik's role, and how in the wee hours of the morning, he'd kept his promise and awakened the young man with the good news.

"Wow." Alison's renewed color faded as she processed the implications. "If any of those pieces hadn't fallen into place, I wouldn't be here today. Especially Erik's piece. I think I owe him a package of supersized Hershey bars."

"I'm sure he'd appreciate that. But now I want to talk about you and me." Mitch set his cup of coffee on the nightstand, then brushed some wisps of hair away from her forehead, loving the satiny feel of her skin against his fingertips. "During the past twelve hours, I did a lot of thinking about us. A lot of worrying that I might lose you. A lot of praying that I wouldn't. And as I sat here beside you through the night, I broke out in a cold sweat every time I thought about how close I *did* come to losing you." His voice hoarsened, and he cleared his throat.

"Anyway, here's the thing. I know we're just beginning to get acquainted, and we haven't had the most normal dating relationship. But once you're back on your feet, I'd like to remedy that. Starting with a lot more trips to Ted Drewes. Because I think we might find God has something special in store of us. What do you think?"

The tenderness in her eyes, and the sweet smile that tugged at her lips, tightened Mitch's throat and sent his spirits soaring.

"That sounds perfect. But there is one small problem."

Her caveat tempered his sudden elation. "What?"

"If things develop as I suspect they might, for the rest of our lives we're going to have to listen to Cole gloat about how he set us up on that first date."

The tension in Mitch's shoulders eased and he smiled. "It would be worth it, don't you think?"

She smiled back. "For a happily ever after? Yeah. I think." Putting her free hand on his shoulder, she gave a little tug.

"What do you say we consider everything up until now a pro-
logue and dive into chapter one?"

Chuckling, he leaned close, his eyes inches from hers, her
breath warm and blessedly alive on his cheek. "You're on. So
. . . once upon a time . . ."

And with that, he claimed her lips.

Epilogue

Five Months Later

"I think this is our dance."

At the husky comment and the touch on her shoulder, Alison tuned in to the background music gracing Jake and Liz's elegant, intimate wedding reception.

The three-piece combo was playing "Unforgettable."

Their song.

With a murmured excuse to her aunt Catherine, Alison turned to Mitch, smiled, and held out her hand. "Lead the way."

He twined his fingers with hers, his touch warm, strong . . . and magic—as always.

The magic was important.

But so were other things.

As he swept her into his arms and they began to move in perfect unison to the music, Alison was struck by the apt analogy. She and Mitch were in sync not just on the dance floor but in all the ways that counted. Especially when it came to values.

For both of them, family was a priority. They shared a passion for justice. And faith was the center of their lives. The latter had always been true for Alison, and Mitch had found his way back to the Lord, too, these past few months. She gave thanks for that every day.

"You know, I think the maid of honor is even prettier than the bride." The words were spoken close to her ear, followed by a discreet nuzzle of her neck.

"No way." Savoring the feel of his strong arms around her, Alison snuggled closer and checked out her new sister-in-law, who was enjoying a dance with her groom. Liz was elegant in a long, off-white sheath with scattered silver beads that caught the light as she swayed in time to the music. Her gaze was locked on Jake, her face luminous. "She looks breathtaking."

"True. But you're more breathtaking. I couldn't take my eyes off of you during the ceremony. You were serenely radiant."

A smile tugged at her lips. "You wouldn't have said that if you'd seen me yesterday while I was trying to deal with three emergencies at work and still get to the rehearsal dinner on time. I was frazzled."

"I'm sure you handled it all with aplomb. Everything okay with Ellen Callahan?"

"Yes. Now that she's earned her GED and gotten a better job, her loan went through. She and the children will be moving into their own house next month. I'm glad things worked out for her."

"How could they not, with you on her side?"

Warmed by his praise, she let out a small, contented sigh and closed her eyes as they swayed, relishing the perfect moment. Wishing it could go on forever.

Far too soon, however, the music wound down. But when the song ended, Mitch released her only long enough to once again take her hand. "There's a nice garden in back. Want to take advantage of the Indian summer weather?"

"Hmm. A moonlight stroll with a handsome man . . ." She pretended to consider it, then flashed him a grin. "Sold."

Smiling back, he guided her toward the side door.

As they crossed the room, Alison caught sight of Cole standing by himself, off to one side, a glass of champagne in his hand, looking very handsome in his best-man tux. He raised the goblet in salute, a knowing twitch tugging at his lips.

334

She made a face at him and nudged Mitch. "Cole has us in his sights."

"Yeah?" Mitch seemed distracted as he scanned the room for his colleague. "He's just jealous. Why didn't he bring a date, anyway?"

"Beats me. He usually shows up with a gorgeous blonde at events like this. A different one each time, mind you. But he seems to be off his stride lately."

"Maybe he's finally looking for a more serious relationship."

"One can hope."

He pushed the door open to let her precede him, and Alison surveyed the small garden as she exited. Lit by discreet lanterns, it was still perfumed by tea roses in mid-October.

She inhaled the fragrance. "Mmm. This is beautiful."

"I agree."

She turned to find him looking at her, not the setting.

Warmth flooded her cheeks at the intimate light in his eyes, and she smoothed the skirt of her knee-length sheath, the bronze silk shimmering in the moonlight. "You'll make me vain with all these compliments."

"You, vain? Never." Taking her hand, he tugged her toward a bench situated beside a small fountain. "Sit with me for a minute."

At the subtle undercurrent of tension in his voice—and the sudden, anticipatory energy crackling in the air—Alison's pulse tripped into double time. She followed without a word, sitting on the bench as he settled beside her.

In the silence that followed, she tried to rein in her growing excitement. For the past few weeks, she'd known this day was coming. Had wanted it to come—sooner rather than later. There was no question in her mind that Mitch was meant for her. She'd prayed about it daily and felt confident this special man was part of God's plan for her life.

Yet when he reached into the jacket of his dark gray suit and withdrew a small square box, her breath caught in her throat.

Mitch took her hand, and the tiniest tremble in his lean

fingers told her he was as nervous as she was. He tried to smile but managed only a tiny, tense lift of his lips.

"You know, this is a lot scarier than I expected. They make it look too easy in the movies."

At his admission, her own lips curved upward. "You have a very receptive audience, if that helps."

A dimple appeared in his cheek. "That's good to know."

He released her hand long enough to flip open the box and withdrew a stunning marquise-shaped diamond on a gold band. The air whooshed out of her lungs as he took her hand.

Although the light in the garden was muted, Alison had no trouble seeing the love in his eyes. It shone bright as a beacon in the quiet night, bathing her soul with brilliance and illuminating all the places in her heart that had been dark for too long.

"I'm not the poetic type, Alison. I wish I were. You deserve beautiful words at a moment like this. All I can do is tell you how I feel, straight up. So here goes." He took a deep breath. Let it out. "The truth is, I wasn't looking for romance when we met. My job always came first. But you changed that. Because you captivated me from the start."

His voice roughened, and he cleared his throat. "Over the past few months, I've fallen in love with your kind heart. Your strength. Your steadfast values. Your faith. Your love of family. Even your independence—most of the time." One side of his mouth lifted, and he gave her fingers a gentle squeeze. "So if you're willing to spend the rest of your life with a less-than-perfect man who adores you and who will promise before God and our families to love you all the days of his life, this ring is yours. Will you marry me, Alison Taylor?"

He held up the ring. His hand wasn't steady—but Alison knew his love was. And that it always would be. For this was a man of honor, who kept his promises. A man of strength, whose integrity was steadfast. A man of deep compassion, whose tender heart held a depth of love and caring that had already enriched and blessed her life beyond measure. No matter how long she lived, she would never forget the day he'd buried her beloved Bert, or all the times he'd calmed her when she'd called him in the wee hours of the morning after horrifying nightmares had wrenched her awake. Or all the other ways he'd demonstrated his deep, abiding love these past few months.

Alison extended her left hand—which was none too steady either—and managed to whisper a single word. "Yes."

He slid the ring on her finger, then drew her to her feet and looped his arms around her waist. And as he pulled her close, the joy in his eyes was mirrored in her heart.

She smiled up at him and found her voice at last. "There will be much celebration in the Taylor family when we announce this news, you know."

"You think?"

"I *know*. Before you claimed me for that last dance, Aunt Catherine was counseling me not to play hard to get. She said, and I quote, 'That young man is one in a million, Alison. Handsome inside and out.' My mom agrees with her. And just for the record, so do I. My family is sold." She put her arms around his neck and studied his face. "How do you think your dad will react to the news?"

Mitch smiled. "I already know."

She arched an eyebrow. "How come?"

"Because I told him before I left for the wedding that I was planning to recruit a new Musketeer tonight."

Grinning, she tipped her head. "And what did he say to that?"

Mitch chuckled, and as he bent down to seal their engagement in the most traditional of ways, he murmured his answer. "He said it was about time."

Acknowledgments

As with all my suspense books, *Deadly Pursuit* was a research-intensive project. It took me to places I've never been—and hope never to visit in real life! I can't imagine writing a book like this without the internet.

But online research only takes a writer so far. In the end, you need real people—experts who can weigh in on situations unique to your book. And in that regard I've been incredibly blessed with every suspense book I've written. *Deadly Pursuit* is no exception.

So I'd like to offer my sincere thanks to:

Lieutenant Tom Larkin, Commander of the St. Louis County Police Department's Bureau of Crimes Against Persons, who not only answered my many, many questions with patience and promptness but gave me a deeper appreciation for the nuances of criminal investigation and for all the men and women who dedicate their lives to bringing justice to the victims of crime.

The St. Louis County staff of the Children's Division/Department of Social Services, who provided answers to my questions about Alison's job, especially Program Manager Mary Beth Carpenter.

Captain Ed Nestor from the Chesterfield, Missouri, Police Department, who remains my go-to person for amazing sources. Ed, you are the best.

The fabulous team at Revell—especially Jennifer Leep, Kristin Kornoelje, Twila Bennett, Michele Misiak, Cheryl Van Andel, and Deonne Beron. It's a joy to work with you.

Finally, love and thanks to my parents for their unwavering support and enthusiasm, and to my husband, Tom . . . always. The dedication in this book says it all.

Irene Hannon is a bestselling, award-winning author who took the publishing world by storm at the tender age of ten with a sparkling piece of fiction that received national attention.

Okay . . . maybe that's a slight exaggeration. But she *was* one of the honorees in a complete-the-story contest conducted by a national children's magazine. And she likes to think of that as her official fiction-writing debut!

Since then, she has written more than thirty-five contemporary romance and romantic suspense novels. A five-time finalist for Romance Writers of America's coveted RITA award (the Oscar of romantic fiction), she took the golden statuette home in 2003. Her books have also been honored with a HOLT medallion, a Daphne du Maurier award, and two Reviewers' Choice awards from *RT Book Reviews* magazine.

Irene, who holds a BA in psychology and an MA in journalism, juggled two careers for many years until she gave up her executive corporate communications position with a Fortune 500 company to write full-time. She is happy to say she has no regrets. As she points out, leaving behind the rush-hour commute, corporate politics, and a relentless BlackBerry that never slept was no sacrifice.

A trained vocalist, Irene has sung the leading role in numerous community musical theater productions and is also a soloist at her church.

When not otherwise occupied, she loves to cook, garden, and take long walks. She and her husband also enjoy traveling, Saturday mornings at their favorite coffee shop, and spending time with family. They make their home in Missouri.

To learn more about Irene and her books, visit www.irene hannon.com.

Three siblings bound by blood
and a passion for justice. . .

Three determined killers. . .

Three protectors who don't
intend to fail.

MEET THE

GUARDIANS
of JUSTICE

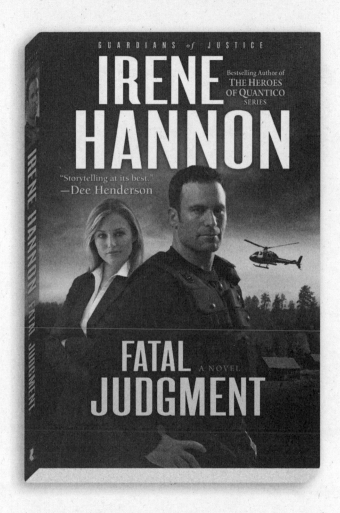

"I've found someone who writes romantic suspense better than I do."
—DEE HENDERSON

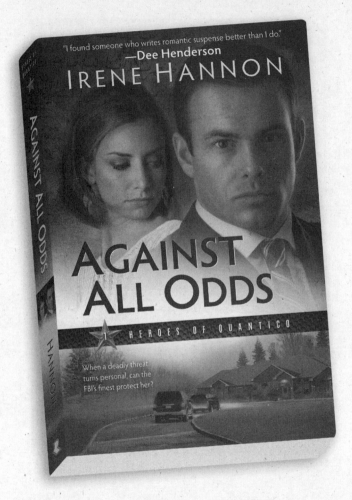

Enter a world of danger and romance where lives—
and hearts—are on the line . . . and time is running out.

Another Action-Packed Novel
from RITA Award Winner
IRENE HANNON

Award-winning author Irene Hannon brings readers another fast-paced tale of romance, suspense, and intrigue in the can't-put-it-down second installment of this exciting series.

Final Installment of the Bestselling Series
HEROES OF QUANTICO!

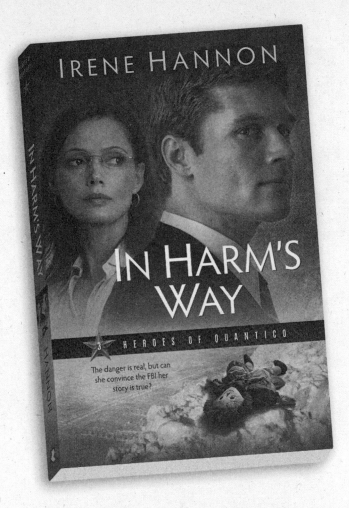

A terrified woman . . . a skeptical FBI agent.
The danger is real—but can she convince
the FBI her strange story is true?